AND THE DESERT SHALL
BLOSSOM

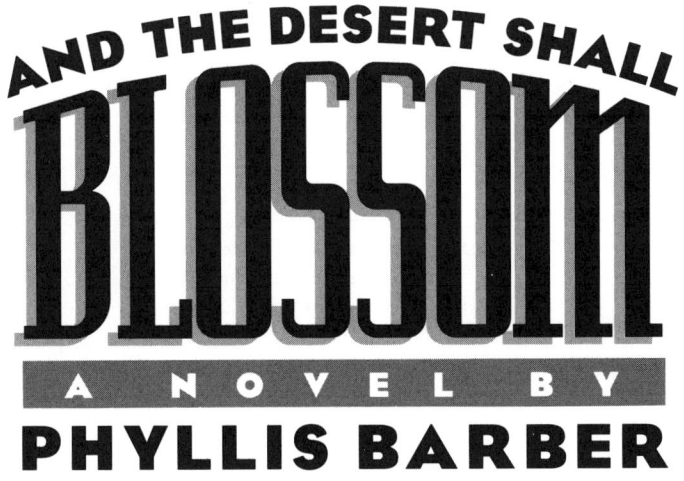

AND THE DESERT SHALL
BLOSSOM

A NOVEL BY

PHYLLIS BARBER

SIGNATURE BOOKS
SALT LAKE CITY
1993

This book's story and characters are fictitious.
The setting is the construction of the Hoover Dam, southern Nevada, 1930-35. Certain
public and company officials are mentioned by name, but when any characterization
takes place, the names and characters are imaginary.

SPECIAL THANKS TO:

Dennis McBride for his research
Marion Allen for his song
G. W. Hawkes for his editorial suggestions
Gordon Weaver for his encouragement
David Barber for his support

Cover art by Royden Card, *Fall Cottonwood*, acrylic on canvas, 1991
Cover design by Brian Bean

Author's note: A portion of *And the Desert Shall Blossom*
appeared in the Fall 1968 isuue of *Ellipsis* magazine.
An earlier version received a first prize in the annual Utah
Arts Council Literary Competition in 1988.

© 1991 UNIVERSITY OF UTAH PRESS. ALL RIGHTS RESERVED.

PUBLISHED BY ARRANGEMENT WITH THE UNIVERSITY OF UTAH PRESS;
ORIGINALLY PUBLISHED BY THE UNIVERSITY OF UTAH PRESS
ORIGINAL PRINTING IN CLOTH

SIGNATURE BOOKS IS A REGISTERED TRADEMARK OF SIGNATURE BOOKS, INC.
∞ PRINTED ON ACID-FREE PAPER IN THE UNITED STATES OF AMERICA.
97 96 95 94 93   6 5 4 3 2 1

ISBN 1-56085-036-1, PAPER
ISBN 0-87480-363-2, CLOTH

LIBRARY OF CONGRESS CATALOGING-IN-PUBLICATION DATA
BARBER, PHYLLIS, DATE
AND THE DESERT SHALL BLOSSOM / PHYLLIS BARBER.
P.   CM.
ISBN 1-56085-036-1
1. HOOVER DAM (ARIZ. AND NEV.)---HISTORY---FICTION. 2. NEVADA----
HISTORY----FICTION. 3. MORMONS----FICTION.   I. TITLE.
[PS3552.A59197A83   1993]
813'.54----DC20   93-13570

To Elizabeth Hortense

Flowing from a basic tenet of occidental philosophy that nature, distinct from man, exists to serve him, is a strong and pervasive view of man as a manipulator of nature. . . . Arguments for controlling the flow of the Colorado . . . to make the desert bloom reflect the view that an uncontrolled resource is a wasted resource and that if man has the capacity to control and completely utilize the waters of a river he should do so. . . .

National Academy of Sciences
1986 Report on the Colorado River

When a man is in turmoil how shall he find peace
Save by staying patient till the stream clears?
How can a man's life keep its course
If he will not let it flow?
Those who flow as life flows know
They need no other force:
They feel no wear, they feel no tear,
They need no mending, no repair.

Lao Tzu

INTRODUCTION

One drop of water. That's how the Colorado River began. The drop escaped from a crust of snow and fell to the frozen ground where it quivered, as if it were a liquid jewel. Other drops followed until a mountain niche was filled to overflowing.

Timidly, the water trickled over the edge, then gained momentum until it rushed over cliffs and sprayed the air. It swirled and leapt and gathered strength until one day, Lieutenant Cardenas and his men, the first Spanish explorers, peered over the lip of a canyon and watched this water churning like a devil's belly far below. The *conquistadores* knelt, crossed themselves, then turned back to warn others away from the river none could possess.

Many tried to cross, and many failed until Father Silvestre Vélez de Escalante's leather boots squished the soft clay of the river's bank as he paced back and forth, waiting for slow water time. He barely survived at *El Vado de los Padres*, but his accomplishment gave other men ideas.

In 1857, the U.S. War Department sent Lieutenant J. C. Ives to build military posts and an avenue of transportation for immigrants to California. He traveled 400 miles from the Pacific to watch his boat, *The Explorer*, collide with rock and crumble while the sheer black cliffs echoed violently. "It seems intended by Nature," he wrote, "that the Colorado River, along the greater portion of its lonely and majestic way, shall be forever unvisited and undisturbed."

Brigham Young tried several ways to use the Colorado for God's purposes. He assigned John D. Lee to build a ferry crossing—a route for Mormon settlers in and out of Arizona and Mexico—and Jacob Hamblin to cross the river and tame the Indians with the gospel of Jesus Christ of Latter-day Saints.

And because he had claimed the Mormons would make the desert blossom like a rose, the advent of the Civil War forced him to find alternate routes for supplies and immigrant converts. He assigned Anson Call to scout the Colorado, build a settlement with a steamboat landing, and cut a road into Zion. Call's party dug out a horseshoe nook in the river's bank, named it Callville, and rode their horses north to build St. Thomas and St. Joseph—links to the Pacific for Zion.

After several attempts, a Sacramento River pilot successfully navigated the steamer *Esmeralda* upstream and landed at Callville in 1866. Service, however, was only possible before and after high water. The rest of the year, the river and roads were impassable. The crossing and recrossing of streams in high water, quicksand, hostile natives, and malaria caused the once-triumphant *Salt Lake Telegraph* newspaper advertisements for the steamship company to be discontinued two months after *Esmeralda*'s first docking.

Other explorers became bolder after 1869 when the one-armed John Wesley Powell, with his wooden dories, barometers, and sextants, battled the length of the river through Hell's Half Mile, Flaming Gorge, Grand Canyon and their nightmarish cauldrons of white water. But four of the nine-man expedition didn't make it to the mouth of the *Rio Virgen* where a Mormon bishop from St. Thomas brought a wagon of melons and other luxuries to the survivors still deafened by the roar of water in their ears.

Robert Brewster Stanton dreamed of a railroad to haul coal from Colorado to California, but could convince no one after he led a float trip from Green River, Utah, and lost three of his party, including the president of the railroad company. They swirled away in sucking pools. The Colorado continued to repel men and women with ideas of settling, conquering, and channeling.

In 1904, however, the actual course of the river was challenged by Imperial Valley entrepreneurs who decided to reroute the river. They had serious machines and a righteous resolve to grow crops for the nation. The California Development Company cut into the bank of the Colorado just below Sharp's Heading in Mexico to carry water into the Imperial Valley and away from the Mexicans. Without approved plans or sufficient funds, they cut directly to a dry channel with the hope of keeping their company solvent and placating farmers who'd believed the advertisements about this fertile delta and bought acreage.

The river seemed to scoff at them. It followed the easy shortcut, then crashed through the man-made headgates and canals and plowed its own course to the Pacific. It rolled across newly planted crops, through furnished houses, and under men's beds. It chewed up meager ditches, tossed pails and sandbuckets aside, and finally settled in the saucer-shaped Imperial Valley in the basin of the ancient Salton Sea. Before it was returned to its original channel by desperate men, the river left behind a 500-square-mile sea which had previously been a mere 22.

As the seasons continued to change and the river flooded and sometimes ran dry into the sand, farmers, engineers, and entrepreneurs gathered their forces. They sent surveyors to the river. They knocked on Department of Commerce doors and pleaded with Congress. In March of 1928, the Swing-Johnson Act passed both houses: "A mighty river, now a source of destruction, is to be curbed and put to work in the interests of society."

Considering the project too massive for a single corporation, six companies—Utah Construction, Henry J. Kaiser, W. A. Bechtel, MacDonald and Kahn, Morrison-Knudsen, J. F. Shea & Company, and Pacific Bridge Company, thereafter known as Six Companies—bid for the contract. The heads of each of these organizations met in the St. Francis hospital in San Francisco where the president of Utah Construction was taking Coffey-Humber cancer treatments, all the time swearing he'd be well enough to be on the job which was, after all, only another dam. He'd proven himself on Hetch-Hetchy near San Francisco, and Guernsey in Idaho without the benefit of gasoline-powered equipment. He'd hauled a concrete mixing plant into Deadwood River, Idaho, by horse-drawn sleigh. "By damn," he laughed, "we'll make this desert a helluva flower! We've got internal combustion now."

Irritating the hospital staff with their cigars, chalkboards, and a cumbersome wooden model of the dam, the company heads spent hours writing and rewriting numbers and calculations and the cost effectiveness of producing cement near the damsite rather than shipping it. Because of this uncanny prescience about cement, they were low bidder at $448,890,995—five million dollars under the next bidder and $220,000 under the government estimate.

On March 11, 1931, as the first snow was melting in the high country, Six Companies was awarded the contract from the United States government. Immediately, they organized the Boulder City Company to handle housing, feeding, and a commissary, and the Hoover Dam Transportation Company to handle purchasing, administration, and transportation. After a confused beginning with too many bosses giving too many directions, an executive committee was formed to limit the number of commands, hence confusion, flying into the nebulous space of desert and sage and lizards. The Boulder Canyon Project would shortly be well ordered and under control even though the water flowed on and on.

•　　•　　•　　•　　•

223 East Second South
Brigham City, Utah
April 4, 1931

Mr. A. P. Watkins, Vice President
Six Companies, Inc.
Boulder Canyon Project
Las Vegas, Nevada

Dear A. P.

It's been a long time since I saw you in Brigham City. I'm "little" Esther (Carpenter), (not so little now), John's daughter, the one everybody remembers because of the fire.

My Alfred can't find work to feed us. He's tried everything. Beets, shoe sales, butchering, the mines, even a cosmetic line that did well for a while. We've been living at Mother and Dad's but you've heard about fish and company smelling after three days. If there's anything for Alf, we'd sure be happy.

Congratulations on your big position with Six Companies. You and your brother Bill never dreamed Utah Construction would be helping build the biggest dam in the world. Sorry to hear he has cancer. Sorry about that.

Well, my baby's crying. Bye for now.

Esther (Carpenter) Jensen

P.S. Alf will take anything he can get, but he's a good seller and does a good job with meat and produce.

4

1

The horizon slanted, a bold slash across the bluest sky Alf had ever seen. Standing on the ridge of a hill, he leaned to the right to adjust the angles. He'd never seen anything so bizarre—impulsive rock formations, cracked arroyos, offset mountains that looked like the Creator's five-minutes-to-midnight-on-the-last-day's decision. Somebody must have been too tired, crumpled up the blueprints, and laughed in a fit of exhaustion.

Exhausted . . . like me, Alf mused.

A breeze slid up from the shadowed side of the hill, cooler than the 100 + degrees of hilltop air, less dusty too. Alf pulled it into his lungs, filling his chest. He removed his rimless eyeglasses, massaged the bridge of his nose, and hooked the glasses back over each ear. He touched his toes to relieve the cramping in his legs. One too many of Esther's deviled ham sandwiches, he thought as he loosened his belt to the last notch.

Esther. What had happened to Esther, the flesh he called his wife who sat in the car behind him with his children? She'd given up trying to calm Inez. The baby had been alternately screaming and squealing like a rat since the family waved good-bye to Esther's aunt and uncle in St. Thomas this morning, ever since they turned onto the Arrowhead Trail and into the Valley of Fire. He, Alf, the father of a squealing rat. He once hoped something magnificent would grow from his seed to redeem them all, but chances didn't look too good at the moment.

Esther was a smudge. She'd lost sharp definition in this heat, almost like she was a mirage of a wife. Before he'd gotten out of the car to assess the lay of the land, she'd given him a comforting pat on the knee, but her eyes were dabs of regret and her face and arms were bloated with resignation. Even though she'd sung to the baby all day, her songs weren't "Rock-a-Bye" or "A Little Boy Went Walking" like she used to sing to the others. They were hymns, those damned hymns she'd been singing ever since they'd left St. Thomas and driven into heat unlike any they'd ever felt.

"This town will be drowned when the dam's built," she said before she started in with the singing. "Just like no one was ever here or ever mattered."

"Look at Uncle Woolley's withered almond orchard," Alf said. "Those branches look like they'll snap right off when the water hits. Not worth saving."

"If he can't make them grow, no one can." Esther hummed for a minute. "This desert . . ." she said, and the hymns began. "I need Thee every hour, most gracious Lord," and the words seemed to frighten the baby, not calm her, as the car followed the Arrowhead around grotesque shapes of rocks: petrified fire.

Now, through the prism of late afternoon light, Alf squinted to see pieces of the Colorado—sections of serpent lazing its muddy path through lava and sandstone, a mirage of tranquility. He'd heard about this river: Big Red, the destroyer. He'd come to help tame it. At his back, bulldozers and tractors shoved sand and sagebrush to prepare the foundation for Boulder City, the eventual home for the dam builders and the fortress for combating the river that looked so innocuous to Alf as he stood on the ridge.

How many years on the move, trying to support a family that hasn't been the return on my money I'd expected? How many jobs, trying to bring home the bacon to mouths always asking for more? The concrete factory in Brigham City, his fifth retreat to his hometown and in-laws, had been the last straw. He'd been treated like the gravel in the hoppers, funneled, strained, and ground under the feet of his superiors who could give his job to any ten men who stood in line outside the door. The crops, the economy, the times had failed Alf. That is, until now.

Here by the Colorado River, this was the time for Alf's flowering. His intelligence, his wit, his common sense, even his flare for the finest when he could afford it—all his potential had been purified by his struggle. He'd only been preparing himself for the main event and was ready to prove himself to Esther, except in this heat she seemed totally disinterested in everything, not even willing to make Inez stop crying. Maybe she'd revive when the sun disappeared and they'd settled in somewhere.

He inhaled more of the cool air and tried not to think about the man with layers of grit in his sand-colored hair who hadn't been smart enough to know who Alf was. After all, Alf was related to two of the top officials in Six Companies, builder of the dam that would tame the mighty Colorado. He should have been treated with more respect.

"No jobs," the stranger with the shovel had said. "Ain't you seen the notices posted all over the county?"

"What notices?" Alf controlled his widening eyes.

"The notices that say, 'Warning to the unemployed: Jobs connected with the construction of Boulder Dam will not exist for sixty days or more.' In other words, mister, stay out."

"But I have a job," Alf said, pushing his glasses to the top of his nose.

"Come on now. Nobody much has a job. Hundreds of folks is strung from Las Vegas to the river and you're trying to tell me—"

Alf reached into his shirt pocket between the sweat-soaked layers of cloth, then unfolded a limp piece of paper with care. "See this signature, my friend?" Alf pointed to the blue ink scrawl. "That says A. P. Watkins. He's a Vice President of Six Companies, and his brother's President. This letter says, read it with me if you like, 'Yes, we will find a place for your husband, Esther. Have him report as soon as possible. The River Commissary needs a man with retail experience.' A man with retail experience," Alf repeated, stretching himself to his full five-foot-seven. "That's me."

"Well, ain't you somethin'?" The stranger raised his eyebrows with contempt while sweat leaked from his close-cropped sideburns. "That's called kin lickin' where I come from."

"Call it what you like, sonny. Where can I find Mr. Watkins?"

The man spat into the sand. The stray threads where he'd ripped the sleeves from his shirt fringed his sunburned arms. "Your relation is probably back in Las Vegas, sitting in front of an electric fan, resting his feet on a big desk while you and I stand here sweating. He's writing more letters to kin, what do you bet?"

"Just tell me where I can find a place for my family. We've come clear from Brigham City, Utah. My wife. This heat. June isn't supposed to be this hot."

"This is nothin'. It's mild today. If you can't take this, better go back to Utah. You one of those crazy Mormons?"

"A place to stay?"

Gesturing toward the desert, tractors, and stacks of lumber, the man laughed. "The Ritz and the Savoy are full up with lizards and vinegaroons tonight. There ain't no decent place for men with families, so you better take your sweaty little piece of paper and head back to Utah, the rest of your wives, and the saints." He almost cawed. "The saints. Ain't that arrogant calling yourselves saints?"

Somewhere in Alf's figuring, connections with the top meant a smooth ride, though A. P. had cautioned them about extremely limited facilities. Esther had been the one to insist: "We're going anyway. We know about hard times."

"I know there's a place for us," Alf said calmly.

"Well, ain't you something. A peacock." The man puckered to spit again and aimed at a spot near Alf's shoe. Alf didn't flinch, and the man finally pointed with the handle of his shovel. "Follow the tire tracks—the well-worn ones. If you turn right at the fork and go down to the river, you'll get to Ragtown. Families are squatting there. Most don't have jobs, but figure since it's close to the dam, they'll be first in line. You could try McKeeversville, an old survey camp over to the left, but it's mostly railroad men now. A little rough for young ears."

"Thank you." Through the years Alf had studied the mannerisms of his superiors and their tendency toward arrogance, all the while he followed their orders. He'd even polished his intonation with a hint of British accent. "That wasn't so hard, was it?"

"Choose your poison, Mister." The man pulled off his hat, revealing a mass of greased hair speckled with sand. "By the way, I wouldn't be mentioning my relations if I were you. People around here don't cotton much to that sort of thing. In fact, it makes 'em real mad."

Alf had stalked to the car, angry at his reception. He slammed the door and ground the obstinate gears, nauseated by smells of deviled eggs, sweating children, saturated diapers, and stale car sickness. Trying to get the impudent stranger off his mind, Alf drove recklessly past the beginnings of Boulder City—men and mules plowing a path for iron rails, tents, shovelers, surveyors, foundations with footings, half-built walls and piles of timber. He parked, told everyone in the car to wait one last time, and trudged through coarse sand to where he now stood on the ridge of the hill, trying to get a glimpse of either McKeeversville or Ragtown. Too much turbulent geology to see much of anything man-made, though.

What kind of people would live in a place called Ragtown? But then, the only option was close proximity to the dam site. That much he knew. Who did that smart ass think he was anyway, calling him a kin licker? Why hadn't he told him a thing or two about respect? The remembrance of the cocky bastard with sand stuck to his hair oil grated against Alf's new resolution, the one he'd rehearsed as he drove from northern Utah. This move was his now or never. He'd been moving "now" around to suit his convenience for years, but he was running out of time. He'd stick this one out in this land of scrap wire foliage and scaled reptiles determined to survive—compatriots with Alf. His hide was hammered and scored from hard times.

Now is everything, he repeated to himself. *Don't dwell on the past. Begin again, right now. No more starting over. This is the beginning—right this minute.*

•   •   •   •   •

The car shook violently as it hit a stretch of washboard. Alf took the car out of gear and let it idle.

"The best choice, my dear," he said, staring at the dashboard, avoiding Esther and the crying baby, "is a camp about three, four miles farther. Ragtown they call it. What a name."

"A camp? What does that mean?"

"No places for families on the ridge," he said.

"Not a hotel or abandoned cabin or anything? Not even an old warehouse like in Ely?"

"No, Esther."

"Nothing?"

He drew initials in the dust on the dashboard. "We could go back to Las Vegas, but the drive back and forth to work would cost us more than we'd make."

"A. P. should have been more specific," she said, bouncing the baby in both hands to keep her from crying.

"Esther, you've said three hundred times we're lucky to have a job and that we've freeloaded on your parents for the last time."

"I know, Alf. It's just that. . . ." Esther stared at nothing in particular.

"Don't go changing your mind now, not after all we've gone through to get here."

"You decide, Alf." She leaned her head sideways onto the window glass and surrendered the baby to solo in her lap. "Let's just get out of this stinking car and this firetrap."

Alf made the mistake of looking into her eyes. Trying to erase the connection he hadn't wanted to make, he shifted into first gear and craned his neck to see through the clouds of floating silt. He'd done pretty well, considering. He was still by her side. He was still trying. But why, every time he looked at her, did he feel like some sort of miniature jackass? Those big doe eyes focused him small, accused him. *I've done my best*, he thought, *and Esther still looks at me with those eyes. Why can't she just say thank you once in a while instead of being so sure I'm a bad deal. Why does she think I need to feel worse than I already do?*

"I'm hungry, Daddy," Mary Elizabeth whined.

"You're always hungry," he said.

"Me too," said Rebecca, starting a chant of *I'm hungries* and *I'm thirsties* in the back seat.

"Not one more sound out of you girls," shouted Alf. "I'll whale the living daylights out of you!"

They seemed to know their limits. Even the baby stopped fussing for a few minutes while the car tilted, jerked, and crawled in and out of the flood-carved gullies. The silence was thick as the wheels struggled through the sand and gathered stickers on the tire treads.

"Look, girls!" Alf said, excited, acting as if he hadn't just yelled at them. "A jackrabbit. Did you see it?"

"I don't see it," Rebecca said.

"Over there. Behind those bushes." Alf pointed.

"What bushes?"

"Use your eyes!" Alf yelled. "There he goes."

"Where?"

"Open your damn eyes." Alf shook his finger at the rabbit's fast-changing direction.

"Rabbits, hares, rarebits, or hatters," said Esther. "Are you even sure it matters?"

Alf felt a smugness growing at the corners of her mouth. "Damn your hide, Esther. I'm trying to make things better, and you make your wise-ass rhymes."

"You're all heated up about nothing. A little jackrabbit." Esther squeezed her lips shut with one hand.

"There it is," Alf yelled.

"I see it," Rebecca squealed.

"See, Esther," said Alf. "A rabbit."

Esther still squeezed her lips together like miniature plates. Alf glanced sideways at her profile, and for the first time since St. Thomas, he laughed. Something needed to cancel the sickly odor and the futility of this insignificant vehicle carrying a crying baby, two other daughters, and two adults into a land where the sun could shrivel a body in three hours' time.

"What are you laughing about?" Esther asked incoherently, still trying to hold her lips together.

"Everything." Both hands and his forehead against the steering wheel, he kept laughing, even chanced a glance at Esther and saw signs of her will crumbling. "It's funny," he said. "From the frying pan into the frying pan. A tin can with wheels chasing a rabbit. We're insane!"

First her shoulders convulsed, then she laughed out loud until tears rolled through the fine dust on her cheeks. Then she had a coughing fit which, when it ended, had somehow cleared the car of its congestion and stale resentment. Everyone leaned forward like horses toward evening hay and strained for glimpses of the river and their new home. Even the baby's crying softened to a whimper.

"Home means Nevada, home means the hills," Esther sang her first non-hymn of the day as if the hand of God had picked them up and set them down again, everything behind them now—the washboards shaking the frame of their car and sucking air from their tires, the bends, curves, switch-backs, and ruts, the flat tires, the endless curse of another day traveling.

Suddenly they saw the end of the road. Absolute. Abrupt. Individual tire tracks veered off into greasewood and sage to the place where they stopped as if forever in the deep, hub-high sand. Lean-tos were constructed against Fords and Chevies, their running boards transformed into cupboards for dishes, coffee, and flour. Over the tops of half-buried two-by-fours, sheets were stretched into ceilings and, at their sides, cardboard nailed into walls. Crazy quilts hung over lengths of rope, pegged at the corners like pup tents.

A few people stared out of their shelters as Alf drove slowly past the makeshift housing, sifting the desert floor anew and resurrecting puffy clouds of dust. He noticed weathered eyes, raggedly clad bodies, stubborn jaws, and folded arms.

In the center of the jerry-builts, a wire of a man in uniform emerged from a canvas tent surrounded by a proprietary square of whitewashed rocks. He motioned Alf to stop. Alf braked and waited for the spiraling dust to settle before he opened the window.

"What do you think he wants?" Esther whispered, quickly covering the baby she was trying to nurse. Inez's tiny mouth rooted for food Esther didn't have.

"Beats me." Alf rolled down the glass.

"Where you folks from?" The man leaned into the car, his hat brim almost touching Alf's face. Fingers of perspiration caressed his cheeks.

"Utah. Brigham City," Alf said.

"You have a job?"

"River Commissary. I'll be managing the Commissary. I have a letter if you need to see it."

"Might be a good idea."

Alf eased the wet letter out of his pocket.

"Too many folks are crowding in here," the officer said. "No means to take care of themselves. Government's worried. River water's not potable—too much silt. We have to truck it in from Vegas, but with all these people, the task is near impossible."

"Here's the letter, sir."

"Thanks." He leaned his elbow on the open window and picked the wilted paper apart.

"So ma'am, says here you're related to Mr. Watkins?"

"Yes sir. He's my second cousin." The baby kicked frantically. Shielding her breast, Esther rearranged the diaper so Inez could have air if not food.

"Fine man, Mr. Watkins."

"Yes," said Esther. "A fine man."

"Glad to have you here." The man looked past Alf, touching the brim of his hat in deference to Esther. "Just find yourself a place to shove some sand aside, and pray for Boulder City to get built in a hurry. Nothing should've started before the city was ready, but people in need lose their senses. Williams is the name. Jess Williams, Sheriff."

"We're the Jensens," Alf said. "I'm Alfred, this is Esther, our three daughters, Mary Elizabeth, Rebecca in the back seat, and that's Baby Inez on her mother's lap. Our big boys, Herbert and Jack, will join us later . . . when more jobs are available that is. Right?" He turned back for a smile of approval from the sheriff.

Williams hadn't heard. He had other business.

Alf took his foot off the brake. The car rolled past the whitewashed rocks, past mattresses on the sand, past a few scattered children in mismatched shoes or none at all.

"This is as good a place as any," Alf said, as he stopped the car. "Choose a bush and let's unload."

As ragged as the settlement appeared, the boundaries of Ragtown were maintained at a respectful distance from the river. Alf guessed no one dared settle close to the banks that might be undermined by water or demolished by a flash flood in seconds. The car doors sprang open simultaneously.

"This one," said Mary Elizabeth, running to a creosote bush she'd chosen as the cornerstone for their new home. It looked like all the others with its sporadic covering of furry seed pods.

"Look at this plant, Alf," Esther said, holding the stem of the bush's branch between two fingers. "The Indians used the resin to repair pottery and glue arrowheads to their shafts. Did you know that?"

"Not now, Esther. There's too much to do."

She guided Inez's finger to stroke a leaf. "Leaf, Inie. It's called greasewood. Did you know that, girls?" She snapped a small twig from the bush.

Rebecca kicked the crust of the desert into chunks with the curled toes of her shoes. Mary Elizabeth chased a lizard until Alf ordered her to help him untie the knots securing their belongings to the roof of the car. Packing boxes, wooden orange crates filled with dishes and pans, one ancient steamer trunk full of clothes, tin storage cans tucked under a canvas tarp, a large double mattress and coiled springs on top of that.

Esther kept rubbing a tiny creosote leaf between her fingers. "This savvy little leaf has it all figured out, Alf. The sun and the wind kept stealing its water supply, so it found a way to survive."

"Idiotic knot," Alf said, his temper rising as the unyielding rope brought back memories of another time, another knot, the useless feeling of fingers wrestling against time and a knot.

Mary Elizabeth slipped away from her father and chased after Rebecca.

"Come back here, you numbskull," he shouted.

His papa had been lying on a hard bed of coal—limp, gone, his life erased—and the knot tight against his shirt collar was too strong for Alf's small hands. He couldn't focus on it anyway, the tears warping the shapes of things—the oblong, then square belt buckle; the round, then oval shirt buttons; his father's sad, then twisting mouth: uncertain shapes.

Esther pressed Inez into her neck and chest and held the clump of creosote out like an offering as she approached her husband.

"Alf, did you know this little leaf manufactures an oily liquid to protect its moisture? It needs some for the dry times. Remember Jake Horlacher at the meat market in Ely? He told me about that. Said desert plants were smarter than most people."

"You trying to tell me something, Esther?" he snapped. "Another one of your upbraidings?"

"I didn't mean anything by it, not this time."

"Well I happen to know Mexicans don't think so much of that plant.

They call it 'little bad smeller.' Damn this rope." His shirt was collared with sweat.

"I was trying to find something to hold onto, Alf. I wasn't after you, honest."

"Mary Elizabeth," he yelled, "get over here or hold the baby so your mother can." He looked around to see if anyone in Ragtown was watching this circus. "I've got to get out of here."

Before Mary Elizabeth could answer with a "yes" or "no" or a smart remark, Alf was moving away like a man pursued, the sand slipping and sinking under his weight until he neared the river. There, the dampness changed the sand to a soft clay outlining each of Alf's steps rather than swallowing them, and the sound of the water began to relieve some of the pressure in his mind and at the back of his neck.

"I've heard about you, river," he said. "Stories since I was knee-high. Brethren speaking from the pulpit about Indian scouts and colonizers for Zion, everybody trying to get around or across you. We'll get you this time."

Alf fingered the thorns on a catclaw bush and read the weathered wooden sign that read "Boulder Boat Landing." Beyond that, the wide arc of river curved into Black Canyon with its steep-sided mesas. It looked like a former battlefield, once active with some furious blasting from the inside of the earth that shoved matter upward, cracked it, thrust it into every angle possible. Some huge clash of continents, buckling the earth and scattering the afterbirth—a sea of rocks scored with massive scabs, fissures, obscene warts.

Volcanoes. Lava. Black coal. Black fire. *Coal in a shed. Black coal framing a white-shirted swaying body. Black coal bedding a fallen man cut from rope.* But he had been alone. Alf was only a boy. What else could he have done? Left the body swinging? How could he cradle deadweight in his arms, pry knots, yank stubborn hemp and ask, "Why, Papa?" all at the same time? Black coal. Lava. Knots.

Suddenly, Alf was startled by a massive explosion. Clouds of tumbling smoke and dust poured out of the canyon. And then a second discharge. Someone was already blasting into the petrified lava of Black Canyon.

A chill burrowed into Alf's spine. Something big was happening here. No peon, third-rate stuff. No measly little attempt to mine a poor vein of gold. For once, Alf knew he was in the right place at the right time. This was history that mattered.

He slipped his hat from his head. Sweat bathed his forehead and underarms and oozed under his belt. The essence of heat seemed to distill here where the canyon walls rose out of the flat plain. Not even the wind chased its usual dust devils through the dead mass of air that pressed against the rocks and the water and Alf.

He blinked into the afternoon sun, its perimeter expanding until it almost touched his face. Circles of luminescent blues, greens, and violets whirled behind his eyelids. And then he saw a point of light moving across the river, whiter than hot fire. If he'd been more inclined toward visions as Esther and his mother were, he might have thought it was the finger of God. In the back of his mind he heard his mother Kristina reading the story of Moses and Mount Sinai cautiously in her half-Danish English. "And the sight of the Lord was like devouring fire on the top of the mount. . . ."

But then he heard a stronger voice: "Your trials have not been in vain, Alfred. Open your eyes to accept your destiny. Thus saith the Lord."

Ice and fire at the same time, Alf shivered. God talking to him? Alfred Jensen? No. This was some hallucination. But then, he hesitated, God had talked to Ezekiel, Joshua, Daniel, Joseph Smith, and Brigham Young before him. God and Alf. Personal revelation. He laughed out loud. If God had spoken to him directly, he didn't have to listen to any more intermediaries, any Mormons who postponed living in this life for the next one. Bishops, stake presidents, prophets and presidents. Even his wife, Esther, or his son St. Herbert. *God and Alf. Pals. God saying, "Rise to the heights of glory, my son. You are blessed. Alfred L. Jensen. Accept your destiny."* Nobody else needed to translate God's word if he had it from the horse's mouth.

Quickly, Alf cancelled that last thought in case God was listening. And just as quickly, the light extinguished itself in the river. Alf scanned the river's surface for traces and wiped the perspiration from his neck, throat, forearms, and hand upon hand until he realized there was no way to dry himself.

He was alone, a small man standing by a large river. Those were the facts. But against his better judgment, he touched the skin on his face, wondering if it was luminous like the skin of Moses after his visit with God. There was stubble on his cheeks after the long day of driving. His skin was clammy too. He took one step and lifted his foot to see its outline in the red river clay. The same as before. The same size. The same shape. Then he slogged through the sand to his family, knowing he was the same man, but hoping maybe he wasn't.

• • • • • •

15

Esther handed the baby to Mary Elizabeth who was making no headway with the knot.

"Let me try," she said halfheartedly, her vitality disintegrating even further in the unrelenting heat. She wished her son Herbert were here to help her, to say some gentle thing about perseverance or endurance or faith. And she wished snow would fall from somewhere onto her face and eyes, down inside her dress, in her shoes. As she struggled with the knot, she slipped into memory: snow scrunching under her mother's boot soles as she walked out the front gate. Mama leaving again, always going somewhere. A public-minded woman. The snow. Mama leaving. The fire all around Esther, burning her skin to black charcoal. But Esther was in Nevada, standing by the car in the desert, fighting a knot that held her mattress and her family's belongings on top of a Model A.

Making no progress, Esther lifted the canvas in a few untucked places and poked at a five-gallon tin of winter wheat from her mother's basement in Brigham City. The weevils were probably hatching by the score in this weather, but she'd ground their legs and bodies into flour before. She'd heard they were nutritious.

Once again she pried into the knot with her hapless fingernails, but the job needed someone with more persistence than Esther had at the moment. That much effort cost her. She breathed heavily, and perspiration blotted her dress between her breasts and under her arms. Heat surrounded her shoulders like a wet wool coat; it shimmered around her edges like she was a loaf of bread in an oven. And she was on fire again.

"Watch the fire," Mama had said to her brother Henry on that snowy day in Brigham City. "Don't let it go out. It's extremely cold today."

"I won't, Mama," he answered, turning another page of *From the Earth to the Moon*.

"And don't let Esther out of your sight. She's still little and curious."

"Yes, Mama." Henry's eyes were riveted to the page.

Esther felt the desert sun bore into her back. Water trickled down her arms and her torso in uneven lines until the perspiration found a streambed in the creases of her hands and the rolls around her stomach.

"Give me the baby," she said to Mary Elizabeth. "I'm not getting anywhere, so we might as well wait for Alf. You keep track of Rebecca."

"Don't ask me to do anything else after this, please Mama. I'm tired of you asking me to do everything."

"Shush. Things'll even out. Run along now."

Esther cuddled Inez next to her, trying to blot out this heat and that fire. Esther had been dressing her doll that day, slipping pearl buttons in and out of the crocheted buttonholes.

"I'm cold, Henry." She felt the wind sliding under the door, whistling and rattling windows. "Henry, my baby doll is cold, too." He flipped another page in his book.

"Henry, there's no fire."

"The fire's out?" he asked, still reading.

Esther shivered as she stood in the desert, the sand burning the soles of her shoes. Inez, a slippery waterbaby by now, kept sliding down her arms.

Finally, Henry had grabbed the coal bucket and walked down the cellar stairs, still reading. Without him, the room seemed colder. Esther, with the doll in her arms, moved closer to the embers and touched the ashes for warmth. Wind pushed the front door open and sprayed snow on the carpet. Pulling the afghan from the sofa onto her shoulders, she crawled back to the fireplace to touch the ashes again, but they feathered the air and floated on the wind.

"Mama is singing at the Tabernacle," Esther said to Inez as if she were the doll she'd clung to that day. She dragged the afghan to the front door and put both hands on the glass knob with its prisms of deep purple and flashes of yellow. She pushed her weight into her heels and leaned against the door and strong wind. When the latch finally clicked, she sank to the planed floor and wrapped herself tightly in the afghan. But she failed to notice the live coal caught in a yarn flower that smouldered until tiny flames bloomed at the hem of Esther's dress. Both hands covering her face, she ran through the rooms of the house, tugging fire behind her, trying to find Henry, and then she woke up stiff and straight and wrapped like a mummy.

Esther lifted Inez's stubby fingers to her face. "My face, Inie. Feel my face. The fire didn't get my face."

Just then a truck pulled in next to the Jensens' car with a six-foot-square tin box strapped and bolted onto its flatbed and a hose coiled like a snake on top of the box.

"You new, ma'am?" the driver shouted.

"Can't you tell?" Esther asked.

"You arrived in the nick of time, I'll tell you." The whiskered driver dressed in half-buttoned long johns and rumpled khaki pants climbed out of the cab. Though he kept trying to use the tear in the top of his underwear as a buttonhole, he was unsuccessful and finally stopped trying to make himself presentable to Esther.

"Got a bucket?"

"You need a bucket, sir?" Esther patted Inez's back and pulled her closer.

"No," he laughed, "I don't need no bucket 'cept you need one. Or a desert bag of some kind."

"Why?" Esther couldn't make the connection—too much heat, too much newness, no home, a place called Ragtown, this man talking about buckets.

"Lady. That baby's gonna get mighty thirsty if you don't drink lots of liquid. Nothin' to suck."

Esther blushed. The man was bold.

Then she heard the painful, colicky crying again.

"Lady. Do you want water or not? You can't drink that stuff in that river, 'less you like red mud in your teeth. Not real attractive when you smile."

"Of course. I'm sorry. I'm not myself. Haven't been for a long time." Confused by the baby's crying, Esther stared into the sky for an answer that might be written there, then tiptoed through the sand to the far side of the car. She was an actress in high heels, trying to remember her part—where she was going and what she was doing—rummaging under the canvas for a bucket she wasn't even sure she had.

"Don't cry, baby." The truck driver bent over to touch Inez's cheek. "Where you from, ma'am?"

"Brigham City. I'm Esther Jensen. And you?" Balancing Inez on one arm, Esther stretched to tug on a large cardboard box tied with hemp and marked "Bottled Fruit."

"Blackie Winn. Came in from West Texas about a month ago to wait out a job on this here dam. Establish residency, you know. I'm delivering water for Murl Emery over at the Boat Landing."

"Nice to meet you." Esther held out her hand tentatively to the white-haired Blackie.

"Ma'am, pardon me for saying so, but you can't get under that canvas until the mattress and springs is on the ground."

Esther swayed with her baby who wouldn't be calmed, looking for Alf, then for her daughters, who were probably tracking a scorpion. She wouldn't think about them.

"You want help or not?" he asked. "I'm strong as a ox."

"I wanted Alf to do it this time. I've done it so many times by myself." She bounced at her knees, up and down. "Baby, baby, baby," she sang. "Baby mine, don't cry, Mama's standing by. Mmmm, mmmm. Baby, baby," but the crying continued.

"I'll help you, ma'am, but let's get going."

"I'm not weak, Mr. Winn, not in the ways that count." She opened the car door and laid Inez on the floor. "You'll have to cry by yourself, then."

Blackie pulled a screwdriver out of a metal toolbox on the front seat of his truck and wedged it into the knot. It yielded immediately for him. Then he directed the process. "You stand on that side." Esther obeyed. "Ready now? One, two, three, heave."

Esther's muscles bulged slightly while the undersides of her arms hung loose. She hoisted the creaking coils, tightened her eyes to give her strength, and grunted toward the nose of the car as Blackie barked directions. The load tilted and slid to the ground.

A bed in the sand. Springs and a blue-striped mattress with stray buttons on long strings. It looked strange, framed by gray sand and scattered pebbles. A common ceiling and common floor with everyone else in the world.

An explosion ripped out of the canyon, startling Esther. She bent over protectively and folded her arms across her chest. "Blasting the adits for the diversion tunnels, Mrs. Jensen." Blackie put his arm around her shoulders. "Don't you worry none."

Suddenly Esther heard Inez's crying shift up to screaming.

"My baby!"

Maybe it was Blackie as an audience who helped Esther remember what she was supposed to be about, his standing there, reminding her of her role as a mother. She lifted the scrawny Inez from the car floor and laid her on the striped mattress. "Your T-shirt is stained. Dirty diapers again. Mama's gonna fix up her little ragamuffin." She was on stage again for Blackie Winn from somewhere in West Texas. She could perform when she had an audience. She could rise to a public occasion just as her mother had always done. Remember her lines, remember how to be a responsive mother.

When Esther smoothed the talc on the baby's prickly heat rash, Inez was suddenly quiet, knowing her mother had finally yielded to her demands. For the first time all day, Inez was peaceful except for the convulsive after-gasps that broke from her. Esther listened to that peculiar quiet, not ready to trust it.

"Mrs. Jensen," Blackie said quietly. "I don't have all day."

"Water. That's right. Water. I can't remember if we brought a bucket.

Hold Inez, Blackie. She's got a clean diaper now. Hold her, please. Carefully. She's been upset."

She lifted Inez into his outstretched arms and walked around the car as fast as she could, dipping into the sand with each step, but then the baby started to cry again, frantic to have her mother who had only just become available to her.

"I'm coming, Baby. Just a minute." Esther untucked the entire canvas and uncovered suitcases, the leg ends of an army cot, a Coleman lantern, another box labelled *Dishes* and a carton labelled in red crayon. *Bathroom items. Towels, washcloths, handsoap, toilet paper.*

"I can't find anything. Not a thing. I can't even think about anything right now. When's your next water run?"

Blackie was trying everything to calm the baby, tickling her, holding her close, dangling her away from his body, but nothing worked. "Twice a week," he yelled over the baby's noise. "Hope we can improve the schedule, but folks is moving in so fast. My load capacity ain't that big."

From nowhere it seemed, a dark-tanned woman in sleeveless cotton appeared with a bucket.

"Use mine," she said.

"We couldn't use your bucket," Esther protested, rescuing the hysterical Inez from Blackie.

"It's extra," the woman said.

Alf reappeared carrying some narrow boards on his shoulder. "Look, Esther. I scavenged these from one of our neighbors." Then he looked at the mattress and skewed springs on the desert floor. "How'd you get the bed off the Ford?"

"Blackie. Mr. Winn," Esther said, trying to mask her confusion. "He's waiting for our bucket. I can't find it, Alf. I can't find anything."

The woman stood with her arms folded, the bucket hanging over one wrist. "Do you want this bucket or not?"

"What's going on?" Alf asked.

The woman stepped forward and placed the bucket handle in Alf's free hand. "For you. You need it. Blackie's waiting." She was lean, graceful. Her eyes were strong like they could burn, like sunlight through a magnifying glass.

"Thank you," Alf said, taking the bucket. Esther observed the admiration in Alf's eyes, the respect he showed to this woman who had definitely caught his attention, and she pressed Inez close under her chin.

"Return it when you find your own. I live in the tin-roofed shack over there. Serena's my name."

"Usually the water's three cents a gallon, twenty-five cents for ten gallons," Blackie said. "Being's you're new, I'm givin' it to you free this time."

"How can we ever thank you, Blackie?" said Esther. "Your patience. . . ." She was shifting into a role again, almost as if she might hold out a lace handkerchief to the hero of the melodrama and bid him adieu.

"Nothing, ma'am. Return a favor to someone else someday."

Blackie drove his truck with its homemade water tank back up the hill toward Boulder City and raised gritty clouds of dust as the wheels labored. Esther sat in the front seat of the family car and pulled a limp breast out of her dress. No matter how insufficient it was, Inez began to suck. And while they baked in the car, Esther listened to the sounds of the river for the first time, the soothing, steady sound of water that never stopped. And she heard murmurings from the river and wondered about the rocks, the fallen trees, the reptile skins and bird feathers—things that were once alive and were now part of the river.

"The fire didn't get my face, Inez," Esther said softly. "Mama won't let it get you either." She shaded the baby's face from the sunlight that roared through the windshield.

•　•　•　•　•

Low murmuring from the scattered homesteads and a rare summer breeze floated through Hemenway Wash that night, the name of the area before someone christened it Ragtown. Alf listened to the river lapping its edges and raised up on his elbow to see the reflection of the waxing moon in its blackness. The warmth of the night rubbed velvet on his bare arms and legs.

He touched the hair low on his belly, holding his penis that had been ignored in the anxiety of traveling and settling. He needed a woman. He thought of the supple one who had handed him a bucket. He thought of his wife and her scarred flesh.

Esther was still beautiful, her face especially. Her liquid, faraway eyes. Sad eyes as she looked at Alf who had promised her stars, a trip to the Panama Canal on a steamship, a home of her own. He thought of the rest of her, the skin he'd never really seen but only felt with his hand in the dark. He'd mainly heard about Esther's body from her—how it was covered with shiny, purplish stretch marks from the fire and her nine pregnancies.

"Esther," he whispered. He pushed his cot next to hers—they could manage. The squeaking, the wooden crossbars stretching canvas, might wake the children sprawled together in free-falling sleep on the big mattress. His daughters might see them if they woke, but he had to have release, and not by his own hand this time.

He pictured a high desert bluff covered with fine sand, soft for a bed. There she was, the woman with the bucket, lying on the sand, three buttons left to undo. He kneeled above her, outlining her nipple with his tongue, her breasts exposed to the moon, shining.

"Esther?"

"Unnh?"

"I want to be close. It's been a long time."

Silence from the cot, the sound of indecision or sleepiness, he didn't know.

"Esther?"

"No babies," she mumbled. "No more babies, please." He was good at that, even if he failed at other things. "Do you have a condom, Alf?"

"Of course."

"It better hold."

"You're still nursing the baby anyway. Double precaution," he said.

"Alf, haven't we had enough?"

His arm extended across the dark to knead her flaccid breast. He rolled toward her, awkwardly, impaled on the bony wood frame of the U.S. Army cots they'd found at a surplus store in San Diego, and looked over at the children covered with cheesecloth to protect them from scorpions and tarantulas. None of them showed signs of waking.

Alf kissed her lips, closing them, stopping further words, and cupping her face with his hands. He examined it closely and knew he'd seen her before, but maybe not. Old territory, new territory. Every time old but new. His hands drifted across lace and fabric to the place where she was bare and alive and fluid. He straddled her flesh, onto his knees, looking for a home. *Let me in.* He closed his eyes, and Esther faded from his mind.

"Alf, I can't. I just can't." Her legs opened anyway, obedient to his insistent hands.

Alf arched over her, poised. Esther, habitually submissive, pelvis tipped forward, took his penis in her hand to guide it. The silhouette, the man and the woman, about to imitate the eternal round, the thousands of years of anticipation, legs bowing, legs astride. Alf and Esther sharing the same pleasure as kings and queens in royal chambers, the king touching the queen with a curved finger, her hair flowing, her skirts falling, her eyes saying, "Yes." The same riches, the same wealth.

Alf probed deeper. And then, he was home—rocking, swaying, all's right with the world until he became aware of the singular life beneath him again, still considering the matter, hesitant. When would she stop wondering about life and start living it? When would she recognize that the real celestial king-dom was more about making love to this world rather than saving herself for a starched white afterlife? He looked at her limp head on the pillow, her refusal to be taken in by the passion which had betrayed her too many times, her disgust at her clitoris that made her tremble, that set it all in motion—the moistening, the breathing, the forgetting, the next child.

"Alf, roll over. The heat."

A breeze drifted over Alf's nakedness, drying the matted hair on his belly. He'd show her. He'd turn her limp head. His time had arrived.

2

Two and a half weeks in southern Nevada, half-awake on the army cot inside his cardboard-burlap-and-bedsheet contraption of a house, Alf listened to the others leave for the early shift. He'd join them as soon as he could grope through the morning fog in his brain.

He squinted at his clock. 4:10 A.M. He was lucky to have this shift—the best of two evils until Six Companies added graveyard, the only time of day to avoid sunstroke. He reminded himself that power lines would soon be strung into the canyon to replace the diesel compressors that powered the essential tools, not such luxuries as Alf's fan. Then, whatever hours he worked, Alf's electric fan would hum and blow cool air into his little sweatbox. His fan and cool air, nice things to think about while he avoided the morning. But a jumble of unwelcome thoughts muddled his brain: Esther; his three daughters; money; food; Esther again, unable to rise out of the doldrums; the sun that was dropping people in their tracks; his small baby.

He imagined his fan blowing the worries out of his mind and cooling his face and lifting his hair into wispy spikes. Then he pictured the men outside of his makeshift house—the whites of their shirts, the early morning shadows under the brims of their hats, new portraits in the gallery of his thoughts.

Some of his neighbors were lifelong construction stiffs, children of labor bureaus with their dusty chalkboards advertising romantic, pie-in-the-sky adventure in the armpits of the continent. They were hardened by pick-and-shovel work and the wheelbarrows they'd lifted and pushed. Others were soft-bodied expatriots from the world of stocks and bonds and paper dreams. Alf fit somewhere in the middle of these types—a touch soft, preferring indoors to outdoors, though not a stranger to manual labor. No matter where they fit on the spectrum, every one of them would be wearing a hat of some kind, probably a felt one. And because none of the trucks had gauges and because an empty tank meant walking papers, anybody who was a driver would be pulling out a dipstick to check his gasoline level. Then they'd start up their bulldozers and steamrollers and flatten Hemenway Wash with link treads, cloud it with burls of dust, and steam away from the graceful arc of the Colorado into the lava of Black Canyon. Others would jump onto running boards draped with torn, Arabian-style sheeting under their hats, their noses slathered with zinc oxide.

There were drilling crews too, some headed into Black via the Boulder Boat Landing, others floating on barges tethered to cables while they drilled anchorages for a bridge or an adit for a diversion tunnel. There were high scalers, affectionately known as cherry pickers—a loose assortment of Apaches from Arizona, mountain climbers, high-wire artists from the circus, and daredevils born of hunger like his neighbor, Ed Bishop, husband of Serena The Beautiful who had loaned her bucket to the Jensens. They scrambled across cliff faces to scrape the walls free of unstable rock. Armed with drifter drills and diamond bits, they were lowered over cliff edges in bosun's chairs to chip and drill holes for dynamite moorings. Before they lit the fuses and kicked themselves away from the face, they fondled the silver crosses and medicine bundles around their necks. Ed carried a rabbit's foot in his pocket. Alf saw it once when Ed was counting change in the commissary.

There were bridge builders who stretched suspension footbridges and high-tension cables across the murky water from Nevada to Arizona. And there were railroad men hacking track bed out of solid canyon wall and laying rails on debris blasted from cliffs. This foundation of man-made talus was supposed to support 33 million tons of live load. The numbers boggled Alf's imagination. Everyone tossed big numbers around as if they knew what they were talking about, but he couldn't think—or even dream—in those kinds of figures.

Even as Alf reminded himself to get up and move, he heard dynamite blasting and jackhammers drilling like bees on a hive wall. How would his family fare in the soon-to-be around-the-clock noise, let alone survive the night that spread over the Wash like a blanket and trapped the heat of day beneath? It never floated away or thinned into the moonlight. It was still, always still, and thick with something more than heat. 4:20 A.M. and the temperature had risen maybe five degrees as the sun moved closer to the horizon.

A few weeks. We can make it through a few weeks. People can do almost anything for a few weeks. He tossed on his army cot, rolling in and out of the pools of perspiration under his head and back until he couldn't avoid the clock any longer. He rolled off the mattress, crept past the sleeping children, washed in a bowl of tepid water, slipped into his clothes and out of their shelter he couldn't call home.

Alf, the manager of the River Commissary, the man who was not quite sure he'd been saved by grace, trudged toward the river along wind-polished desert pavement and felt slightly claustrophobic when he peered into the canyon. The towering walls hedged him in. Igneous, pyrogenic, lava. They blocked portions of sky. Black coal in a shed. His father again. His wife on fire, too. Her face like the center of a flower wreathed in petals of flame. And he remembered that face in a mahogany picture frame—her pure face on the mantel at her mother's house where she was once sheltered from the world. *Forget that picture, Alf. Everyone has to lose her innocence somewhere along the way. You can't change that.*

His feet plowing through the loose gravel and shattered rock, Alf reached the Six Companies River Camp at Cape Horn, a precarious group of wooden boxes tacked to a landslide with stilt legs. Above the barracks, two water tanks were lodged in the slope and surrounded by huge boulders that looked as if they could roll into the river if a workman snapped his fingers too loudly. A barge carrying a portable compressor floated by. Murl Emery, the barge-man who'd operated a ferry across the river long before anybody had ideas about a dam, waved at Alf.

"Mornin'," Murl yelled.

"Too hot already to say good morning."

Murl Emery smiled like he'd seen it all before. "Gets worse." He dipped an oar into the muddy water and steered toward midstream.

Alf felt the closeness of the small store even before he entered. Stuffy air. Suddenly the door swung open on its own. Carrying a bedroll, Gordy Weaver, the afternoon manager of the commissary, bolted out before Alf could get inside.

"What'd you do?" Alf asked. "Sleep here last night?"

"Had some thinking to do," he whispered, on the run already. "This is worse than hell, and I'm getting out. For good!" He tried to run, but the waterworn rubble gave him no assistance, bruising his calves and ankles at every step. Sweat dripped from under his hat into his eyes even though it was five in the morning when the world should be cool. Slowly, he made distance.

"Good luck," Alf called after him, then stepped inside.

How could anybody sleep in here? He opened two windows even though he'd have to close them soon. When the mercury passed 100, the windows changed into fire-breathing heat ducts. Already, the thermometer registered 112, but Alf liked the idea of open windows for a little while anyway.

Alf dusted, straightened, and moved the kegs out of the way, still wondering about Weaver sleeping in the commissary. He was crazy to stay in this tight box, but maybe he was riding the edge of his mind about now, so many people snooping in and out of places, no firm walls or doors to keep strangers out, and too many crawling desert creatures to feel safe on a rock somewhere.

He certainly hadn't done much to clean up. Kegs were scattered throughout the room, and leftover stools shoved out of the mess hall into the commissary after yesterday's Sunday meeting when Parson Frank read from the Bible and revived everybody with singing, clapping, and hallelujahs. *Kegs for religion.* Alf laughed. They'd been confiscated by Sheriff Williams on a bootleg raid in Ragtown and emptied into the sand. Kegs were Alf's true religion, try as the Latter-day Saints might to keep him from his ways. He bent to sniff one, his nose, his tongue remembering.

The door opened. His thumbs in the straps of his well-used overalls, Alf's first customer was a Mormon Alf had met when he overheard him talking about St. Thomas in the commissary. Of course, Alf wanted to know if the man knew Uncle Woolley. Yes, he did. That same afternoon, Bill Parker walked over to Ragtown to meet Esther and the family, and Alf decided he liked the unassuming Parker well enough, better than some other Mormons he knew.

"Good morning, Parker."

"Morning to you, Alf. Looks like another scorcher. July's supposed to be worse than anything we've seen yet. Got some Dentyne in today?"

"Not yet. Fresh supplies tomorrow." He dusted the remaining chewing gum with a rag he'd brought from his household supplies.

"How soon's your house ready up in Boulder, Alf?"

"About a month. They're building a house and a half every day up there. Whole crew gets fired if they don't keep to schedule."

"Excuse me for saying so, but your wife doesn't look too good." Parker pulled a toothpick out of his overall pocket.

Alf opened his cash box and cracked open a roll of dimes. "Heat's hard on her." Esther would wake up yelling about the fire, how it was going to burn her again, and then lie under wet sheets all day long. "Besides that, she's worried somebody will steal her shoes if she takes them off."

"Yeah, she looks kind of like the worry might eat her alive. Ain't easy with that new baby and all the rest."

"I wish my son Herbert were here. He knows her better than anybody." Alf had watched Herbert sit at Esther's side for hours after they'd left the Root House in Ely when everything in the world seemed to be caving in and pressing against her. His son had a way of petting her forearms and hands, as if he were an animal trainer with a skittish cat. 'You can trust me,' he'd say to her, and Alf felt a tinge of nausea as he remembered the two of them together, almost like lovers, whispering things they'd never say to him.

Parker interrupted his thoughts. "Good luck, brother. Something about your wife really gets to me. I'm glad I left mine back in St. Thomas where she's at least got a house and the sisters to quilt with. But as soon as Boulder City's built, I'm bringing her down. She'll like Esther, I'm sure."

"I would have left her. . . ." Alf poked his finger into the cage of his fan and whirled the blade. "Not too many days now, this thing'll be turning by itself. Cool air. What do you think?"

"I'll be here, letting it fan my chin every chance I get. Hey, you hear the state mine inspector was around the tunnels again last weekend?"

"I'm hearing it now."

"Says everybody's too loose with the dynamite. Somebody's gonna lose a hand or an arm. 'This ain't a daredevil circus,' he said."

"Sounds reasonable," Alf said.

"Foreman didn't think it sounded so reasonable. And especially the carbon monoxide business. Helluva argument about federal jurisdiction. Nevada ordered Six to obey state mining laws forbidding gasoline engines in the tunnels. Six brought in an arsenal of U.S. attorneys and got the feds to rule in its favor."

The door squeaked open again and a bright slash of light cut across Alf's eyes. His pupils contracted to sharp pencil points.

"Camels?" The new customer's pants had been wiped on like a hand towel until no washing could hide it. He wore a black undershirt and an expression to match.

"Sure." Alf chucked a pack onto the counter.

"Cornstarch?"

"Prickly heat?"

The man grunted.

"Sprinkle it between your sheets. It'll sooth the itching."

Somewhere on the project dynamite exploded.

"When in hell is Six Companies going to improve things around here?" The stranger slapped his palms on the counter. "We get paid four dollars a day in this damn hellhole, explosives going off all around our ears. One of those big black boulders could crash through this shack anytime. Four dead from falling rocks already. And a man could die wanting something cold. Everything's hot—the soda, the milk, and the water full of red grit."

Alf listened to the man whose massive forehead and flat, bushy eyebrows crowded his already small brown eyes. His nose hung long above a curveless mouth.

"You hear about Frank Camoin?" the man continued.

"No, can't say I have," said Alf.

"The doctor at Six Companies's hospital said he had influenza and died of pneumonia. Hell, I was with him two days ago and he was breathing fine."

"Where'd he work?" Parker asked.

"Driving trucks around those explosions. Some tunnel, I think. Probably got gassed. What's it to you?"

"Nothing." Alf made mental notes. He'd heard rumblings about agitators and didn't like the idea of one so close to his hard-won security. "Just wondering."

Parker settled onto a keg. "Of course, you heard about Red Schroeder and the Hercomite?" he said in a one-up tone of voice.

The stranger wiped the perspiration from his forehead onto his pants.

"Well, Red was tampin' black powder into this hole, see, getting it ready to blow. Bosses told him to use a wood tamp, but no, he used metal. A little overeager, and blam, the stuff exploded. Killed both Red and his partner. Wounded three others."

"Nevada or Arizona side of the river?" the stranger asked.

"Nevada, poor soul," said Parker. "Too bad he didn't get blasted into Arizona. Better insurance. Cheap lizards over at Nevada Industrial."

"A week ago?"

"Give or take a day."

The stranger unbuttoned his back pocket, pulled out a notepad and a two-inch stub of pencil.

"How can you write with that thing?" asked Alf. "I've got some new No. 2's. How about one?"

"Mind your own business." He flipped his notebook closed, tossed company scrip onto the counter, grabbed his change, the cornstarch, and Camels, and slammed the screen door.

"Dismal sort," said Parker.

"Sounds like a troublemaker to me," Alf said. "Somebody was telling me some Wobblies are being sent in here to stir things up, as if we don't have enough to deal with already."

"The I-want-whiskey, I-won't-work boys, huh? Speaking of Wobblies, I better wobble on back to them cliffs. Curse the day I climbed my first tree and thought I was a monkey."

"You know my neighbor, Ed Bishop? He's picking cherries up there, too. You boys are getting pretty close to heaven." Alf leaned his elbows on the counter and settled into the palms of his hands. "Ask God to give you the real lowdown if you see Him, would you?"

"If I don't fall the other way!" Parker laughed brashly, a countrified wag.

"What do you think God'll say, Bill? Do you think all this Mormonism is the only way to get to the main event? Do you believe it line for line?"

Bill laughed again, a laugh honed in the jagged terrain of vermillion cliffs and red clay in Muddy and Virgin River country and protected from the domesticated ways of Salt Lake or Brigham City with their third-generation pioneer airs.

Listening to his laughter, Alf thought he might have a friend here, a free spirit maybe, somebody like the unforgettable white-haired missionary he'd heard speak at church when he was nine years old. Brigham Young had sent this man to teach Indians in the badlands of Arizona, and the ancient scout told tale after tale of Navajos, Moquis, and how he traveled with a Welchman to see if they could find a trace of Gaelic in the Indian language. Brigham Young wanted to solve the riddle of the Lamanites, the inhabitants of America before Mormon's golden plates were engraved.

And he talked about the many times he crossed the Colorado at Lee's Ferry, and how Bishop Roundy lost his life, and his group of settlers lost two wagons and all their provisions to the Colorado. He even talked about smoking peace pipes, a surprise to Alf who was used to hearing the abstainers pounding their fists at the pulpit. Alf preferred the missionary scout with his stories about Indians and tobacco at the Brigham City Second Ward when he was young and smart enough to know the difference between alive and dead. That's why he was drawn to Parker who spoke with the same kind of southern Utah, dry-wash drawl.

"Now, Alf, why do you bother with questions for God?" Parker said. "It's all outlined in the scripture. Clear as high mountain water. Just listen to the brethren."

Alf was startled out of his romanticizing. Parker was spouting the standard line of doctrine, words that weren't supposed to come out of his mouth.

"You know old Joe Smith said it was folly for a man to want any station other than the one he's been appointed to by God. Trust and obey, Brother. Leave everything in God's hands like the brethren say."

Alf searched Parker's face for a trace of irony, but he found none; his jaw was set like a steep-sided canyon.

"But why do I have to listen to the brethren?" Alf was still framed by the vee of his hands. "Why do they know so much more than I do?"

"They were called by God. You know that."

"What about *my* ears and eyes?"

"I say listen up and be patient till God lassoes and hogties you and takes you to a higher elevation. That's what I say."

In the back of his mind, Alf could hear the ghostly sound of Esther's collar rustling as she shook her head and said: "He that believeth not shall be damned." But he'd answered her, tit for tat: "Who really knows the mind of God?" And then her tat again: "Certainly not you or me," but he knew that deep down she thought she did know the mind of God because she obeyed the church leaders and because it was her responsibility to guide him into the path, either with coaxing or a reprimand. Stiff-necked Mormons had to have their own way about things. Even Parker with his good-natured hick ways who had just lost Alf's trust. Alf decided not to tell Parker that God Himself had appeared to him on his first day on the site.

"Say a little prayer over yours and Ed's bosun's, Bill. I wouldn't want to take in more wives, though Serena Bishop wouldn't be a bad deal."

"Don't go lusting after other people's wives, widows or no." Parker wagged a bony, sun-tanned finger. "Polygamy's out." Now Parker sounded a little like the chickens Alf had raised from time to time, the high thin gizzard sound of a rooster safeguarding his pen, proclaiming the territory as his, thinking he knew the boundaries for everyone who associated with the name Mormon.

"Take care of yourself, Parker." Alf dismissed him.

"Same to you, Alf." He hurried out, oblivious to his dismissal.

Disappointed with Parker's narrowness, Alf pressed the wrinkles from the scrip and added it to the pile in the drawer. He thought the two of them might have been friends. And then the words started pouring into his head again, the words about God and obedience and failure and determination. He had to find a way to escape them before he drowned.

He looked again at the scrip in the drawer. *Scrip.* He'd heard the men complaining about it. They didn't have any money to buy things except at the company store. Six Companies paid its employees with scrip. Not good at Emery's or anyplace else, it could buy everything under the roof at the company store.

Last week after his foreman was put to bed to recover from heatstroke, Alf scraped a loan together for Tex Jones, another high scaler, out of the commissary drawer. Luckily, Tex won the poker stakes at the Boulder Club and repaid Alf the next day. But Alf wouldn't take that chance again. He'd suffered. No sleep as he watched his hand pull money that wasn't his out of the drawer, over and over during the night. It was just that Jones was so positive Lady Luck was smiling on him after a 12-foot-square slab of cliff broke off next to his scaffold and dropped 600 feet into the river. Alf had to believe him. But no more loans after that, at least until he had capital of his own. The scrip-for-cash idea did, however, have possibilities.

Alf figured if he could get enough capital together, he'd exchange it for scrip and turn a five percent profit. After a day of explosions, dust, and savage heat, a lot of men wanted to escape the reservation into Nevada's jurisdiction which closed its eyes to the 18th Amendment. The two-laner to Las Vegas had its bevy of roadside attractions—honkytonks, bootleg liquor tents, and cathouses. Alf became aware of his shirt clinging to his chest and shoulders and of how he held his breath while he figured. He'd find a way to do it. He might talk to God about it, but if God decided it wasn't a good idea, maybe he'd have to reconsider. But God had given him his brain, hadn't he?

The outside heat poured into the commissary, almost liquid. It oozed into ceiling corners, crowded into middle space, settled on the floor, and left no room for anything else. Alf closed the windows and plugged his fan into the socket, secretly hoping, but not surprised when there were no whirring blades.

The box with the fan was delivered on the same day Red Schroeder tamped the powder too hard. Alf had watched parts of Red fall like gentle rain into the Colorado and wash past him and the Commissary like driftwood. Twirling the fan's blade, Alf kissed the slight whiff of man-made air.

What he wouldn't give for a cold beer. Good thing Prohibition was on, keeping him a semi-straight arrow for a while. A cold bottle of beer appeared on the third shelf to the left of Alf's counter, icy beads of Eskimo sweat dribbling down its sides. Lifting it from the shelf, Alf unbuttoned his shirt and held the coldness to his chest, then rolled it from nipple to nipple, back and forth in praise. He pressed it to his cheeks, closed his eyes and turned it upside down to suck the rim and pull the ale through his teeth and over his tongue. *Mush, you huskies!*

The door opened. More heat and two men.

"Good morning, Alfred."

"Mr. Watkins. Well! Good morning," and Alf was happy the beer was only a mirage. This was only the second time he'd been in the man's presence, and Alf wasn't sure if Watkins was a straight-backed gentleman of the Church or not. Nobody knew for sure, since he was always away on a construction job, unable to be in town for Sunday worship. It was also rumored that his wife was a secret Christian Scientist raising their children her own way. She had been ostensibly Mormon when they married in the Salt Lake Temple, but the relatives surmised she kept the truth from her husband about the Christian Science practitioner who'd prayed for her when she was young and ill and left her a copy of *Science and Health*.

"She lost her marbles over that Mary Baker Eddy woman," one aunt said, this topic being a favorite in the whisperings of the more distant Utah relatives.

"Alfred, meet Walker Young, Construction Engineer for the Bureau."

Alf held out his hand with a slight hint of formality he'd adopted to keep his supervisors guessing. "Nice to meet you, sir."

Young didn't return the greeting. His mind seemed on another rail. Owlish glasses wrapped around his straightforward eyes and ears that looked waxed. His hair was cropped close to his head like a skullcap, one inch above his ears, and he wore a bow tie.

"Alfred," said A. P., "we have some questions."

Alfred was mesmerized by the white-haired Watkins—a big man with a heavy head of hair. There was no equivocation in his questions or demeanor. He knew what he wanted, when, and how, probably ever since the turn of the century when he and his brother hauled freight in wagon trains for a railroad contractor who went belly-up before his particular stretch of the Transcontinental was completed. Determined not to lose the pay they both needed to put food on the table, the brothers begged a local banker to trust them with that section of track. After dozens of sessions where the talk turned from corrupt to successful relatives, Alf knew the Watkinses' story backward and forward.

He wondered if the story was true about A. P. riding by stagecoach from Price to Watkins, Utah, where the brothers started a coal mine. The coach driver drove A. P. straight to the stables rather than to the hotel because of knee-deep mud. Watkins told him he'd better do some quick thinking: one of them was going to get muddy and it wasn't going to be him. The driver could either saddle up the horse and take him across the street to the hotel or carry Watkins on his own back.

Alf wanted time to analyze this legend he'd heard so much about, find out his secrets, understand why he didn't equivocate about things, why he could just walk out and get what he wanted. Where did a man get that kind of moxie?

"Alfred? Are you listening?"

"Sir?"

"I'll get to the point. Mr. Young and I've heard rumors about certain labor activists infiltrating the project. I told Mr. Young you could be trusted to keep our interest quiet, being we're related by marriage."

"Yes sir. Of course."

"Have you seen or heard anybody agitating about conditions here?"

"Everybody complains, sir. A man can't draw a full breath for fear of burning his throat."

"I mean, anything out of the ordinary?"

Alf took a deep breath of his own and waited for the burning in his lungs to pass. "There was an odd one in today."

"Yes?"

"New to me. About six feet tall, I'd say. Brown hair. Didn't wear the usual blue shirt. But I get new men all the time."

"Why did you mention this one?" Mr. Young's eyeglasses duplicated his eyes: two terraces of blue pupils.

"He talked about a man named Frank Camoin, a man who died yesterday. Implied he hadn't died of pneumonia like the officials said."

Walker Young seemed to be a man more comfortable with blueprints and compass-drawn arcs than human beings. "Where on the project did Camoin work?" he asked. His presence affected Alf's breathing.

"Driving trucks close to the explosions is all I know. Something to do with carbon monoxide and no ventilation to clear the blast particles away. Too many people come in here for me to keep things straight."

Young mopped his neck with a plaid handkerchief, then his temples. "We've got to nip any labor-organizing activity. Can't get off schedule. This dam is the largest government project since the Panama Canal. No room for any kinks."

"I understand, sir." Beads of sweat pimpled Alf's cheeks and forehead. Young's eyes looked severe behind the horn-rims. They reminded Alf of someone else's eyes, the scolding eyes of a man at Church who towered over Alf as a little boy. He'd been playing marbles under the wooden pews at sacrament meeting, disappointed when the missionary hadn't come back to talk about peace pipes. The elder collared Alf afterward, righteousness in his eyes, and called him a "dumb Dane with the manners of a boar." Alf remembered a button and thread stretching across the man's Adam's apple until the thread broke and the button flew.

As perspiration ran from the bottom of Young's ears down a muscle in his neck, Alf wondered if he was the kind to get physical if he didn't like someone. But no, this man lived with paper and pencil lines that could be erased even though he wore a tight tie and a stiff shirt collar with a three-inch ring of sweat around his neck.

"You do a good job for us, Alfred," said Watkins, "and you'll get that greengrocer's job we talked about. You'll be out of this canyon and Ragtown as soon as possible."

"Thank you, Mr. Watkins. Esther's not holding up too well."

"You never should have brought her and the children down, but people do what they have to do; I understand."

"Dumb Danes, right?" Alf said to the side.

"What, Alf?"

"Nothing, sir. Is your brother doing better with the cancer?"

"He's still taking the treatments and swearing like a trooper he'll be on the job. Still handles all the correspondence and directs the project from his hospital bed."

"I hope he'll get better."

"As long as the Hoover Dam contracts keep coming in, that's his best cure." Watkins touched the rim of the useless fan on the counter. "We'll have electricity in here as soon as we can. In the meantime, keep us posted. And give my regards to Esther. I remember when she was wrapped in cotton for a whole year, poor thing. Lots of people prayed for her."

Young opened the door, and heat blasted in like a wind.

"Before you go. . . ." said Alf. "That man had a notebook and jotted down a few things when Parker talked about Red Schroeder."

"Parker?" asked Young.

"Parker. The high scaler. I'm sure you heard about the explosives accident, didn't you?"

"Yes, but who's this Parker?"

"He's not a Wobbly if that's what you're thinking. He's a friend I met on the job. A Mormon fellow from St. Thomas."

As Young turned to leave, Alf observed the thinness of his lips. How could a woman or even his mother find anything to kiss? There seemed no generosity to his face.

"We'll see," he said.

"Get more information as you can, Alfred," said Watkins. He was in his late seventies and still reeked with authority. "Remember the greengrocer's job."

After the door banged shut, Alf thought his fan might turn magically on its metal axis in celebration. Two and a half weeks on the job, and chances for a promotion looked good. About the right timing for a man of destiny. A man of destiny. Yes, just as God had promised him even though Alf had begun to doubt his encounter with God as he'd seen the effects of heat on others around him. The sureness of his vision had slipped through the pores of his mind like water into the sunbaked desert hardpan. But now it was sure again. A Calling Made Sure through the auspices of A. P. Watkins: VIP; kind patron.

Only a few weeks ago the Model A had dipped in and out of sand hills, rattled through dry washes and around the tules on a road no more than two tracks through the desert, Esther moaning they should have stayed in Brigham City.

No more Brigham City for Alf. No more stooping in beet fields, thinning, pulling, cramping his back. No more cement factories or newspaper distributorships. No more looking at the untarnished Esther smiling out of the picture frame on her mother's mantle—soft, lovely, the charmed daughter who had lost her way by following Alf. No more standing at his in-laws' doorstep with his hands in his empty pockets, hearing his wife say, "Can you put us up for a little while?" No more looking into their hard faces that didn't conceal their lack of enthusiasm for him. Esther wouldn't want Brigham City anymore. This time she'd be happy. He'd do right by her. He'd buy her a fine dress for dancing, one with black bugle beads crowded on black jersey, heavy layers of bugle beads tight to each other, no skimping on quantity, heavy on her breasts. Once again he believed.

No more rentals, no more warehouse homes, no more tents. He perched himself on top of a keg to think about the good things to come. And then the door opened again. Back to business at hand.

"Can't find the doctor anywhere," the breathless man in a sweat-drenched shirt said. "Sam Cookson dropped dead in the kitchen. Just like a fly in midair."

• • • • •

The baby pumped at Esther's breast, flailing her arms and fretting. Perspiration pooled between Inez's cheek and Esther's flesh.

"I can't breathe," she said out loud.

The sky shimmered fire white outside their shelter. Heat smothered her pores and pressed the cotton to her skin even though she sat near a newly wetted sheet, hung over a split of clothesline to cool the air.

"I can't stand it anymore." Her upper torso rocked in agitation. She jerked Inez from the nipple and pressed her, bawling, flatly into the dresser drawer that served as a cradle.

"Shut up, baby. Shut up. Heaven have mercy, I'm so hot." She grabbed a pie tin for a fan and tried to move the immovable air.

"I'm gonna die."

Sun seeped through the brown cardboard roof, the sheets, the burlap, and the nailed two-by-four frame Esther and Alf had pieced together. She dipped into the day's water supply with the long-handled scoop, thinking she should have stayed in Brigham City with the apricot and peach trees and the water running in a ditch in front of her house, with her mother who had already seen too much of her in the many retreats homeward to birth another child or when things rotted between her and Alf.

And I never can wait to get back to him. Ass you are, Esther. Ass. Stupid ass. Why did you ever pass Row 5 at the Elberta Theater anyway?

She had dressed carefully on that evening so many years ago—long sleeves, laced cuffs and collar. The black straw hat with white roses nestled in its brim flopped as she walked down the aisle, already a professional singer like Mama, at eighteen.

Passing, Esther noticed some locals jockeying for the aisle seat on Row 5.

"Esther. Esther Carpenter, my dear." The speaker swooped in a low bow, cap in hand. "May I have the honor of your notice?"

Her hat bobbed as she flipped her head too quickly, looking straight ahead, trying not to listen.

"See that girl, Esther Carpenter?" he said. "I'm going to marry her some-day, just wait and see if I don't."

While the projectionist rewound the film, she sang, and the pianist rippled arpeggios like streams over the keys. There, on the aisle, Alf grinned, eager, handsome, acting like he owned the world plus the moon, and she could have felt the tendrils wrapping around her legs if she hadn't been so engaged in singing "Me and My Gal." The piano tinkled tin sounds and last chords. She stepped forward into the lights and the applause, and with a generous flourish of her arm, said thank you. The movie flickered onto the screen. She smiled condescendingly at him in the half shadow as she left the theater.

Stupid ass, Esther, why did you ever smile back at him? Everybody said he was no good, but, no, Esther, you never listen to anybody. Meek, but headstrong mule of a woman.

The baby gasped for breath between her bleatings. Esther stared at the anger in the tight fists, but ignored her baby, walked to the makeshift window with no glass, and peered out. No one was in sight. No one laughed or traded gossip with their foot resting on the bumper of a parked car. The sun was bleached dead white and dimensionless.

"Shut up," she screamed, jabbing her fingers into her ears.

On the cot, eight-year-old Rebecca woke from a troubled sleep, her hair coiled in wet ringlets against her cheeks. She dipped her hand into the bucket and bent over the dresser drawer. "Suck baby," she whispered, tapping the baby's lips with her finger.

Esther slumped onto the other cot next to Mary Elizabeth whose back was turned to her. Nothing else to do in the middle of these insane days where the sun crowded the entire sky. The smart, intelligent women stayed in civilization, waiting for Boulder City to be built, packing three clothes changes into cardboard, kissing their men good-bye and reminding, "Send for us when you get a job and a place to stay."

Esther heard a car toiling to a halt. She lifted the canvas flap to see Alf slamming the door of a borrowed car, home too early.

"Alf, what's up?"

"It's Sam Cookson."

"What happened?"

"Too hot. He came out of the vegetable cooler where he makes out menus, walked into the blast of those oil stoves and keeled over."

"Why'd you come home?"

"We need you, Esther."

"What for?"

"The doctor's at the other end of the project and can't be reached. It's Hades down there, and you know what that means for a corpse. I told them you'd dressed the dead before."

"Alf, does it matter to you I'm dying?"

"My songbird. Wilting in this desert." He patted her breasts.

"Alf, don't patronize me." She pushed his hand away. "You're in charge of the commissary; big man now. You do it."

"I need you, Esther." His face was set.

She sighed and then rummaged through the orange crates for soap, scissors, and washcloth. "Bring the family Bible, Alf. Rebecca, watch the baby until Mary Elizabeth wakes up." She grabbed her hat, its satin ribbons blotched with water stains, and tied it in a bow under her chin.

"I'm ready."

"Somebody measured 134 down in Black Canyon yesterday," Alf said as they climbed into the car. "The heat bounces off the lava and intensifies. They say it's never been this bad. Lucky we don't have to sleep in that canyon. Fifteen degrees cooler over here."

"Alf."

"They say there'll be some houses ready soon." The engine turned over, and everything in the car vibrated. "Cooler by seven degrees up in Boulder City. More breeze."

"Soon, soon. Always soon. Alf, I didn't want the baby."

"You'll feel better by tonight when the sun goes down. We'll invite Jack over to play his sax. 'Dark Town Strutters' Ball.' We'll sing. And guess what? A. P. came in and said the greengrocer's job at the Boulder City Company Store looks like it'll be mine."

"I'm too old for that baby," she said.

"You're a spring chicken, Esther."

"I am the gizzard and the neck, the plucked skin pimpled with half-plucked feathers."

The car tilted to the left and battled soft sand with one wheel.

"When we move to Boulder City, I'll bring home crisp vegetables. Greengrocer A. L. Jensen. Greens, Esther. Crisp carrots and celery stalks blooming with green. Butter squash, crookneck, zucchini. Apples to crunch your teeth in; firm, red apples to leave a big white bite in while the juice drips down your chin and hangs there waiting to fall to your hand. It will be fine, Esther. Fine."

She stared at the dust reeling over the window glass and powdering her cuticles brown.

"Let's get out of here, Alf."

"Things are good now, Esther. They like me on the job."

"They always like you in the beginning."

"Esther," he glared at her, his eyeglasses mirrors of desert landscape. "Your mouth." He geared down over the last hill. "I try to believe in myself and you're always there with your mouth."

He drove the car as far as it would go until the newly blasted talus became too obstinate for tires. Then they walked and hobbled over the rocks piled against the canyon walls until they reached the river camp. They climbed the barracks' wooden stairs in silence.

Three men stood inside the door.

"Thanks for coming, Mrs. Jensen. He's in here."

Wood flooring echoed the shuffling, muffled the whispers in honor of the deceased.

"Bring me some water, Alf." She noticed Cookson's boots by his bed, crusted and crimped with dried river sand. "This heat doesn't do him any favors." His stomach had bloated; his blood had pooled. Esther pulled his eyes closed, but one opened again.

"Any coins, big ones?"

One of the men handed her a fifty-cent piece. "He won't need this long will he? That's an hour's work."

"Don't worry, Mister, it's yours again when the coffin lid goes down."

Esther closed the eye that stared and put the coin over the socket. As she cut open his undershirt and tugged off his pants, Alf returned with a basin. Esther's hands swished the river water and coolness lapped at her elbow. She reached for the soap, turning it over, sliding it under her wedding band and over her knuckles, rotating it in the nap of white washcloth. She mopped Cookson's stillness, lathered his neck, his chest, and groin. The men looked away as Esther lathered the soap to peaks. Esther, nose to nose with life gone limp.

"Fresh clothes?" she asked.

"Right here, ma'am." A white shirt, short sleeves, flat pearl buttons, washpants, clean underwear. Esther dressed him for a new day. Cookson was ready.

"The boys will have a box here soon," someone said. "Not long now."

"Until then," Esther said, "leave this Bible right here." She placed the heavy book on his stomach to flatten the distention, then laced her fingers with Cookson's before she folded his hands across his chest.

41

"Tell God to send for me," she whispered in his ear as the sunlight erased the panes on the window behind her. Then she turned for the door and the heat and the river that was flowing steadily, wide water that frightened her with its sullen power. Esther stopped to listen and thought she heard murmuring in the water, voices garbled by the swift current, and she wondered if God lived in the river because it never stopped flowing and God couldn't be trapped, could he?

Maybe she could go to God right now. Slip off the rocks and say, "I give." But Alf was holding her firmly by the elbow.

"Let's go back, dear," he said. "You were brave in there. That's my Esther."

3

When he heard the triangle ringing like a fire alarm in the dark he didn't panic. The LeTourneau Construction crew had moved into camp, complete with a triangle to waken their early morning crew, and he'd been waiting all night for its sound.

Alf paced outside his disreputable house, waiting for Ragtown to come alive, even his own family which actually should stay asleep, especially Inez with her colic and Esther who'd been morose since she'd dressed Cookson for his departure three days ago.

When she was awake, she sat crosslegged on the cot and stared. Dressed only in her temple garments which stuck to her like soaked newsprint, she sat like a statue—no word, no response, not noticing Mary Elizabeth who brought Inez to her for feeding, then took her away.

"Esther. Snap out of it," Alf had coaxed. "Get dressed."

"Mama. That's enough." Mary Elizabeth tried shaking her alive.

Nothing seemed to move through her eyes or ears. She sat as though a shawl of oblivion had been thrown over her back and shoulders and head, like a peasant woman gone blind and deaf and immune. No, Alf wasn't going to waken her now, afraid she'd sit up and stare at him again as if he wasn't there.

A few weeks. People can stand anything for a few weeks.

He examined his puffy face in the dark reflection of the cracked hand mirror. *Old man at forty-six. Tired old man pretending he can start again.*

"Mary Elizabeth, Rebecca," he crept next to them and whispered close to their ears. "It's time. They're starting to cook already." He noticed Mary

Elizabeth under the sheet, her curving spine protecting her breasts and stomach from his eyes. His daughter—a woman soon to become someone's dream, someone's lust. She'd curled her hair in old rags. His daughter learning the game of allure without a teacher, the rules stamped inside of her somewhere. More daughters following, falling in line, the same game, born to listen to their hearts and wombs—those illiterate organs—instead of their heads.

Mary Elizabeth pulled the sheet up to cover her ears. "Go on," she whispered. "I'll be there in a minute."

"You sure we're going to have bacon, Daddy?" Rebecca asked as she had the night before. Everybody had talked about it all week long—The LeTourneau Road Construction 4th of July Chuckwagon Breakfast Celebration.

"Can't you smell it cooking?" Alf said. "Mary Elizabeth, it's time to get up."

"I said I'm coming. Just go ahead. I'll be there."

"I'll be waiting," Alf whispered as he went outside to watch the increasing activity.

Rebecca's whispers were not so quiet as she buttoned her dress and cleaned the sleepers from the corners of her eyes. "Hurry up, Mary Elizabeth."

"Don't boss me around. I'll come when I'm ready."

"Miss La-Te-Da," mocked Rebecca as she lifted the canvas flap and reached for her father's hand. "Good-bye, Mary Elizabeth," she yelled.

"Shhh," Alf said. "You'll wake the baby."

Together they walked toward the growing crowd at Jess Williams's tent where Alf could see the tip of the sheriff's rifle silhouetted in the early light. The gun cracked the air, and its echo ricocheted off the labyrinth of Black Canyon walls.

"Jess is paying tribute to the Declaration of Independence, Rebecca. That means our freedom. America, you know." She grabbed tightly to Alf's hips when the rifle fired four more shots.

"My little love, don't be afraid." He pulled her along gently, sidestepping mesquite and beavertail, and lifted her onto the hood of a dusty Chevy. "I think you can see from here. It looks like the sheriff made us a flagpole last night."

Williams's flagpole was a crooked stick, barely tall enough to keep Old Glory out of the dust, apropos for Ragtown. While the sheriff lashed the rope to the pole, Alf contemplated the red, white, and blue, the stars, the stripes, his flag, and cursed the patriotic swelling in his throat. He needed to maintain a calm voice and appearance.

"God bless America, land that I love." A few started to sing and urged others to join in, but both the flag and the song hung limply in the heavy air. The crowd seemed permanently dusty—dust under their fingernails, in their hair, on their eyelashes, and under their collars. The dry silt from Big Red seemed to coat the vocal cords of the people who sang, "Stand beside her, and guide her."

"Breakfast, provided today by the generous LeTourneau Construction Company, will be served right soon," Williams announced, "and after you've eaten, we'll have a few games for the kids, young and old, a three-legged, a potato sack, maybe a wheelbarrow race if anyone's up to that. You may be interested to know that LeTourneau is offering big prizes—pea coats, snow-shoes, and hot water bottles."

Alfred Jensen, intense while the others chuckled at Williams's announcement, opened and closed his mouth like a guppy, anxious for an opportunity to speak.

"Sheriff." He waved his index finger for attention. "Sheriff Williams. Do we have an orator?"

"Orator?" someone yelled. "Left that monkey business back in Kansas."

"Independence Day," said Alf, "is not Independence Day without a tribute to our founding fathers."

"I hadn't planned on any speeches," Jess said, "but looks like you might have, Alf."

"I'm your man." He smiled a quick smile, stepped into the arena next to Sheriff Williams, who appeared to be a stretched wire next to Alf's softer contours.

"Hey, Alf," yelled Ed Bishop with a steaming mug of coffee halfway to his lips. "None of your bull."

Alf's downturned palm tamped the opposition. Before he cleared his throat, he noticed Mary Elizabeth at the edge of the crowd in a pale peach dress with a hint of censorship at the corners of her mouth.

"Seven score and fifteen years ago—" preacher-sure he spoke, proud of his midnight calculations, proud that Esther's mother had been his example, polished him up, taught him elocutionary technique, "—our fathers brought forth on this continent, a new nation, conceived in liberty. Now we are engaged in a great civil war—an economic one this time."

The crowd shifted uneasily, wondering how this had happened to their party.

"Gentlewomen, gentlemen," he said, "be grateful for your country. And, today, we should be grateful for the honorable Jess Williams. Ragtown, though temporary, is not a suitable name for our burgeoning settlement. We are not rags and dregs as the name implies. Therefore, I move we pay tribute to Williams." Alf looked straight at the wiry man. "Let's name our settlement in his honor. After all, when he's smart enough to lead a raid on the bootleggers in these neighboring canyons and dump the hooch in the river, he deserves our appreciation."

Alf tried not to laugh at his cleverness, but couldn't help it when there was enough other laughter to cover the extent of his pleasure.

"I'm not so sure that was real smart," Ed Bishop wisecracked. Everyone laughed again, this time a bit uneasily, aware of the public posture expected for Prohibition, especially on this government-controlled reservation.

"What do you say?" Alf asked, spreading his arms wide open to the crowd. "Williamsville? After all, he's the lawkeeper appointed to protect our homes. . . ."

"From snakes-s-s-s-s-s?" someone hissed.

"How about the heat? Can he do something about that?"

"Time to eat, folks," Williams announced flatly, avoiding Alf's eyes.

Center stage shifted like so much sand as people lined up for pancakes, syrup, bacon, and coffee. Alf watched his careful plans fade into a ray of morning sun and float skyward with the camp's cigarette smoke.

"Ragtown is henceforth called Williamsville," Alf yelled to the few still standing near the flagpole. "Do I have a second?"

No one answered, occupied with plates and forks and spoons and the smells inviting them to feast.

Then he noticed Serena Bishop staring at him. "Serena," Alf yelled again. "How about a second from you?"

"I'll give you your second, Alf." Her voice was low, a sound from the sand and the river. Her dark eyes measured him as she spoke, framed by her brown hair pulled straight back and tied with a blue bandana. She stood apart from the others, someone sure of her ground and her footing, a woman not bound to anyone or anything, at home in her body as if she'd been there for five lifetimes, a woman immune to the gravity beneath her. She seemed to know Alf. She probably even knew that God had pointed his finger at Alf and singled him out. He suspected she recognized the real Alf. She had eyes to see.

Alf forgot about asking for yeas and nays. His eyes wandered the range of her sinewy legs, long and well proportioned and obvious. She was one of the few women who wore walking shorts.

"Thank you, Serena." He moved closer and felt the energy of the woman, her power to ignore the insignificant details that occupied most domesticated females. "This tawdry crowd is lucky to have someone like me, right?"

Serena's smile spread like a slow hand.

Alf raised an oratorical fist for a parting shot to the people in line for breakfast. "May our nation, under God, have new birth, new life, in spirit and upon the face of this desolation."

"Cut it, buster," someone mumbled.

Serena winked at him. "See you later, Alf." She slipped into line next to the pancakes and Ed.

Then he noticed a pair of scuffed shoes he'd seen before, the hem of a pale peach dress, and looked up at an expression that both mocked and tolerated him. As he briefly studied Mary Elizabeth's face, he noticed Esther's arch of brow and the suggestion of her in the eyes, and yet the color of the eyes was Alf's as well as the shape of the forehead. A synthesis. Two in one. Splintered selves gazing back at him, Alf Jensen. But she ignored him when he approached her. She grabbed the arm of the closest person.

"Will you be my partner for the three-legged race?" Alf heard his fourteen-year-old daughter say to a ratty-looking construction stiff, an awkward man in his twenties with too much bad weather on his face.

"Sure, sweetheart," he said to Mary Elizabeth. "What's your name?"

"M. E."

"Me? Is that your name?"

Alf didn't stay to hear the rest of their ridiculous banter. He'd already warned her there weren't many women around. He figured the hour was too early and the weather too hot for problems, but he couldn't handle them right now anyway. Sometimes a man had to throw up his arms and surrender to the inevitable. He stepped over bedrolls and mattresses in the desert sand, walked past the lean-tos, packing boxes, and nailed sheets, and opened the burlap flap of his misbegotten house of cardboard and two-by-fours.

"Esther?" he called. "The girls are out already. Come on."

"I can't."

"Yes, you can. Can't you smell the bacon?"

"I can't."

"I delivered the 4th of July oration."

"I heard you."

He watched her bury her nose deeper into the pillow. "I'll be outside," he said. Then he sat on an isolated nail keg and rested one foot on his knee.

•   •   •   •   •

When Esther had heard LeTourneau's triangle clanging, she turned over on the cot, still dressed in the same clothes she'd worn to wash Sam Cookson. She curled into a fetal position and wished the Founding Fathers had signed in the springtime when everything else was born and the thermometer read thirty degrees cooler.

She used to love the Fourth when her mother recited the Declaration of Independence at the Brigham City celebration. Stirring people to pride, Zina Carpenter, in the voice of an oppressed colonist, recited the grievances as if they were her own.

Frail in a white pinafore and long sleeves of flowered chintz, Esther sat next to her mother, always at her side after the fire. The platform drooped with yards of patriotic bunting and sagged with the weight of the city, county, and state dignitaries seated on folding chairs. The year before, Esther shook hands with a senator who patted her on the cheek. "You have wise, sad eyes for a little girl," he told her.

While her mother recited, Esther kicked her legs back and forth underneath her chair and watched people's faces. If someone's attention wandered, Esther glared at them. After all, her mother was speaking. Esther had to listen and so did they. Sometimes, it worked. A lady in a flowered sunbonnet would feel a pair of eyes boring into her and look up at the platform, slightly alarmed.

After the audience sang "The Star Spangled Banner," Zina's voice soaring above the rest, the Box Elder Stake president closed with prayer. Then everyone praised and congratulated Esther's mother. She walked proudly underneath a flouncing hat brim while Esther pushed the baby buggy, a token hot dog in her hand. The bun was never long enough to cover the frank that overlapped the ends. Mustard and catsup dripped onto Esther's white pinafore and sometimes onto her little sister's fat cheeks. Then baby Marian cried, and Esther laughed at the creative design on her face. Even then, Mama kept talking, stopping only to tell Esther to push the carriage more slowly or quiet the baby.

Sometimes Esther tired of waiting and found the three Grandmothers—Grandma Nettie, Grandma Rebecca, and Grandma Sylvia—"Grandpa's used-to-be wives." They were always together, and even though Esther had never seen them apart on holidays or at family gatherings, no one would explain the trio to her. She pieced the story from conversations exchanged over the top of her head.

"After they outlawed polygamy, if you can believe it," her mother was telling a visiting cousin one day, "the government told my father to choose one woman. But how could he choose one when he loved them all? You tell me that."

Any conversation on this subject always turned to whispers at that point, especially when Esther was within hearing. "He just pretended to choose one of them," Aunt Mildred once said loud enough for Esther to hear. "I've seen him slipping in the different back doors. He still loved and protected those women honorably till the day he died, but the eastern newspapers and their nosy reporters, Congressmen too, kept butting their noses in, trying to make Grandpa and the others like him into lusty, carnal slavers, not having any clue about The Principle."

The grand matriarchs sat on the same bench at every Fourth of July celebration. Always, one of them would drop a dime into Esther's hand, and she'd want to ask them about the brown blotches on the backs of their hands and why Grandpa used to sneak in their back doors. They collectively patted baby Marian and told Esther what beautiful eyes and what a talented mother she had and wouldn't she like an ice cream cone?

She wandered past the band shell, drawn to the beat of the bass drum that passed through her skin and into her stomach. Even now as she thought the thought, she felt the throbbing of the faded drum as she lay on the cot and listened to the milling outside in the Nevada desert, the disembodied celebration. This was not America. This was the end of the Earth. She heard her mother calling from across the years, "Esther, put your bonnet back on. Too much sun will hurt you."

Her skin, once a charred black, then red, purple, then shiny and translucent smooth, had shriveled with age. An ancient hide, strangely puckered and drawn. Thank the Lord, Esther often reminded herself, she had the holy garment of the temple to cover her body, the garment she promised to wear to the grave when she took out her endowments with Alf, the reminder of her promise to upbuild God's kingdom here on earth.

Actually, she didn't need a reminder. She took pleasure in serving God—singing at wedding receptions and funerals, baking bread for neighbors, teaching stories of Jesus and Joseph Smith's first vision in Sunday School, embroidering garden trellises on pillowcases and days of the week on dish towels for Relief Society bazaars.

Alf said she was a blind sheep and didn't think for herself, but he missed the point, the simplicity, the fact that an individual was only a part of things, not a lone star in the sky. If only he could surrender to the whole. . . .

But listen to her talk. Esther Carpenter Jensen. She mused over the perfect picture she'd drawn of herself—a generous woman, all-loving, a gracious instrument for God—so far from the truth. How could she judge anyone else when she couldn't even get off this cot to console her scrawny baby who must feel very lonely in her disinterested arms? *Stop it, Esther. Where's your charity?*

Their marriage was sealed for time and eternity, beyond death. Esther and Alf. But what if his rebellious ways meant he'd resist God's will in the hereafter, too? What if he never would understand the law of obedience which had its beauty if he could see beyond the obvious clichés of sheep and blindfolded followers? There was divinity in pure trust.

Which kingdom of glory would he inherit then? Certainly not the celestial. Maybe the terrestrial. Hopefully not the telestial, the closest thing to hell Mormons had, except for southern Nevada.

Because she was his wife, would she be barred from the celestial kingdom if he couldn't go? Would she have to follow him wherever? Or could she be assigned on her own merit?

It was Alf who seemed less and less interested in the proposition of eternal togetherness, Alf who strained at the bit. She'd yelled at her mother who said Alf was beneath her and could never give her what she needed. She'd covered her ears when her father asked her to please listen to her mother. Secretly, she'd had her own suspicions before they drove to Salt Lake City to be married, the way his truth telling would slide sideways to fit an occasion. Nothing mean-hearted, just slippery.

After the ceremony, however, she definitely knew things were out of order as she gazed at the ornate doors of the temple, at the handiwork of God, and looked up at the golden Angel Moroni blaring the gospel news from his trumpet. While she closed her eyes to feel the inspiration wash through her veins, Alf pulled her sleeve and said, "Let's get out of here."

"But Alf," she said as he pulled her out the gates and onto South Temple Street.

"It's you and me now, Esther. I'm your husband. Not God."

She'd cried in the bathtub of the Albany Hotel after they'd made love, saying "He doesn't care, he doesn't care," over and over. She'd slept toward the edge of the bed, but woke up the next morning with her stubbornness intact. Esther never backtracked on her word, and she'd given Alf and God her word.

But maybe I've failed to love Alf, failed Christ in that regard. Stubbornness isn't love at all, only stubbornness. God's punishing me for that. He'll send Alf to glory while I drown in the waters of my self-righteousness. Judge not, Esther.

But why all this investment, anyway, in a hereafter everyone at church spoke about with a wistful, faraway look of knowing? What would a resurrected body look like? Would Alf still touch her and come inside her? Or would sex be streamlined into a certain smile or a code word? What would everyone do? Would there be carpenters and seamstresses and apricot trees? *Stop turning things around, Esther. Find your courage to get up and move.*

But it hurt to be with Alf, this erratic man who had a tin ear for truth. A man eating himself, feasting at the wrong table. She could help him if he'd listen, but there was the matter of his pride. He had that, and who was Esther to be director of anyone else's life when hers seemed so ill-made most of the time? *Expand my heart, Father. The gift of charity.*

She reached inside her dress and touched the laced edging of the garments she could barely stand in the heat, the wet cotton clinging to her skin, never dry, making her feel like an infant bathed in its own urine. But she'd wear them always. They protected her from herself, always close, a thin covering of fabric, God's hand guarding her except for the times when Alf reached for her in the night and slipped them off her shoulder and past her hips. He'd stroke her belly which he'd never seen, only felt in the night, some of which had no feeling but only patches of responsiveness. He'd tempt her with his words and closeness, and sometimes she'd squeeze her eyes and think of a world away from this one where no God was peering down at her, a world where she could scream and bite into Alf's flesh, where she could dance naked across the room with billowing silk scarves and her imperfect skin. At those times she knew she was woven of the same fabric as Alf. When he came inside of her, she begged him deeper, every bit of him, his fingers, arms, and shoulders inside of her.

But then she'd feel for her garments that had been cast aside, draw the cloth into her fingers, and, of course, she'd never, ever show him the skin, the grafted patching that puckered and gathered in skewed patterns. He'd have to guess at it with his fingers, use his imagination. The garments and the skin. Two shields to help her hold to God's word.

She gave way to a watery sleep, floating in red-brown waves through rapids, surrendering to whirlpools where the circling water kissed her arms and breasts and caressed her hair and cheeks and stomach. And then the calm. The soft lapping waters against a canyon wall, an eddy that gave refuge to water and Esther and kept them from rushing into mad cataracts. It was quiet there; the sound of water lapping the shore, back and forth, steadily. Esther heard whisperings that soothed her as she slept, indistinct answers to something she needed to know but couldn't quite hear when awake.

·　·　·　·　·

Two days after the 4th of July, Esther suddenly sat up and blinked her eyes as if she were a new doll. No heavenly messengers had come to take her away.

The baby, Inez, sighed gently in her sleep.

"My baby," Esther said out loud, the first words she'd spoken in a long time. "Somebody bring me my baby."

No one was there to waken the baby and carry her to her mother. Esther edged off the cot and bent over the dresser drawer lined with a worn apron. She touched the prickly heat rash on Inez's cheek, the matted hair on her head, and the channels of sweat that filled the wrinkles in her neck.

My baby. She's beautiful. God will give me strength. He won't let me fail this child.

"Sleep, pretty baby," she whispered until the blanket of heat started to smother her will.

Water, Esther. Get your hands in water.

Carefully she poured a measured amount of drinking water into her washtub; she wasn't supposed to, but she was tired of the grains of silt that never left the river water no matter how long she let it settle. Then she rummaged for the bar of Fels-Naptha and the chipper from Fels & Company in Philadelphia—free and postpaid, upon request. She carved the fragrant soap and watched the golden chips dissolve in the water and coax dirt from Alf's workpants, the girls' and her underwear, and the baby's diapers. Clean clothes. The cooling water. Grace.

Just as she finished wringing the excess water from the clothes, Inez awoke with a jerk and kicked her legs wildly against the harsh heat boiling her skin.

"Come here, Inie." But when Esther cuddled the baby, Inez's bare chest stuck to her exposed arms and neck. Their skin ripped like adhesive tape when either of them moved. "You'll have to wait, Inez." She laid the baby on the large mattress and changed her in the rumple of sheets.

Damn this heat. Damn it, and Esther wanted to sink into the cot again and melt then and there. But she wouldn't fail God. Things would be good for her baby.

She found her purple-flowered dress wadded behind a cupboard where it had fallen, slipped it over her head, and borrowed Mary Elizabeth's hairbrush. Scraping across her scalp and through her abused hair, the bristles felt like salvation. She tied her straw hat under her chin, balanced her wash basket on one hip, then Inez on the other. "Ta da, here we go," and she stepped into the desert furnace to hang clothes on a rope tied to two bushes. She sorted the clothes with one hand, folded them over the line, and cherished that small portion of time between wet and dry. Each time she grabbed a clumped diaper out of the basket she held it against Inez's cheek and against her own neck and eyelids. "We'll put our toes in the river when we're finished, Inez."

"People can't work in conditions like this." A man's voice cut into their pleasure, someone in another cardboard box house close by. Then she heard another voice.

"Bud Anderson's been trying to organize everybody, spends his time selling *Industrial Solidarity* and *Industrial Worker* at the Boulder Club ever since he got laid off his job as truck tender. Looks like it could be a general strike."

Esther put her hand over Inez's mouth. Alf had told her to listen for any talk about strikes and to remember names if she heard them. This could be their chance to get one of the first houses in Boulder City and the greengrocer's job.

"Naw, Fred, there ain't enough sympathy. Too many men waiting in line for your job if you're lucky enough to have one."

"Anderson claims he's only organizing for better hours, pay, and conditions. Seems okay to me."

"They're anarchists," said a new voice. "You know that. Put 'em back on the Red Ark. Get 'em out of here before we get big trouble. What can a damn Wobbly do about this heat, anyway? Government only started construction early to help some people find jobs. Who're they supposed to be? God?"

This was the conversation Alf had hoped she might hear.

"Fred, look at the River Camp. It's unfit for a mongrel. No showers, everybody has to bathe in the river. Drink from the river. Pure silt until it settles. While it's doing that, it multiplies into tons of bacteria."

"What do you expect, man? They've promised cooling systems as soon as possible."

"Fred, they shouldn't have started. Mongolians are the only ones who can handle these conditions, and Six Companies will only hire American-born workers."

"Poor shame," said the man Esther thought must be Fred, "if our veterans don't have enough stamina to withstand some hard times."

"People are dying, Fred. Do you understand the word? Maybe it's part of the job when a guy like Dave Sanford gets disemboweled by an explosion, but when people drop in their tracks, that's pretty dismal stuff. Paula Casey, Fern Roberts and her daughter, all dead the same day. Fern's daughter started decomposing right in front of my eyes. Couldn't get her to the mortuary fast enough. They've sent for some Harvard expert to provide a few answers, but it's a little late, wouldn't you say?"

Esther held another wet, balled-up diaper under her chin, then to Inez's nose. She hadn't heard about those women. Three in one day. She'd been wishing while they'd been dying.

"I don't care who went to Harvard," the same voice continued. "Nobody but the Almighty can turn down the heat."

"Give me ice," said Fred. "That's all I want. Ice."

"Esther. Esther Jensen." She recognized Serena's low voice, though something was different about it. "Esther. Oh God, please help me."

Esther didn't stop to fasten the diaper, but carried it with her as she tripped through the sorry pavement of broken rock toward the sound of Serena's voice. She scratched her ankle on the spines of a shrunken and discolored beavertail. "Even the cactus can't survive, Inez."

Serena stood on a hill, motioning Esther with both arms. She'd disappear behind the rise, then reappear, waving her arms again for Esther to hurry. Esther cradled Inez against one breast and hurried along in her broad-heeled black shoes which hadn't seen polish since June.

"I'm coming, Serena. Just can't move too fast."

Esther had never seen Serena perturbed in any way—always a cool woman, sure of her place, her self, but Serena's face. . . .

"You won't believe this, Esther."

As Esther climbed, her shoes slipped in the rocky sand and filled with sharp pebbles and splinters of tumbleweed.

"This boy," Serena wailed. "This boy."

When Esther topped the hill, she saw him. Stretched out, tied to four stakes, his legs, arms, and bare chest scratched, a young boy burned silt red.

"I can't untie the knots, Esther. Some maniac tied them tighter than hell."

"The heat shrinks rope like hides. Here. Take Inez."

Esther bent over the boy, shading him with her hat and wringing the last drops of wash water from the diaper onto his lips puffed like baked apples. She slapped him gently on the cheeks and felt for the pulse in his neck. It was still there, thank heavens. Laying the diaper over his chest and her hat over his face, she started in on the knots, but they wouldn't budge, just like the ones on the mattress the day she'd first met Serena.

"Let me have one of the baby's diaper pins, Serena."

Serena held the diaper closed with her fingers while Esther jabbed the pin into the rope to loosen the tight-fisted maze of knots.

"Daddy," the boy moaned. "Daddy, don't hurt me."

"I'm not your daddy," Esther said.

"Daddy. I didn't do it. I didn't take your wallet. Don't hurt me."

"You'll be all right, son." Esther loosened one knot, wove the end in and out of the tangle, and employed the pin as a blunt needle through the maze.

"I heard them arguing," said Serena. "I told myself it was none of my business, but look at this boy. Look at him. How could I ignore this?"

"You found him, didn't you?"

"I'm going crazy. Even me. I'm starting to hallucinate." Serena clung to Inez. "Baby, baby, little baby."

When the boy was untied, Esther held him like he was a baby, too. She rocked him. The four of them swayed in unison, their eyes closed, strings of sweat framing their faces, each trying to comfort and be comforted under the sun spreading across the sky.

"Where's my daddy?" The boy was hoarse. "I'm sorry, Daddy."

"You owe no apology," Esther whispered back. *Neither does your father, really.*

Esther put his limp arm around her neck and lifted his deadweight from the waist. "Help me, boy," she said, but when he couldn't, Esther lifted his shoulders from the ground.

"Serena, put my hat back on for me, please."

Serena seemed lost and unsteady; her hand shook as she lifted the woven straw to Esther's head.

She's never had a child with colic, Esther mused. *Crying all night until her sanity is shattered. Maybe this man, who must have loved his son, was pushed past his outermost bounds. And he gave his son as his answer to God—"This is too*

55

much. You've asked too much"—*a son stretched spread-eagle, a drying animal skin. But God has shown his face. He sent Serena, and he sent me. Just as with Abraham, the man's hand has been stayed. It's God's love.*

Esther trudged through the sand, her black-soled shoes leaving deep tracks behind her as she pulled the boy, his heels dragging a path across the desert's crust. Serena walked silently by her side.

She cupped her hand into the Colorado's water and smoothed it onto his face and neck. Then she let the diaper float on the river's surface before she wrapped it like a turban low on his forehead to protect him from the sun.

Cupping her fingertips into the water, she sprinkled several drops on his face and on her face. "I baptize you to new life, boy. In the name of the Father and the Son and the Holy Ghost, I baptize you, me, and I baptize Alf who needs a new start, too. We're all forgiven. We're all new. Unblemished lambs for God."

"A mighty fortress is our God," Esther sang out suddenly. "A tower of strength ne'er failing." Her contralto voice was a rich copy of her mother's against the panorama of spare branches. Serena harmonized with Esther though she didn't know the words, both of them oblivious to the fact they were singing in the church of the open sky accompanied by the sound of the Colorado River and an occasional explosion.

4

The commissary was packed with steaming bodies. Nobody had room to move, and when they tried, the smell of sweat and stale tobacco in the folds of their skin made Alf feel like a fish in a small can.

Everyone was talking about the arrest. Bud Anderson's. He was the man whose name Esther had passed on to Alf who'd sent it along to A. P. who'd deliberated over it with the other officials of Six Companies.

"They got him in front of the Boulder Club a couple nights ago," Bernie Wilson said, a lanky tunneler whose work pants were tucked into unlaced boots. "He told the *Las Vegas Age* there were three hundred Wobblies at the dam."

"That's not true," Alf boasted. "Maybe there's five at the most."

"So how do you know so much?"

Alf recognized the massive forehead and bushy eyebrows and the voice of the man who'd been in the commissary the day A. P. came in to check out the labor situation. His name was Bill Burroughs. Alf had asked around.

"Nobody should be arresting Anderson," Burroughs yelled over the din. "Twenty-two people have died since we started in May. That's over two months of a bad record for Six Companies."

"Where do you get your figures, hot shot?" Bernie Wilson's height didn't account for his short stick of dynamite temperament. "The conditions bother me the same as you, but I'm sick of all this bellyaching."

The commissary felt more and more like the inside of a can, and the oiliness seemed to slide from man to man, everyone wondering who was speaking, what kind of threat this was to their safety that wasn't feeling so safe, and whether or not it might help for them to get a few dollars in their pockets and a tank full of gas to drive to a mountain or seaside or even a clump of trees for shade or anything offering different weather and employment. But they were caught like embalmed sardines, the tin strip tangled, and the key stuck halfway around the can. They had no money to buy gas nor the stupidity to hold their felt hats like offering plates and say, "Give me something for good luck, just maybe you have something to spare?" If only they could swim back to something they knew, some familiar, cool water.

"Most of the deaths were from heat and carelessness," Wilson said. "Anderson blamed it all on 'capitalist exploitation.' That's nothin' close to the truth." He seemed to rise out of the sea of men, maybe because of his height or his insistence. "The *Journal* said *The Age* was doing its usual yellow journalism number again. There's no three hundred Wobblies and no threat on this dam, and any Wobblies in this room know the rest of us ain't riled up or interested either."

"Have you tried to get something cool to drink, Mister?" Burroughs's eyebrows straggled down over his eyelids like leafless vines.

Alf watched the match between Burroughs and Wilson and the men who watched and listened. They all seemed familiar to him now, those who'd passed scrip across his counter, asked for chewing gum, Sen-sen, Murine for the dust in their eyes, cigarettes, Fairyfoot to dissolve their bunions, Borax for their dirty clothes, sometimes for loans, even advice. They were survivors like him. They were uneasy with these words, this arguing. They wanted things to be right with Six Companies, their employer, their hope for dinner, rent, and maybe a new blouse for their sweethearts.

Alf sided with Wilson. He, too, was tired of complaints. He sweated like everybody else—dark, wet spots on his shirt, front and back. He'd listened to these guys on all the jobs he'd been on in the last twenty years, and nothing ever came of whining. The only reason he'd been unable to last at his jobs before now had nothing to do with any complaining on his part. It had to do with his finer sensibilities about how things should be done. He suggested these finer ways to his bosses, but had a problem with timing, not picking the right moment and then shouting to be heard and surprising everybody who paused to look at his red face before they said, "You're out of here, Mack."

Mack. People used that name after he'd shouted, as if there were one Mack in the world who was a loser and everybody knew who he was. "Mack, get lost." Alf didn't like being called Mack, but just the same, he'd never groused on the job like Burroughs was doing.

He looked out his window at the high scalers rappeling down the sides of the cliffs. They were specks of men whose lives hung on a few twists of hemp. Why weren't they in this squeeze box of a commissary complaining?

"The law sloughed two other guys yesterday morning," Burroughs continued, "just after they left the telegraph office in Vegas. Vagrancy charges for walking out of a telegraph office? Come on, now."

"Probably sending a wire to Communist headquarters." Bernie Wilson stood his ground like a bull. A few hands applauded the dark-tanned man with a two-day stubble. "Nobody messes with the U.S. Government, especially not commies like you."

"Bull Wilson, Bull Wilson," somebody chanted.

Wilson's two legs were as solid as thwarts between a boat's gunnels. His hands were stiff in his pockets, and his face expressed no doubts. Wilson. Bernie Wilson. Alf was duly impressed.

"Says who?" Burroughs yelled back. "Not only are people dying, there's disregard for your safety. You've been breathing carbon monoxide in the tunnels, doing overtime and double shifts; you don't have crappers or cold water, and you've got red silt stuck in your hair and your gut. Nobody'd ask the same of an animal. Wise up, you idiot."

"Nobody's gonna call me an idiot," Wilson shouted. "Especially an idiot like you!"

In ordinary circumstances, fists would have flown, but their words spiraled into the air and went nowhere. Too many men separated the contenders.

When Alf heard the screen door squeak open with yet another customer, he winced. Walls and tempers would burst any minute now. "I'll need some of you fellows to clear out," he yelled.

"Look who's talking," Bill Burroughs said, pointing at Alf. "Did you boys know this runt is related to a plute, none other than the vice president of Six Companies? Did you know that fact? Alf Jensen. The Prince of Patronage. Hundreds of men waiting barehanded in the sun, and this little man walks right in."

Alf had been covered with perspiration before, but now it spattered his forehead and merged into a thin stream down the sides of his cheeks.

"What about the others who got here first, Mr. Big Man?"

The squeak of the screen door again. Alf would have to oil it as soon as these sweating, stinking bodies and this jackass Wobbly cleared out. Alf knew his name. The guy wouldn't be good for much around here after Alf got to A. P.

"The Ingersoll-Rand, the compressor," a man with grease-covered overalls was shouting from the door. "It's on fire!"

The crowd sifted out of the commissary like fine sand through a large-holed sieve. Everyone ran, including Alf. Their legs worked like pistons through the muck from the tunnels, the ever-changing shoreline of the river. Everyone struggled across the uneven fill toward the small floating platform with three compressors side by side, one of them being swallowed by flames.

"How'd this happen?" The supervisor grabbed the shoulder of the operator's shirt and pulled it in a bunched knot. "Damn it to hell, we can't lose any air to the tunnels," he shouted. "They're drilling like sixty in there."

"Gasoline on the surface. Spontaneous combustion," the operator said as if he disbelieved his own words. "The fires of hell are popping out of thin air like black magic. *Ignis fatuus.*" He crossed himself. "In the name of the Father and the Son and the Holy Spirit."

"Stop your gibberish," the supervisor yelled. "Where in the hell is a fire extinguisher? Can anybody find me something for this fire?"

"I've got one in the commissary," Alf shouted and started back across the muck, sinking up to his calves with every step, thinking of fire, Esther's scars, and of his father hanging in the dim light of a winter afternoon, a bed of black coal six inches from his swinging toes. "Fire. Damnable fire," he muttered, his ankles turning sideways in the loose ground.

"What about river water?" someone else shouted. "Where's some buckets?"

"Water'll cool the compressor too fast." The supervisor was hoarse, his shirt totally wet. "Break it down even worse."

No one knew what to do except wait for Alf and the extinguisher. The high scalers on the cliffs, the muckers at the edge of the adits of the two diversion tunnels, the rodmen, all suspended their activities to stare at the strange fire engulfing the source of air that kept their hydraulic tools at work.

"You ever touched any metal in this canyon?" Bernie Wilson asked the man next to him, turning his back on Burroughs. "Burn the epithelium right off a man's fingers."

Burroughs shook his head. "You idiots. Think you can work in this place. Think you're in the hands of the Good Master. Well, this good master didn't prepare all too well for this job. Too big of a hurry to get going, get their money rolling in, all in the name of jobs for the jobless."

No one paid attention to him. Alf was attempting to run through the broken talus with the heavy cylinder, but its weight buried his legs even deeper. He ran but he wasn't running because his legs sank into the loose holes of rock, sand, gravel, and remains of Mesozoic slime left by dinosaurs and flying reptiles and fishes with hard rhombic scales. Alf struggling through centuries to get to another fire, Alf alone until he reached the first man who seemed to have forgotten that Alf was hired by a relative and had failed at most every job he'd ever had. The man held out his arms as if Alf was his equal, his brother, and the differences seemed to slide into the centuries beneath their legs. And behind the first man was a brigade, men with more outstretched arms ready to help Alf get the red metal tube to the fire. It was handed from man to man to man, then to Burroughs, then to Wilson with no pause for arguing, to another man in overalls with no shirt, and finally to the supervisor on the temporary landing where the compressor was turning blacker in a bowl of flames.

For the moment, every disagreement was forgotten, Alf and his relative not a fact to consider, nor the Wobblies or union cards or what would happen tomorrow or the next day. All distraction was set aside for the compressor. It was vital for the drilling which was vital to the project, and somehow everyone sensed the importance of the battle against this unpredictable river that could rise a foot in an hour after a flash storm. For a moment, everyone disregarded the torturing heat that roasted their flesh and the black walls of volcanic rock that intensified it like a Bunsen burner.

Alf felt a tinge of personal pride as he watched the fire smother. And he noticed the men with their mouths open and heads stretching forward in anticipation, forgetting themselves and their irritations. He and the fire had been the initiator of this brotherhood.

In his head, he replayed his run to the commissary, his luck at knowing where an extinguisher was, his chance to be seen as he should be seen—a man of action, always available in a crisis. But even Alf was swept back into events and out of his self-concern. The moment lifted him out of self-absorption, out of Alf, the uneven man who sometimes broke promises and spoke half-truths, who most of the time preferred hooch to the sacrament he took on Sundays.

Heat from the fire increasing the heat of the day. The compressor, the men, the river lost in a cloud of fumes. The shouts. The applause. The sweating men putting arms around each other. Alf felt hands on his shoulders, hands in his hands, congratulations in his ears.

Tonight, they'd sing. He'd get Esther and Serena and Ed together, maybe invite his son Jack down from the dormitories in Boulder, and they'd harmonize, sing about good times and lose themselves in music, the next best thing to booze. He'd avoided the bottle for two months now, not especially a triumph because Prohibition had kept temptation away, but he was doing what he'd promised himself. Doing a good job and making a name for himself and his family. *Alf Jensen. He was the man who helped save the compressor. Alf Jensen. I don't care if he is related to some official. It's good he's here on the job.*

•　•　•　•　•

The music that night!

Alf walked in the burlap door singing "Carolina Moon" and scooped Esther into his arms. Esther, who'd been waiting all afternoon to tell Alf about the young Rafferty boy stretched out flat between stakes on the desert—how a mob tried to lynch his father and how Sheriff Williams had paid for a tank of gas and told the man never to show his face again—forgot to tell him because of her surprise when he hugged her Hollywood style.

After their dinner of navy beans with a hint of ham begged from the mess hall, and while Rebecca and Mary Elizabeth put the clean plates with chipped edges into the box labelled *Dishes*, Alf pulled Esther tight to him again. He rubbed against her breasts.

"Carolina moon," he began. And then they both sang like movie stars, lips close to each other, two gilded actors promising springtime on lint-flecked celluloid. Each of them played to their young audience, animating the romantic. The girls giggled. The baby cooed from her bureau drawer bed.

"You're beautiful, Esther," Alf whispered in between a phrase. He rubbed his hand over the uneven lumps on her hips, the shelf of behind she'd put on over the years. "Shining for my one and only love," they sang.

Esther smiled as she had when she was sixteen and Queen of the Elberta Theater. "Alf, I haven't seen you like this since . . . I can't remember."

"My beauty, we've arrived. All of the pain of the past has been preparing us for this. It'll be good now, my sweet. Good for you. No more wondering about a job and the next dime."

Esther rewet the sheet she kept over Inez and said yes to her girls who wanted to hunt horned toads before the sunlight was gone.

"Alf, I like the life in your face."

"I was my best today." His eyes were bright like new coins. "Like my mama said, patience, and your time will come." *When the world's mine,* he thought, *it's Esther's too, and then I don't have to see those 'you promised me' eyes.*

They held each other as only those who both love and hate can. They'd seen each other's worst; they'd been foes in battle. Now they paused: Truce. I give. Let's not fight anymore.

Alf had searched her eyes ten thousand times, yet here he was again, still hoping to understand them. He saw traces of sweet innocence in Esther's eyes tonight, and he was glad the two of them could harmonize. Alf the bass. Esther the contralto. They could sing. Thank God for that. When they sang, everything else—their troubles and old wounds—disappeared. Beautiful music.

A refreshing breeze picked up and carried the smell of rain. The steel grey clouds were backlit with heat lightning, and wind flapped the burlap-covered windows. Out of breath, Rebecca came running back with a lizard captured in her hands.

"Mama, I need a jar with a lid. See my pet?"

"It'll suffocate unless you poke holes in the lid," Esther said, pulling herself from Alf's arms. "Find me a nail and the hammer and we'll punch holes in one of the Mason lids. Mary Elizabeth, get me a jar out of that box of bottled peaches. Should be an empty one in there."

Jack, their oldest son who'd gotten a job driving trucks in and out of the canyon, appeared at the door. Everything seemed to lift at the same time—the weather, their spirits, their good fortune at having Jack with them, who just happened to have his saxophone case in his hand.

"How about a celebration?" he said. "I heard my daddy was a hero today. Savior of the Compressor." Jack had midnight hair with a blue shine to it, smoothed back tight to his scalp. He walked easily, more confident than Herbert, who was still up in Ruth, Nevada, working in the copper mine offices. Jack had always been the easier of the two. Everyone relaxed when he walked in the room.

"Put 'er there, Dad." Alf shook both of Jack's hands.

Esther gave him a bearish hug and pinched his cheek. "Pull out your sax, Jackie. The sun isn't blazing, praise the Lord, and our desert bag is full of water tonight."

"The household god in its temple?" Jack laughed.

"I want to hear some good-time music." She started snapping her fingers and moving her shoulders to a rhythm that hadn't been played yet.

Alf had seen music transform Esther many times into something alive and vibrant. Without music, she was uncertain, melancholy, and too focused on the difficulty of everything for everybody. Music seemed like the kind of sunshine that warmed Esther when she was cold, instead of the kind that burned her skin and lungs the way the desert sun did. *Thank God for music, Alf thought.*

"All God's children love music." Esther closed her eyes and beat her head side to side with the imaginary tune she seemed to hear inside her head. "Music, Jackie!"

The saxophone began. Jack danced out of the cardboard house like the Pied Piper. Esther followed. "Come on everybody." Putting the jar with the lizard on the ground, Alf plucked Rebecca off her bed and twirled her under his arm until she was dizzy and fell laughing onto the bedrock floor that had been cleared of desert sand and pebbles.

"More, more, Daddy!"

"It's Mary Elizabeth's turn now." Alf pulled her out of her usual nest cluttered with drawing paper, charcoals, her hairbrush, her hand mirror, and then pulled her close to him. He felt her budding breasts under the sheer cotton blouse and for one moment, before he remembered he was the father, wondered if her nipples would respond to his closeness. She danced tightly, her arms rigid at her sides.

"Loosen up, honey," Alf said. He shook her shoulders and pushed her from side to side with the rhythm of Jack's "Dark Town Strutters' Ball." "I'm going to sing those Jelly Roll Blues," he sang, "and dance off both of my shoes. . . ."

"Hey, Alf," Ed Bishop appeared at the door, a dark shadow against the orange-peel sunset. Serena peeked over his shoulder.

"Stay outside," Alf said, brushing past the burlap door. "Breeze is good tonight. You met my son, Jack? Serena and Ed Bishop, Jack Jensen. He's a gearjammer hauling muck out of the canyon. Oldest son. Hot lips on the sax."

"Don't stop on our account."

Alf moved their two folding chairs and several wooden crates out on the sand while the rim of the sun played across the outline of dusk-blue mountains.

"Jack plays in a band out at Blue Heaven on weekends," Esther said. "Play it, Jackie." She was in rare form.

Before long, Serena was dancing with Mary Elizabeth, Esther with Alf, and Rebecca with Inez, all of them bumping together on their small dance floor hedged by mesquite bushes. Dust sifted up from their high-stepping feet and filled the air while the door of the lean-to billowed in and out to the rhythm of Jack's music.

Ed looked around to see if anybody might be watching, then pulled a flask out of his back pocket. He took a swig and offered some to Alf. When Alf started to reach out, he seemed to catch his own hand in midair. Even in the midst of the music she loved, Esther stopped smiling and dancing. She looked at Alf, at Ed, then at Alf again. Jack stopped playing. The children looked up, wondering where the merriment had gone. Nobody said anything. Everyone studied the flask in Ed's hand as if it were an object from an ancient culture. Esther coughed a polite cough. Jack silently fingered the buttons on the sax.

"Go ahead, Alf," Ed said, holding out the dented flask. "Nobody'll catch us."

Alf looked like a self-conscious, newly shaven adolescent as he lowered his eyes and fiddled with his belt buckle. Everyone waited. Then he tried to play bandleader, beating some snazzy rhythm with his hand to get Jack back into action. Alfred's children stood quietly. Esther, too.

"It's been so long," said Serena, swiping the flask from her husband's hand, throwing her head back, and letting some of the whiskey run across her tongue and down her throat.

Everyone stood as if in a photograph.

"Did I tell you about the boy I found today, Ed?" Serena whispered to her husband, pulling him close to a bush and away from Alf. "You know I want a baby, Ed, and there was this boy left in the desert, stretched and left for every bone to bleach. After Esther and I took him to Sheriff Williams, Jess found the boy's father and literally kicked him in the backside. Told him never to show his face again. He's gonna take the kid to the juvenile authorities in Vegas. Can we take care of him, Ed? He needs somebody."

Ed took the flask, drank some, and put it back in his pocket. "You know I don't want kids," he whispered. "I can barely take care of us, baby. It's you and me. That's enough."

"Music, maestro," Alf said, beating a mean cut time for his one-man band, something to recapture the atmosphere before Ed's flask appeared. "Put another nickel in. Let's live right now. Who knows about tomorrow? Burroughs could get to me before I get to A. P."

Jack obliged with the music, but Esther didn't yield so easily. "Who's Burroughs?"

"Let's not talk about it right now."

"I bet he's a Wobbly." The music had drained from Esther's face. "One who knows about you and A. P. I'm not forgetting that Gans-Nelson world title boxing match in Goldfield when some rabid Wobbly shot an everyday man like you."

"I'm sorry I mentioned it, Esther. Everything's okay. We've got a breeze, some music, some good friends. Dance, sweetheart. Dance it out of your worried head. I love you tonight."

"I don't want anything to happen." She hugged his upper arm like she hugged Inez and then seemed to remember cautions she'd heard about being too cloying with Alf. She broke from him with a burst of forced energy. "Of course, it's ridiculous to worry," she said.

Alf stood with his arms folded while Esther danced alone with Jack's stark melody line. He listened to the sound of the clouds rushing elsewhere and the heat settling back down on him and these people. *It always comes back to this. It never changes.*

"I'll show you the Lindy, Alf," said Serena, boldly pulling him back to the center of the dance floor. She tucked her arms against her sides; her hands beating time like miniature wings flapping. "Learned it in Chicago. Pick up the tempo, Jack." She leaned to the right. "Slow, to the right, slow, to the left, then quick, quick. Right, left. Try it again. Slow, slow, quick, quick. Come on, Alf. Show your stuff."

Esther laughed at this new game. She lined up behind Serena, watched the teacher's feet until she got the idea, and then did the slow-slow-quick-quick until it looked as if she'd known it forever.

"Teach me, too," said Mary Elizabeth, obviously tired of being cooped in their makeshift house which was like a house of the dead during the day. Dark, still air. Everyone's hair pressed wet and flat to their faces, no desire to sit or stand or move. Nothing to do except lie under a tent of wet sheet, draw on her Big Chief tablet with charcoal, or read from the family Bible.

Jack tootled on his saxophone while everyone else rocked back and forth, working on the new dance step. Serena lined everyone up except Ed, who eased himself against a Joshua tree where he could nurse his flask.

"How about a little game of monte instead?" he asked.

"We're dancing tonight," Serena said, taking her place in front of her newly acquired students. "Right foot first. Then rock onto your left. Step behind with your right, a quick ball change. Slow, slow, that's right." She clapped her hands to the rhythm.

Esther, Mary Elizabeth, Rebecca with Inez in her arms, and Alf all followed Serena's lead and were soon rocking in the same direction at the same time.

"Look at this family," said Serena. "You two make beautiful babies. Dancing fools, too." She looked over her shoulder into Alf's eyes. "Let's try it together, now." She took his hand and arched under his arm, then showed him how to curl her into what she called a cuddle position. "Now try it with Esther. Okay?"

Someone's head poked out of their house. "We gotta go to work at 4:00 a.m. Cut the noise."

"We just got started," Rebecca whined.

"Well, just get ended. Consider your neighbors!"

"Okay, okay," Esther said. "Bedtime, everybody."

Jack's music and the pleasures of dancing faded into a shuffle of feet and night sounds—crickets, a coyote, the river. And everyone seemed to close like morning glories at the end of day except for Ed who whisked Serena away from the Jensens and didn't take much care to keep his voice down as they walked away. "What the hell you talking about babies again?"

"I only want to help this Rafferty kid. He's over at the Williamses' right now. Needs a place."

"I thought we'd been through this before. Dozens of times." Their voices dimmed as they walked past the yucca whose stiletto points glowed silver in the stark moonlight, the vainglory clouds having blown over without a trace of rain.

Jack snapped shut the clasp on his sax case, tucked his younger sisters into thin sheets on their beds, and kissed Mary Elizabeth on the cheek. "You're getting pretty good looking, Mary Eliz. I better come down here more often and keep the wolves away." He saluted his parents and climbed into his borrowed car.

"Bring your girl next time, honey," Esther said.

"Depends on her shifts."

When the sound of the car toiling up Hemenway Wash had disappeared, Alf put his arms around Esther who stood at the doorway watching the egg-shaped moon.

"We do make beautiful babies, Esther. Did you have a good time tonight?"

"Look at me. I can do the Lindy." She started into the slow, slow, quick, quick steps. Alf wrapped one arm around his wife, took one hand in his.

"What's going to happen with the Rafferty boy?" Esther asked. "I wonder if we should take him in?"

"Don't worry about him. You've got enough to handle. Besides, it's cooler tonight than it's been since we got here. You forget how you feel when that monster sun comes out."

"When things are like they were tonight, I can handle everything, even more children, God forbid. Even you! Were you proud of me for not worrying about Burroughs? I wasn't too heavy, was I? You always tell me I'm heavy."

"Come to bed with me, Esther."

The night had a palpable texture, almost as if Alf or Esther could reach out and wrap its velvet around them, a sumptuous cloth in which to lose themselves. Esther stepped out of her dress and let Alfred uncover the rest of her in the dark.

"Good music, Alf."

•　　•　　•　　•　　•

Six Companies cut wages the first week in August. Muckers, nippers, and cherry pickers down to four dollars a day, cabletenders hit with an even bigger cut—from 5.60 to the same four dollars. They'd been working through one of Nevada's worst heat waves, and their wages were cut.

According to the government meteorologist, the average maximum temperature from June 21 to August 5 was 120 degrees fahrenheit, the absolute maximum 128—in the shade. He didn't mention the numbers recorded in sunlight, though stories circulated about people who'd seen the mercury soar to 140 in the bottom of the canyon.

Labor efficiency was as low as the temperatures were high, tunnel work being the most difficult. Groundwater and condensed heat combined to overwhelm the comparatively insignificant men with their drills, shovels, and jackhammers. Even when electric mucking machines and electric locomotives were brought in, the crew's efficiency was so reduced by the heat that installation was next to impossible.

Though construction was under way on a permanent water treatment plant, the water supply was still plagued with silt. Refrigeration was a marginal operation. Fourteen hundred men were jammed into 4,000 feet of canyon and their numbers were being chiseled away by falling rock, asphyxiation, and heat prostration. They kept disappearing, small pieces at a time, and those remaining started to complain—louder and louder.

When Bill Watkins, the frustrated president of the operation, heard about the complaining, he slammed the telephone into its cradle and thrashed from side to side in his hospital bed. "I've never had a labor problem in my life. What the hell's going on down there? Nurse," he shouted, "get me the hell out of here. Nurse?"

Meantime, the project couldn't wait for Bill Watkins any longer. An executive committee was formed to make decisions in the interim—Henry Kaiser as chairman; Stephen Bechtel to oversee purchasing, administration, and transportation; Charles Shea in charge of field construction, legal affairs, feeding and housing; and Felix Kahn to mastermind the finances.

"Crowe needs some help," Kaiser announced at a committee meeting in San Francisco.

"I'm on my way," said Shea. "But don't worry about Crowe. He's been on irrigation and dam projects for both the Reclamation Service and Morrison and Knudsen for twenty-five years. Give him a little slack."

"This project's coming to a standstill. We can't have slack. No way in hell."

"But look at what's working," Shea insisted. "There's the railroad being built from Las Vegas to the rim of Black Canyon and then the other standard-gauge rail line from Boulder City down into the canyon which, as you know, has no natural shoreline; the compressor plant has about twelve more days' work before it's ready; the city's going up—more dormitories, the mess hall and company store, thirteen houses now, sewers, streets, waterworks, septic tanks, and warehouses. Crowe's main problem is in those diversion tunnels. Everybody's suffocating inside that rock, but we can provide each heading with better ventilation as soon as we get the power from San Bernardino which is any day now. It's timing. Everybody's so damn impatient. And the weather will change before long. Count on it."

But the fact remained. Wages had been cut. On August 7, 1931, a general strike was called. Walkout. Four o'clock shift. All tunnel workers except ten. Four hundred workers met at the River Camp cookhouse.

"Stand up for your rights," the speaker said, then looked over at Bill Burroughs who stood at the back of the room like a puppeteer. He leaned against the wall, wiping his hands on his workpants sometimes, folding his arms smugly at others.

"We've been working like subhumans," the speaker continued. "Eight people already dead from heat prostration, let alone the cables snapping, wires falling out of the sky and gaining momentum with every foot of free fall, rocks raining down on our heads. We've been putting up with impossible stand-ards—the heat, lousy sanitary conditions, no decent water, machine drills being used instead of hand drills in the tunnels, disregard for mining safety laws. And in case you didn't know, the *United States Code 321* reads, 'It shall be unlawful for any contractor to require or permit any laborer to work more than eight hours in any calendar day, except in case of extraordinary emergency.' You men have all been putting in double shifts and a lot of overtime. And now a decrease in pay from a company who's making money out of our hides. It's time to unite. You won't regret the price that might seem high right now."

They voted unanimously to strike—even Alf, who hadn't planned on raising his hand—and filed out of the cookhouse to evaporate into the evening.

Alf's hand just floated into the air as if he were one of Bill Burroughs's marionettes. He touched the hand that betrayed him, each of the fingers, the thumb, and knew he couldn't face Esther that night or smell the smells accumulated in his mockery of a house. He couldn't face himself, either. He thought he knew who he was and had surprised himself when his hand went up at the meeting. Who was Alf Jensen? What did he stand for, if anything? How could he bite the hand that fed him, A. P. who'd helped him? But something inside him pulled the lever that raised his arm. "For the good that I would I do, not; but the evil which I would not, that I do"—one of the few scriptures Alf had memorized. St. Paul. Alf. Brothers in humanity.

"Real important I go see Jack," he told Esther, all the time holding onto the car door handle, acting as if matters were too urgent for her to stop him with questions. But instead of looking for Jack at the dormitories where he would have been, Alf drove to Blue Heaven where the proprietors did their own bootlegging in a mechanic's garage out back. He was well lubed, overcoming the bitter taste of yeast at the bottom of each of the moonshine beers, before other workers drifted in, buzzing with talk of the demands presented to "Speed-Up" Crowe and the now fourteen hundred men on strike.

That includes me, Alf thought, swishing warm beer over his tongue. *Me with a hand that raises to vote while the rest of me is looking on in surprise.*

In addition to the scrip he still had from last Friday's payday, Alf had one valuable dollar he wanted to keep and forty-seven cents change besides to finish out such a night as this, a night for blurring everything, fuzzing the edges of a day too discouraging to think about. Suddenly, his focus sharpened on a diminutive girl who sat down on the next stool. She had curls across her forehead like commas in a row. Her eyes were streamwater clear, and Alf thought he could see way into her soul when she said hello.

"God's perfect creation," he said. "He was in a good mood on the day he minted you, Ma'am."

"My mother thanks you," she said. "You work on the dam?"

70

"You're a tiny little thing, aren't you? What can I get you to drink, sweetness? Beer? beer? or beer? Might be able to find some sloe gin if I talk just right."

"Anything with ice. That tinkling sound in my glass just drives me wild. That feeling of cold cold against my teeth."

"So, you want ice on the rocks?"

"Ice on the ice. We'll ice skate together. 'Ice Skaters' Waltz.' I can sing it while we skate."

"Ice is nice, ice, ice, ice, ice." Alf sang "ices" up and down the scale in his basso profundo.

"You're feeling good, brother. You want to come with me and feel even better? Rock you in my crib. Make you feel good all over."

"I could use feeling good," Alf said, swirling the ice and admiring his reflection in the glass. Then he whispered. "What if these strikers foul up everything? All my plans? Why are they screwing with my future when I had everything squared away? Bastards made me raise my hand."

"Let little old Cynthia take care of your worries. I know how to put them away in a tight, tight box where nobody can see them. Not even you."

Alf pulled out his pockets. "You take Six Companies scrip?"

"Sure, honey. That company store is opening any day now, and then I can buy anything I need. But you know, it's not quite open yet. You think you could spare that dollar in your hand?"

"I have a baby to feed, Cynthia. A little baby and two other daughters and a very sad wife. And you want to take my dollar?"

"Little old Cynthia needs to feed a baby too, honey. Did you ever think about that?"

Alf was lubed, but he didn't miss the puff of a nimbus cloud sailing into Cynthia's clear eyes. Then he noticed the slight, hairline cracks in her porcelain cheeks and a suggestion of terror in her eyes.

They walked through the tables thick with cards and hands holding more cards and cigarettes, and Alf followed her through the back door to a narrow shed built of planks.

Alf looked at the bareness. No flowers. No pictures of uncles or grandfathers. A stark wooden floor and a thin mattress with one sheet and no pillow. A candle being lighted. A skirt falling to the floor. A blouse half unbuttoned.

"I'm a decent man," he said. "I try to keep my promises. I do. You hear me?"

Cynthia sat on the mattress to unhook her garters and roll her stockings into limp rings. "I keep mine too. I promised you I'd help you forget."

"But I can't forget for long enough." He squatted on his haunches and put his hand on her breast—a breast just full enough to fit the curve of his hand. He shifted his weight to his knees, bent over the opening in her blouse, and dragged his tongue across the salty taste of Cynthia.

And he tried to forget. His children, Esther's eyes, Bill Burroughs, A. P. Watkins—the man who could give or take his life away—the strike that could blow everything apart, his hand floating into the air to vote "yes, let's strike." Six Companies could lock everybody out now, including him. There were enough replacements waiting on the lawns in Las Vegas right this minute. He thought how nice it would be to be lost in a bushel of breasts—breasts against his cheeks, his arms, and his thighs, a total surrender to the pillows of life. Breasts to shield him from the enemy. No one would find him in there, in that basket of fresh tits.

He felt her nipples harden like diamonds under his tongue, and he said, "Thank you, Cynthia. Thank you very much." He held out his last dollar.

"That's all?" she said.

He kissed her on the cheek as she folded the dollar between her fingers and found Blue Heaven's back door in the dark.

•　•　•　•　•

The next morning, "Speed-Up" Crowe closed down the project indefinitely. The chief accountant of Six Companies, the paymaster, and two payroll clerks had worked at their oak desks through the night, their fingers flying across the keys of their adding machines, their swivel chairs creaking as if to complain of the trouble. They had checks ready in the morning for everybody on the job. They'd show them how quickly they could be replaced.

Alf drove into Boulder after he heard the news. If Big Six kept total control, Alf could probably ride the crest. After all, he'd concluded after a night of tossing covers, A. P. never saw him raising his hand, and he'd sworn during the night that he'd work under whatever conditions, anything to keep his family in one piece. But he hadn't expected a general shutdown. He'd better take a few precautions.

After the teeth-jarring ruts of the Hemenway Wash road, he drove onto a smooth, newly paved section of highway and thought about Blue Heaven and last night. Somebody was sure to bend Jack's ear about some little chippy and his father, make the story sound worse than it was.

But Jack knew about Esther and Alf and their different philosophies. He went through the paces for his mother, just as Alf did, sometimes going to church to please her, trying not to swear or ogle a shapely pair of legs in her presence, but religion hadn't taken with him, either. Jack would understand a slight indiscretion like booze and Cynthia if Alf could get to him before somebody else did, but Herbert never would. He'd be indignant. "How could you do this to Mother? Where are your principles?" Thank goodness he was still up at the copper mines. He was too much like his mother—too serious about Mormonism and any departure therefrom. Thank the Lord for one ally: Jack. Alf intended to drop in on him after he talked to A. P., to set matters straight.

Men were standing in line outside the Six Companies's offices. Alf recognized some of them—Ed Bishop, Bernie Wilson, Bill Parker—in the middle of a continually changing mix of people. He parked his car off the road, pulled on his hat, and pushed into the crowd.

"Hey, Alf. Afternoon," said Ed. "You ready for the federal troops? I'm told they're just waiting for Young to blow the whistle."

"You sure?" Alf asked. He was glad he'd come. Make sure he wasn't whisked out of Boulder with the flood of strikers, sent on his way, nameless, faceless, for being in the wrong place at the wrong time.

"Who knows for sure? Everybody's lining up to get their paychecks, and the maddest ones are gathering at a place they're calling Camp Stand, eight miles out of Vegas. The Central Labor Committee in Vegas has promised to feed everybody while they're waging war, but I bet Six hires new crews as soon as they clear out the strikers. Crowe said they didn't mean to be arbitrary, but they wouldn't discuss the matter with anyone. 'Our conditions or none at all,' he said."

"Hell, is that what Big Six is saying?" Alf asked, hiding his satisfaction that they were taking a hard line.

"The very words of Speed-Up," said Ed, "who says he is speaking on behalf of the board of directors. But he caught me by surprise when he said there weren't any accidents in July. How come there are six men and two widows drawing comp from Nevada and Arizona for that month?"

"Maybe death from heat prostration and drowning don't count," said Alf, drily remembering how his hand had betrayed his intention to support Six Companies all the way. Maybe his body knew something his head didn't.

"And of course," Ed continued, "the Trio of Dead Ladies at Ragtown don't count, seeing's they're not on the payroll. Six is sending strikebreakers down to River Camp right now. Clubs and guns, I heard. Guy named Joe Fulevich is holding out with a contingent of Wobblies down there. If the government stays neutral, Six Companies may be up shit creek."

"But it doesn't sound like they're going to, does it?" Alf asked, suddenly anxious. But then he remembered Walker Young from the Bureau of Reclamation alongside A. P. in his commissary, both asking him to look out for strikers. The government wasn't going to remain neutral, he was sure of it. He relaxed.

"Ed, I gotta see if I can find my son Jack. Keep me posted, okay?"

"Sure, Alf."

Alf moved off in the direction of the single men's dorms. After he thought he was lost to Ed's eyes, he cut back to the Six Companies's office. Maneuvering his way through the dense crowd, he heard every kind of rumor flying. He whistled to soften the sounds of the dissatisfied men and their edginess. He had purpose, something that protected a man, and had better things to do than stand around and relay rumors larger than the last one. He felt a nudge against his shoulder.

"Hey, Jensen!" Bill Burroughs, the last person Alf wanted to see, reminded him of a bare-knuckles brawler. "How's the little big man? On your way to patsy the big boys with your fine face?"

"Why aren't you down at River Camp with Fulevich and your friends?" Alf asked, not turning his head in Burroughs's direction. "What kind of dissident are you, making everybody else do your dirty work?"

"Tough cookie, Jensen. Tough for a kin licker. I see you've got the info ready to pass."

"I'm looking for my son, thank you."

"More kin, huh?"

Alf slid behind two tall, lanky boards of men and waited until Burroughs lost interest in him and started another lecture about The Cause to keep men from sliding back into security.

Alf slipped into the Six Companies's office where brown metal fans sat on tables with green linoleum tops, rotating back and forth, whirring cool air over the crowded room, the addressograph, the adding machines, the switchboard, the typewriters. The electricity from California had made it this far, if not to Alf's commissary.

"May I help you?" a stenographer with precisely measured finger waves in her hair asked. He felt surrounded in this sea of orderliness. Slide rules, reports, charts, typewriters. Another world. A different ocean.

"Mr. Watkins?" Alf said. "Is he in?"

"He arrived this morning on the train and will probably be in meetings for the rest of the day."

"But this is important."

"Your name?"

"Alfred Jensen."

"I'll see."

The typewriter desks were brand new, miniature metal tables with drop-leaf ends. Alf noticed two safes in the corner and a switchboard confused with myriad cords, lights, plugs, noise, and the operator's fast-moving hands.

A. P., older than he should be for a job like this, limped out the door and motioned for Alf to follow him into the corner by the water cooler.

"Be brief, Jensen." A. P. was wound like wire on a spool.

"Why are you limping, sir?"

"A broken leg. In June. Slow to mend, but let's not waste time."

Alf looked down at his shoes, once brown and shiny, now ghost white with dust. "Bill Burroughs is the key man. Get him and you've nipped the movement."

"We can't hire or rehire until we've got every last one of those agitators off the reservation."

"He's your man. Get him and you've got the canker."

"This damn strike had no business happening." A. P. held a paper cup under the spigot and turned the handle. "We can't control the weather, for hell's sake. We've always treated our men fairly. We're feeding them like kings."

"I'm sure, sir."

"Bill Burroughs, you say? Next house ready is yours. Take my word for it."

"But," Alf said with some hesitation, hedging his bets, "when do you think this will be over?" Maybe he couldn't feel sure about anything made of words, not until he was dressed in a green apron at the company store or living inside a house on the Avenues B, C, or D, next to the other workers with families.

"The federal marshal won't let us employ force, but, between you and me—and swear to top secrecy on this one—the government's on our side. Tomorrow, Young is delivering an order to vacate the reservation, and he'll send in trucks to transport the troublemakers out of here."

"Sir, with respect, I heard Six Companies was sending in strikebreakers right now."

"Disregard that idle gossip, Jensen. Just get me every last name you can."

Alf thought of the strikers at River Camp and the strikebreakers Ed said were on their way there with clubs and guns.

"Buzz Bodell's our new deputy marshal," Watkins continued, "and will be swearing in all the government bosses he can. Giving them pistols and a badge. We can't get stopped on this project. It's too important."

Alf knew about Bodell. The bandy-legged tough guy had managed the Boulder Club in Vegas and had a healthy appetite for trouble. His ivory-handled revolver, a permanent fixture on his right hip, and his pit bull named Musso—for Mussolini—were favorite topics of conversation in the commissary. Nobody messed with Buzz Bodell and walked the next day.

"You've done your best," he said. "I know you have, sir."

"Damn rights we have, and these troublemakers are just making things worse. Drawing national attention to something that's going to be remedied any day now. Weather'll ease off in September, at least I hope it will. Electricity is almost connected down at the River Camp. Lights. Fans. Water coolers. We're killing ourselves to get things ready and then everybody throws sticks at us. Anyway, you've been helpful."

"Thank you, sir."

"You understand our dilemma, then?"

"Of course, Mr. Watkins."

"If you get more names, Alf, give them to Bodell." Watkins paused between Alf and the conference room door. "Any questions?"

Alf's saliva tasted bitter. *My arrangement is with you, A. P., not Bodell.* Was Alf an enemy to himself as well as the men he worked with? He'd put up with as much hell as anyone, his family squatting in a cardboard house for six weeks, living off spoiling canned goods from his mother-in-law—peaches, mustard pickles, cherries, applesauce, tomatoes, apricots; cooking around a stone-ring fire on nights when they could scrape up some hamburger or chicken. He hadn't asked for any favors from this relative except a job, and what man wouldn't do that if he hadn't been able to find work? Maybe he wasn't a he-man blasting into the diversion tunnels, but he earned his pay, sweating, his lungs burning with every breath when he stepped outside the commissary barrack on the precarious slant of landfill above the river. Why was Watkins matching him up with a lowlife like Bodell?

Maybe Watkins wasn't all that different from Burroughs. A bigger big man, maybe, but he didn't seem to be giving Alf the full picture either. Choosing information to fit the ears. Using Alf for his own purposes. Knowing what Alf needed and pressing ever so gently. Alf trotting into the trap because he needed the meat. Little big man.

Two sides of a coin. Burroughs. Watkins. Both big men. Tall men goading Alf to play their rules.

And Alf was a little man staring up at his father swinging from the rope, his father who had decided enough was enough, that he couldn't face another day and wanted to hear the music of silence. "My little man," his mother had said when he went to her speechless, pointing in the direction of the coal shed. Little man trying to find words for what he had seen, though none would come to him, even when he tried to say *Papa*. His finger pointed in one direction only, and his mother followed that finger to its logical conclusion and screamed for five minutes solid while the little man covered his ears with his fists.

A neighbor had cut the rope while his mother softened his father's drop, falling with him to the coal. His mother, Kristina, with black coal on her face. Once, he liked drawing on paper with coal—billowing clouds and sometimes sheep in a meadow—but that was before his father lay crumpled on top of it and made him feel small. And here was Watkins treating him like a notch on a flywheel.

"Any questions, Alf?" Watkins said again as he hovered near the conference room door and made Alf feel anxious and ready to apologize for his thoughts. He hadn't meant them. He wanted this job. He needed it.

"I hope it's over soon," Alf said, "for all our sakes."

"Regards to Esther." The inner door closed, and then Alf found the doorknob of the outer door that returned him to the bleached white day. Even after the pupils of Alf's eyes shrank to a pinpoint, everything remained as stark as when he first stepped outside. No colors in the clothing or the men's faces. Everyone faded in the white light. No one saw Alf on his way to his car. He was invisible, a ghost of light.

• • • • •

Even after the government made the Six Companies's strikebreakers put away their guns and unload the trucks they'd crammed full of workers, and even after the U.S. deputy marshal told the strikebreakers they had no authority to move men without a warrant, the federal neutrality didn't last. At a meeting in a government warehouse, Alf listened to Walker Young order the obstinate strikers off the reservation. The laborers, assuming federal authorities were acting in a neutral capacity, left without a fight. Alf watched the government trucks roll out of Black Canyon, removing 200 of the most obstinate men to Camp Stand, the place where they thought their cause would be won.

But Alf knew all along. The Feds were not neutral at all, neither was the state of Nevada. They were agents of something bigger than even Six Companies, or the other road-building, railroad-building, Boulder City street-laying companies. The agitators didn't understand. A river had to be tamed. The interests of society were at stake, and Buzz Bodell had the names of twenty-three red cardholders, courtesy of Alfred Jensen, a servant of higher law when all was said and done.

The employment office was moved to Las Vegas, away from the entrance to the reservation. A large gate was installed across Boulder Highway with a painted sign: *You Are Entering the Boulder Canyon Project Federal Reservation. You Are Subject to All Regulations of the Reservation.* Lines of cars waited at the gate while government employees, deputized and armed, checked credentials and issued passes.

The changes after the strike: River Camp was abandoned; Alfred Jensen put on a green apron at the Boulder City Company Store, plucked heads of lettuce out of boxes shipped from California, and lifted packages of meat from Reno out of dry ice. He arranged bottles of milk from Moapa Valley—"Anderson Brothers" painted across the glass—on the shelves of a walk-in refrigerator. And sometimes after hours, he went home to Ragtown and brought Esther and his children back to Boulder City for their favorite entertainment—to stand inside the magic coolness of the walk-in.

5

Esther rubbed the black ink stain on the pocket of Bill Parker's white shirt. She'd decided to wash other people's laundry to cool herself down and refill the blue ceramic teapot. It was emptied in Brigham City when Esther decided their only chance was Hoover Dam. Alf didn't know about the teapot. She'd said the money was a gift from her mother.

When Esther swirled the cloth and her hands in the water, she swayed and sang bits of familiar songs from the Elberta Theater days. "Peggy O'Neill." "A Bicycle Built for Two." She turned collars with her eyes closed and smiled at her audience. Faces full of emotion for the words she sang, some people moving their heads in time to the piano's tempo. She'd been good. Darn good, though she'd never said that out loud.

"Rebecca, honey, I need your help hanging these shirts out."

"I'm in the middle of solitaire, Mama. I'm winning."

"No you're not," Mary Elizabeth said. "You're cheating."

"Shh, girls. Inez is sleeping. Remember? Go get the clothespins, Rebecca. Mary Elizabeth, you check the clothesline. See it's stretched tight."

"In a minute, Mama." Mary Elizabeth was curled up on her bed—a thin mattress on top of boxes—sketching on her Big Chief tablet again with a stick of charcoal. No one was allowed to see what she was sketching, having been told in no uncertain terms to keep their eyes to themselves. Esther suspected heart shapes with Mary Elizabeth's initials inside, or perhaps horses, or perhaps pictures of green trees, a creek, or maybe a bushel basket full of peaches from Grandmother Carpenter's orchard. Or maybe it was a drawing of a house, a fence and a chimney, ivy clinging to its whitewashed walls.

They'd had one home of their own once. The Root House in East Ely, Nevada. Nobody knew why it was called the Root House, whether or not the original owners were Mr. and Mrs. Root, or whether somebody dug a root cellar and built a house on top. Their first home. Not a rented apartment or a partitioned warehouse like the one they'd had in Ely proper, not a room in a relative's house or basement. It was a bought house, actually owned by the bank but that didn't matter, just like the reason for its name didn't matter when compared to the pleasure of pointing out to someone: "That's my home."

It had a bay window with a seat for looking out at the weeping willow in front, at its slender branches under white snow or fringed with bursting buds. It had a real dining room. Table, chairs, even a shelf for china if there had been any. And the stove in the kitchen. After Esther banked the fire at night, their dog, Pal, cozied up to the side of the black cast-iron stove and soaked up the heat until morning when everyone skimmed over the cold floors and warmed their feet on his back.

The magic year of the Root House. The year Esther began stuffing coins and a few greenbacks into her blue ceramic teapot, saved from her washing and ironing for the neighbors. For once, Alf seemed satisfied. Ely Meat happened to capture his attention and Jake Horlacher tolerated Alf's opinions better than most employers.

"Alf in his prime," Esther smiled. He'd been called as the branch president of the East Ely Branch of the church. Under a gray veil of stale cigarette smoke from Saturday night's crap game, the members met in a vacant store on Sunday mornings to shake hands, partake of the sacrament, and discuss the celestial kingdom.

"Brothers and Sisters," President Alf Jensen would say as his unframed octagonal eyeglasses reflected the light spilling through the storefront window, "how glorious it is we can gather here to worship the Lord together and partake of the sacrament in the remembrance of our Savior, our Lord Jesus Christ. Leave your weariness at the door."

The congregation of thirty-four shuffled their feet on the naked wood, coughed, pulled their wraps tighter, their chairs closer, and hushed the children.

"For our opening song, we will sing, 'Now Let Us Rejoice,' led by Sister Esther Jensen." Alf carried his three-ring binder like a prayer book to his chair where he sat with mannequin precision. In his notebook, he'd written the names of the people who'd be giving the opening and closing prayers, the sacrament gem, and the Sunday morning talks. He'd written hymn numbers, announcements of who was sick and who needed help, who was visiting, and who needed to be fellowshipped. He was the chosen leader given special powers and blessings to serve this tiny flock.

Esther stood with a brown hymnbook, *Deseret Sunday School Songs*, raised her arm and traced in the air a 3/4 beat pattern she'd learned from a Brigham City chorister. No organ swelled in the dingy light, only Esther's voice, an unhesitant contralto that held the song and the singers together, urged them to sing their troubles out and away from themselves, sing with all their hearts to the God who'd given them everything:

> When all that was promised, the Saints will be given,
> And none will molest them from morn until ev'n,
> And earth will appear as the Garden of Eden,
> And Jesus will say to all Israel, "Come home."

Esther remembered her boys, Jack and Herbert, sitting in the congregation, shined like silverware, and proud to be sons of the leader. She glanced over at Alf who had once been lost in the middle of eleven children, some dead, some alive, the son of Mama Kristina who never talked about her husband after Alf found him in the coal shed. Tiny Mama Kristina squeezing eleven squalling bodies into life. Alf was glorious as the leader; Esther knew God moved in him despite the contrary evidence.

Brother Horlacher, the owner of Ely Meat, blessed the sacrament. He took the crystal glass of water to President Jensen, who left his binder open on his knees while he caressed the sacramental cup with both hands. Then Brother Horlacher passed it to the two counselors, to Esther, and to the members in the room. Some of their mouths were painted with bright lipstick, hidden by a moustache, or reddened by a running nose; yet each mouth pursed at the rim of the glass to drink the symbolic blood of Christ. The community. The branch, bound together by the rim of a glass of sanctified water.

Esther missed those things now, even though they hadn't lasted long. Alf had tired of posing as a religious man after ten months of that game and said "It's time to move again," even when Esther glared at him and cried for him and said, "No, you can't take this away from us. It's all I've ever wanted. A house. Some roots. All of us together in the church, and some harmony for a change. Please, Alf."

Then, to make his decision stick, he rubbed his favorite heresy into Jake

Horlacher's good will while they ground and hacked beef behind the meat counter.

"Joseph Smith started polygamy just to satisfy his own sexual appetite," Alf said. "He wasn't given any divine plan to re-establish the original church. He just read the Old Testament about Abraham and Isaac and all their wives and said, 'This is the way I can have all the women I want. Marry them.' Smart old fox, I'd say. What do you think, Jake?"

"It was a revelation from God to establish a divine form of marriage. Don't bring it down to that low level of thinking, Alf."

"If it was so divine, why did the leaders drop it as soon as they got pressure from the government?"

Jake could stand only so much sacrilege about his Prophet, Seer, and Revelator. Soon the Jensens were packed and headed for Idaho. But something gave way in Esther then, as if she was a limp rubber band. Grey shades of light in her eyes and in the way she moved.

After that, she stored her pictures in boxes instead of hanging them, unwilling to face the nail holes or the crumbling plaster that ravaged the walls. Sometimes, the nail came out clean, but still, there was the nail hole. Nothing more empty than a room bereft of furniture and full of holes.

As she rubbed the stained pocket against the bar of Fels-Naptha, the ink faded except for a subtle darkness stamped into the cloth. *My life is like this. Memories fade but never completely. Everything waits in traces of memory.* She squeezed the water from the shirt and cranked it through the wringer.

Their family hadn't had anyone to hold church with in Ragtown except for the one Sunday after Esther dressed Cookson and had stared into space for days. Alf had panicked. He told Jack to bring his new friend, an elder who was also a barber, from Hurricane, Utah. They broke the bread and blessed the sacrament together, and Alf gave a short sermon about repentance, apparently willing to do anything to stop Esther from staring holes through him and everything else.

But since that momentary surge in family worship, Esther felt empty. She needed some kind of fellowship and a chance to sing again. She smiled, remembering her audacity last weekend. She'd heard the singing and guitar strumming floating across the Wash and couldn't stay away from the open-air meeting and Parson Frank, a Congregationalist. She joined in with every hymn, even though she didn't know the words and felt guilty worshipping among gentiles. Her first time ever. Afterward, everyone wanted to know who she was and would she come back and sing a solo for them sometime soon.

That was her happiest time here, except, of course, for the night when Jack played a smooth saxophone and Serena taught them the Lindy. Now, people in Ragtown—or Williamsville as Alf still called it—said hello to her, waved at her when they saw her looking for a child or carrying a bucket to the water truck.

As she cranked the last of the shirt through the wringer, Esther heard a car stop outside and then the sound of rushing feet. No one ever ran out here. They usually moved like tar and barely arrived at a place.

"Esther," Alf was breathless. "The house. . . . A. P. was in today. He said we could have a house. One on Avenue B. Block 29. Beautiful lady, we have a home! Indoor plumbing. Wood floor. Shingles on the roof, not tar paper or tin. This'll be just like Ely," Alf said, eagerness everywhere on his face.

The thought of a real place to stay, a home like the Root House, sank into her slowly. She looked at the lingering hint of ink in the shirt and decided maybe she should try one more time, give it one more blueing, until the spot was pure white again. Such things must be possible if she had a real place to stay.

"Oh, Alf," Esther said, holding out her arms to the man who represented too many things to her. He was like loose sand under her feet, slipping every time she took a step; then he was impenetrable with sunlight reflecting off his glasses and other hard surfaces, and then he was a soft cloth body with no hinges in his arms. Awkward. Vulnerable. Esther felt confusion when she hugged him, flustered by the pull toward and away from him at the same time. Inside, there was a young girl who once sang at the Elberta Theater. This girl still looked at Alf as though he were handsomely new and full of promises she could believe, though Esther, the seasoned veteran, knew better than to trust this creature who slid in and out of her affections like the white of an egg.

"A. P. said I was instrumental in breaking that strike which could have broken the back of this project." He grinned. "Your Alf made a difference. What do you think, my sweet?"

"A house, Alf!"

"Damn rights."

"Heavens to Betsy, we made it! Mary Elizabeth, stop drawing on that pad. Get over here and hug your father. Did you hear what he's done for us?"

"It's too hot, Mama." Mary Elizabeth didn't look up.

Alf walked over to his eldest daughter's side of the room and leaned over her work. She slammed the tablet to her chest. "Nobody sees my drawing."

"Come on. Let me see, honey. This is your Daddy."

"You're my father."

"Let me see then. I'm proud of your art. You know that."

"Privacy. There's none of that around here." She scrambled over the edge of the boxes, bumped Alf, and rushed out into the sun.

"For hell's sake, Esther! Asinine little prima donna."

"Leave off, Alf. It's been so cramped and impossible. It's a miracle we're still walking around."

"Who does she think she is?" Alf stormed out of the burlap door and started yelling after Mary Elizabeth, who ran to the river with her tablet tight to her chest, her head bowed as if she was facing off with the north wind.

"Get back here, Miss High Horse. Get your ass back here."

"Alf, please," Esther called after him. "Everybody's going to hear you."

Inez, startled from her sleep, started to cry. Her arms hit the edge of the drawer which was getting too small for her. She screamed even louder. Esther picked her up, ran back to the doorway. "There, baby. There now. Everything's all right, little one."

Alf unbuckled his belt and slipped it out of its loops. "You get back here you little snot, or I'll whip you."

"Alf, stop it. Please. We have a home. A home, Alf, and you have a job as a greengrocer. Remember. Apples, celery, lettuce. Cold crisp carrots. Alf, she just hasn't any privacy. Please, sweetheart."

His face reddened like a newborn. "Will you let me run my own household, woman?"

"You're not whipping Mary Elizabeth." Esther pushed past him, slipping in the grainy sand.

"Don't get in my way, Esther."

Esther struggled along in the sand while Inez bounced and cried, and Mary Elizabeth ran along the edge of the red river on the smooth, worn sand of the bank raised by the last flash flood. Suddenly, Esther tripped on an exposed root and fell on her hip, still holding Inez.

Inez cried louder than ever, and Alf stopped, indecisive, more inclined to move forward than back.

Esther was not lithe. She'd had three miscarriages, and seven children counting the twins who'd lived for two days. She'd been pregnant so many times—full-blown round—that she forgot which figure was really hers. She rolled forward trying to stand, but hanging on to Inez and getting up was a greater exertion than she could muster, and she rocked back and forth, trying to get to her feet with some dignity.

"I won't ask Alf for help," she kept saying to herself. "I'll do this myself and hang him."

Finally, she laid Inez in the sand, leaned on her left arm and struggled to her feet before Alf arrived with his glad hand and his sweet-talking apologies she'd heard too many times.

"You and your temper, Alf." Esther shook the sand from the folds of her dress and the creases at the back of her knees. "You lose all your sense."

"I'm sick of Mary Elizabeth's attitude. A nine-day-old fish. That's how she treats me."

"Stop it, Alf. You're torturing yourself and your daughter."

"I'm sick of you females. Delicate sensibilities. Cultured. Who feeds all of you?"

"Alf, remember your good news? The house? Alf, everything's solved with the Avenue B, Block 29. You've secured us a house."

"The house. Yes."

"Things'll be better, Alf. Not so crowded. Cooler. Fall's coming too. Apples. Celery. Your job. Forget your daughter. She doesn't have enough to do. It's like everybody's been on a shelf in a steam room, getting all the wrinkles, the starch, any will a body ever had, steamed out of their systems. Too hot to move around or believe in anything besides heat. Everything will be better, Alf. Forget Mary Elizabeth."

The belt hung loosely from his hand. He snapped it once before he tucked it back into its loops. That snap seemed the only sharpness of the day, everything else gone slack in the heat, and it cut cleanly into Esther's senses, another memory.

• • • • •

Dingbat houses. Two carpenters plus one helper built one and a half of them every day under instructions that the crew would be fired if they didn't stick to schedule. The houses were not meant to be permanent. They'd be razed when the dam was completed, but regardless, Esther thought 216 Avenue B was maybe the most beautiful thing she'd ever seen, even though from a distance it looked like a section of a giant white caterpillar stretching across the wasteland, identical to every other house on the street. People were continually getting lost in the rows of dingbats, each of which had screened porches on two sides and windows set in the middle. There were no street signs yet, only replica after replica of white cottage with a loosely plowed yard of dirt, broken sage, and lizards, scorpions, and vinegaroons skittering to find new homes. To everyone except Esther, the only redeeming feature of the cottages was the indoor plumbing and the cooler daily temperature.

When she carried the box of photographs and pictures inside 216 B, she knew she would unpack them this time. These walls were brand new, not covered with crumbling plaster or full of empty nail holes.

Before tackling the boxes of dishes, soaps, the remaining jars of canned peaches, or even her own clothes, she pulled the string from the box of pictures and photographs. She wound the string in a tidy ball and folded the tissue from each picture into a neat square.

There was the Three Grandmothers—Grandmother Nettie and her two sister wives, Rebecca and Sylvia—and Grandpa, the patriarch, his hand flat on his heart under his lapel. There was the oval watercolor of the Salt Lake Temple with its gold-leaf frame and convex glass. Esther thought of herself there, kneeling across the altar from Alfred, facing her man and her womanhood at the same time, shy as she'd never been before, unable to lift her eyes to meet those of her husband's at the beginning of their time and eternity together. And there was Alf with his brothers and sisters, young Alf standing proudly at his father's side, the picture taken three months before the man died. Waxed moustaches. Razor-clean cheeks. Pomaded cowlicks and side-burns. The Danes, most of them fair-skinned, except for one daughter and Mother Kristina. Who knew where the dark flashing eyes had come from or the olive skin that contrasted with the other pale Danish eyes and complexions? Esther thought of her son Jack with the same dark eyes and black hair. A Ute Indian chief once asked to adopt him. He'd never really been her own as Herbert was, and Herbert would be coming now that they had a home. She was counting the days.

Esther dusted each one carefully and placed it on the floor to decide the best arrangement for hanging. When she lifted her Grandmother Nettie's engagement photograph out of the box, she pressed it next to her heart as if to feel the photo's life. The people she'd never known, designers of Esther and her children and their children, passing on strengths, quirks, and oddnesses.

Nettie had a hint of melancholy on her face through her bride-to-be smile. She was the last of Grandpa Carpenter's three wives, Esther's very own blood grandmother, looking as if she was wondering what it meant to be a third wife and have no man to call her own. Esther rotated the dust cloth absentmindedly across the face in the face of the glass.

Mary Elizabeth stumbled across the threshold carrying a box too heavy for her. Esther could see a corner ready to give way where her daughter wasn't supporting it with her hands. Old beaten boxes. Twenty-six moves in some of them. She slid the picture gently to the floor and hurried to help her daughter.

"Where's your father? You shouldn't be carrying this by yourself, young lady."

"He's out there talking to some guy about scrip. How he can give him cash for a percentage or something like that."

"That man's always got some scheme. Here, put this box in the other room."

"Mama, when will Herbert be coming? He's my best friend. And he never stares." Freed from her burden, she danced through the four rooms as if imagining them grand halls of a castle.

"Who stares at you, honey?" Esther unwrapped the last picture and stood to study the arrangement of photographs, sweat trickling down her elbows.

"Oh, nobody really. Except sometimes—"

"Sometimes what?"

Mary Elizabeth put her hands on the laundry tub which had its own built-in space in the kitchen, and leaned forward, her back leg kicking into a low arabesque.

"Do you think I'm pretty, Mama?"

"Of course I think so. Your eyes and smile especially. You're a magnet. Wait till you start high school in Vegas."

"Nobody notices me, except sometimes Daddy."

"Your father has an eye for beauty."

Mary Elizabeth looked down at her breasts which were full like her mother's.

"Why do men like breasts so much?"

"What do you know about men liking breasts?"

Mary Elizabeth dampered a broad smile. "I've just noticed they do."

"Men can't help it. Memories of their suckling, that softness and warmth, their mother's heart beating steadily while they filled their empty stomachs. I wish to heaven men could separate a woman from her breasts, but honest to goodness, I think males are attached by invisible breast strings."

Mary Elizabeth filled her hands with her own breasts. "They're just fat, Mama."

"Where's Rebecca?"

"Out digging in the sand. She's got her sunbonnet on, I checked."

"I worry when she's out there. You saw the rattler whose head the carpenter chopped off the other day. He's got its head dangling over the spare tire on the side of his truck."

"Mama, she's got to breathe a little. You've kept her in since the first of July, worrying about the sun. She's got to run. Six weeks of that is a long time."

"Has it only been six weeks?"

Alf ran into the house carrying Rebecca in his arms. "So what the hell you doing in here? My little girl's out there courting a tarantula, and you're in here gabbing."

"Well, Alf, you were out there with her."

"I was doing business."

"I see. Hanging up pictures in a house is not so important as you talking to some neighbor?"

Rebecca struggled to free herself from Alf's tight grip. "We were talking business," he said. "She's okay, thanks to me. The nick of time."

"What kind of business, Alf? Some kind of lending scam again? I thought you learned your lesson in Ely."

"It's legal. I can trade cash for company scrip. With me they lose only five percent. Any establishment besides the company store takes ten percent. I'm doing them a favor."

"For a percentage, right, Alf?" Esther, hands on her hips, stood with her feet apart.

"What's wrong with that, Esther?" Alf moved in closer. He had a three-inch height advantage over his wife. She could see the glistening oil in the pores of his nose. "You're always complaining we don't have enough and then you sit on everything I try to do if it doesn't fit into your morality."

Mary Elizabeth covered her ears with her hands and stamped her feet. "Stop it. Stop it, you two."

"Just cause you're in a house now, don't forget to pay attention to your children, Esther. Don't get lost in here mooning over the past: your fine pioneer family. Those upstanding citizens related to somebody who happened to be in Brigham Young's first wagon company into Utah. Right, Esther?" He kicked the picture of his father's family with the toe of his shoe and destroyed the symmetry Esther had arranged.

"Our pictures, Alf!"

"Who needs these people breathing down our necks, Esther? I saw enough of my family to last me a lifetime and you insist on hanging them over my head. I know what was going on just before this so-called pleasant picture was taken. My father had whiskey on his breath and was yelling at everybody until the photographer said to smile."

"It's our heritage, Alf." She squatted to straighten the picture back in its place. "The children need to know."

"They should forget."

"I refuse to argue anymore," she said. "This is the first day in our new home, and we're going to do it right." She stomped her heels hard against the wooden floor as she walked to the kitchen door, then turned on gentler heels.

"You're right, Alf. I should have been watching Rebecca, but I thought she needed freedom after being cooped up so long. We're in our new house. You've been working hard. I'm sorry."

"A lion. A lamb, Esther. I never know about you. One extreme or the other."

Suddenly, she sat in the middle of the floor on the rough, unplaned boards. "The weather. Make the heat go away." Tears rounded out of her eyes. "Alf, make it go away. I'll never be angry again if you'll make it go away."

"Geez, I married a crazy woman. One minute you're Attila the Hun, then you're looking at me with those sloppy wet eyes."

"I'm sorry, I'm sorry."

"Stop saying you're sorry. It makes me gag."

"Hug me, Alf."

"I can't change from hot to cold like you do."

"Hug me and say everything's okay. Please?"

She held up her arms to his. He held them stiffly at the elbows.

Why does it fill me—this feeling that nothing will ever work and why go on trying? Its poison fills my body and stretches my skin until it hurts. She looked at the pictures on the floor, her hands still in Alf's. *Maybe Alf was right. Maybe the ancestors are wearing masks. "Look closer," they're saying. "Look behind our eyes for the real story."*

You're evil, Esther. You hate the sun that warms others and makes things grow. You resent your own baby and never find enough good in your husband. You run from God's face to hide in a dark cave. The Prince of Darkness, Esther. Is he your savior? There's fire in God's face as well as in Satan's arms. No place to go. No coolness, not even in death, not even in goodness.

"Forgive me, Alf," she said in a monotone that flattened her emotions. "Are you driving to Ragtown for another load?"

"Yes." His voice was hoarse.

"Could Rebecca ride along? Inez will be waking soon."

"Of course," Alf said. "And you come too, Mary Elizabeth."

Mary Elizabeth shot a dark look toward her mother. "Do I have to?"

"Help your father," Esther said with no equivocation.

When the car disappeared in its own tail of dust, Esther sprawled in a corner next to the mattress where Inez lay sleeping. Beautiful child, thought Esther, stroking the tiny forehead with its liquid crystal beads of sweat. Smooth skin. Peaceful child.

"Now that we're in a home, I will love you," she whispered to Inez. "I promise. I won't let the poison take me away. You'll be my tether. Soon the weather will be cool, and we'll go for walks, you and me. The city streets will be in soon, and we can walk without sinking in the sand. We'll go up to Tank Hill and look at the Colorado which won't be the Colorado much longer. It's startling from a distance, Inez. Red winding water. It's ours, Inie. Remember how it soothed us at night, going on and on, a moving picture never changing, not really, the sound of a thing going somewhere, always moving? And the rain, the drops pitting the ground, and how we could almost hear the sand swallowing the drops of water? It sustained us. We've been to hell, baby, like Persephone. Now we're back and we'll stay back. Your mama will love you. Your mama will be calm and love her baby."

Esther outlined the child's lips with her fingernail. Inez opened her eyes and gave her a fragile, wispy smile. Esther bent over her, kissed both cheeks, and lifted her breast out of her dress.

"Your mama won't hate you anymore, I promise. I'll make up for everything, sweet baby. Forgive your mother, please baby."

6

────

Esther seemed a new woman. She made cupboards from orange crates Alf brought home from the grocery and nailed a temporary sideboard together for the kitchen. She stacked the few remaining jars of her mother's mustard pickles, tomatoes, and peaches, alphabetized her bedraggled spices, and bought two bottles of Certo in anticipation of canning the Utah peaches Alf said he'd order into the company store.

After debating whether or not to keep the Germozone that had protected their chickens from disease in Ely, Malad, and Price—chickens and eggs often-time their only meal in a day—she decided to trust in their new future. She tossed the Germozone, but did keep the Hires extract she'd carried from pillar to post. The children loved the root beer made from the extract and Brewer's yeast, especially when she let them press the long-handled bottle capper and squeeze the metal caps flush with the lips of brown bottles. When Herbert arrived, she'd throw a root beer party. Maybe Jack would drive to Vegas and find the bottles she needed.

Then she started to dig holes for spring bulbs until her neighbor reminded her that no one in town could use water for anything but drinking and household purposes. She put her mother's precious bulbs back in the paper sack and set it beside the blue teapot. She'd have to wait, but when she had daffodils and apricot trees growing in her yard she'd have the whole of her dreams. She wouldn't have to grow things in her imagination anymore. Green grass, daffodils, a home, and apricot trees were all she needed. Even though the houses were desolate, unlandscaped cottages plunked down between mounds of freshly turned earth, they were clean and orderly, and $30 a month, payable to Six Companies. And they were multiplying.

Esther's mind calmed as civilization emerged from the bulldozed terrain, and she even allowed herself to feel some pride. After all, she'd lasted through events she once thought would be the end of her—twin babies turning blue and bruised-looking before they had a chance to pull themselves across a floor or even cry very much. Gone away too soon. Inez, born when she should have stayed in God's care. Ragtown, the heat, unpredictable Alf, and her own mercurial emotions that dragged her all over geography, but mostly down into a deep blackness of soul. But now she'd find a balance. She knew she could. Her life was shaping into softer contours—pictures on the wall, curtained cupboards, the look of settling, and even new neighbors.

Bill Parker's wife, Dorothy, had finally moved from St. Thomas. She was a round, red-faced woman who wore crystal spectacles with frames of the lightest gold wire. Esther wanted to greet her in the way she knew best, with a loaf of home-baked bread.

She slid the pans into the oven at five in the morning in order to cool the house down by seven when everyone would waken. Four rounded loaves of whole wheat bread, springing back to the touch, done to perfection because Esther felt like a new woman and because baking was a reflection of the baker. Good times: fresh bread, the sound of the knife against the hard crust before it cut through to the insides, one hot piece for herself, generous amounts of butter and honey.

She was on Dorothy's doorstep by eight.

"A little something to say hello," Esther said, her big eyes full of the charity preached in Relief Society.

"Why, I thank you," Dorothy said, wiping her hands on her apron while two small children peered out from behind her. "Can you come in?"

"It's early," Esther said.

"We're always up at dawn. Farmer's habits, I guess, though you need to be up way before dawn in this territory. Sit down." Dorothy offered Esther an oval-backed chair upholstered with horsehair. "I hope this won't itch you. Depends on what you're wearing."

Dorothy settled into a rocker and pulled a child up on her knee. "Say, have you heard about Six Companies and the U.S. Government deciding to bus our kids to school in Las Vegas?"

"Those powerhouse minds just plain overlooked school in all their planning for the dam. Yes, I've heard some talk that that's their weak-kneed solution to the problem."

"Well," Dorothy said as she rebuttoned her child's shirt, "I'm not having any part of that plan. Don't mind my teenagers taking the dusty ride to Las Vegas, but not my little ones. Never know what'll happen so far away, and they can't take such long days. I've taught third grade and know those kids' limits."

"It's a shame they didn't think about the children," Esther said.

"Men and their ways," Dorothy said. "Always wake up too late."

"That's for sure." Esther turned the hands in her lap, noticed the prominent blue veins, and decided to risk what might seem like arrogance in front of this down-to-earth woman. "I'm related to the Watkins brothers, you know, some of the top officials of Six Companies." Esther looked away as she said this, trying not to be obvious about family ties. "I'll see what I can find out."

Dorothy beamed, her shiny red face looking like satin in the early light. "Could you really do that?"

Esther nodded.

"That's just the thing to do, then. We'll eat your bread while you solve the problem." Dorothy laughed and bundled her little girl in her arms. "The bread looks and smells delicious, by the way."

"I hope so," Esther said, rising out of the chair that was making her back itch.

Dorothy squeezed Esther's wrist. "You seem to me a very fine woman."

"The feeling's mutual."

Later that day, Esther asked for A. P. at the Six Companies's home where the directors lived when they visited—a spacious Spanish stucco with a view of Hemenway Wash and the snaking Colorado.

"He's back in Ogden," the receptionist said, "nursing the broken leg which isn't mending like it should." The finger waves in the receptionist's hair made her look like a timid sculpture.

"And how's his brother Bill?" Esther asked while the receptionist stamped "Received" on the incoming mail with purple ink from a new ink pad.

"Not well," she said. "The others have pretty much taken over his responsibilities. Mr. Kaiser, Mr. Bechtel, you know. Why are you asking?"

"I know them distantly." Esther kept an official expression firm on her face.

"He should be back a week from Monday. Any messages?"

"I'll come back," Esther said, wanting to get past the high, squared archway where she could keep her disappointment to herself. A. P. and his brother Bill: shadows behind stenographers, nurses, hospital walls, subcontractors and other company heads when all the time she'd imagined them at the center like a dual hub, her relatives pointing directions for everyone else. They were becoming background, not the front-and-center entity she'd begun to accept as her due. A. P. Watkins. Bill Watkins: a disappearing act. Now you see them; now you don't.

But she wouldn't allow herself to sink into despair. "Life will not upset me. Life will not upset me," she repeated as she walked to the Boulder City Company Store to purchase a sheet of stationery. She still had herself, and that was something after all was said and done.

I do hate to bother you again, she wrote and then erased. The legs on the kitchen table were uneven, and the table rocked back and forth. "Bold resolve, Esther," she reminded herself as she found a piece of cardboard to level the short leg. "Firm, bold resolve." *You've been so wonderful to our family, I thought I might ask if you've heard of any plans for schools in Boulder City. Many of the mothers are concerned because Las Vegas is too far for young children to be bussed. Who can I talk to here?*

I know you have more important things to do, but, then Esther erased that sentence. *I'd like to invite you to dinner the Friday after you return. Herbert is arriving in town, and we're celebrating. I hope you can spare the time.* One more sentence to erase. *I hope your leg is better soon.*

After Esther sealed the envelope, licked the stamp, and walked to the post office, she decided she'd spearhead the neighborhood mothers into organizing their own one-room school in their own homes. No more wasting time feeling sorry for herself. This was definitely a time for resolution.

A few days later, the first session met: Dorothy Parker taught the primary grades; Thelma Black over on D, who'd taught high school English in Peoria, Illinois, took grades 4-6. Esther volunteered to teach music two mornings a week while holding Inez on her hip. "Home Means Nevada" was the first song she taught. She stuck one hip out, balanced drooling Inez there, and exaggerated the shape of the words for the children sitting in a circle on the floor. Rebecca sang loudly, clearly as she'd learned to do in Primary, and Esther dared feel another small burst of pride.

• • • • •

"Know what happened at the employment office, Esther?" Alf said one afternoon after work. "Six Companies is starting construction on the diversion tunnels, and the word's out. Five hundred men are waiting in line for every job given. Some of the men are signing up under several names they're so desperate. We're lucky we got here when we did."

"We sure are."

"By the way, I saw A. P. who said he's happy to accept your invitation to dinner. Says he has some news on the school situation."

"He's coming?" Esther grabbed Alf's elbows, then embraced him with unusual enthusiasm.

"You're happy, Esther," Alf said.

"I am, and you seem to be, too, Alf."

"This climate I could do without, and there's something about this project's different from anything I've ever seen. . . . Oh, Claude Rader over at Mrs. Mears' boardinghouse taught me some of a song he wrote, probably hoping I'll get Jack to play it out at Blue Heaven. Hit tune or something."

"How does it go?"

"Something about the thousands who knock Six Companies, saying they're cheap, but the chaps who came in the beginning are going to stick it out no matter what."

"Sing it to me."

"Wait a minute." He shut his eyes for concentration.

> And the fallin' rocks can't scare us, or the scorchin' rays of sun. We've rode the rods and brake beams, ragged and on the bum, and they gave us jobs and fed us when we needed it, you bet. And we all are truly thankful with no feelin' of regret.

Alf looked good to Esther at that moment. He wasn't angry or laced with alcohol, and she felt that hook Alf had in her take hold again. Maybe it was the music; maybe it was the half-light shining on him through the window, blurred by the blowing sand outside; maybe it was the way he was talking. She liked his philosophical moods, dimestore philosopher notwithstanding.

"You looked at Inez lately, Alf? She reminds me of your mother. Brown eyes and olive skin like both you and her. You've got some handsome children, Mr. Jensen. Like their father."

"That's what Serena tells me. You heard she and Ed got a house over on D?"

"When were you talking to her?" Esther tried to keep her voice in a casual range.

"That's what she said the night they were dancing to Jack's music in Ragtown. Don't you remember?"

"Who told you about their place on D?" Esther could feel the wind blowing against their house. Suddenly the walls seemed thinner.

"It was Ed. Saw him in the store."

"Oh." Esther rearranged the hair on her forehead and then stroked her neck. "I haven't seen Serena since we left Hell's Hole. Glad she's out of it too." Esther's body relaxed, her breathing deepened, and the walls of the house seemed to thicken again. "Is Ed still working as a high scaler?"

"Yes. I hope he'll be okay. Some of those Apaches scramble over the cliffs like spiders, but Ed doesn't seem natural to that terrain. He's not saying much, but I think he's scared. Big piece of rock broke off last week and carried two of his buddies home to God. Now he's talking about omens."

"We'll have to get them over for some more dancing when we have our party for Herbert. After dinner, when A. P.'s gone, we'll get comfortable. Let our hair down." Esther raised her arms high and shook her hips, bumping all the bad luck away. She saw Alf smile. Then she teased the tip of his nose with her little finger. "They'll want to meet our Herbie, wouldn't you say, Alfie Baby?" She accentuated the last four syllables with her hips.

"You're flying high today."

"Everybody's got their own place to sleep. No one's rolling over on anybody at night. The baby's sleeping through the night, and we've got fresh vegetables and fruit, and Herbert's coming. And know something else, Alf? You can hardly see it, especially in this dust storm, but somewhere it's autumn. Leaves are coloring up in the mountains near Brigham. I can feel them changing, and the weather crisping the apples. It's always been my best time, Alf. I can feel the autumn somewhere. My alive time."

She wasn't tall, maybe five-foot-four next to Alf's five-seven. She wasn't slender, though some of the weight from the baby had disappeared from her hips and thighs. Her skin had lost much of its resilience, but no one noticed once they saw her eyes. Even when she smiled, her eyes seemed to exist apart from her face. She herself compared them to the teacup eyes of the dog who guarded the tinderbox in the Hans Christian Andersen tale she'd loved as a child. Water at the bottom of a cup, she'd say of her eyes. They dominated her face, and people were usually ashamed to look closely at her—her soul was too naked. But for the moment, they sparkled with thoughts of autumn.

"So Anderson Brothers said they'd take Herbert on?" she asked.

"Probably. They're still in temporary quarters, but should be in their new place soon. He'll have to stay with us to establish residency for a couple of weeks—procedure to keep the nepotism accusers quiet—but then Jack can help him get in the single men's dorms. Once he's inside Six Companies, maybe he can get on driving trucks down at the dam site. Better pay."

"But Herbert could stay here. He likes the babies and Mary Elizabeth."

"He's eighteen, Esther. You can't keep him under your wing. He's not a babysitter."

"But he knows how to make us laugh, Alf. Always surprises the girls with some treat. And he needs the extra money he'll save if he lives with us. You know he wants to go to college."

"Dreamer."

"But he's a bright boy. You know how he always gets on first-name basis with the librarian in every town we've ever lived."

"Kid's soft. He should live in the dorms with the other men instead of being mollycoddled next to your big bazooms." Alf tweaked the tip of Esther's breast and flustered her.

"My country, tits of thee," he teased, then his hands were on her waist, hips, and sliding down her thighs, and Esther and Alfred tussled with each other in the kitchen. The washtub rattled as they scuffled across the floor, Alf grabbing at her breasts, Esther swiping back at his crotch.

"You're supposed to surrender, Esther. Don Juan here. Give me your hand, your arm, your elbow. Let me nibble at your soft shoulders."

"I'll bite your nose off." But Esther laughed away her edge in the battle. She switched from offense to defense, doubled over to protect herself, and wrapped her breasts in both arms. "Rebecca!" she called out in the falsetto of the pursued heroine. "Where are you? Save me." The little girl came running from her bedroom with a long rope of modeling clay wrapped around her wrist. She grabbed Alf's leg. When he tried to walk, she hung deadweight, a tether of stone.

"I give. Uncle. I give. Rebecca is an Amazon warrior." They fell to the floor, and Alf rolled over on the rough strips of flooring to play dead. Then, one eye opened under an arched eyebrow, he cradled his head in his interlaced fingers.

"Did I ever tell you the story of the Spartan general, young lady? When two of his soldiers—who were very stern soldiers—caught him playing horse and rider with his infant son, he begged them, maybe even threatened their lives, I'm not sure, never to tell what they had seen until they were fathers themselves. What do you think of that?"

Rebecca straddled Alf's stomach and started to bounce, a rider with reins held high.

"Your brother Herbert's coming this weekend, Rebecca." Esther picked the frying pan lid off the drainboard to wipe it with a towel.

"Her-bert, Her-bert," Rebecca chanted.

"Goin' to dance out both my shoes," Esther sang, waving her arms, the towel, and shaking her hands like tambourines in a minstrel show until the front door whipped open. Mary Elizabeth rushed into the room. Strands of hair were pasted to her face, and a light dusting of sand powdered her eyebrows and cheeks.

"Look what the wind blew in," Alf said from his horizontal position on the floor, Rebecca still riding her hobby horse.

"Fun-ny." She slammed the door and threw her books down on the wide-armed rocking chair. "I hate it here. I hate it."

"So, what's wrong today?" Esther asked. "Yesterday, it was diagramming and your stupid English teacher."

"Have you looked outside? Everybody's wash is black. I can't even see where I'm going and almost walked into the wrong house because everything looks alike, and besides that, I don't have any friends. I can't stay after school because I have to catch the bus back to this stupid place. I can't be in the Spirit Club because they practice after school. I can't do anything."

"Just a minute, now," Alf sat up as the sandstorm, which had begun in little gusts and slight whistles around the corners, blasted with full force. It sounded like an assault of miniature hail pitting the walls of the fort.

Esther suddenly felt her good mood vanish and the perversity of the desert move inside herself. Nature dealt the cards how it dealt the cards. Nobody could tell the sun how to shine, the clouds where to move, the wind when or where to blow. She felt an odd sense of detachment. *Blow, Mary Elizabeth*, she thought with contempt. *Blow wind. Blow everything out of my ears and mind until I'm a skull bleached white on the desert floor. None of this matters.*

"Mary Elizabeth," she said sharply. "Stop complaining. Of course you don't have friends. You've only been going to school for a couple of weeks. These things take time. Don't expect a silver platter."

"Can't I even tell you how I feel?"

"No, you can't. Everybody's got to pull their own weight, and the less said the better."

"You drag me all over Utah, Idaho, California, and Nevada," Mary Elizabeth yelled, "and expect me to smile and say thank you. I hate this family!" She scooped her books out of the chair and threw them on the floor next to her father.

"Mary Elizabeth," he said, a calm counterpoint to Esther's surprise offensive, "you'll be all right. You've always had friends before. They're waiting for you now even if they don't know it." He lifted Rebecca off his stomach and stood up.

"Herbert's coming," Rebecca said, hugging her big sister's waist. "Herbert's coming, and we're gonna have a party." Then she marched around the room playing an imaginary trombone, imitating the slide, raising it to the ceiling, pointing it at the floor.

Mary Elizabeth almost smiled.

"This weekend," Alf said, patting her on the shoulder with fatherly affection that wouldn't offend her. "But don't get any big ideas. Herbert has to work now, and he won't be able to spend much time with us."

"You don't know his schedule," Esther said, glaring at Alf and vehemently paring a potato. "How do you know so much?"

"He can share our room," Mary Elizabeth said.

"There are already two of you in there," Alf said. "And Inez will be moving in as soon as she stops crying at night. There's no room for him to stay long."

"We'll make room!" Then Esther rinsed the potato and spoke with more restraint. "It's not like Herbert doesn't have his faults," she added, "but at least he cares about us and the Church. All Jack cares about is his saxophone and Gloria, that frizzhead from Okmulgee, Oklahoma. Can you imagine anything good coming out of Okmulgee, Oklahoma?"

"We'll see about Herbert," Alf said, pronouncing each syllable loudly. "What's under your skin, Esther? You were okay a few minutes ago."

The air outside was brown with silt—a nine-bucket storm, ten being the point where everything moveable was carried off the ground and over the next ridge. It was blowing hot, scattering scraps of planed wood and curls of pine, lifting sand from one mound to the next one. As Esther set the table with the blue-striped china, she listened to the storm destroying whatever it could. And she saw that her china was chipped and nicked, just like everything else, just like her children. She'd tried to keep them whole and protect them, but they were chipped and nicked, nobody could control that. Like the time a strange man grabbed a fistful of Mary Elizabeth's skirt and pointed at the erection jutting out of his pants. *What my children have had to survive.*

Once Esther tried to provide a tidy life. She took her children to Sunday School and Sacrament Meeting every Sunday, to Primary every Wednesday, and to Relief Society on Thursdays when they were too young for school. She taught them to recite poetry and to pay attention to manners she'd learned in her own home in front of a china plate and silver-plated knives and forks. But as they moved again and again, her notions of how the world should work leaked out of her hands. In Ely, Malad, San Diego, McGill, Ruth, even in Utah where things were supposed to be ordered.

She'd dreamed of budding scholars in libraries or lawyers like her father, but her sons sold newspapers to help feed the family. Their regulars were transients, half-wits, prostitutes—one of whom was knifed to death while the boys stood trembling behind their newspaper bags with *Salt Lake Telegram* stenciled across the front. The red-light district in Ely had been a profitable place for the boys, the ladies not only buying papers, but giving them candy and extra coins. They'd been as generous as the sisters in the Relief Society, always looking out for Herbert and Jack and even asking after Herbert's health when he was in the hospital with scarlet fever. But the illusion lost some of its magic after the boys saw one of the sweethearts of the night pushed onto the rutted main street of Ely, blood instead of lace at her throat.

Esther dreamed of her daughters playing piano in a drawing room and embroidering silk petals on pillowcase flowers, but instead they'd learned to banter with obscene comments that Esther in her wildest dreams could never imagine being spoken. Esther never caught her at it, but had heard reports that Mary Elizabeth sometimes sang in the streets for money; she had a polished vaudeville act by age eleven, given impromptu when a passing crowd seemed lively. Her girls had also seen their own father stumble through the front door, his only tie and shirt wrinkled after a night on the floor, his breath rotten. Her babies. Her hopes for them. *Be in the world but not of the world,* she heard at church, but she had no choice in the matter. Alf brought the world stumbling in their door and the need for money kept her children going out.

Occasionally, Esther reasserted her determination to hold to the rod, the word of God. Something to save her children in this life and the next. Something that was stable, ordered, the truth. This resolution was her only remaining gift to her children when everything else had been warped beyond recognition.

But, even so, she was suspicious of herself at times, and Alf couldn't be blamed for everything wrong. At odd moments of the day when she was off guard she wondered if she might be the flaw in their marriage. She'd tried so hard, but praise God as she would, she had strange veins inside that strangled her will even as she tried to pick them out of herself with prayer and supplication to God to become perfect even as He was perfect.

When she tried to shield both herself and her babies, when she'd say, "Don't you ever, ever go near that place," she had her own quiet insurrection, one that wanted her children to know all of life, good and ill, and wanted them to defy her, to stand up for themselves. Sometimes, she was glad when Mary Elizabeth used the swear words she never could. Her daughter swore for her mother, took God's name in vain as Esther wished she had the courage to do without frightening herself, without looking up to see if a swift hand was moving in her direction to smash her. And she wanted to stamp her own feet sometimes, not let other people crush her with their grand designs and threats of God's frown, grimacing at her every wrong move.

She thought of Alf battling against the elders and church leaders. She complained to his face, but all the same, this seditious part of her was glad he stood up to her and to them. She'd never let him know, but she didn't like anybody running over anybody else, not even when she tried to combat Alf with her righteousness. That's what she'd liked about him in the beginning— the way he laughed at her and told her to live for the moment.

Maybe this odd twist in her took root during the year she lay in a protective covering of gauze and waited for the courage to bend her elbows and knees so she could race wildly on the outside in the sun and rain and snow and whatever else might be out there.

Right at this moment, she felt the same contempt for perfection that she felt for the wind blowing against her sturdy house. No one was perfect, and those who aspired were only pretending. "No man is good save God."

Stop it, Esther. Only Satan mocks God. Stop it. She was letting Satan worm into her integrity like the sand was seeping through the windowpane in this storm.

But maybe God had struggled as she was doing: "As man is, God once was," Joseph Smith once said. If that was true, Esther could overcome her humanness and her rebellious veins. She could. After all, she now had walls to protect her; more Latter-day Saints were moving into Boulder City to gather on Sundays and partake of the sacrament together; Herbert was coming. What more could she want? She'd curb her impulses—the only way, the only road. She'd calm her mind, make it peaceful, right this very minute. No more mutinous thoughts. *God will help you through, Esther. Be grateful. You've got so much. Be Serena. Toss your hair and drape yourself over the chair. Nothing can change your direction. Nothing.*

There was something like a knock on the door that could have been the wind. But the door opened before anyone could answer. It was Jack.

"Mother," he said, the door at his back and the inside doorknob in his hand, "have you heard yet?"

"Jackie. I've been wanting to talk to you. Come on in the kitchen. Can you play your saxophone when Herbert gets here on Friday? I thought maybe we could have a dance like we did in—"

"Mother, A. P.'s brother is dead."

"Bill Watkins?"

Alf came out of the bathroom, adjusting the notch on his belt. "Hey, Jack. Can you stay for dinner?"

"Dad. Bill Watkins. The cancer."

A new storm seemed to enter the room. Esther could feel everything being chipped and nicked again. A link in her lifeline was gone, and right after she'd been so foolish with her thoughts about God. She looked over at Alf who seemed very small, his belt buckle still in his hand. He was vulnerable, a little big man standing there in a dingbat house on Avenue B in Boulder City, Nevada, the tongue of his belt in his right hand. Her protector. The words Jack pronounced threatened her and her plans for daffodils and apricot trees.

Alf seemed to speak from far away through the dust whirling around Esther's head. She wanted to hear him, but was surrounded by this storm that wanted to carry her away where it was safe and still.

"We're here now, Esther. I have a job. Jack has a job, and Herbert is coming. Remember, Esther," he was shaking her shoulders, "Herbert is coming. Looks like he has a job. All of us have jobs, and you're helping with the school. Remember?"

"A. P. is mortal, too." The white-haired brothers shriveled in her mind like tumbleweeds rolling and disintegrating. She sat on the edge of the rocking chair to fold her arms around herself. And then everything was with her again—her dress on fire, the twins. . . . And the beginnings of three babies falling out of her safe womb, falling away from the place where they could grow and be born out of her at the right time. Three babies not ready. Esther had failed them. She failed three of God's spirits and kept them from coming to the earth to receive their bodies because she was too tired or too nervous to let the babies grow safely. The twins had their bodies but not their lives. She had failed them, too. Five babies she had failed, and now one of the Watkins was gone. Her foolish thoughts. Everything failing until Esther looked up at Jack, Alf, Mary Elizabeth, Rebecca. They were all standing before her, breathing, watching. *They* were alive. *She* was alive.

The dust storm paused for a breath, and Esther remembered her mood of a few moments before. *I could be Serena tossing my hair. I have my home. Indoor plumbing. These people are alive. I haven't failed them.*

"It's okay," she said to the concerned faces that relaxed when she spoke. "You're right. It's not up to any of the Watkins now. It's up to you and me. All of us. Right?"

She looked out the window. The center of the storm had blown elsewhere, and a gigantic goldfish cloud swam across an entire half of the sky. Its nose was slanted toward the horizon, diving into the deep blue of the evening. The rest of the sky was covered with clabbered clouds, and Esther smelled rain.

•   •   •   •   •

It did rain, so much that Esther was sure flash floods would close the roads and keep Herbert from arriving on the bus. Rumors were that the river had risen twelve feet in two hours and that the diversion tunnels were in jeopardy in this supposedly slow-water time.

She tried not to worry, but it was as natural as breathing to her. Her worry fed upon itself and enlarged like a black hole which Esther might have fallen into except for one diversion: a letter from her mother, Zina. As she sat at her lopsided kitchen table, she read that at least one person, Bill Watkins, was beyond worry now. The thought cheered Esther.

His brow was relaxed. The mortician made him look peaceful, Zina wrote. *You should have seen the truckloads of flowers and all the dignitaries from the Masonic Temple, mind you, not our own church authorities. Bill was not a church man. Too bad (as we've said before). There were state officials, Six Companies's executives coming in on the train from San Francisco, important politicians. But they didn't ask me to sing. Even though I live forty miles away in Brigham City, I somehow thought they'd remember family. I've been the mainstay of funerals around here for over forty years.*

Incorrigible vanity, Esther thought as she looked at Bill Watkins's obituary Alf had pinned to their kitchen wall, the one that didn't mention any cousins, not even Wilbur P. Carpenter, Esther's father, Zina's husband. Nevertheless, the obituary was a reminder, not only to themselves, but to any visitors who might ask why it was pinned to their wall. *Bill is peaceful in his death; be peaceful in your life, Esther. Stop worrying.*

But when three days of rainstorms toyed with Esther's peace of mind, she began slipping toward the black hole in her spirit again. She tried to anchor herself with fervent prayer—two times a day on her knees and while she stood to prepare food. She mumbled pleas to God while she rolled dough for pastry canapés and while she undersalted the aspic that needed to chill for over twenty-four hours before it would quiver spectacularly on A. P.'s plate. She wanted everything to be perfect and mustn't fall into that hole again where everything was black and where failure was larger than anything else.

"Don't touch anything," she kept yelling at Rebecca, Mary Elizabeth, and Alf. "Keep your hands to yourself. Off limits." But the hands kept touching and taking. The war escalated, and Esther was so captured by the battle she barely noticed the end of the rain and the warmth of the sun that baked the caliche and hardened the roads. "Don't touch," she kept saying, and then she noticed the stain in the tablecloth. It would never be presentable.

When Herbert walked in the front door and put his suitcase in the corner, it was not her finest hour. Six of the canapés had disappeared in the last fifteen minutes, her apple pies were convex, and she was sure the roast would be too tough and give A. P. indigestion. He'd never come to see them again.

"Mom," Herbert put his arms around her. "You're upset, and I just got here!"

"I'm sorry, Herbert." She hugged him with all the strength she had left and pushed the hair back from her forehead. "I wanted to make everything so nice, but I can't do it. I can't cook anymore. Go tell A. P. to come another time. Go on. Right now."

"Now, Mother." He dropped his overcoat on the sofa and followed her to the kitchen. "I'll help you. Everything's fine. I'll guard the canapés." He opened the Kelvinator. "Look at that aspic. It's beautiful. The way you designed the cucumbers, pimentos, and green olives. You're an artist, Mom. And these pies." The sunken pies were lined up on the window ledge.

"Should I throw them out, Herbert? They're a mess."

"No, they're not. They've got apples in them, don't they? Just settle down."

"After dinner, probably after A. P. leaves, Jack will play his sax and maybe we can dance a little. I can forget all this."

"Dancing and singing. That's you, Mother. You should have been a star. A thousand-point star! Forget cooking."

"You really think so, Herbert?"

"Absolutely."

"You always know how to make me feel better. How do you know how to do that?" She kissed his cheek. He kissed hers.

"Heaven only knows."

At dinner, A. P. was so full of talk about the past few days on the project, he didn't seem to notice the cucumbers, green olives, and pimentos jellied in aspic. He ate the canapés as if they were saltines—fast and without comment. But he did chew the roast with consummate patience.

"The water was clogged with silt," he said between bites. "Mucky, mucky stuff. Flooded the ledge where we sharpen our rock drills and where we have our transformer. And it got one of our steam shovels. I saw it tossed around on the foam like one of the toy boats I used to put in the creek when I was a boy. If we're getting floods like this in October, what in hell's name'll happen next spring?"

Rebecca and Mary Elizabeth said nothing, except hello when asked by their parents to respond. Jack separated the olives out of the aspic with his fork, keeping to himself. Herbert asked a few questions, but mainly A. P. talked about the project, the project which totally filled his head and animated his hands.

"How did Six Companies first come to be?" Herbert interjected while Jack extracted the sixth olive.

"Old Harry Morris of Morris & Knudsen in Boise joint-ventured with Utah Construction on Guernsey Dam in Idaho in '27. Morris came to me and Bill, rest his soul, with the idea of consolidating brains and manpower to build the biggest dam ever. Then they lined up Shea and Pacific Bridge before the big boys—the Bechtels and Kaiser—ever came onto the scene. We had to wrestle with my brother Bill, who said, 'If we can't do the job alone, to hell with it.' Thank the Almighty that his banker friend, Marriner Eccles, talked him out of his stubbornness."

"And how did you get the bid?" Herbert asked, having done his homework before A. P. arrived. "There was a rumor that the Six Companies's men panicked on the train ride to the bidding in Denver and shaved two million from the bid while crossing Nevada."

"No, it wasn't the most expensive train ride in history, as the joke goes, but people keep talking like it is. You should have seen our chief engineer, John Q. Barlow, figuring everything longhand in the bid work, no calculators or adding machines. He came up with the miraculous figures that blew the opposition out of the water. It's the way we figured the concrete that made the difference.

"Hell," A. P. said after he took a sip of the root beer Esther had made, "we pledged our damn sheep herd to secure that bid. Sheep! Did you hear that?"

"Is that a fact?" Herbert said. "Sheep for a pledge?"

"Sure enough."

"Speaking of sheep," Herbert said, "that reminds me of something I've been wanting to ask, if you don't mind. It's a change of subject, and," he hesitated, "it's personal."

"I've got nothing to hide. Go ahead."

"I've been wondering why you Watkinses broke with the Church?"

Jack started cutting his olives into slivers with the tip of his knife. Alf pulled at the knot in his tie and rolled his eyes. "Let's go sit in the other room," he said. "We'll have our dessert in there." But Herbert didn't catch the import of Alf's manuever.

"I've always wondered what soured the Watkinses on the Gospel," he tried again when everyone was settled in the living room. "You're such fine people!"

Jack looked ready to strangle Herbert, but A. P. was in a talking mood. "You ever hear of the Morrisites?"

"Yes," Herbert said before anyone else could.

"My father was a bishop when Brigham Young ordered the State Militia to bombard the Morrisites in Weber County. This offended the rest of the Saints up there. I know Joe Morris was trying to set up a state within a state, but they shouldn't have used their cannons in the name of religion." He put his hand on Esther's shoulder. She sat next to him on the davenport. "I hope I don't offend you, Esther. You're truly the kind of Mormon I respect, but even though I think the Gospel's true, it's the way people live it offends me. Thinking they're the only ones with tickets to the pearly gates. Forgive me for saying so."

Jack twisted a rubber band around his index finger.

"You're a good man, A. P.," she said. "That's what counts."

"You're a good woman, Esther. A good family here. You've been through a lot. And I've heard many stories about your singing. Would you mind singing something before I go? I've got to catch a nine o'clock meeting."

"First tell me what to do about the school situation?"

"Oh, that." He stroked his jaw. "There are plans to build a full-fledged elementary school next year, but in the meantime everybody, mainly the almighty U.S. Government, seems to be dragging their feet. I suspect a little nudging from the citizens, especially the mothers, will hasten action. Why don't you call on a Mr. Nichols over at the Bureau of Reclamation? Go as a mother, not as my relative. You'll be more effective."

"Thanks, A. P. You're the greatest." She grabbed his hand and kissed his knuckles. "Now what song would you like to hear?"

"One of my favorites is 'God Bless America.' "

"Mind if Jack accompanies me on his saxophone? You should hear him play."

"Whatever pleases you," A. P. said. "And by the way, thanks for dinner. I know you went to a lot of trouble with those fancy do-dads, green olives, and all. I'm beholden."

Esther blushed while Jack, who seemed glad to have something to do besides listen to Herbert cut his throat, retrieved his sax from the case. He used the "My home sweet home" phrase as his introduction, clear and lonely as he often played. Seated on the sofa in the Jensen family home, Esther and Jack rendered a plain, simple, and unplanned tribute to A. P., his company, his project, his United States of America—all the things in which he believed.

A. P. acted as if the tear in his eye was an itch, rubbed it out, and stood to go.

"It's been right nice," he said quietly. "I'm glad we're related. God bless you," he said, his mane of white hair brushing the door as he limped out the door. "Those sheep, too."

As soon as Jack heard the sound of A. P.'s car starting, he blasted into a furious jazz rendition of nothing in particular, the notes coming out hard and fast.

"Play something soft," Esther said. "I'm exhausted."

Jack kept playing every note on his sax as if he were shouting in a different way with each one of them, as if he never could find the words to match the sounds he was making.

"Jack," Esther said again. "Softly."

"See you later," he said, slamming his sax in the case.

"But we were going to have a little celebration for Herbert."

"Got a date."

7

Every time Alf saw Ed Bishop in the grocery department, he was talking about bad omens. Ed would toss an orange back and forth between his hands and talk about "one smart Apache who happened to be the best cherry picker on the entire project." The Indian spoke a respectable English and had told Ed that the white man was on the path to destruction because he didn't honor the land.

"So, why are you working on this dam?" Ed asked him while they sat in partial shade under an overhanging rock and worked their teeth on a hunk of beef jerky.

"Long Sad Face," the Apache grinned, "no one can explain their reflections of the universe. You sit in a different place from me when you hear my words."

After a few of these conversations, Ed transferred over to truck driving. He was nervous cleaning canyon walls at the end of a dangling rope and lighting sticks of dynamite with nothing supporting his feet but hot air. "Leave it to the ex-sailors, circus performers, and the Apaches," he told his superintendent, who liked him enough to help him get another job. But even after his transfer, he thought about the Indian's talk, about how the white man was too proud of the gifts he thought came from his own effort rather than from the Great Spirit.

Given that, he made a predictable mistake. He backed his fifteen-ton mucker to the edge of a rock cliff to collect his cargo. His rear wheels sank into loose rock and started to spin. The whole chassis tipped toward the edge of the world while Ed tried to regain control. He should have given up sooner.

When he opened the door to step outside, the truck was sailing toward the river. Big Red swallowed them both for a little while. Ed. His truck.

"Ed wasn't a religious man," Serena said to Esther after they sat down in Serena's living room, Esther bearing a loaf of hot bread. "He was afraid of something. 'There's something bigger than me,' he kept saying. Pray for him, Esther. I know you're religious. He needs somebody out there who'll wrap him in Big Arms. He was shaking those last few days, like he knew."

Esther nodded. "The veil gets thin when you're ready."

"I need you to sing, Esther. I need to hear your beautiful voice fill up that empty mortuary room where all they have are metal folding chairs and a pump organ. You can still smell the sawdust from the newly planed floor-boards. But I'm glad they finally built one here, Esther. I couldn't make it into Vegas with my Ed laid out across the back seat, not talking to me or making jokes or sneaking sips from his flask."

"Alf and I have sung together many times. Would you like both of us, Serena? I know Alf is partial to you and Ed, the only two friends we made in Ragtown. I'll never forget the night you danced with all of us. Taught us the Lindy."

"Ed and I got in a big fight that night. Biggest one we ever had. About that boy, remember? I could have loved him, Esther. He needed some love. His dad going stark mad like that, tying him to stakes like some primitive sacrifice. I about left Ed then, told him I was going to Seattle to find a man who would help me make a baby. Or I'd adopt one—with or without him. Jesus, he was a hard one to live with, Esther, but I stayed with him." She pulled her hair in a tight, fisted knot and squeezed her eyes shut as if they were doors against pain. "Why I stayed, I don't know. I honestly don't know. What am I going to do now, Esther? I've got to start all over again."

"You'll get this funeral out of the way, and you'll rest for a few days before you decide anything. I'll send Mary Elizabeth over with your dinner."

"Esther, I can fix my own dinner. I'm all by myself." Serena sat alert as if she could hear something.

Esther stood up behind Serena's chair and put her arms around her shoulders. "Don't make any decisions for a few days. Promise me? What you decide now won't hold water in time."

"I'm fine, Esther. Don't you mother me."

"Serena." Esther bent over and looked as fully as she could into her face, forgetting how her eyes with the naked feelings made people afraid. "Listen to me. I've been through this a few times."

Serena trembled. "I don't know if I loved him, Esther."

Esther tucked Serena's head next to her ample bosom. She smoothed the tangled mahogany hair with the palm of her hand and combed it with her fingers.

"Somebody, let me have my Ed back. I'll be nicer to him. I promise. He was enough. Why did I keep pestering him about a child? Why couldn't I just love him?"

"Shh," Esther said. "Quiet now."

Serena pillowed her head against Esther like a newborn. "I'm so ungrateful, Esther. Maybe your God knows how ungrateful I was and took Ed away from me."

"No, Serena. Please don't talk now. Everything will change if you'll rest. I'll go home for a few minutes to get Inez from her nap, and then I'll come back."

"Don't wake your baby. She needs the rest. She looks like a little old man, Esther. Have you seen her eyes? Little girl baby with grandfather eyes. Little baby. Oh, I'm sorry, forgive me."

"Serena," Esther straightened up and pulled Serena to her feet, "I'm staying right here until tonight. Rebecca can tend Inez. I'll fix dinner, and you go into your bed and get some sleep. Don't talk anymore. Please. You're just hurting yourself."

• • • • •

Poor Serena, Alf thought as he held his hat in his hand and waited to shake hands with her. The mortician must have been a novice, sent out from Vegas to keep the newly built Palm Mortuary nailed together until the finish carpenters could find their way out to Boulder City. He seemed to know more about carpentry than embalming. Ed looked tight. Waxen. Pancake makeup slabbed across his cheeks. Serena's Ed who'd lent Alf tools and a sip from his flask once in a while: swollen tight with formaldehyde.

Then Alf noticed Sid Empey, the city manager, hovering in a corner of the room, uninvited, but then no one was invited to funerals. He was a sour lemon of a man whose eyes burned like those of an eagle. Empey's prey, however, was people like Alf. People with imagination. Sid Empey, exemplar, judge, jury, and avenging angel, appointed by Secretary of the Interior Ray Lyman Wilbur to run the city, to issue business and residence permits, and see to it everything was well ordered. He'd already drafted a proclamation, "Causes for Expulsion from the Reservation," a document specifically aimed at drunkenness. With these rules and a rubber-stamp advisory board, Empey found ingenious ways to control people's lives. Alf wished he hadn't come today. He was like an eagle masquerading as a benevolent King Solomon, his claws wrapping around larger and larger areas of control. Alf felt the shadow of his wings as he tried to concentrate on the funeral, Serena, and Ed.

The funeral director invited everyone to be seated, gave a brief sketch of Ed's life, and asked Alf and Esther to come up front and sing "In the Garden."

Their rich bass and contralto voices filled the new chapel and enhanced the smell of new wood and the aroma of the flowers sent by the high-scaling crew. While they sang, the Apache sat apart from the others, fingering his medicine bundle and chanting softly. Everyone else looked tight in their collars and polished shoes, even Herbert and Mary Elizabeth who were used to Sunday clothes.

> He walks with me and He talks with me, and He tells me I am His own.

Everyone bowed their heads, some looked at the walls, some cupped their heads in their hands. Sid Empey just sat there, no feelings on his ill-chiseled face, his arms folded across his chest. His presence ruined the song for Alf. He couldn't get next to the emotion with Empey sitting there, making him feel he had something to hide, when, damn it, he didn't.

"Not our best," Esther commented when the service was over, "but we tried. I'm going home to rescue Rebecca. See you later."

Alf was the last in a three-car caravan toward the Las Vegas Cemetery, Esther unable to make the trip because Inez needed a nap and quiet nursing. No one had thought to build a cemetery in Boulder City yet; there were too many projects to complete for the living.

Serena, he mused the minute he was on the road. *Serena*. He'd been wanting a quiet space to contemplate Serena. She had something he admired. While Esther was a vulnerable creature, almost without skin, with no place to hide her feelings, Serena had a harder surface. She wasn't about to let anybody or anything stand in her way, and it was good Ed was dead, Alf suspected, because he would have been in Serena's way before long. Serena wanted a baby, for one thing. Maybe Ed was afraid to give her up to anything so demanding. Not that Serena was the type to use a baby for a doll and dress it in frilly clothing. That's not what Ed was afraid of. It was the aliveness that frightened him—more life inside her body, growing and kicking. All that life sparked by his semen, and then he would lose control—the source of life too large to stay within the boundaries of her womb, too much to be confined inside anybody.

Alf liked to make babies, plant his seed, and make it grow in warm places. He looked down at the rise in his pants. *Serena.*

She'd made a few overtures to him: telling him he made good babies, coming in to buy lettuce and potatoes in his department, asking him to sing at her husband's funeral. She had a body vibrating with sensuality beneath a jaw set to keep everybody at a distance. Her long glossy hair seemed to swim around her face as she walked or talked to people. Always in fluid motion. A challenge to get inside a woman like that.

The road out of town was graded and oiled now, though not paved yet, and the loose gravel and rocks spun up and hit against his wheel wells, spokes, and the chassis. The funeral caravan paused at the guard station built after the strike scared officials into martial law. For a while, they'd posted twenty-four-hour armed guards, though they were down, now, to two rangers at the guard station who waved most people on after they stated their business and showed their government-issued passes. They were more cautious with people in out-of-state vehicles.

Alf slowed to salute the rangers, then stepped on the gas pedal with more force than he had meant to, unknowingly spraying dust and pebbles on the sign that said, *Boulder Canyon Project Federal Reservation. STOP! U.S. RESERVATION OFFICERS!* A sense of freedom washed over him as he drove toward Cooper's Still, hidden from the feds in the rocky hills west of the Pass. The Department of the Interior thought the whole area was an unbroken section of public domain, a wide-open opportunity for federal land grabbing, but didn't know about the mining claims adjacent to the city limits of their new town. Some big corporation decided to forget about precious metals and try a new-style gold mine. They built a giant casino—The Railroad Pass. Twenty-five ceiling fans. A five-piece orchestra in which Jack now played. Roulette. Big Six. Craps. Their own brandy. The new establishment was committed to relief for the hardworking man and disdain for the Sunday School rules of Prohibition and Sid Empey's federal reservation. Too much law. Too many people willing to obey it for fear of losing their jobs. Dangerous times when free spirits got locked up too long; the world got out of balance.

He'd been out to the Pass drinking a few times, even inquiring after Cynthia, who'd moved in from Blue Heaven for a while. But she'd been run off by the government with all the other girls except for Big Thelma, who managed to ignore or bribe the rangers and stay in business in the shacks on the side of the mountain. In general, he'd been busy settling into town, fine-tuning his lending business though he didn't have much capital to work with.

The question was: how to stay inside the law, how to help out his fellow man who needed cash sometimes instead of Company scrip, how to get his hands on some greenbacks of his own. Home was a better place for him, too. Esther had relaxed in the cooler weather and shortened her "I-think-I'm-going-to-end-it-all" speeches to "Sometimes-I-wonder." She stopped calling herself "the whale lady," and the extra weight she referred to as her blubber seemed to have eased off her hips; the only bonus of the Ragtown trauma. She was alive again, singing around the house, and joking about the walking wounded.

Serena. She needs somebody. Alf remembered her dancing the Lindy with Mary Elizabeth, remembered how he thought she looked like a housecat who occasionally condescended to ask for food while everyone else had seemed so squalid and pathetic in their half-soled shoes and wash-thin clothes. No matter what she wore, she seemed independent from even the clothes on her body.

Alf looked at more shanties thrown together in clumps along the highway, other versions of Ragtown though not close to the river or to the incredible heat trapped in Black Canyon. He could pull over and tell these people they were fools to come here when there wasn't enough work yet, but they'd just say it was bad everywhere, that they were satisfied to squat and wait for something better.

When the procession arrived, Alf shook his head at the pathetic cemetery's wiry, uneven, scarce grass, a joke when compared to the cemeteries Alf had known in Utah and Idaho, where people irrigated and had a more sympathetic sun. It was laid out next to the old adobe fort the Mormons had built when they established an Indian mission in 1855. A mission in Las Vegas, Spanish words that meant "the meadows." What kind of blind visionary named this place The Meadows? Alf's father had known John Steele, one of the missionaries set apart by apostle Wilford Woodruff to convert the copperskins in this part of the territory—the Pahgat, Moapat, Pahrucat, Quoeech, and Mohave Indians—and had told him stories of how Steele seemed to work magic with the natives, converting them from savage ways to the Gospel. The Church of Jesus Christ of Latter-day Saints. The only true church, so Steele and all the faithful ones said.

Cottonwood trees marked the course of the ditch winding through alkaline banks next to the fort. Many times as Alf had crisscrossed the Great Basin, he'd seen tall stands of cottonwood trees, lacy against the late evening sky, sketchy shade during the day. They were shrines, temples to the people he'd grown up with. Spring and early summer were the only times water could be seen aboveground, but cottonwood trees always meant water to travelers, even if it was hidden from the sun under the ground.

Alf surveyed the headstones, the solemn people, Serena, the pine box, his own hands holding the felt brim of his hat. Edward Smithson Bishop was lowered to darkness, out of the blinding sun at last. Off the high cliffs. No more crowbars to wedge into unpredictable fissures. No more manila rope knots to check under his bosun's chair, but no one to carry on his name. Serena wiping her eyes—what would she do now? Where would she go? Serena weeping openly, but probably not for Edward Smithson Bishop. Alf knew this about her, maybe because he knew it about himself. They were survivors of the same breed. They weren't like Esther, caught up in manners and in treating people right, sponges who were molded and destroyed by people's fickle opinions. Serena had steel in her backbone. She'd be a challenge for a man.

"My condolences, Serena." Alf put his hand carefully on her shoulder. "Esther and I will help you any way we can. You'd better not make any rash decisions right away. Lean on us for a few days."

"Alf, you've been so—" Serena started.

A woman in a broad-brimmed black hat interrupted to tell Serena how sorry she was and how she knew things were hard because she'd lost her own husband five years ago.

"I know just how you feel, Serena." The woman's cheeks were streaked with mascara and her eyes filled with pity that seemed more for herself than the new widow. "It's the damnedest, loneliest time when the one you've had there, isn't."

"Thank you, Jean." Serena patted the woman's hands and held them for a moment. "I'll be all right, I promise."

"If I can do anything for you at any time," the woman said as she turned away and picked her way through the uneven clots of grass in clay, "you know where I live. You'll get lonely, Serena. Don't think you're different, honey."

"Bitch doesn't know how I feel," Serena said so softly that Alf questioned whether he heard correctly.

"I'll help you forget, Serena. We'll dance again. If you feel like laughing it out of your system, come on over tomorrow night. I'll get Jack to play his sax again."

"You're something, Alf. Nobody proper invites fresh widows to parties, especially at the cemetery. What about widow's weeds, all that. . . ."

"What's proper? Come on, Serena, I know you better than that."

"What do you know?"

"More than you think." And Alf was glad Sid Empey and Esther had chosen to stay behind.

Serena's brother, who'd driven in from Barstow, finished his conversation with the minister, tucked a bill in the man's coat pocket, and walked over to Serena.

"Alf Jensen, Sammy. Sam Konevic, Alf. My only kin now."

"Nice to meet you," Alf said, and turned his hat brim ninety degrees under his fingers and felt the heat under his necktie and collar.

"Likewise."

Sammy Konevic had the same detachment as his sister. More important things to do, it seemed, than stand in a cemetery and feel the pain about a man who had never registered in his debit column. Something smooth about Sammy. Harder, yet weaker, than Serena.

"Let's go blow it out somewhere, Sammy," Serena said. "You can get some hooch at the Pass, I know."

"Thank the Lord for criminals," Sammy said, flipping his cigarette over the fence into the ditch. "They make it easy for those passing over the bumps of life."

"The government would make us bear our pain nobly." Serena put her hand on her chest and arched her head like a patriotic statue in a city park. "Let's get out of here."

"Join us at the Pass?" Sammy asked Alf.

"I'll think about it," Alf said, knowing what his decision would be but deciding to keep his cards in his hand for a little longer. Things had been going better at home, and he wasn't sure Esther was ready to be gracious toward an infraction of the rule he'd stretched so many times. But he'd been toeing the line lately, maybe too much. Maybe he was getting to be Esther's pet dog again. Well-trained. Obedient. But he thought of her eyes and felt a deep river of pain in his chest. She needed somebody loyal who could love her as she should be loved. She was a good woman who happened to live close to the margins all the time, but damn, he couldn't always be there to keep her away from the edge. She had to take care of herself. Why did he marry such a delicate, tightly wound string so close to breaking? He couldn't be responsible for holding her together all the time. His thumb in her dike. Soft dike, good dike, he laughed to himself. He had to think of his own dreams too. And he liked to laugh, get down-and-out obscene and say all those things Esther thought were disgusting.

Disgusting had its merits, Alf laughed to himself again as he drove his Model A in a line of Model A's—few people drove anything else—past the Meadows Casino where he'd heard they had armed lookouts guarding the booze and gaming, past the Texaco Bar which fronted as a service station and lunchroom, past the road leading to Texas Acres which operated illegally on government property. A bordello, bar, and casino right under the feds' noses, breaking their laws on their land. No wonder Secretary of Interior Wilbur turned up his blue nose at Vegas as a site for the dam-building community. They'd never have been able to have the kind of control Sid Empey exercised on the reservation. Alf on a reservation. Improbable. Chief Alf; papooses; squaw Esther. Rules all around. A dictator. Tight security. A man had to have a place to breathe if he was going to work every day and bring home the bacon. He didn't surprise himself when he turned into the dusty parking lot at the Pass or when he arrived home at 11:00 that night to look into Esther's face and questioning eyes before he had to look away.

8

Mascara; rouge; Miracle Red lipstick. Esther was dressing her best, carefully applying the Mary Ellen makeup she once thought would be the key to the fortune that kept eluding her. She'd done well enough selling the cosmetic line in Utah, but gambled too loosely with the distributorship in San Diego. It had been Alf's idea, actually. Alf: always looking for the bigger, faster, and better way to make money instead of plodding along on consistency and salary. He was a gold miner at heart, jumping from claim to claim. *Forget that now*, Esther sighed. *Tonight, we laugh.*

For the recreation hall's Inauguration Dance, Six Companies had hired Tommy Nelson and the Engineers of Rhythm from the Pass, the band Jack played with now on weekends. Esther smiled thinking of Jack: he was probably in front of a mirror at his dormitory this same minute, knotting his tie and sucking on his reed to make it pliable. He'd talked about some of the new tunes his band had worked up for the gig when Alf took the family on a tour of the hall earlier that day.

Esther had felt like a visitor at the king's court, standing at the edge of the highly glossed wooden floor, full of Thanksgiving dinner and satisfaction, marveling at all the pool tables lining the room. The mirrors over the soda fountain reflected Hamilton Beach milk-shake machines and bowls of apples and oranges. Someone had polished the ceramic tiles underneath the counter to perfection: squares of pale green and rectangles of jet black. Bottles of Mission orange soda were stacked in pyramids across the top of the mirror casing, ten on the bottom, one at the top. With her finger, Esther set six vinyl-covered stools spinning at the same time on top of their high, slender metal poles, then sat on one and spun around, holding her knees high to keep them from crashing into the next stool. "Whee!"

She saw Alf looking at her, as he sometimes did, as if she was this unfathomable creature—one minute drooping, her every pore satiated with despondency and a flattened sense of possibility, the next minute acting like a free and unregarded child, oblivious to judgment on how a grown woman should act. Her abandon seemed to inspire Alf, who bought her a Zagnut from the new candy vending machine and felt uninhibited enough to mention something he ordinarily would have kept to himself.

"It was only a poker game with the carpenters between breaks," he said, "and then, out of nowhere, The Official Frown, Sid Empey, arrived and pronounced shame on our heads. 'No gaming allowed on this reservation,' he said just like he was Caesar. That hunched-over, grasshopper of a man who looks like he was left out in a blizzard as a child. Never got over it. Never does smile. He caught me holding a good hand even." Alf unwrapped the red paper and broke off a small piece of Zagnut for himself. "But, funny thing; after that, Buzz Bodell set up a few games and I haven't seen Sid around here since. Bodell must have worked some sweet deal."

"Heavenly Father," Esther prayed while she curled her eyelashes and rolled up her only pair of silk stockings between her thumbs, one of them marred with two runs and dabs of nail polish to keep them from lengthening any further. "Please keep Alf out of trouble. He can't keep from putting his finger in the pie cooling on the windowsill, and that big hand is going to reach out and slap him down if he doesn't watch out." *No, don't think of those things, Esther. We're dancing tonight. A full band. Dancing, Esther. Music. Inauguration time for the recreation hall.*

The hall gleamed even brighter at night, the varnished ceilings reflecting light from the hanging lamps. Everyone at the dance gleamed too. Shiny hair, no doubt rinsed in vinegar, ties knotted under the collar of every white shirt, slicked, tidy, everything shiny like chrome. A sense of something safe at the dance, hard times locked outside the door and the reservation for a few minutes. Excited nervousness. Something like arriving at the big times, something about feeling new and fresh and ready to take on the world and every challenge it could hurl. Something about the moon shining in the big empty sky, clear as the sound of good crystal. Crisp night, slightly cool, everyone excited, nervous, filling up with something that was rising toward their throats to burst out, either in hearty greetings or "da, da, da, das" to the beat of "Margie," the song the band played. Everyone walking a bit tightly in their best clothes, buttoned, girdled, harnessed, belted, tied, brushed, lacquered. Some of the women sported tight waves pressed demurely to their scalps; others wore soft curls, undoubtedly crimped with rags rolled and tied into their hair.

Herbert, Mary Elizabeth, Alf, and Esther had walked to the dance because the night had a clarity and brightness that seemed to make promises. They detoured over to Avenue D to pick up Serena, who, in order to keep her house, had taken in a chuck tender as a boarder and had been promised a job waitressing at Browder's soon-to-be-open luncheteria. Now they stood at the threshold of the Six Companies's Recreation Hall in their best clothes, watching everything and everybody else dressed in their best. High heels, a couple of tuxedoes taken out of mothballs, white shirts everywhere, some suit coats. Flashy ties. The oddest thing of all was no men wore their felt hats, which they never parted with otherwise. Maybe that was part of the excitement, thought Esther: no hats.

No sun shining down, trying to blacken people's skin or fry their brains. This was a dance, and hats hung on hooks and rested under chairs. The sight of foreheads, hairlines, colors of hair seemed new, fresh, and above all, magic. What was it about hairlines and the way they defined a man's appearance? Receding hair. Slick hair. Long, careful parts at the side or in the middle.

Some women had been transported from Las Vegas for this dance, and for the first time in a long time, Esther witnessed the age-old drama of boy-asks-girl. Everything seemed softer tonight, less harsh. Boulder City was gradually coming together. Each new building and each new business was anticipated like a baby's first step. The city was everyone's child, even though Sid Empey seemed to think it was his alone the way he skulked at the sidelines like a high school chaperone.

The band stopped playing and Esther suddenly realized she was being waved over to the platform by Jack. "Mom, over here. 'Moonlight and Roses.' You can do!"

Esther blushed, the color rising above her beaded collar. Unwittingly, she placed her hands on her soft stomach like a young girl wondering whether or not she was real or imaginary, and felt embarrassed at the prospect of standing in front of everyone and singing. Momentarily, she was the Whale Lady she'd joked and moaned about all summer, beached in the desert, fish body, no waistline, no delineation of figure anymore, her skin slack in soft rolling ridges.

"Come on, good lookin'." Jack raced up and down an F scale, his brass sax flashing diamonds.

"Go on, Esther," she heard Alf saying. "You do a good job with this song. Go on."

She looked at Alf curiously, somehow commanding in appearance even with his diminishing hair and limited build. He was still the man she loved more than she hated. Surreptitiously, she took a reading on Serena, her olive smooth skin glowing with a suntan in November, tossing the gypsy rings in her ears as she talked with great animation to Alf. Then she settled her attention on Herbert, her man-child who measured everyone and everything around him and walked as if he would break glass if he moved the wrong way. He tried to assume a mask of composure, but she could see straight through to his unsureness as if it were a red thumb on a pale hand.

"Come on, Mom," Mary Elizabeth was saying. "I'll go up there with you." She was ready to jump through hoops or turn cartwheels—anything to please an audience. She'd inherited a stage thirstiness from somebody, probably Esther, who was pretending to be bothered by the fuss everyone was making.

"Okay, you come with me, Mary E."

Jack smiled a go-ahead to Tommy Nelson, who delivered the upbeat for the musicians. Esther and her daughter wound through the crowd holding hands while the band played an inviting vamp. Esther's blood raced, and she felt it in Mary Elizabeth's hand—the excitement that could make knees shake and throats dry out, everybody looking her way, craning their necks, wondering what was happening. Jack clapped his hands and leaned into the microphone.

"Fine little singer, here, ladies and gentlemen. All the way from Brigham City, Utah, with her daughter, Mary Elizabeth. We bring you Esther Jensen."

The band had almost played the vamp out. Esther's and the band leader's eyes connected, waiting for the moment when they were ready to start. She closed her eyes for a few seconds, trying to get the rhythm inside herself. *Hell, why did Jack do this to me? I'm not even warmed up.* She held her eyes shut and listened to the sounds of the crowd. What was she doing up in front of these people, ex-lawyers and businessmen who were now hammering nails into Six Companies houses, government engineers who worked with figures and numbers all day long to calculate the best methods of preventing distortion and cracking in the concrete for the dam-to-be, mechanics, powder men, miners, pipe fitters, electricians, railroad builders who blasted and carved a snakelike path for rails and ties and chipped away at the edge on their way to the bottom of Black Canyon?

When she opened her eyes, she saw the much-talked-about Bernie Wilson in the crowd, the "Bull of the River," who'd devised a jumbo rig to drill the diversion tunnels and had thus come into some local fame. His picture was in all the papers next to his miracle machine with thirty-two drills mounted on its cumbersome frame Sheriff Williams was there and had waved carefully at the Jensens when they'd first come in. The head construction superintendent, Frank Crowe, his wife holding his arm, too. Newspaper pictures, alive. Some of these people were high government officials—Walker Young in a stiff bow tie talking to Henry Nelson and his wife dressed in solid pink. Six Companies's executives with their cigars and confidence. She recognized Felix Kahn in his scholarly horn-rims and blue-with-gold-stripes tie. He was the West Coast financial wizard from MacDonald & Kahn who'd helped build the Mark Hopkins Hotel in San Francisco. His pocket handkerchief stood in stiff peaks against the breast of his jacket. He, A. P., and Steve Bechtel were clustered with a small group of men who looked like San Francisco, money, and power, and who were too engrossed in conversation to notice Esther standing there. There was a mix of people like the mix of the aggregate for concrete. The sayers, doers, inventors, movers and shakers, and Esther stood above them.

"Mom," Mary Elizabeth said, "you want to join me or not?"

The same old invisible wall was between Esther and what she'd been asked to do. It was always taller than Esther, and wider. She took a huge, deep breath, and fell through it and into her song.

"Moonlight and roses." Once again, silk floated out of Esther's mouth. Mary Elizabeth put her arm around her mother's waist and slipped into a smooth alto harmony. "Bring wonderful mem'ries of you." Esther had made it yet another time, and here she was, full into the song, given away to the music, and relieved to be there.

"My heart reposes." The harmonizing sounded incredibly fine. The mother looked down at the young woman by her side, grown up already, a surprise to Esther who hadn't been able to see much of anything this past summer. Mary Elizabeth, the unacknowledged apprentice who had noticed everything all these years. She knew every move. Every gesture. She bloomed next to Esther's side at that moment—a rose, a dahlia, a sunflower—and tears started down Esther's cheeks, springing from some unfathomable gratitude for a world where things grew despite a gardener who could not always be there with trowel in hand. This young woman could sing and move and sparkle, and Esther hadn't seen it before, not in full flower like this.

Alf beamed, his round face lit with what Esther interpreted as the adoration she'd seen on his face when she first met him at the Elberta Theater. And A. P. stopped talking shop, looked up at Esther, raised one finger in greeting, and smiled. She was in her stride, her element. No whale lady when she sang. No thought for the shape of body she lived in. She was something more than her body, something flying out of herself, and she knew she was there, if only for a few minutes.

Esther and Mary Elizabeth repeated the song again. "June light discloses—love's olden dreams sparkling anew." Most everyone was dancing to the music now, even the executives and their wives, their faces turned toward their partners, signs of accruing affection in bashful grins and side glances.

Why am I always afraid in the beginning? thought Esther as she sang the words so familiar to her she didn't have to think about the next one. *God takes care of me, and I'm still so afraid. Always afraid. Here I've got this amazing sidekick I didn't even know I had, my baby grown big.*

Then Esther saw Alf and Serena dancing together. She wanted to be happy for Serena, who had been through so much in the past few months; she wanted to smile beneficently at them, glad Alf could help someone out. *Do unto others as you would have them do unto you.* Esther wanted to feel generous. She'd seen her polygamous grandmothers living contentedly with each other, loving their sister wives even though it wasn't always easy. She wanted Serena to have some love in her life too, but her heart clenched, a dull thud in the middle of her chest. Alf was laughing, his eyeglasses sparkling with the overhead light. He was holding Serena close, leading her backwards at the moment, leaning into her almost. Esther could even imagine the words he was saying to her, the ones he sometimes spoke to her when he had that look on his face.

"Moonlight and roses," Mary Elizabeth and Esther finished their song, "Bring mem'ries of you."

The dancers applauded enthusiastically, and the two singers waved goodbye to Tommy Nelson and tossed kisses to Jack.

"Thanks to Esther Jensen," Tommy Nelson said into the microphone that looked like the planet earth surrounded by celestial orbits, "and her lovely daughter. 'Moonlight and Roses,' ladies and gentlemen. Now how about 'The Sneak?' Ha, ha, do you know 'The Sneak'?"

Tommy Nelson peppered the air with high notes from his trumpet while the drummer rolled his snare. Jack stood ready with his gleaming sax. Everybody roared and hunched over, in position to sneak with their partner.

From the middle of a crowd of dancers, Alf pointed one finger in the air like an auctioneer. "One more with Serena, and then I'll be back."

"This dance please, ma'am," Herbert whispered in her ear. Herbert, her gentle, pale-eyed boy, knew every nuance in her repertoire of responses. And Esther and her son sneaked into the sea of dancers, the sea of salvation.

•　•　•　•　•

How to make the concrete that would keep the river from its destructive course; how to build mixing plants close to the project when the formidable geology of the cliffs seemed to prohibit installation of any substantial proportion; how to supply aggregate to the concrete mixers in exact quantity and size for four years running; how to mix the ingredients together with more efficiency and speed than anyone had ever seen before; how to deliver the mix to the building site without it setting and having to be chipped out by hand, piece by piece, with a hammer and chisel: these were a few of the problems facing the government engineers.

The Bureau of Reclamation needed more concrete than it had used in all the dams they'd built before 1931, and, on top of that, their calculations had to deal with a 100-degree temperature differential between winter and summer.

Herbert followed the account of the dam's progress day by day, talking to engineers and gandy dancers alike in the mess hall as well as after hours in his father's vegetable department. He wanted to know what was happening, how it was happening; this project was important to him, and he had a feeling that someday the information he gathered might be important to someone else. Progress or delay on the project was Herbert's personal success or failure.

"It's that consarned Black Canyon," he heard some surveyors discussing over coffee and french toast while he was wiping the next table. "We keep moving further upstream every day, and there just isn't a place on those cliffs for a four-story concrete mixing plant. We've got to get the plant as close to the project as possible, or those buckets of slosh will harden like a stiff, just like that." He snapped his fingers. "It's a damn nightmare."

"I heard just last night that somebody found a crescent shelf on the cliff that could be blasted out with jackhammers and dynamite. Little further upstream than they'd hoped, but it will work. They'll use that for the Lomix plant. Must have discovered it on the shift after yours."

Before Herbert could catch himself, he heard himself butting into the conversation that wasn't his. "What's a low-mix plant?"

The man looked at him as if he were a strange bird, but then shrugged his shoulders and warmed his hands on his coffee cup. "Lomix will supply all the concrete for the diversion tunnels and for the first two-thirds of the dam, boy. Himix will be on top of the cliffs, later. It'll handle the final mixing for the dam."

"How will they get the rocks to the plant?" Herbert asked, the wet rag in his hand.

"Conveyor belts, trucks, trains, you name it. Storage bins will siphon them into batchers—cake mixers to you, boy—where the ingredients will be blended to make the finest dam on the menu. Could you excuse me now?" the man said to Herbert. "I've got to catch my lorry, if you don't mind."

"Sorry," said Herbert. "Here, let me take your dishes for you."

Herbert was all ears at every meal, disregarding the term "boy" and picking up bits and pieces about the dam because he couldn't be there himself. He'd asked for a job on the site, but had been told to stay where he was because he was too light to handle the bone-crunching work. So his ears were like vacuums, sucking in facts, figures, stories of the glorious dam.

"Three hundred fifty tons of structural steel's arriving today," he heard at lunch. "They're delivering it to Three-Way Junction to build the framework of the gravel screening plant."

"They'll be throwing up those girders like Tinker Toys, now that they're here."

"The network they're building for the gravel production and screening'll be sprawled all over Hemenway Wash. Daddy-long-legs supreme."

The words gradually seduced Herbert away from the long tables, the ever-sticky salt and pepper shakers, the dirty dishes with cigarettes ground out in leftover eggs. One night he told his mother he'd be late and not to worry about him. He needed to be close to the dam, close to the work, not just to the pancakes and hash browns that went into men's gullets and fueled the hands that made things happen.

He found himself balancing on the iron rails at the switchyard and walking among the shadows at the warehouse. He passed row after row of gasoline drums, the empty "track shifter" railroad car that rescued derailed locomotives, piles of lumber, spools of cable. Shadows of the dam, fingers and hands of the dam, parts of the dam. And he heard the whistle blast of a locomotive pulling out of the yard. It was pulling nothing except itself, a vessel setting out to the sea of moonlight on its own, the perfect carrier for Herbert.

Before he could think about it, something wild in him made him run for the black engine lumbering out of the yard, whistling, chugging off into the desert, and he caught hold of the railing at the end of the locomotive and pulled himself up to a small ledge where he became a part of the locomotive and the steam and the rumble.

He pressed his body flat against the engine to escape being seen, but the iron was freezing and shots of cold pierced through his cheek and into his sinuses. Herbert didn't care, though. The fierce wind blew against everything he owned, lifting his hair from his scalp, his gooseflesh rising high, but Herbert Jensen was riding the rails, a bold man, an adventurer.

The moon was a brittle wafer in the sky, and it whitewashed the landscape and the train chugging through the stillness where creatures hid beneath scant limbs and rocks. Shadowy spikes of sagebrush appeared on the sand that looked white and blown instead of gray and broken as it did during the day.

Herbert Jensen was flying over the desert almost like Pegasus; the landscape raced past him and he was part of the wind that whipped across the desert and made bushes bend low to the ground. He was the king of the desert; he could fly; he had wings, and he almost let go to test the feeling that he was not an ordinary mortal anymore. But he remembered he was Herbert Jensen holding onto the railing with every ounce of his strength, worried about sudden stops, worried he might be found out and fired from Anderson Brothers.

And then the locomotive slowed to a stop. Three-Way Junction, a white sign with black-painted letters said, and Herbert saw a field of acetylene torches, their sparks of light flying into the darkness, and he could hear the cold clanging of hammers on steel. A maze of girders and pipes and catwalks rose into the sky like black skeletons next to pyramid piles of rock and sand.

And Herbert breathed the smells of steel, gasoline, and sage. He jumped off as close to the back of the engine as possible and huddled in its shadow until it labored off toward the canyon. And he imagined the architecture of the steel rising even higher, tall beams rising into the clouds and disappearing into the far-off sky. These men were preparing to build a dam that was almost as big as God. Herbert shivered. The wind was screaming through the girders and seemed harsh enough to break a piece from the brittle moon.

Before he was discovered by someone who might pause from welding or from hammering steel against steel, he wrapped his thin sweater tightly around himself and turned to walk the miles back to town. He didn't care how many that might be. Tonight's time didn't matter. He was part of the dam. He could feel its insides growing, materializing, becoming. He was happy and in awe. He was a child at the foot of a very tall edifice which went up and up until it disappeared from view. There was nothing more he could say about it at the moment.

· · · · ·

Gradually, the committee of The Mothers for the School Children of Boulder City came into being: Dorothy Parker, Thelma Black, and Esther Jensen, concerned citizens. The committee was formulated more by their own concern than by any election. Families were crowding into town. Sixty elementary school children in September; 190 by December; 500 projected into May. By December, they were ready for action.

"Before Christmas gets any closer," Esther said, "we've got to walk together up Denver Street, up the hill to the administration building, and find Mr. Nichols in the Bureau of Reclamation. That's what A. P. said to do. Let him know how fast the numbers of children are multiplying. There's no way we can teach them all."

"Yup," said Dorothy. "Can't believe they didn't think about school. Danged engineers."

"That's water under the bridge," said Thelma with a midwestern, solid certainty Esther admired. Thelma seemed more sure of herself than Esther or Dorothy. "They need to hear from us now, the real people who live in their model city. They've got no sense of much but the river and how they're conquering it. One-track bureaucratic minds."

Esther was appointed chairman, even though Thelma was more articulate. After all, Esther had the relatives. But she worried incessantly about what she would say when they walked into the air-conditioned building to ask for a man who'd probably built government projects the world over. What did she know, compared to him?

She'd been educated well enough in Brigham City, her theologically inspired hometown, but she worried that the real knowledge, the necessary ways of the world which one should understand to make it through life with some style, had never made it to northern Utah. She knew the national anthem and the Golden Rule. She knew Aesop, Shakespeare, and much of the King James; she knew the Norse and Greek myths, reading, writing, and the manipulation of simple numbers. She'd memorized a few arias from

Mozart, Puccini, and Bizet, enough to whet her appetite for the Big Times where sopranoes stood in spotlights and awed those in the shadows. But her growing up had an insularity. Her schoolteachers were Latter-day Saints, as was her voice teacher, the grocery store manager, and the theater owner. Everyone in Brigham was Mormon to one degree or another. Underlying everything, even Esther's decision not to try for the Big Times, was the communal belief that nothing was more important than serving God's purpose. Anyone who thought otherwise was a pawn of darkness.

When Esther, a willing chalice for God's glorification, was tossed out into the world with her less willing husband, she was frightened. No one understood the intricacies of her faith or comprehended her words. Her mind was inhabited by prophets who received revelations from heaven, by Joseph Smith who had a vision and talked directly to God the Father and Jesus Christ the Son, by aunts, uncles, and neighbors who spoke in tongues and healed with the laying on of hands.

Uncle Woolley, before he was called on a mission to grow almond trees in St. Thomas, had laid his hands on Esther's fever when her father was away on business. He pronounced her well in the name of Jesus Christ and by the power of the Holy Melchizedek priesthood.

Not many shared her view of a personal God who bent over with a hand cupped to his ear and listened as she knelt in secret prayer, nor could they comprehend the Three Nephites who could appear out of nowhere to tell a righteous man to move his horses before a storm toppled a tree in that very spot, or the guardian-angel presence of her three grandmothers who stood by, even whispered as she washed dishes, "Keep going. Endure. Be brave."

Esther's inner world became more hidden and tenuous as her tether stretched farther from Brigham, farther away from those who understood her spiritual sensibility and too close to strangers who could never fathom the world according to Esther Jensen. She felt like invisible ink, only perceptible to those who knew about the Urim and Thummim—the seerstones that aided Joseph Smith when he translated the Book of Mormon from golden plates. She felt herself disintegrating, crumbling like an Egyptian mystery on brittle papyrus. Thus reduced, she forgot her faith that had never failed her when she was a young girl walking the unpaved streets of Brigham City, staring up at umbrellas of peach blossoms, and wiggling her toes in cold irrigation ditches.

She worried incessantly about everything, including the committee meeting with Mr. Nichols, the public relations coordinator for the Bureau. Could she speak his language? Would she make a fool of herself?

In her petulant worry, she was unable to see the larger picture: the nature of politics, the science of applying force from two different directions to turn about a third, the application of leverage. She couldn't see far enough to accept the fact of hard-ball, dollars-and-cents negotiations between the Bureau and Six Companies.

"Eighty percent of the employees here in town are employees of Six Companies," the government was insisting in meetings and memos to the executive committee Esther didn't know about.

As Esther rehearsed the words she and her committee would say to Mr. Nichols, she failed to put her responsibility in perspective.

She got up early for three dark December mornings in a row to write her presentation. "Dear Sir," "Mr. Nichols," "Dear Bureau of Reclamation Representative. . . . We the people. . . . We, a few of the citizens of this great land. . . . On behalf of the children of Boulder City. . . ."

She'd never pled a case before a non-Mormon and thereby convinced herself this was a more challenging encounter than singing to an audience or giving a two-and-a-half-minute talk in Sunday School. "People are people," she told herself, but somehow didn't quite believe it.

Thelma Black, Dorothy Parker, Esther Jensen—dressed carefully, modestly, and primly—listened to their heels echo on the marble flooring in the two-story-high foyer and introduced themselves to the receptionist who told them to take a seat, that Mr. Nichols would be right with them.

"I'm Esther Jensen," she said after the three women were directed upstairs to the mezzanine, ushered into a small office at the back of the building, and seated in three straight-backed wooden chairs. "This is Dorothy Parker from St. Thomas."

"How do you do?" Mr. Nichols shook each woman's hand.

"And Thelma Black," Esther said. "Peoria, Illinois. You certainly have a lovely view of the river from here, by the way."

"And what can I do for you ladies?" Mr. Nichols had a pleasant face, like most of the government employees Esther had met, yet seemed on the serious side. Not a man given to joking or b.-s.-ing like the construction crews, she concluded.

"The Mothers for the School Children of Boulder City is the name of our committee," Esther said, unknowingly brushing her fingers across her throat as she spoke. "We are aware of the increasing numbers of children moving into the city, and though we've tried to meet the problem with co-ops, the numbers are getting too large for us to handle."

"And?" Mr. Nichols said.

"Well," Esther felt the wetness of her palms and hid them behind the purse on her lap, "we know you've been busy trying to work against the river, so we don't want to press you, but we've been wondering when the problem of a school is going to be addressed."

"She's trying to say," Thelma Black said, seemingly impatient with Esther's round-about approach, "that no one is paying the least bit of attention to the schoolchildren. There's a problem here, and the buck keeps getting passed. We talk to someone in Six Companies, and they say to talk to you."

"We don't mean to intrude," Esther apologized, trying to regain leadership of her committee in the only way she knew, "but we wonder if we could have some kind of statement from you regarding your plans for education of Boulder City's children."

"Not some kind of statement," Thelma Black interrupted. "A definite answer."

"Right," said Dorothy Parker.

"Yes," said Esther.

"We're more aware of this problem than you might know," Mr. Nichols said. "But, as you yourselves said, there have been many pressing matters. The most I can tell you at this time is that we are in negotiations with Six Companies to get the school situation handled. Most of the young ones are children of men employed by Six Companies, hence not our problem. Can you understand our dilemma?"

"Of course," said Esther, too quick with her sympathy.

"No," said Thelma. "There are children hanging in the balance here, and you're playing hot potato politics. We need a public facility right now, tomorrow, next week. It's not fair to the children."

"Okay, Mrs. Black. I hear what you're saying, but these things don't happen overnight."

"Look at everything you've done, like building houses in a day and a half. So why can't you do the same with a school?"

"That's Six Companies, Mrs. Black. Our buildings are built to last. Theirs are only temporary."

Esther watched the words go back and forth like tennis balls. She was quietly crucifying herself for her lack of assertiveness, her loss of authority, while at the same time trying to listen. She'd primed herself for several weeks, and it was someone else's ball game now. Just like that! Gone! She looked at the piece of paper on her lap with all the points outlined. Maybe she could find a way back into the action.

"We've thought of having fund-raisers," she said. "Maybe selling baked goods and candy to help out. But there isn't a lot of pocket change around these days." She laughed nervously, and looked to Dorothy for a nod of acceptance.

"But that's peanuts compared to what we'll need." Thelma had a strong jaw that seemed stronger when she said the word "peanuts." "Isn't there some way you can build one in a hurry?"

"You're talking about an act of Congress, Mrs. Black." Nichols moved his paperweight in circles with the tip of his finger.

"What about a vacant building?" Esther asked, the words rushing out of her mouth in a hurry before she missed this conversation. "Someone's old office, maybe? What about the Rangers? Aren't they just about ready to move into the municipal building?"

"Now, there's an idea." Mr. Nichols' face seemed genuinely responsive for the first time, the pleasant boredom changing to interest.

"What a good idea, Esther," Thelma Black said, nodding her head in affirmation.

"I think we might be able to do something about that," Nichols said. "Now that's what I call a creative solution!"

The celebration inside Esther! A party with triangle hats and paper confetti and rubber balloons. She might not be a forthright leader with pummeled fists and steadfast knees, but she had a mind that could cut corners, erase lines, find answers in the unexpected. *Congratulations, Esther*, she told herself several times. Elation zipped through her. *You can hold your own. You're not just a small-town Mormon girl who doesn't know her ass from a hole in the ground. You don't have to take a back seat to anybody.* And the party was so loud inside her she had a hard time coming back to the meeting with composure.

"I'll check with my superiors," Mr. Nichols was saying, "but I think we've got a temporary solution here. And, I wish to assure you," he directed his words to Thelma, "we'll have a more permanent answer in the next few months, even if we have to involve the Secretary of Interior and Congress to make Six Companies pay their share. Will that make you happy?" Something had happened to Mr. Nichols. He was a booster for The Mothers of the School Children of Boulder City. Esther had found a way out for him.

"Absolutely," said Thelma Black, unsnapping her black purse and pulling out a plaid-bordered handkerchief to wipe her nose.

"Sounds good to me," Dorothy agreed.

"I'll be talking to you, Mrs. Black," Nichols said as he shook her hand. "Come back in two days, and I'll have an answer."

"Thanks to you for your good idea—Mrs. Jensen, is it?"

He had trouble remembering Esther's name. "We'll all come back," Esther said as the ladies walked out the door. "We're all on this committee."

"Of course," Mr. Nichols said, already leafing through a stack of papers in the wooden incoming box on top of his filing cabinet. He seemed satisfied with his day's work that might earn him some notice at the next "school problem" meeting.

And Esther used her own satisfaction to shore herself up against her disappointment for not leaving a firmer impression on Mr. Nichols. Why was she invisible like spilled water on the sand? She wanted to count and be seen. She had an inner strength; if only people would stop to notice or look at her a second time. Why couldn't she be more straightforward like Thelma? More certain?

But by nighttime, she was immersed in thoughts of Christmas—giving instead of getting what she wanted, what to buy everybody with the savings in her teapot. This could be one of their nicest Christmases if everything stayed in balance.

When she knelt for bedtime prayers, she remembered to be grateful. "Thank you, Heavenly Father," she whispered. "Thanks for being with me today and giving me the idea about the old Ranger station. I almost took the credit. And forgive my ambition, my wanting to be the leader and bask in the glory. Help me accept whatever instrument I am, Father. I thank Thee that Herbert is here with us now. And I thank Thee for all of my children. Bless Mary Elizabeth and Jack that they won't wander from the fold. They'd be so lonely without Thy guidance. In the name of Jesus Christ, Amen."

9

On Thursday night, while the boarder who made it possible for Serena to keep her house played solitaire in his room, Serena's brother Sam bought Alf's idea: trading cash for scrip with a five percent margin. Sam had certain connections. Pounding his fist on Serena's kitchen table, he declared he could come up with more cash than Alf could ever set aside from his wages.

"We'll get the thing going." Alf was excited, using the voice he automatically slipped into when he tried to impress someone—a cultivated, high-blown British affectation, though he'd never seen one inch of England. "It'll be self-supporting once we have the up-front infusion of hard cash."

Sammy, smooth and streetwise on his surface, could be taken in by someone who sounded more urbane than himself, and Alf did have that talent of sounding sophisticated to someone who hadn't had enough experience to differentiate between the real thing and its imitation. Sam had bounced around California mining towns for years trying to find the right deal to set him up for life. The sound of an entrepreneur voicing his own pipe dreams had something to do with how Sammy assessed a deal.

"How much do we need for starters?" he asked, sliding down in the kitchen chair.

"A thousand?" Alf raised his eyebrows as if they helped him to figure. "That's about twenty-six clients. Say a man gets paid five dollars a day for six days, than he'll have company scrip worth about thirty dollars by the weekend. Say that's the number. Then we give him twenty-eight fifty cash so he can go out to the Pass and have the kind of good time he's been dreaming about ever since he got cooped up on this reservation, and he'll be a happy man. What more could we be doing for our fellow man?"

Sam slid his finger slowly down the center of his forehead to the tip of his nose while he listened.

"And then we buy goods from the company store, all for the price of scrip, and sell them in the little outlying camps for a profit—Oklahoma City, Pitcher, Hooverville near the cemetery in Vegas, McKeeversville, too bad Ragtown's cleared out now—to all those folks not privy to Six Companies's goods and prices. You know how everyone's still stacking up in this territory now there are more jobs available, though Six'll never be able to hire all of them. We'll be doing them a service. They won't have to use gas to get into town."

"And you want me to run the goods around this desert in my flivver?" Sam asked, scratching his jaw and both sides of his neck.

"For a while. Maybe we can find a better way to use the scrip, but for now, it seems a pretty good possibility. What do you think, Serena?"

An irregularity in his breathing always surprised Alf when he looked straight at Serena, full-faced. Green fathoms for eyes, her pupils almost the shape of small marquise diamonds, almost like cat's eyes that could open and close out the light. A survivor. Street smart.

By contrast, Esther's eyes were either sad, anxious, or accusing. When they did invite his tenderness, they still kept him at bay. Sure, he'd made false starts and been the fuse for some blowups and major disasters, but mistakes were part of learning. He could give her what she wanted if she'd take a deep breath and stop self-destructing by riding every wave until it crashed against the shore. But even though Alf stroked her in the night to calm and reassure her, she talked incessantly, her words tumbling out of her mouth, unsure, her hands never still. Too much worry about everything, fearful of her life sinking to the bottom of the sea where it could never be salvaged. If she could only relax, but she seemed tied in a knot of anxiety. And she was getting worse. Her eyes were more bold with fright. Her thoughts collided with each other until they disintegrated into tears, so many tears it seemed she was a natural spring. "The burns," Dr. Spilsbury said when Alf had taken him aside at the rec hall and told him he was worried. "It's a wonder the doctors kept her alive. Too much nerve damage."

Serena, on the other hand, wasn't anxious to get anywhere; she was more like a sunning creature, happy to be on a rock with Old Sol infusing her with heat. And her heat showed in sultry, desert-slow ways. Slow hands and fingers. A slow tongue, Alf imagined.

"Sounds possible, Alf," Serena said, shifting her eyes to her brother who looked like yellow clay in the stark light of the bulb hanging over them. "Where you think you'll get the money, Sam?"

"Some guys I met in Vegas. Talked to them last weekend, you know when Alf and me went out to the Boulder Club for a little rest and relaxation. Alf's been working hard with all those vegetables. Needs to experience the real world, get his hands on real coins, real metal, you know. Alf got into the dollar poker hand; I played higher stakes."

"I didn't escape the vegetables actually," laughed Alf. "Sorriest poker game I ever played."

"Well, there were two high rollers in my game looking for a place to put the money they've been making. You know, the Cooper brothers who run Cooper's Still out by the Pass? Just across the highway?"

"You'll have to take me out there sometime," said Serena, crossing her legs at the knees, accentuating the slow curve of her calf. "They got guns beaded on comers?"

"Hell, I know 'em now, so they'll let us pass. Pretty vicious rocks out there, they told me. Sort of a maze to give any snoops a bad time."

"Let's have a picnic on Sunday afternoon, Alf. I'll make sandwiches, you can bring some oranges and apples. Coopers'll supply something to wet our whistles. You want that, Alf?"

"I have some obligations then, Serena. I promised Esther I'd take her to church this Sunday, but maybe I could leave early if we wouldn't be too long. I mean, this is important. We've got to get our business started on the right foot. All the partners should be there for the negotiations. Right?"

Sam unscrewed the ring on the Mason jar, his complimentary bottle of potato gin from Verl Cooper, who had swept all of Sam's poker chips to his edge of the table. Cooper'd felt compassion for Sam sitting there with only two chips to his name. Sorry little stack. Not even enough for a stack.

"I shouldn't," said Alf when Sam passed the bottle. "Dinner's waiting for me right about now."

"But this is our partnership inauguration, Alf," said Sam. "We're going to be bona fide partners this Sunday when we shake hands with Verl and Split-T Cooper, and maybe we already are because we've been talking about this like it's a sure thing."

"Split-T?" Serena burst out laughing, choking on the gin that hadn't gone down yet.

"He tells it like this," Sammy said.

"No story could be as good as that name." Serena uncrossed her legs and leaned into her knees, still laughing.

"Hey, you two," Alf broke in. "I've got to get home. I'm always there for dinner. It'll hurt Esther too much."

"She'll understand," said Sam. "Doesn't she want you to be successful?"

"Of course, but she has her own ideas about how and when. I need to go easy on her with this. Can't spring it on her all at once. 'Sleazy,' she'll say, especially if she finds out who our backers are. 'Under the table,' she'll say. She doesn't understand economics." Alf adjusted the cheesecloth stretched over the top of the jar for keeping the bugs out of one's mouth and sniffed a deep lungful of the aroma before he tipped it to swallow.

"She seems pretty tough to me," Serena said. "You should have seen her untying that boy out at Ragtown. Remember that awful time when everybody was afraid to go outside for fear of dropping flat on their faces? She was one amazing woman. Went right in there next to that boy, calm as could be, ministered to him like she'd been doing that her whole life. I'll admit, she's the saddest woman I've ever seen. Those eyes! I see her walking up and down the streets like nobody else is alive, almost like she'll find something if she walks far enough, but she was one cool lady then. Like she knew how to carry the hardest kinds of troubles when she had to."

"She's not easy to understand," said Alf, softly, almost to himself. "I can't just say she's one thing or another. Every time I decide who she is, she shifts out of focus."

"I admire her, Alf." Serena leaned back and folded her arms across her midriff. "She doesn't have much use for me, I'm afraid. She's got righteousness on her mind. Integrity. I'm full of different stuff, but I admire her, believe me I do. We're going to sing together someday when I feel like singing again."

"Yeah," said Sammy. "I want to hear you sing again, Serena. You know how to make people stop talking, that's one thing I know if I don't know much else."

"I've got to go," said Alf. "I'm already an hour late, I think. What time is it, Sam?"

"Quarter to eight."

"Oh hell, you're not serious? And I've got this stuff on my breath."

"Sure as the guy's name is Split-T Cooper. Remind me to tell you about his name next time."

"See what you can do about Sunday, Alf." Serena bent over to pass him the bottle once again. He could see past the top button of her V-necked dress into deeper territory, shades of flesh, skin folding and unfolding as she breathed. "I haven't been to a picnic for years. You'll come, won't you?"

He held the bottle in both hands, feeling the Mason logo under his palm and holding a whiff of the jar's aroma in his lungs before he let it all out again and took another drink. "I'll try."

And then he drove down to the dam site in the moonlight to give himself a few more minutes before opening the door to his humble home. There's no place like home.

•   •   •   •   •

The next morning as Alf was misting the lettuce with a fine-spray nozzle, he decided that the cogs of the dam-building machinery were cooperating with him and his plans right on schedule. The different parts of the process were slowly twisting toward each other to interconnect with the whole: the grand finale when gigantic turbines would be dropped into place to process infinite tons of water through their blades.

One cog was the screening and washing plant at Three-Way Junction in Hemenway Wash, almost ready for its test run. It was Henry Kaiser's brain-child, the reason Six Companies presented the United States Government with the lowest bid. It would provide five sizes of aggregate—sand, three sizes of gravel, and cobbles—all free of dust, lumps, flaky particles, shale, alkali, loam, and mica.

Earlier in the week, Alf heard some railroad men talking about a Shay-geared locomotive purchased from the Tamalpais Railway Company near San Francisco for specialized gravel hauling. It had arrived at the switchyard in Boulder, yet hadn't moved one inch further. Last night, on his detox loop around town and down to the dam, Alf noticed it was still idle in the yard.

"Why?" he asked one of the brakemen who came in early to buy some ruby red grapefruit.

"Just on hold until the last of the tracks is connected from the gravel plant to the Arizona gravel deposits. There's a big debate going on. Should they use a conveyor belt to carry sand and gravel across the river, or should they use railroad cars on a wood-pile-and-trestle bridge? Just this morning they started building a bridge, so that locomotive'll be moving out soon. They decided a bridge could wash out four times for the cost of one conveyor belt."

Another cog: a thirty-seven-mile standard-gauge railroad line to transport sand, gravel and concrete, to move loose rock and muck to disposal areas, and to carry other necessary materials to the dam site.

Upstream from the dam site, railroad builders spread track like threads of a web to connect many points: Himix, the cement mixing plant on the Nevada canyon rim; the gravel plant where sand and gravel would be processed into aggregate; the Arizona Gravel Pit, upstream and across the river, where the Colorado had deposited silt, sand, gravel, and boulders over its thousands of years of passage, ironically providing the dam builders with the material they needed to change the river's course; and Shea, which was downstream at the upper end of Black Canyon. At this point, the weblike tracks melded into single-ply thread.

"It's like the most delicate vein," the same brakeman told Alf in the aisle for fresh cucumbers and green peppers. "It's propped on top of landfill. The canyon railroad—the most expensive and hazardous little stretch of track around. We're working on two tunnels to get the tracks into Black, cutting shelves out of solid rock and mooring ties to loose rock. This vein'll pump sand and gravel into Lomix."

"Lomix," answered Jack Lamey, a tunnel supervisor, when Alf asked him what was top priority at the moment. "It has these damn tilting mixers'll turn out a cubic yard of concrete every nine seconds." Lamey was buying a banana for breakfast after his graveyard shift.

"Why do they need concrete this soon?" Alf asked Jack as he chose a banana flecked with brown.

"Gotta line the diversion tunnels. And we'll be doing some preliminary pouring for the actual body of the dam before long. Everybody's getting competitive down there, trying to see if they can drill faster than the other crews. River's going to be partially diverted pretty quick now."

Everybody kept talking about the dam, the cogs meshing and turning, the excitement high. Up and down the aisles of yellow onions, potatoes, and melons, Alf heard the road builders toss anecdotes about their graders, steam shovels, rollers. They bragged about the cliffs they were cutting to lay a long ribbon of asphalt deep into the canyon. They shaped pictures with their hands to show the severity of the hairpin curves on their twisted-S road which would carry muck and workers, executives and superintendents, secretaries and senators in and out of the New Hell, to the blast-fire furnace in late spring, summer, and fall, and icy winds channeling through the canyons in winter.

And everyone talked about the diversion tunnels being near completion, two tunnels actually "holed through," though the miners were still hacking into the andesite tuff breccia referred to by miners as "dead," the kind that broke true if dynamite holes were placed with accuracy. Because the rock was volcanic, each completed tunnel would stand its total length without any timber supports.

Since May, when they first perched precariously on shelves dug out of cliff walls to blast the first entrances, fifteen hundred men had wrangled with these tunnels. Now the crews bragged about their record month of January, 1932, almost 7,000 feet dug, almost 450,000 cubic yards excavated in thirty-one days, the drilling going full steam ahead, four tunnel headings at the same time. Men were blasting, digging, and mucking twenty-four hours a day in three eight-hour shifts, sometimes eighty of them in one heading during a shift—miners, chuck tenders, nippers, a safety miner and foreman; a mucking crew with a shovel operator, an oiler, a pitman.

The same Bernie Wilson who'd taken on Bill Burroughs in the defunct River Commissary, was now a demigod. He usually played pool in the rec hall every night with the same few men, but always stayed aloof, which added to his mystique. He'd thought of a way to streamline the drilling process in the tunnels. Built in the shape of horseshoes and mounted on wheels that traversed ninety-pound rails, the jumbo carriages he'd invented had twenty-four drills mounted on tri-level platforms. That way, the drifter drills could bore shafts simultaneously, the thin narrow pockets for sticks of forty percent gelatin dynamite. Then, the carriage backed out and the miners made quick, clean exits. After the blast, crews waited exactly five minutes before moving in with the mucking equipment, just enough time for the powder smoke to drift to the vaulted ceiling and for blowers to discharge piped air to remove the accumulated gases.

Everyone checked their timepieces while they waited. They weren't going to be caught leaning against the door of their truck or jawing idly when Lamey, their supervisor, gave the go-ahead with a waving arm. They were ready on the second. Nobody could afford to lose one of those. The schedule had been planned with all due respect to the unpredictable itinerary of the river, and no one could fall behind. A man could lose his job if he did. The entire project would be ruined if they didn't stay on schedule and one step ahead of the Colorado.

The top and bench headings cleared, invert carriage drills followed behind to change the horseshoe shape of the tunnel into a circle. Trimming jumbos, chipping away at the overhang and rude projections of rock in each tunnel, followed behind all the others. Important cogs in the machine: Bernie Wilson's jumbos.

And Boulder City was the hub. It had paved streets, its principal buildings were near completion, and concrete sidewalks lined most of the avenues and streets.

The story circulated around town that after the frightening heat of 1931, the Secretary of Interior pleaded with Congress to release more funds for a gardener and a decent landscape for Boulder City. It needed to be a model of order and serenity, an exemplary mecca for the engineers, government officials, and tourists pouring in from the world over to watch this major assault on the Colorado, the most ambitious American engineering project since the Panama Canal. Meccas needed shade, not scraggly, clawing vegetation or dust-blown plazas. Someone needed to plant trees, shrubs, flowers, anything that would grow in that climate, in order to create the illusion of a real city with established trees and a pleasant history.

Alf had smiled about all of it coming together when he'd driven around the city and out to the edge of Black Canyon last night after his meeting with Serena and Sam. He'd watched the toy men and their tools far below, each a necessary cog to make this machine run smoothly. His after-hours business was part of this too, a minor gear maybe, but nonetheless a part of the machine. He had big hopes for his business. The town seemed new every day. New workers with new accents—southern, Texan, Minnesotan. New possibilities. A kaleidoscope of opportunity.

There were those people who knew him to be helpful when they needed loans, and they'd tell others. The scrip exchange was bringing in more money than his greengrocers' job, though it was turned back into profit for more profit. He hadn't revealed the exact complexion of his business to Esther. He'd been vague: "Lots of opportunities around here if a man has sharp eyes and ears."

To his relief, when Alf got home last night, she seemed happy for a change, even though he was unusually late. Maybe it was the January chill or the committee to get an elementary school opened for the coming fall. A. P. said she had his blessing to rally more women and make all the necessary noise, and that he'd mention the problem to the executive committee again.

In this brief window of clear skies with Esther, Alf felt safe to drop a hint: "People appreciate a chance to borrow money sometimes," he said, intuitively knowing she'd be content to let things glide by.

She passed her rare contentment to Alf with a kiss on his cheek and a dreaminess in her eyes. If he hadn't known better, he'd have suspected new love in her life. She even hummed "Carolina Moon" and pinched his bottom.

"Make love to me, Alf. I want you to hold me."

"So, what's come over you?"

"Do unto others as you'd have them do unto you, Alf. Why not tonight?"

"I'm going to make you happy, Esther. You'll see," though he had no idea she'd met Conway Mitchell that day who'd already made her happy when he said Esther was a mirror of souls and an artistic woman with beautiful eyes.

All he could think about that Friday morning in the vegetable department was how he could turn every cent he could get back into more loans. He'd use only a little of the cream for himself and his business associates after hours at the Pass. The new car and property in Vegas would come later, along with the black bugle bead dress for Esther. So it didn't matter as much as it might on Saturday night when Alf arrived home five hours later than his promise and when he tried to make sense to Esther even though the alcohol numbed his tongue. He was filling the cracks of Esther's dreams. Before long she'd notice she had everything she'd ever wanted. She'd say, "Alf, you've done it. You're a genius. I'm sorry if I've ever said anything about your judgment, because you've really proven me wrong. Alf, you amaze me!"

•   •   •   •   •

It was Sunday evening. Esther walked toward the site of the movie theater, the wind biting her ears. Last Thursday, the same day Alf sealed his deal with Sam and Serena, she'd stopped in front of this soon-to-be Boulder Theater. Tonight she noticed the progress in the framing for the two-story walls and in the additional forms for the arcade and Spanish arches that would soon grace the sidewalk. She wished Conway Mitchell hadn't told her he'd be showing the new talkies when the theater opened, though she didn't regret meeting Conway, not for one minute.

Esther shivered in the piercing wind on Arizona Street and absentmindedly listened to the sound of last Thursday's hammers. The sound warped as the wind curved around corners. Conway hadn't taken away all her hope, but if she understood about talkies, she wouldn't be standing center stage between flickering movies. She'd been hoping to sing in the new movie house after her baby was weaned, but maybe she was a relic of the past already, discarded from necessity because she'd been away and because people kept inventing new things such as talking films.

As cold as she was in the wind, she lingered in front of the theater and mulled over the word "archaic." Esther. The silent movie stars, too. Past tense already. She'd spent hours studying Clara, Theda, and Rudolph, their soulful eyes, their moist expressions of love, their poised hands, their alphabet of emotions, and now they all would be replaced. Hollywood orchestras would drown Esther's voice like the reservoir behind the dam would drown St. Thomas, Uncle Woolley's orchard, and even the gravel screening plant where Ragtown had been. Talk and special effects would erase the art of gesture and blot Esther and the stars out of the sky. Thank heavens for church and funerals, those would always be there, but why did everything else have to change constantly?

Once she'd thought there was safety if one worked hard, learned to sing, took in ironing, washed clothes, kept children neat, kissed one's husband when he came home from work, but now it seemed nothing was reliable, not even the promises of the brethren at church who told her if she was faithful to the end everything would be all right.

The blowing sand stung her face and forced its way into her eyes while she thought of the bishop, his counselors, and the other priesthood holders who couldn't change the fact that this morning she'd sat in a Sunday School meeting in the Palm Mortuary with tears running down her cheeks. Alf had spent their tithing money for a new suit. When he was dressing for church, she noticed the stiff newness around his shoulders, the sharp crease in the pant legs as he preened in front of the bathroom mirror.

"I need the right image," he told her. "Give me your blessing, Esther."

But blessings were for the faithful, Esther thought at the time, and even more so now, not for someone like Alf who was in and out of the state of devotion to his family and the church like quicksilver in a thermometer. Schemes were his only religion. As long as he had a scheme, life was a good idea.

He'd gone with them to church this morning, probably to show off his new suit, but he left early. He said he had important business but didn't say what. He just said, "Excuse me. I'll see you later this afternoon."

"But we just got here," Esther whispered as he stood to leave.

She sat next to his empty wooden folding chair, trying not to cry. How could she have married a man who belonged to the congregation of vacillation, who shifted from job to job, plan to plan, someone who didn't feel dependable?

After the meeting, Bishop Vaughn stopped at the end of Esther's row of chairs and waited for her to sidestep her way to the aisle. Putting his arm around her shoulders, he quoted a passage from Mormon scripture. "You remember what the Lord said, Sister Jensen? 'Provoke thy husband to good works.' Be firm about it, and try to get Alf out to church more. It's not only your salvation at stake here."

He looked patronizing, and Esther knew he'd seen her crying. He only wanted to help, she decided. *God should bless a man for that impulse.*

But after Esther shook his hand and nodded a tentative "Yes," she turned away to cover the internal warring against what felt like the bishop's smugness. *Who is he to think he knows the answers for everybody? What does he know about me and Alf? Something I don't? Our marriage is our business! Besides, Bishop Vaughn, it belittles a man for a woman to provoke him. Belittles a woman too. I watched Mother. Always performing while Father stood by. Mother staying after church to hear everyone's compliments on her vocal solo. Father wanting some quiet where he could read a book. Mother in the limelight; Father at the edge of the beam. Mother martialing everyone into their Sunday best which wasn't as nice as her Sunday best. After all, she was in the public eye. Everyone buckling their shoes and brushing their teeth while she said, "Hurry, hurry. Have respect for the Lord's House by being on time." Mother mixing God with her need to be recognized, to be treated with deference. Mother pulling Father, Henry, me and Miriam along, telling us to hurry, to love God by cooperating with her. Harsh words to Father. Why couldn't he take more responsibility? Why didn't he embrace the Gospel with a full heart? No, Bishop Vaughn. I won't provoke Alf to good works. Don't ask that of me.*

"Where'd Alf go?" Sister Parker pried as she pulled her overcoat over her shoulders after the meeting and grabbed the arm of an about-to-run-away child.

"He's not feeling well today." Esther felt like a painter trying to cover the fact that her large canvas of faith had been stretched too tightly and was splitting at crucial points.

The church. She wanted it to give her comfort—the hymns, the sacrament, handshaking and the backpatting—but she didn't like sitting alone or feeling her troubles were a matter of spiritual speculation for the bishop or the congregation. She knew Mormonism was not for halves, quarters, and shaved bits of families. It preached Unity. Harmony. Togetherness in praise of God. But hers kept splintering like the wings of a balsa wood airplane, fragments and curls and bits of wood fraying the already rough body of her family. Esther had vowed to hold it in one piece, though Alf and Jack and sometimes Mary Elizabeth stretched her definition of a one-piece family out of shape, especially when Alf left church meetings early and came home with alcohol on his breath, like last night.

Last night. She'd wondered just as Sister Parker had. "Where's Alf?" she asked the clock when he wasn't home at the close of his shift, not for five hours. "He wouldn't stay at her house this long," she said, painting over her worry. Esther had seen him walking down Serena's Avenue D when she was on her way home from grocery shopping. "He's with Jack now. Of course, that's it. They're celebrating the fact they just holed through the second diversion tunnel down at the dam, the first one on the Nevada side. Tunnel No. 2. Everybody else is celebrating and acting like the workers are small miracles who just finished building the Sphinx."

The Sen-sen on his breath couldn't cover the smell of alcohol when he walked in the door. "I'm developing contacts," he told Esther. "I've got a plan to make us some big money. Don't you worry, my little Esther. I'm taking good care of this family now."

"Sid Empey'll throw you out of town if he smells your breath, Alf. It's Prohibition and this is a Federal Reservation. Who are you kidding?"

"You just wait, sweetheart. Everything's in hand. Full of promise. You worried about your little Alfred?"

"I don't worry, you know that, Alf." She turned her face to the wall.

Last night while she slept at a stiff distance from him, she listened to Satan whispering in her ear that her prayers were stopping at the ceiling of their home on Avenue B, that Alf wasn't worth her prayers anyway. And she was filled with nightmares of water rising swiftly, a hundred feet a minute, rising and pouring through the tunnels, crushing in the sides of railroad cars, ripping ties from the track laid at the edge of the river, carrying away steam shovels and trucks and drills and mechanics and truck drivers and her Herbert, Jack, Mary Elizabeth, Rebecca, and Inez. It was rising above the cliff tops and fingering its way toward her home, flooding into her body and her life.

But when she opened her eyes this morning, there was no Satan in sight or no high water trickling across her bedroom floor. Only bright sunshine and stiff wind. So today, after a terrified night, everything had an odd sense of dignity, and no one, not even the bishop, was going to take that from her.

After all, Esther thought, tucking her windblown hair back inside her hat, the family was better situated than they'd ever been. Alf wasn't talking about moving, for the first time in years; Herbert was dressing every day in his white shirt and tie and reporting to Cox, the supervisor at Anderson Brothers Mess Hall, even though he desperately wanted a job at the dam. His paycheck was making a difference. Rebecca was content at the neighborhood school being held in Dorothy Parker's house at the bottom of Avenue B. And Mary Elizabeth was the star at the Las Vegas High School talent assembly. Everybody had told her so. A languid torch singer draped across the top of an upright piano with a long, purple net scarf wrapping her neck, the ends clutched tightly to her bosom while she sang "Cuddle up a little closer, lovey mine." That made up for the fact that she was a 15-year-old in a women-scarce city with eyes following her steps everywhere, that she looked back over her shoulder when the wolf whistles curved in her direction and was as subtle as a lighthouse, that she was standing outside the rec hall yesterday with a strange man's arm around her, his fingers stroking bare skin just inside her blouse. Esther wouldn't think about that just now.

The wind charged like a dark knight ready to spear everything on the point of a lance. It seemed as if it were a thief stealing shingles from the pile near the theater and warmth from her body. It blew as the sound of old sheets tearing, singing like a lunatic, no hesitations. Nothing could keep the wind-chill out, not even Esther's warm wool coat that for fifteen years had pro-tected her from blizzards in Malad and Brigham City.

Extremes, thought Esther. Maybe there's a license to be extreme here. Maybe that's what's plaguing Alf—these extremities coaxing him further out on a limb. Almost as if he thinks, If Mother Nature and God can act this way, so can I. She'd seen him follow Serena to her house last evening. "Maybe," Esther tried to be charitable, "he's trying to help her adjust."

Somehow, Esther and Serena, except when they'd untied the boy from the stakes and talked after Ed's death, never became close friends, though Esther baked bread and delivered several bottles of canned peaches to Serena's house. They were too different—Esther's Mormonism and demand-ing family; Serena, a seeming child of the breach, wary of anyone cornering her into a solidified view of life.

She'd heard Serena say she wanted a baby, but she'd be wanting it to hold, a connection to another life that would help anchor her own, maybe. Esther's babies were for the purpose of building the Kingdom of God on Earth. Esther, a conduit for God, contributed her share to the glory of her Maker. She'd made a covenant in the temple to multiply and replenish the earth. Her babies were born for a larger purpose which sometimes kept her from loving them in simple ways. Serena was not interested in the higher way of living. She and Esther were obviously too different to need each other.

147

"So, how's Serena Bishop?" Esther asked Alf late last night when she served his warmed-up leftovers.

He slid his chair up to the table, squinted at her through frameless eyeglasses, and turned his head airily. "She's fine. She's been into the store several times, trying to get me to do business with her brother, Sam, who's staying with her now. I stopped by their place after work to see what they had to say."

"Well?" Esther asked, still holding the plate of meatloaf and creamed carrots in one hand, a glass of milk in the other.

"Could be good, we'll see."

Esther felt it coming on again, his restlessness and shifting focus. A man with no sense of permanence, who thought there was always something better if he looked hard enough.

She knew the signs and tossed all last night to scatter them from her mind. But then the nightmares came, repeated dreams of rising water flooding every crevice around her. The Colorado crept out of its riverbed and flooded the wrinkles of her bedsheets and the corners of her eyes and marooned her children in tiny dinghies with waves swamping the sides. "Mother," they called. Rebecca trying to paddle with her hands. Mary Elizabeth falling out of her boat, clinging to the sides, tossing a purple scarf for someone to catch. Inez tied to an inner tube, crying as it spun like a wheel.

Esther had finally forced herself out of bed and tiptoed to the kitchen to find a piece of paper. It was time to advertise. No more word-of-mouth business. It wasn't good enough. She wrote the ad several times, wording it just right, erasing, editing until she felt satisfied. She took it to the company store after she left Sunday School meeting. *Expert washing and ironing. Starching to suit your taste. Especially delicate with fine cottons. Contact Esther Jensen at 216 Avenue B.* It was time to fatten her blue ceramic teapot, not just line it. Time to advertise and stop counting on Alf.

And now, she'd returned to the beginnings of the Boulder Theater, a place that felt safe. A movie theater was sacred—a place where stories had endings, where love was stronger than people, where one could cry over a sad life and leave it behind. Esther longed for the day she could disappear inside the two-story walls and compare her smile to Jean Harlow's and listen to Walter Huston speaking lovingly to her through a substitute actress. Maybe she'd get to sing here someday, somehow, but most of all, she'd have an escape from the sun. Even as she stood in the freezing wind and watched the mocking red blaze on the horizon, she knew the February wind and cold temperature were only diversionary tactics.

As she surveyed the ghostly innards of the theater one last time, she closed her eyes to remember the words and nuances she'd repeated so often since last Thursday afternoon.

"Good afternoon, Ma'am." The tall man had tipped the brim of his hat while he held the crown tightly with his other hand. "I'm Conway Mitchell, owner of this soon-to-be theater. You've been standing out here quite a while. Aren't you frozen stiff?"

"Oh," she'd blushed, embarrassed. "I used to sing during intermission at the silent movies in Brigham City, Utah. I like theaters."

Mitchell was a big man, over six feet tall and penguin-shaped, a wide leather belt around his middle and a silver dollar slide on his bolo tie.

"I'm building a stage in front of the screen," he told her, and much as she didn't want to, she felt hopes rising. "Vaudeville. Special attractions on their way to somewhere else." He laughed. "I've got chandeliers ordered. Wall sconces for a nice gentle light to shine up the length of the two-story pilasters."

Esther's eyes had glowed at the thought of dimming lights and the anticipation she could almost feel now, waiting for the curtains to open and the reel numbers to flip past. Darkness. No harsh light. That's got to be heaven, she'd thought, not burning bushes and a God too bright to see with human eyes. Something easy on the senses. That would be her choice if she could choose God. The idea of a dark, cool theater sounded like the celestial kingdom.

"I'm putting in a swamp cooler too, Ma'am. First one in town. People will pay me to come in out of the heat."

"You sound like you know what you're doing," Esther said.

"So you sing, huh? Could be we could use you sometime."

"I can make people get next to their emotions with my music. That's one thing I can do even if I have a hard time holding it all together myself. I sing with my husband, Alf, sometimes too. We've got a good repertoire."

"You know there are thousands of movies being made right now, Ma'am. Hollywood's turning them out like hotcakes. We're going to change movies four times a week." His attention began to wander to a workman.

"Sounds like you don't need much live entertainment." Esther had turned away to give the impression she had more important places to go.

"Probably not." He left her side to check one of the carpenters. "Make that arch a little higher, Wetherell. It's lower than that one over there. This is going to be the biggest and best theater in the whole state. Help me do it right, okay?"

Esther did an about-face to walk away, embarrassed and hot around her neck, believing he'd wanted to talk to her. He doesn't have much confidence in Brigham City, Utah, she thought, humiliated to be dismissed so summarily. Got to be flashy and brassy for entertainment in Nevada. Too close to Hollywood. But I'm good. If he could hear me. . . .

"Hey, Ma'am," Mitchell ran after her. "Why'd you leave before you told me your name? I might need you sometime in a pinch. Right?"

He hadn't dismissed her, then. He'd heard her. And believed her! Esther suddenly felt petite next to him. He was a big man, but sensitive. Esther saw it in the slant of his cheekbone. He looked directly at her, and Esther felt that, just maybe and after all, he found her appealing, even if that thought had been abandoned by her as foolish a long time ago. Five living children. A set of dead twins. Three misses.

"Excuse my boldness, Ma'am, but you have beautiful eyes, a mirror of souls."

How poetic, Esther mused.

"Tell me your name, okay? I really might need somebody."

"Esther Jensen. I'm on Avenue B with my three daughters and one son. My husband is one of the greengrocers at Boulder Company. You may have bought a head of lettuce washed by him, or," Esther began to mimic a Shakespearean actor, "a grapefruit stacked with the aid of his fine sense of proportion."

They'd laughed.

"I've seen you walking past before," he said. "Come by again, okay? I've got to do some overseeing just now. You're an artistic woman, I can tell. You'll like my movies. The best, okay?"

"Okay."

The wind was so cold now, Esther couldn't stand it any longer, and she gave in. But before she turned for home, she pulled her coat tighter and imagined rows of seats lined up on the inside of this theater. Row after row. People eating popcorn. Crying. Laughing. Then she stepped onto the loose boards serving as a sidewalk until Laskey's Friendly Shoe Store and the

Boulder Theater were finished. The sound was hollow, but she had other things to think about besides hollowness which reminded her of futility, a much too common subject in her mind. These boards were only temporary. Soon, they'd be cement. And she could use the new sidewalks to walk to the movies, and maybe to see Conway.

10

Esther's watery nightmares turned into real rain. The earlier flood was nothing compared to this one that carved deep furrows in roadbeds like an apprentice butcher might. The Colorado rose forty-six feet this time. The silted water once again flooded the ledge where the transformer shed controlled power and light and where the blower house supplied fresh air to the tunnel workers. But it also washed away the new trestle bridge connecting the Arizona gravel deposits and the Nevada gravel screening plant. Water poured into the portals of the diversion tunnels and scared everybody mindless, the way it played with the diligent workers as if they were small mannequins and their steam shovels mere sticks. It flowed in legend-making proportions, and machines and materials floated away on the hackles of the water dragon's raised back.

An era of urgency came to Boulder City. Floods in summer were one thing—bothersome yet half-expected—but flooding in the middle of winter when Rocky Mountain waterfalls were supposed to be hanging over the edges of cliffs in iced suspension, was another.

The high water pervaded everyone's nights: dry dust whirling around a fiery yellow circle of sun with the roar of water rushing toward them from some unseen place. And it was always at the heart of everyday conversations: "What's the river doing today?" The mighty river; the Colorado.

More than the electrical storms, the winds, the heat, the accidents, and the deaths, this flood became a catalyst which sharpened the lines of demarcation: the river vs. the dam workers; the dam vs. the river.

It drew them out of their personal lives and into a larger scheme. Esther and the other wives had done their wrestling with the basics—food, shelter, a promise of a permanent elementary school built of brick and red tile, a sense of community where they knew each other's names and asked questions of their health. Engrossed in their own survival, they'd regarded the Boulder Canyon Project as amorphous and somewhat mysterious. Who really cared about such things as the incline hoisting railroad, double track construction, a refrigerating plant which would supply cold water to pipes that would cool the cement, the odd shapes of gates, pipe fittings, and hoists rumbling through Boulder City on flatbeds and tracks? These things were something apart from their individual occupation with dinner, school, clean clothes, and lunch pails.

But now, those things which had seemed unimportant to them shifted. The teeth in the cogs of each part were biting into the bigger gears, transforming the project into something much larger than anyone had ever witnessed. Six Companies became We. Theirs became Ours, and a common front faced off with The River.

No one could be lax on their job without an effect on the whole. Their part, their gear in the machinery, mattered. They weren't individuals doing solos on tightwires, shaking in the balance; they were movers of material from point A to point B which in turn affected points C and D. Each man was needed in his place at his designated hour. During each shift, no one lingered over coffee or wandered elsewhere in their minds. Their best was necessary.

The language of the dam became the language of the town and took on mythic overtones because of a river that could rise forty-six feet in a few hours, lash through tunnels and drown thousands of hours of hard manual labor, not to mention an unlucky laborer.

Townspeople forgot Bernie Wilson's real name. He was no longer himself, but "Bull," the Bull of the River, a modern-day Minotaur in the labyrinth of the diversion tunnels. The language became part of the town, a fabric woven by the people to magnify their purpose, a warp of desert-colored, wind-washed, sun-soaked, water-stained threads with bold blues and glaring yellows, strengthened by a weft of steel threads shaved from hard edges of shovels, blades, sprockets, and nail tips.

The language spilled onto the streets where children played: "I went to the dam to get some dam water," the children chanted, "and the dam man said he wouldn't give me any of his dam water." The language fermented in intimate conversations: "You dam driver," a wife would joke to her husband after dinner. "My favorite diversion tunnel," her husband joked back.

The language grew as men rode out of the canyon on truck transports. Spillway tunnels were christened *Glory Holes* on a Wednesday, and the whole town would be talking *Glory Holes* before the end of the week. Rigging crews argued the intricacies of splicing cables and moving loads by pulleys and sheaves at a thousand feet, and an eavesdropper talked *splicing cables at two thousand feet* at his dinner table. Form-strippers, discussing creative ways to remove their forms after concrete was poured, became *strippers* over a hand of pinochle. Some men on the transport talked; some men lit cigarettes, found a spot of shade under the makeshift canvas cover flapping in the wind and soaked up the language without exchanging it; some waited to be dropped at the Six Companies rec hall where they would chalk their pool cue and move the talk around. Some transmitted the new language when they went to the drug department of the Boulder City Company to sniff cigars. They told the clerks how many feet had been tunneled on their shift or how a train had crashed into a pile of rocks on a hairpin curve and smashed a flatbed truck or how a swinging crane had snagged a power line and carried some poles along with it.

The language grew as the monstrous immortal grew between the thighs of black lava in the canyon. It grew in answer to the question everyone asked when each shift rolled into town to be dropped off the truck transport at the Boulder Company Stores: "What happened at the dam site today?"

Boulder City, swelling in numbers and structures daily, became a fortress, a city high on a hill to watchguard the ribbon of muddy red winding through the rocks and bluffs below. Every move by the river was reported on the hill; every countermovement to prevent the river from behaving irrationally was common knowledge to every man, woman, and child.

Herbert carried snippets of each crew's language home to Esther and his sisters along with half his Anderson Brothers Boarding and Supply Company wages. Half of the remaining half was stuffed in a wool stocking at the bottom of his sock drawer, the growing bulge enlarging his hopes of getting into a college somewhere. He was tired of being treated like a busboy, even though he was one, so after hours, he stood in the long line at the employment office, waiting for a place on the truck transports, something closer to the dam itself. Every day they told him the same thing: "The dam's no place for light physiques," but Herbert knew somewhere there was an opportunity to get closer to the dam, a higher salary, and a stocking full of tuition money.

He was undaunted because he had dreams. He not only dreamed of college, a place to escape the cycle of defeat he'd witnessed in his father, but dreamed of a flowing pen in his hand. Words. Words on paper. He observed everything intently, hoping his pictures would flow from the tip of his pen to transport readers from the mundane. And he dreamed of rows of bound covers with his name on the spines, and even beyond that to fame. But in between dreams, Herbert kept working at the mess hall, listening to the men talk, boast, and bend language into new shapes. And after hours, as he stood in line, he acquired more language for his secret cache, sometimes taking notes on a stenographer's pad.

Between Herbert and Alf, the family was supplied with ample Hoover Dam talk. No one was surprised one evening when Inez, at thirteen months, shouted with a mouthful of noodles, "Dam. Big dam."

Everyone laughed and tried to get her to do an encore. Esther fed her more egg noodles and coaxed the precocious Inez until the door opened and the scene changed. Jack arrived with Gloria, his black hair slicked down more than usual and a maroon bow tie with white roses tied around his collar. Gloria hung onto his triceps with both arms and looked like a movie starlet in her flowered jersey dress. White cuffs on the short sleeves. Deep finger waves in her blonde hair.

"You two look up to no good," Alf said, peering over the tops of his glasses.

"How can you tell, Dad?" Jack looked like spring had come, the hint of flowers blooming out of his shirt sleeves and trouser cuffs.

" 'When it's springtime in the Rockies,' " Esther sang, dabbing a spot on the tablecloth with her napkin. "You've decided, haven't you?" she said. "I can see it plain as day."

"Yeah, Mom."

Herbert stood to shake Jack's hand, Herbert always a little unsure around his older brother, always guessing what was appropriate. "Congratulations, Jack. Are you two planning on a temple wedding?"

Herbert may as well have blown a whistle. Everyone at the table stopped eating. Forks were eased onto plates, and everyone's hands found unobtrusive places to rest. Esther, everyone knew, because everyone heard about it at least once a day in the family prayer when they kneeled at their chairs before breakfast, had entrusted her heart to the Lord in the matter of Jack, her wayward one. "Bless our Jack that he may be guided back to Thee." She even bargained. "I'll keep up my end if you'll help Jack change his ways and convince Gloria of the necessity of a temple marriage." Esther wanted everybody together in the hereafter, to stand side by side in celestial gardens and partake of spiritual food superior to anything on this plane of existence. She refused to accept that any of her brood might not be worthy to pass through celestial gates, even though evidence to the contrary seemed to be piling up all around her, including the cracks in Mary Elizabeth which were almost visible.

Alf, privy to the workings of Esther's mind, looked worried about her reaction, which could be hysterical if Jack told her the truth: "No, not now or ever," and furthermore, that he didn't want to be tagged "Mormon" in any way, shape, or form. Jack had stepped into the bigger world and liked it out there. He liked the fact that Gloria was from Okmulgee, Oklahoma, had never heard of Mormons, and didn't care to in this life or the next. Jack and Alf had discussed these things over bathtub gin at the Pass.

Mary Elizabeth crossed and uncrossed her knees, apparently incensed by Gloria who appeared to have no time or interest in any of the Jensens, only for Jack and the mirror of his captivated eyes. Rebecca scraped the floor with her feet, looking hungry still and unsure why her dinner was suspended.

"Big dam," Inez said again, breaking the silence.

"You hear that, Gloria?" Jack took two steps to look closer at his baby sister, as if she were a prize at a carnival. "Hey, say that again, kid."

Gloria followed Jack and wrapped her arms around his waist, a territorial move to keep him on her side of the border.

"So, will you say that at my wedding, Inie? After the preacher tells me to kiss Gloria, we'll bring you up for comic relief. What you say, kid?"

Inez dribbled spit bubbles down her chin; Herbert stood back and smiled while Jack charmed the baby; Esther looked covertly at Gloria who chewed too much gum on one side of her mouth.

"When is the big day?" she asked.

"We thought June," Gloria blushed. "June bride. Parson Frank is going to marry us. Everybody loves him."

"Grace Community Church," Alf told Esther, watching her mood with apprehension and calculating her hair-trigger temper.

"I know who Parson Frank is," snapped Esther, "and where he preaches. You think I don't know anything about this town except what goes on in this family and at church? You think I'm some hick from Utah? Well, Mr. Suave, where do you think you come from?"

"Esther," Alf said, "we have company."

Esther tried to smile, to eat her bowl of canned Elberta peaches from her mother's fall peach crop in Brigham City. She dipped her spoon daintily into the sugared syrup and lifted it half full to her mouth. Suddenly everyone seemed conscious of every move she was making. Gloria was watching her. Alf, too.

"Don't look at me like that," she yelled. "Everybody stop looking at me like that. What am I to you? Some kind of sideshow?" Her eyes were pinpoints of hate. *My first child. My son. Things are splintering, dividing. Mary Elizabeth, too. Finding her own head, talking back to me, laughing at my speeches about chastity, saying I'm an ostrich with my head stuck in Great Salt Lake sand. My plans for my family, ripping, tearing.*

"The temple, Gloria," Esther said. "Has Jack ever told you about the temple and eternal families?"

Gloria stopped chewing her gum and pulled her head back and down into her shoulders, the borders of her crimson rouge spreading.

"Esther's not feeling well," Alf said. "Please excuse her."

"Don't try to excuse me!" Esther yelled again. "Why are you trying to excuse me when I'm talking about our salvation? Alf, you never let me speak. You never let me speak at all, and Jack won't listen. He's never listened to me. You've coddled him, let him go slack. Alf, I needed you!"

"Mother," said Herbert. "Please."

"Big dam," said Inez again.

"You little bugger," Jack laughed nervously. "Can you believe this kid?"

Esther lifted Inez from her high chair and hugged her tight to her body. "Big dam, big dam. What are you going to be? An engineer or something?" She held Inez like a shield, her protection from this moment.

"Mom," Jack said, "I love Gloria. Let's set all this religion aside for a moment and consider my feelings."

"You fool," Esther said, standing and wiping cream sauce from Inez's fingers with her own. "Excuse me. Please." She hurried out of the room, her heels loud on the wooden floor.

"She'll be all right," said Alf. "You know how she is when she first hears news. Give her a few days, and she'll accept things just fine. You've got my blessing, Jack. Gloria."

Herbert stepped forward and put his arm tentatively around Jack's shoulder. "Mine too, Jack." But he couldn't refrain, the religion too strong in him. "Maybe someday it'll feel okay for you to take Gloria to the temple."

Jack slipped away from the perfunctory embrace and words that made his blood rise. "Gotta run, brother. You'd better be looking out for a woman for yourself. Your hair ain't any too thick these days."

Gloria shook the hand Herbert held out to her. "Welcome to the family," he said without looking into her eyes. He was a composite of shyness in Gloria's abundantly sexual presence mixed with resentment at the woman who was leading his only brother away from the celestial heart of the family.

"Nice to meet you," Gloria said, grabbing Jack's arm again and following him out.

The room was absolutely still. Everyone looked at each other and listened to the sound of the door closing over and over again in their minds. No one dared breathe.

"Idiot!" Esther screamed from the bedroom. "Idiot child. I suppose all the rest of you are going to throw away everything precious. You too, Mary Elizabeth, the way you flaunt yourself in front of those strange men. You don't know the first thing about being a real lady. Your father doesn't care either! Not one minute does he care."

Alf covered his face and took deep breaths from the cup of his hands. "Herbert," he said quietly, "you're the only one who can calm her anymore. Go in there. She'll be okay once she settles down."

"She needs to be alone, Dad."

"I said go in there. She needs somebody's arms, and mine aren't large enough."

Herbert's steps whispered down the hall. "Mother?"

"Oh, Herbert." They heard her weeping. "Nothing is sacred anymore. Nothing. Mary Elizabeth is sneaking around behind my back. Nobody cares about the important things. My Jack. He's lost to me, Herbert. Lost. I don't have a dam to stop him."

"Nobody's lost until the end. Keep your faith, Mother."

They listened to Esther sobbing from her room until the sound slowed to a few intermittent spasms of caught breath. Herbert glided quietly back down the hall with Inez in his arms, suggested the girls gather dishes from the table, and told Mary Elizabeth to be more respectful. She'd be sorry later if she wasn't.

•　　•　　•　　•　　•

Winston West, Boulder City's official landscape gardener, appointed by the U.S. Government, had been trying to make things grow. He arranged for the soil to be analyzed and found it free from the usual desert alkali, lacking only humus; he planted deciduous trees and shrubs and lawn with the right mix of seed to survive in the desert; he imported topsoil and laid it a foot deep around the administration building. He was busy making things green to give relief from all the summers to come to Boulder City.

Esther, now a familiar sight in the business district as she carried her daily groceries and sometimes wheeled a baby girl, was friendly to West, Conway Mitchell, Ida Browder who owned the cafe where Serena waitressed, and the men employed to sweep the streets with brooms. She always waved to everyone, making the downtown a comfort zone for her, the dam builders, and the curious visitors from all over the world. As she walked through the weeks and the days, she watched West plant his first saplings along New Mexico Street, then move northward to plant strips of trees and shrubbery on the residential streets, then dig holes for trees and spread manure for grass in the four town plazas.

But after Gloria and Jack announced their plans to wed at the Grace Community Church, Esther felt less like waving, almost like the starch had gone out of her arms.

One day in late April, she would have passed West without speaking. Except she had no choice. Winston West stood with his hands on his hips in the middle of the sidewalk, shaking his head at his experimental rose garden.

"The roses," she said. "I read about them in the paper. They'll survive?"

He rattled the once yellow-rosed bush. The remaining petals and a few leaves scratched the ground when they fell. "I don't know," West answered, lifting his cap to let a draft of air cool his head. "They seem a bit reluctant."

The trees on the residential streets had adapted and appeared semi-sturdy and rooted; the landscape of the administration building was almost thriving in the one-foot layer of topsoil, imported to cover a shelf of broken granite; but the rose gardens on the North and South Escalante Plazas were not cooperating with Winston West.

"A mecca. Nevada's Garden City," he said, leaning on the rubber brace of a sapling on the street side of the walkway. "That's what I'm trying to make this town. Everybody's tired of mirages when they ride out of the canyon wiping the sweat from their necks and ears and foreheads. I'm working to make the real thing."

"Doesn't look like we'll be rolling in grass on this plaza this summer," Esther said. The tied-off squares of grass were sparse here, the saplings thin as premature bones. "Do you think anything here will make it through the summer?"

"All the grass and shrubs need is time and more water. The roses may be a different story. I'm watching them like a hawk does mice. My pet project." He fingered another shriveled bud which snapped off in his hand. "But maybe, not even me with all my college botany classes and piped-in water can convince them to grow here."

The rose bushes were leggy, their green stems hardening to a wood-brown. As West and Esther talked, the heat seemed to rev up and bare its breast. The stems of the roses seemed to calcify while they talked.

"I've watched you since February when you first started planting trees," Esther said. "I've been waiting for the spring flower show, but maybe," she mused, "there's no such thing as spring here. I didn't see it. Did you?"

"Maybe a couple of days." He tipped his cap back again and scratched at his hairline.

"There's nothing gradual here. Just extremes. Hot. Freezing. Windy. Hotter. Boiling."

"I'm not a man to give up easily."

"Bless you for that, Mr. West. The ad building seems to be flourishing though. A few gifts in this life. Right?"

"A few, but this desert is handing me some harsh lessons. I thought I could get these roses to grow with the right nutrients and my special brand of tender loving care. But they don't care for me or this place."

"I'm a rose," Esther said, shifting the weight of the groceries to the top of her hipbone.

"Your mama call you Rosie O'Grady or something like that?" West laughed. "Rose. Lily. Violet. Flower garden of females. Has anybody ever been named Delphinium, I wonder? So your name is Rose?"

"My name is Esther Jensen, but I'm a rose. You just can't see me."

"So what do you need? A little phosphorous, potassium, nitrogen?"

"I don't know what I need for sure. Maybe a few trace minerals. Does love have any trace minerals in it? Do you think when my husband puts his arms around me and says he loves me that I am absorbing the essentials or does it have to be the truth to help?"

"You're a strange one, Mrs. Jensen. As baffling as my roses. Guess men need a few mysteries to solve."

"Good luck with that, Mr. West. Got to get to supper for now. I'm needed, don't you think? Everyone needs me to keep their clothes nice and bake bread and fix dinner. I'm valuable. A jewel in the desert. A rose. I'll pray for your roses tonight. I promise."

West tipped his cap. "Find a cool place to sit, Mrs. Jensen. This heat affects the mind like poison."

·   ·   ·   ·   ·

The grand opening of the movie theater was on Esther's birthday—May 14. "Forty-three years old and still putting on makeup," she said to Alf as he stood behind her and combed his moustache in the bathroom mirror.

"And why shouldn't you?" he said.

"Sometimes it seems like a clown mask or war paint." She laughed with rare pleasure. "But tonight is my night, my dear. Nothing else matters but this occasion. My birthday. And I'm not thinking about the Lindbergh baby anymore. Yesterday is yesterday."

A day of celebration! Boulder City Optical Company and Laskey's Friendly Shoe Store opened as well, construction on the elementary school would begin in two weeks, and all four of the diversion tunnels in Black Canyon were "holed through," dug from the upstream entrance to the downstream exit. Two in Arizona; two in Nevada. None of them were parallel because of the shape of the canyon walls, and they still needed to be lined with concrete, but in a few months the Colorado would flow away from and around the dam site. The town breathed a collective sigh—happy the rock was blasted and blown and mucked out of the gaping holes in the canyon walls, relieved that the river would soon be turned away from their precious dam site.

Even though everyone expected it, the final announcement swept through Boulder City when the swing shift rolled into town and left a party mood in its wake. Everyone wanted to forget yesterday's headlines about the Lindberghs and dilute the pall that had settled over the town. The news of the tunnels made life feel better and helped everyone rock a little easier in their chairs.

To Esther, the perfect party for both herself and the tunnels was the opening of the Boulder Theater. She could escape now to someplace dark, cool, apart. Esther felt as happy as one of the miners who'd been subjected to the eight-hour-a-day shaking of his bones, vibrating for endless hours while his drill bit pierced into solid rock, now free from the jarring and rattling.

There had been times in the middle of difficult nights when Esther felt the buzz of the rock drills within the thin strands of nerves in her spine, almost as if she were a canyon wall herself. Tomorrow there would be more vibrations and more humming of compressed air into tunnels, electricity humming through wires, even more drilling and blasting, but tonight there was rest for the miners, the engineers, and her sympathetic spine. No vibrations sending chills through her body, not tonight. No chalk scraping across the slate backdrop of her dreams. It had stopped now, at least for tonight, and

Esther sambaed out of the bathroom in her freshly pressed yellow and brown plaid cotton with the loose dancing sleeves and white pima collar.

The day before, Esther overheard Herbert suggesting to Alf that he make arrangements with the baker in the mess hall for a three-layer white cake with pink frosting roses and silver-paper leaves. Thinking of the different poses of surprise she might use, she was full of the excitement of someone who knew all about the plans but still had to pretend. Alf even asked Esther for a date to the theater opening, the seven o'clock show, and had sent Mary Elizabeth to stand in the ticket line that morning. She came home with the story of how she had pushed her dollar through the arch in the glass of the ticket cage, and how after two dimes rolled into the change tray and two movie tickets were safe in her hand, Conway Mitchell walked out from behind the double doors and announced that all four performances were sold out.

"It's your lucky day, Mother," Mary Elizabeth said when she fell onto the sofa at home and held up the tickets like a small fan. "You've got me and two passes to the show. What do you think? There was a line down to the corner and I was the last one to get tickets."

"I think you're right," Esther laughed. "It is my lucky day. I've been wanting to thank you for being more diligent about your church meetings lately. Spending more time with the young people at church than over by the rec hall. Thank you for that, Mary Elizabeth. You need to mix with the people who have your same values. Be in the world but not of it. You won't be sorry."

Mary Elizabeth groaned. "No lectures today, Mama. It's your birthday, and I want it to be good for you."

Esther ruffled the top of Mary Elizabeth's hair. "You scoundrel." She caressed her face with both hands and kissed her blossoming daughter who had, when Esther was fair, been a big help ever since they left Brigham. If only she would stop ripening. "Thanks for remembering."

Esther had been dreading her birthday. It was usually the worst day of the year because she waited for everyone to treat her like royalty. More often than not, they didn't even remember the day. And she'd also been dreading the return of the heat, the sun pumping up its bellows. But today, there was magic and a cool breeze in the air. Everybody was cooperating.

She felt very young and light sitting next to Alf in the theater, freshly minted, glowing with the pleasant memories of the day: her forty-three birthday candles, everyone's laughter when she blew them out at last, the taste of the pink frosting roses melting on her tongue, and the sound of the tissue paper being wadded and thrown into the wastebasket before she unpinned and unbuttoned the folded blouse to try it on.

The lights dimmed, and Newsreel filled the screen with footage of Charles and Ann Lindbergh and their empty arms. Esther felt her birthday slipping away, her foolish impulsiveness to forget all her troubles. Lindy's only baby kidnapped. Now dead like her own twins. *But maybe . . .* she reconsidered when Mickey Mouse and his skinny legs strutted across the screen and Mack Sennett's comedy short made her laugh. *Maybe I can be granted one day of pleasure. There are always troubles in the world.*

One long glance at Douglas Fairbanks, Jr., in his opening scene of *It's Tough to Be Famous*, was enough to rescue Esther completely and carry her into a place where everyone's hurts were mended and no one's hearts or lives were broken. Fairbanks—a bit British, proper, a gentleman, honorable and above reproach. She'd watched *Broken Hearts of Hollywood* six times in Brigham City and committed his noble profile to memory.

She surveyed Alf with a side-glance, pretending to watch the film. She sniffed the aroma of hot popcorn, sucked her Jujube to a withered dot, and basked in a moment of contentment. A snatch of heaven. *This is my husband,* she whispered to herself. *Sometimes I forget things have been hard for him, and sometimes I don't understand who he is. But the divine's in him as much as in me. Forgive me, God, for judging. There's nobility in his cheekbones. Maybe he's a bit shorter, more rough complected, but I'd even say there's something of Fairbanks about him. Yes. Alf's handsome. Commanding at times.*

Alf reached out to pat her hand and his mind wandered from the movie to thoughts of his wife. He should have been disinterested after all these years, but Esther could surprise him still. Mulligan's stew. Her rapidly changing moods, her frailty, her devotion to Joseph Smith and Jesus, her repeated attempts to love him from a new angle, her valiant efforts to say nothing against Serena even though this other woman had cornered a measure of his affection. Esther never said anything to Alf except in certain movements she made, but she knew Alf's chemistry, knew how he was like litmus paper that turned passionate under certain conditions. He couldn't hide anything from her, though he had nothing too major to hide, not yet.

He wanted to reach out again and hold her hand. He wanted to take it into his and say thank you for something, somewhere along the long line between them, though he didn't. He knew he had failed her dreams, even his own about love and marriage, but Esther still possessed a mysterious quality that attracted him. She was deep water, not like drops that could be wiped from a surface. He wanted to talk to her and say these things, confess his failures, confess the half-life he'd given her. Out of some perverted sense of respect, he wanted to speak the truth of their marriage, the half-love, pretense, the cycle of being in and out of love and always looking for something better. Greener grass. He knew somehow they both understood, and he wanted to talk about it—congratulate her on her resilience and the reserves she possessed that carried her through all their hard times together.

Instead, he watched the slight movement of her jaws as she sucked a Jujube. He held out the bag of popcorn and watched her pluck a kernel and hold it in her hand. *Little gifts for his wife who would liked to have been a queen. A Jujube crown and popcorn pearls. Queen of the movies where stories are the same at the beginning, middle, and the end, never changed by whim or fancy. Predictable. Stable. Stories on film wound forward and backward around sprockets and reels. Films kept in a round cannister where they stay the same forever.*

He wanted to put her on film right now. She was laughing, pleased, satisfied, happy to have both Alf and Douglas Fairbanks, Jr., at her birthday party. The Birthday Girl. That's how he'd like her to be all the time. Delighted to receive pleasure from him. Happy he was Alf, the man visited by God and the man who could make a difference to people if they'd let him.

He knew what his calling was now. He'd show others there was nothing to fear. Everything—life and death, man-made opinions, and the shifting emotions in a body—was illusory. Everything changed with the weather and the times. There was nothing to fear, not even dying, because in death people would have no will to feel anything, no feelings of sorrow, regret, stupidity. In death there was no feeling. When a man couldn't feel anything, he couldn't feel fear.

Alf would help people when they were down. Lend them money. Trade their scrip when they needed some real entertainment to relieve their relentless work load or when they needed to forget someone or something. He wanted people to have pleasure, to not take it all too seriously. He believed in laughter, a little nepenthe, a dampening of the brain to help make the hard times bearable.

Esther didn't see it his way, of course, but it mattered to him that people should be able to forget when they wanted to, not always be nagged about God watching every move they made. Who knew the truth of these things anyway? Why should he buy into talk of horses stampeding over everyone in the Apocalypse? Why should he buy into fear about the weather and the government and the Depression and a stern God? The sun shone on the righteous and the unrighteous, the rich and the poor. Something was equitable.

Alf was here to help people forget the dark prophecies. He'd seen the darkness of the pit as he looked down between the cracks of coal that cradled his father's body after he untied the knots. He'd seen the blackness. He'd seen the whiteness of his father's face against the blackness of the coal and knew both of them were nothing more than shadow in light, light in shadow, nothing more or less.

His father's breath gone like a snap of fingers. The breath pumping his lungs, the breath heavy with desire as he fathered eleven children, the breath pulling in oxygen while cigar smoke curled out of his nostrils. His breath. Snap. Gone. Neither white or black. Just air. Oxygen. Invisible to the eye, but gone. So noticeable when gone. So still. Pale. White framed by black. A study in still life. White hands relaxed against black coal. And it was nothing to be afraid of because it was quiet. He remembered his father hovering around their family home, sitting in a chair gazing into space. Tired. Gray. A picture of suspension. The moment between breaths. Now crumpled on the coal. Quiet. Telling Alf not to worry about this because there was nothing to fear when you were quiet and still and void of the desire to feel anything.

Looking over at Esther, he knew she wasn't worried about the sun or fire or money or God at the moment. He was happy for her. He held out the popcorn again, asked her how many Jujubes she had left, and how was she enjoying her seat in the air-conditioned movie theater. He knew how to make her happy when he put his mind to it. Things had changed since they'd come to southern Nevada. His footing was sturdier. The ground had stopped shifting so quickly.

And he was making Serena happy, too. Jesus said to love one another, and Alf was obedient to some of the commandments. Though Alf was mainly attending Serena's loneliness, he had one further thought in mind. She wasn't afraid, and he needed to mix his seed with a woman like that. Their child would bring new hope into the world because it wouldn't know fear. It would laugh brashly at the sun. No frightened genes in this child. Alf had always known there was a woman like Serena somewhere, and he'd found her. And he'd make her ultimately happy when the time was right. She'd bear a Tuesday's child, full of grace just like the one in the nursery rhyme Alf's mother recited to him when she tucked the quilt under his chin once in a while when she wasn't too tired. He'd give Serena a child when she was ready. He was good at making babies. He'd be careful of Esther if that happened. He didn't want to hurt her, but surely she could understand his purpose. Esther wouldn't need to know if it happened, except that she would; Esther knew everything.

11

In August of 1932, Nevada's Senator Oddie sent a telegram to Secretary of Interior Wilbur. "The builders of Hoover Dam are abusing their commissary privileges," he claimed, "exploiting the employees and causing unfair competition to the merchants in Boulder City and Las Vegas. Scrip, which can only be used at face value for company store merchandise, deprives workers of the true value of their wages because it can't be cashed anywhere else except at substantial discount. An investigation will be conducted by the Committee of Irrigation and Reclamation, of which I am a member, if conditions are not corrected soon."

Acting Secretary of the Interior Dixon telegraphed Senator Oddie to tell him he'd been seriously misinformed: "Workers are not required to take scrip, but do so at their own election. They receive cash twice a month and scrip in between. Besides," he added, "many of the employees are married, live in their own homes, and are unaffected by mess hall rates. In fact, the postal savings business in Boulder City is booming, which would indicate no disadvantage to the workers."

The text of the exchanges appeared in *The Las Vegas Age*, and suddenly Sam and Serena were advising Alf to look at other options. But as the months and weather shifted into another autumn, the issue seemed to dissolve and float out of sight. No one knew where the buck had stopped, but something was jamming the works, keeping the scrip in print. Alf kept in touch with every shift of political wind and prayed to his god that company scrip would not go away. It served many people well, including himself, of course. However, he did start diversifying . . . a few small loans, but nothing he'd define as a business. Just good will.

"The trouble with lending money," Alf said, leaning his elbows into the lacquered finish of the bar, "is that voluntary return of funds doesn't always happen."

"You're trying to tell me something," Sammy said. His hands caressed the martini glass as if they were cradling a small animal. He stared at the pearl onions stuffed in the olives.

"Dix Ballard. Fifty dollars over two weeks ago, and he promised it back by last Friday. Seven days I'm left holding the bag. It's payday again and he's out of sight."

"Increase the interest."

"And just how does one get that to happen?"

"You need some muscle." Sammy plucked one of the olives from his martini and sucked out the round onion.

"That's not the kind of business I want to run," said Alf. "I'm a decent man. A family man, though I know you don't believe it." His eyes skimmed the room, looking for Dix Ballard as well as Roger Brown, who promised to pay back his loan tonight. "I should have stayed exclusively with scrip. Straight deal on the front end. No waiting around and getting heated up when your money's out to pasture."

"You said you wanted to do it big."

"I do. Of course I do, but this could work into some rough stuff."

"You know I never finished the story about Split-T Cooper, Alf. You wanna know about Split-T?"

"You talking about Split-T Cooper runs the still?" The man on the other side of Sam, dressed in a hard hat, safety belt, and khakis, sat solemnly in front of three glasses, sipping sloe gin from one glass and comparing each level to make sure it was even with the other two. Alf hoped he hadn't been listening to the entire conversation.

"Split-T's mother," the man said with a triple-thick tongue, "thought he was a steak when he was born—couldn't find any brains or eyes or that kind of stuff. No, no. I've got the story wrong. She thought he was the finest meat she'd ever seen. Born with a big red hard-on, splitting her in two when he was born."

Sam turned his back on the man. "Horseface!"

"Nobody's calling me horseface!"

Sammy ignored him.

"Hey imbecile," the man yelled. "I've been up on those cliffs all day dangling like a spider, and nobody calls me horseface. Split-T was a jack-off in his mother's womb."

"You're drunk, man." Alf saw the bouncer pushing his way toward them. "Tell me your bee against Cooper. And maybe you could lower your voice."

"Nobody tells me to lower my voice." The man smashed all three of his shot glasses to the floor. "I don't have no bee against Cooper, little big man, except I hang over cliffs all day while he cooks up potato gin that makes me sick when I swallow all the bugs he didn't bother to screen out. I work. He cultivates bugs. He's yellow. Yellow like his piss gin."

The bouncer was reputed to have been a boxer, but probably in the lightweight division. He came up to the shoulders of the rowdy high scaler and appeared half the weight of the tall timber of a man spewing curses and spittle.

"You're out of here, Scott."

"Who says? Some little runt like you?"

"That's drunk-talking so I'm going to keep my calm. Out of here, fella."

"Your mother's a steak. Fresh meat for maggots."

"You're dead meat," the bouncer said without a change of expression. His fist hit Scott's jaw, and everybody stopped what they were saying to watch the timber fall. The bouncer rubbed his knuckles, then dragged Scott across the wooden floor by his heel.

"Good riddance, don't you think? Hey, there's Brown." Alf raised his arm and waved it impatiently to make sure Brown saw him sitting there, the imperious lender with the upper hand.

"Hell," said Sam, "I ain't ever gonna get that story about Split-T told. He could help you with Ballard, Alf."

"I told you. No rough stuff. I want a decent business."

Brown carried a stack of scrip. "Couldn't get this changed into cash, Alf, but here's the full amount plus five percent. You helped a man in need. Thanks."

"We'll buy a stack of khakis," Alf said. "Two bucks a pair. Use them for drapes. Join us for a gin fizz?"

"No thanks," said Brown. "I sit around you long enough, I'll think I need another loan."

"You seen Dix Ballard around, speaking of loans?"

"Don't know the man," Brown said. "He's not on the highline crew with me."

Sammy jabbed his finger in the middle of Brown's chest. "Well, we've got our eyes open for him. If you happen to meet him, tell him his shadow might be getting stepped on soon. He's two weeks late."

"Hey, Alf . . . you ain't running that kind of a business are you now? That's dirty stuff."

"No, no, don't mind Sam. He thinks I should be a sharper, but I'm trying to get it through his thick head I'm content to provide cash for scrip, end item. That's a valuable service, and nobody gets clipped, either before or after."

"Keep it clean, Alf," Brown said. "You got a nice family and your wife sings into my heart. Heard her at Bobby Turner's funeral last week and can't forget the sound. Take care of her now."

"See you in a few," said Sammy, bored with domestic laundry and Alf's chameleon switches.

"I'm doing my best, Roger bud." Alf lifted his glass in salute. "Speaking of that, I better be getting home. Promised Esther a high-level conference tonight."

"See you around, Alf. It sure feels good to have you paid back. Last time for me."

"Don't apologize for hard knots to crawl through," Alf said. "We all have them."

He drained his glass, then looked twice to check if it was really Cynthia walking his way. She'd been gone for over a year now. Some said she'd been working Vegas, though Alf hadn't seen anything of her since his night when the world seemed too black and weighted down by the probabilities of the strike and Esther's melancholy. Cynthia still had good legs and a way of making him rise up and notice.

"Hey, handsome. Long time no see. I hear you're getting big in the loan business. Sammy tells me about you."

"When did you get back to Boulder?"

"The line-up was getting too hard on me in Tonopah, standing there, waiting to be chosen by some dolt who has no appreciation for the worth of a woman besides her sideshow breasts. I'm ample, no doubt, but there's ample and then there's ample. I'm talking about clear out to China on this one lady named Melba. They all wanted to dive into that." She laughed, coughed on the draw from her cigarette. "You never let me show you how good I can be. Previews—that's all you got. Moon Mama's what they call me."

"You're beautiful, sweetheart. Wish I had some extra time, but I'm pretty close to being scalped if I don't turn my little old Model A in the direction of home."

"Am I getting too old?" she asked, her nose turned up and red at the tip like a very young girl about ready to cry.

"Nothing like that, believe me." Alf crossed his heart. "Promises at home. Things'll be good for you here. You've got style, and they're getting ready to divert part of the river in the next few months. By next spring, the big pour'll start and then the guys'll be pouring in here for you."

"Cynthia, the stopper. The dam on the Colorado, me at the Pass. Should I put a sign over my crib—'Put Your Plug in Here?' "

"You should get a job as a comedian." Alf pocketed the scrip and put change on the bar. "Quick-draw Cynthia."

"Get out of here, you phoney. Say hi to the little woman for me, okay?"

"She'll bring you over a bottle of peaches and a Book of Mormon tomorrow if I tell her about you. A Mason jar full of Elbertas. Kindness bottled in syrup. Then she'll try to convert you to Mormonism. Watch out then. Quilting bees, bazaars, up to your elbows in steam from the food mill. You ready for that? No swearing, booze, tobacco. No interesting sex. All purity, aboveboard. Bowing to God and obeying without question. You'll get on the track and chug right into heaven if Esther gets hold of you."

Alf leaned close to her cheek and bussed her lightly.

"See you later. And Alf, I know it's not my business, but I don't think you and Sammy are suited for each other as business partners. He's got a different set of ideas. I've got a wisdom most people don't respect, but I'd advise you to listen up."

"I'll stay on track. I solemnly promise."

· · · · ·

Four days after he'd been hit by a landslide of ballots marked with bold X's for Franklin Delano Roosevelt, Herbert Hoover suddenly switched his plans. Instead of returning immediately from southern California where he'd visited his son's new home and nursed his campaign wounds, he decided on a one-day side trip to see the Colorado River flowing through Black Canyon for the last time. Its official diversion was scheduled for November 13, 1932. Hoover Dam. The massive construction project he'd sponsored. A symbol of something he'd done well. The people in Washington and the war-debt issue could wait one more day.

The train veered off the main line of the Southern Pacific at Colton, California, where a large crowd cheered him and his words pleading for every

American to unite in the continued recovery of the country. Then he sat back against the plush velvet seat and commiserated with the bleak Mojave Desert and the wind bending every branch away from him.

Hoover's decision was so sudden that the government and Six Companies's officials barely knew he was coming. No chance for gossips or newspapers to carry the story. So Herbert Jensen squinted his eyes as he swept the sidewalk outside the mess hall. He'd been enjoying the feel of dusk gathering and the anticipation of the moon rising, lulled into dreaming by the rhythm of the brush strokes, when he saw a black limousine pull up at the head of a trailing motorcade. Men in suits, ties, felt hats, and wary expressions climbed out. They looked suspiciously at Herbert for a second, then their no-monkey-business darting eyes surveyed rooftops and doorways and alleys and the lone Herbert one more time. A familiar face and body unfolded from the back seat. The famous ruddy face, well sculpted under a felt hat with a grosgrain band. A long black overcoat and charcoal-gray slacks.

Herbert Jensen, alone by himself, sweeping the sidewalks free of empty matchbooks and broken bottles, standing there as if he were Hoover's assigned host. People had congratulated him on having the same name as the President of the United States, and Herbert was proud. Now he'd have a chance to tell Hoover he'd have stood by him and the Republicans if he'd been of age to vote. Had his twenty-first birthday arrived in time, he could have helped.

He'd heard the radio announcers last Tuesday night who sounded defeated themselves as they kept repeating, "Roosevelt, Roosevelt all the way." He'd heard them talking of the quarter of a million people in Times Square, dumbfounded by the crushing assault on their President, the White House, and their futures.

The man walking toward him would always have his vote, but Herbert Jensen was surprised by his mixed feelings. He would have expected to be awed by this man—the smooth pink roundness of his face, the cleft chin, his million-dollar bank account. A few days earlier he would have stared from the sidelines and smiled gently, a conscientious citizen, a man who loved America and its leader. But today, even carrying a broom, he stuck out his right hand as Hoover stepped over the curb—a commoner once again, an orphaned Quaker boy from Iowa who once picked potato bugs to buy fireworks (a penny for every hundred), a man who once delivered newspapers just like Herbert Jensen.

"Welcome to Boulder City," he said. "Herbert Jensen's my name. First name just like yours."

"Good evening, young man," Hoover said, not avoiding his eyes.

"I would have voted for you, sir."

"So, you didn't buy Roosevelt's 'Forgotten Man' jingo, then?"

"No, sir. We might be a battered ship, but we're seaworthy. Right, sir?"

"Right. You carry on, young man. Your kindness is a credit to our nation."

By then, the rest of the motorcade had pulled in behind the limousine. Car doors were flying open everywhere. Stephen Bechtel, Herbert recognized. Felix Kahn and Henry Kaiser. Elwood Mead, the commissioner of the Bureau of Reclamation, and Ray Lyman Wilbur. Herbert looked in vain for A. P. His visits were less and less frequent these days, though the tall, white-haired septuagenarian still commanded respect when he arrived in Boulder City with a VIP or one of his grandchildren whom he wanted to see his greatest achievement. The Executive Committee was sweeping Hoover into the mess hall, through the store and back out the doors where Herbert worked his broom. They slammed themselves into their automobiles and sped off to Hoover Dam—the name everybody had to remind themselves to use. "Hoover" was only a moniker to the townspeople who still called the project "Boulder."

The official name had been Hoover since 1931 when Wilbur pointed out that the building site had been shifted from Boulder to Black Canyon. What better name than Hoover, he reasoned, who had been the chief negotiator between the seven Colorado River states? As one-time Secretary of Commerce and Chairman of the Colorado River Commission, Hoover worked for three years to hammer out an agreement with Colorado, Utah, Nevada, California, New Mexico, and eventually Arizona. As a concerned engineer, he'd been the one to stress the importance of this work to President Coolidge and Congress. This suggestion met with Cabinet and Department of the Interior approval, something of a life buoy in the rising sea of distress, but nobody asked the people near the dam who'd grown comfortable with their new home, its name, and its tendrils of tradition.

The dusty motorcade climbed out of town on the Nevada Highway while Herbert leaned on his broom. He ran inside, begging his boss's lenience even before he found him. "The end of my shift is only twenty minutes away. Please? Hoover said I was a credit to the nation," he bragged to Cox, not meaning to brag, just full of his bursting feelings.

Cox smiled. "Sure. Go follow the dead."

Nothing subdued Herbert as he ran home, finding his mother and Mary Elizabeth in hair rags and bathrobes, the other girls ready for bed. "Come on," he shouted. "Is the car here?"

"Your father hasn't come home yet," Esther said.

"But we've got to get down to the dam. President Hoover's here."

"President Hoover? Really?" Esther tightened the belt on her chenille robe, obviously comfortable with the evening, her old slippers, and the nearness of sleep. "The man's brave to show his face."

"His wife's here, too. I saw her peeking out the window."

"I've heard she's beautiful."

"Hurry up, then. Let's get down there, Mother. This is history."

"Just hold your horses, young man. My body hasn't quite made up its mind to move as quick as you need me to." She laughed. "Come on body, let's move. Herbert's proposing adventure!"

Herbert pushed her gently into the bedroom. *She seems good tonight,* he thought. *Better than she's been for a while. When everything else is dying or going into hibernation, she starts blooming like a flower in the snow.*

"Where's the car, Mother?"

Her nose wrinkled with impatience. "I'm pretty sure your father's over at Serena Bishop's house having one of his business meetings with her brother Sam. Why don't Mary Elizabeth and I get dressed? We'll be ready for you in ten minutes. Go over and get the car, and tell him he can walk home when he's finished with his precious business."

"I want to go," Rebecca insisted, leaning on the bedroom door handle. "Why does Mary Elizabeth get to go and I have to stay home all the time? You always leave me with Inez. Always." Her eyes clouded with moisture.

"I need you, Rebecca. Don't be stubborn."

"I don't want to watch Inez. I want to go somewhere besides church and school or here babysitting Inez."

"I'll give you extra money for treats at the Saturday matinee."

Rebecca had a sweet tooth like her mother. They challenged each other to contests when they went to the movies together: who could stretch their Sugar Daddy the longest before it curled under. So her resolve could always be weakened by certain promises. "Oh, all right," she said, though she embellished her acceptance with a pout and mournful eyes.

"Next time," Esther said. Then she picked up lanky Rebecca and whirled her until her legs propelled out and accidentally hit a cabinet door. "Oh, I'm sorry, sweet Rebecca. I try to make things right, and they go wrong. Clumsy me." She bent over to kiss her daughter's shin.

"Mother, you're never going to be ready." Herbert charged toward the door, yelling to Mary Elizabeth to hurry. He was personally determined his father would be in the car when he returned for these passengers. He sprinted up Avenue B, then slowed to a walk after his breath came hard. *Why can't my father be completely in love with Mother? She's like exquisitely blown glass, but full of life when she feels well. She's a faithful woman who only wants to do right by God, who embodies the ultimate compassion and knows the best way for humans to set oars in rough seas. Why can't Dad yield to her, maybe in just a place or two, and let her know her desires matter as much as his? She'd be enough for him if he'd get his eyes off all the other possibilities and savor the pearl of great price in his own home.*

He rounded the corner onto Avenue D, paused to check for his father's parked car, then ran until he reached the top of Serena's front steps. She answered the door. "Oh hi, Herbert. You looking for your Dad?"

"He's got to come right now. We're on our way to see Hoover down at the dam."

Alf appeared in the half-open frame. "Herbert! What are you doing here?"

"We need you and the car. President Hoover's down at the dam site."

"You're kidding me!" Alf was a shade away from inebriation, Herbert noticed. Maybe Herbert had gotten there in time to keep his mother from something she didn't need tonight.

"No, Dad. Come on. Mom and Mary Elizabeth are almost ready."

"Let me get my overcoat, wash up a little."

"Give me the keys so I can start the car."

"Okay, okay. You'd think there was a fire or something."

Herbert idled the car until it stopped jumping. He hoped cold water would rescue his father. Then he thought of a pearl he'd seen in an oyster once, a dusky seed pearl enveloped in the fleshy insides, almost imperceptible if he hadn't been told it was there. Like his mother. He wanted his father to see something besides the broken shell of Esther which couldn't quite repair itself. Tonight she was vibrant, and his dad should be clear-headed so he'd see it.

After Alf got in the car, Herbert stepped on the gas, zipped to the top of Avenue D, and raced for B without stopping at the corners.

"Take it easy," Alf said. "You'd better let me drive."

"It's my turn tonight, Dad." Herbert pulled up to the curb in front of their home. "Be right back."

He banged through the door. No one was ready, though Esther was in the finishing stages, splashing powder on her face and nagging Mary Elizabeth to hurry. After all, she carped, this wasn't an official reception for the President, no one would be worried about her daughter's appearance and wouldn't she please have consideration for the rest of them and come on, right now.

Then Alf burst in the door, too. "Hurry up, you women."

"Oh good," Esther said. "You're coming too. How wonderful!" She kissed a print of red lips on Alf's cheek. "A printing press of love," she teased. "Everyone will know what you've been doing!" And then she blushed. "I'm not implying anything about where you've been," she added quickly as if embarrassed by the cutting edge of her thoughts.

Herbert hoped that if she noticed the alcohol on Alf's breath, she'd refrain from diatribe. He wanted this night to be magical like the rest of his day.

"Everybody bundle up," Alf said. "The wind isn't strong, but it's full of the Eskimo tonight. You look like you're going on the warpath, Mary Elizabeth. Who's all that paint for?"

"The Apaches on the cliffs, mein Papa. I dibs front seat with Herbert," and she was out the door.

The magic held frail command of the Jensens while the car hummed over the pavement, the headlights reflecting off the white paint of the guardrails. Herbert narrated the story of his chance meeting with Hoover, exaggerating the actions of the Secret Service men, making the whole encounter grand and glorious as the wheels of the Jensen family car rolled toward Hoover Dam.

"Shine on, shine on harvest moon," Alf sang. "Up in the sky," Esther harmonized. "I ain't had no lovin' since January, February, June or July." Alf and Esther looked at each other with eyes that could have been bitter and both decided to smile instead. A miniature truce. Herbert watched the exchange in the rearview mirror and felt happy. November. A walnut-shaped moon. No history for a few minutes.

"Look at the glow!" Herbert said as he opened the car doors for his mother and sister. Hundreds of floodlights with reflectors made from metal dishpans embellished the already generous moonlight. Herbert had never seen this much light after sunset. Usually, when he came here to sit at the top of the cliffs at night to wish he were part of the action, the floodlights seemed eerie and unnatural, the shadows they cast like strange hoodoos. But this was an occasion of light: a waxing moon, dozens of floodlights at the cliff's edge, hundreds of them illuminating the mile-deep canyon. The occasion felt like a wedding, night and day the bride and groom.

"Look, Mom and Dad," Herbert shouted above the sound of trucks, water, and wind. "They're pouring the cofferdam right now!" They all crowded near the mesh-wire fence and clutched it as they tried to see through its patterned weave.

The floodlights below lit a strange configuration of land and water. The low water of the Colorado had been forced into the Arizona half of the channel by a barrier of fill—muck from the Nevada spillway tunnel. Since September, the fill had been poured from the river's edge, out to and down the center of the river, then back to the Nevada shore. Now, the fill was an earthen fence around a rough stretch of barren riverbed where the imprisoned water had been pumped back into the flowing half of the river. At that very moment three electric shovels were digging away at the silt and sand inside the barrier while a long line of dump trucks waited on the construction road upstream for their turn to drive on the wooden trestle bridge and dump their ton of rock into the Colorado.

"By noon tomorrow," Alf said, "the rest of the river in that channel is ancient history. Tunnel number four's going to carry her away from her bed as soon as that rock's poured all the way across and the dynamite blows the barrier at the head of the tunnel. Clockwork at its best. So what do you think of that, Esther?"

"I think it's time to listen to the Honorable Mr. Hoover, who's already started speaking."

"Shhh. Shhh." Alf put his finger to his lips and grinned. "What do you think of that down there? Tell me, my sweet one."

"Shhh, shhh yourself, Alf. You've been drinking again."

Herbert watched her fold her arms and look straight ahead, no redeeming glance for her husband. He wished for once she could have kept quiet, just once on this special occasion. He hated the tension, the silences.

Hoover stood next to a *DANGER—Do Not Throw Rocks, Men Working Below* sign as he spoke to the engineers, Six Companies and government officials, and some dam workers.

"This is not the first time I have visited the site of this great dam," Hoover was saying. "And it is giving me extraordinary pleasure to see the great dream I have long held taking form in actual reality of stone and cement.

"It is now ten years since I became chairman of the Colorado River

Commission. That commission solved the legal conflicts as to water rights amongst six of the states which had long held up any possibility of the realization of these works. Three years of negotiations finally closed with the Santa Fe Compact, the first time that a provision in the Constitution of the United States for treaties amongst the several states was utilized on so great a scale. The compact was ratified by six states and is held open to the seventh to join at any time it may desire.

"I had the satisfaction of presenting, both as engineer and as head of the commission, to President Coolidge and to the Congress, the great importance of these works, as well as a further part in the drafting of the final legislation which ultimately brought them into being."

Herbert's attention was interrupted by his mother who was eagle-eyeing Mary Elizabeth as she unsubtly searched for someone in the small crowd.

"Mary Elizabeth," she whispered harshly. "Pay attention!"

Mary Elizabeth scowled and sidestepped away. Herbert worried about the attention she received from some of the unattached dam workers. He often saw her talking to this one or that, putting her hands on those strange men's shoulders, laughing like a lunatic over some asinine joke.

She seemed to have more energy than her body could contain, erupting out of adolescent chunkiness into an unmanageable beauty. Her laugh, her way of tossing her arms into the air and shaking her hips at convention frightened Herbert. He'd spent many hours talking to her about spiritual matters, about the eternities and how they would always be together if they lived worthily. Brother. Sister. Nighttime promises to remain a united family beyond this earth life. They'd promised each other, their right hands together on a stack of the King James Bible, the Book of Mormon, the Doctrine & Covenants, and the Pearl of Great Price. They'd cherish the Gospel and not disappoint their mother as Jack had.

But when Mary Elizabeth went out in the light of day, she seemed like a weed grown from the seed of good intention. Her promises faded like colored cloth in sunlight.

"To understand its purpose," Hoover was saying, "our people must realize the Colorado River in its freshets from the snows of the Rocky Mountains flows at a rate as great as that of Niagara. In the dry season it diminishes to less than five percent of its maximum flow."

It's as though, Herbert thought, viewing a great man on the descent, *someone in the audience might still be wondering about the massive river ready to be subdued and turned out of its bank for the advancement of humankind. Why's he trying to convince us?*

"Its major purposes are four in number: to stabilize the flow of the river; to provide a supply of domestic water accessible to Southern California and parts of Arizona; to provide an adequate supply of irrigation water to Arizona, the Imperial Valley and other valleys of Southern California; and to preserve American rights in the flow of the river."

Herbert listened carefully to see if the President would say anything about the campaign, but, with one exception, Hoover spoke as if nothing existed except the impressive project surrounding him. The President seemed pacified by this reminder of science and its possibilities, the practical application of knowledge for the advancement of civilization. There was only one note of regret in his speech that Herbert could detect.

"I hope to be present at the dam's final completion as a bystander. Even so I shall feel a special personal satisfaction."

A bystander. An 'even so.' Just because someone new gets elected, a man who started a thing is swept aside, almost like he wasn't there or doesn't really matter when the curtain is drawn. Even presidents and kings are subject to being swept away.

"But the whole of this translates into something infinitely more important." Hoover seemed to recapture a spirit of purpose with these words, to recover from his momentary lapse into the truth of his new position. "It translates itself into millions of happy homes for Americans out under the blue sky of the West. The spread of its values in human happiness is beyond computation."

The applause was long and loud, though thin because of numbers, but everyone was proud, the buttons on their shirts and coats reflecting the overhead moon sprouting ever larger in the black ink sky. "Hoover, Hoover, Hoover," some of them chanted, and the President raised his arms and clasped both hands overhead. The wounding. The healing. The wind flapping the corners of coats and cuffs of trousers. This small crowd and Herbert Jensen— salve for the wounded.

Mary Elizabeth disappeared into the crowd while Esther, Alf, and Herbert shook hands with some of their friends and commented on Hoover's speech, its appropriateness, and the shame of his defeat. But the subject was less black and white than it had been the week before. Even Boulder City, which everyone thought was a solid Hoover stronghold, had gone with the tide of the country and started believing that FDR would save them because Hoover was just plain incapable.

"But Hoover's impotent in a national crisis," Lanny Rector was saying to Esther in a loud voice. Herbert took her arm to steer her away from the ranting. She'd stood by her President through the election and still did. Rector better be careful.

"Remember what you always told me, Mother. Don't discuss religion or politics. It's not safe."

"Don't tell me what I can and can't say." Esther jerked her arm away from Herbert's hold. "I should give that Rector a piece of my mind. And where's Mary Elizabeth? She spent the whole speech looking around for some fresh punk from who knows where, can't wait to get next to a man of any kind. You'd think nobody ever taught her anything about anything."

"Esther," Alf called from across several conversations. "Come over here and meet Scott Nelson." Esther squeezed through the crowd. "Scott here thinks maybe I can find better work as soon as this river is diverted, which is tomorrow. Lots of people needed to scrape the canyon bottom clean. What do you think?"

"Don't you like the greengrocer's job?"

"Well, I've been doing it for a year and a half now. You know that's too long for me."

"But it's a nice job, Alf. You're not far away from home, and you're out of danger of falling rocks and swinging cables."

"But I'd like to be down in the canyon, right Scott? Four thousand men stuffed into five thousand feet of space. Working shoulder to shoulder. Comraderie."

"Why can't you let well enough alone?"

"Why can't you be a little more adventurous, Esther? Something's always too hot, too high, too dangerous—"

"Nobody over thirty-five years of age can stand that canyon, let alone you. What are you blowing off about? And why can't you stay home more. You're always off to some meeting—" Esther broke off her words. Herbert watched her chewing them, trying to swallow them back down. She smiled at Scott Nelson. "Excuse us, Scott. These little domestic issues will pop out sometimes."

No eruptions, please, Herbert prayed. "What about me?" he asked Scott who looked him over carefully. "Afraid you're a bit on the small side," Scott said, then turned his attention back to Esther.

"Didn't mean to interfere, Ma'am, but Alf was saying he was a little tired of trimming lettuce. There are a few openings if he wants to get down there, especially if he already has a job with Six."

"I'm always one to be cautious." Esther laughed nervously and absent-mindedly rubbed her eyetooth in case it had a lipstick smudge on it. "He's been on a lot of payrolls."

"Nice to meet you, Ma'am. Hope we'll meet again. Alf," Scott shook his hand, "we'll be seeing you around. Maybe down there." He leaned toward the riverbed where the Colorado still rushed through the narrowed channel. "That sound won't be here tomorrow."

Herbert saw Mary Elizabeth first. She was holding two hands of a workman and looking straight at him rather than turning her head to the side like a proper female. He pushed through the crowd and took one of her hands. "Come on, time to go," he said, avoiding the young man standing there.

"Don't you want to meet Chris?" she asked, one hand held by Herbert, the other still in Chris's. "Chris Johns from Winslow, Arizona. He's a concrete puddler. Look at those feet, would you?" Mary Elizabeth laughed brashly, the Black Canyon for her stage. "Longfellows. Good for stomping wet cement." She clapped her hands, slapped them on her knees, and sang a few bars of "Mississippi Mud" from one of her self-designed vaudeville routines, a remnant from the streets of Ely. "This is my brother Herbert."

"Nice to meet you." The young men shook hands.

Chris's hand was rough in Herbert's. Herbert who washed dishes, swept sidewalks, and worked in the clerical offices every time he was near an earth-moving project. *These rough hands. How can they move anything inside Mary Elizabeth? What does this roughness feel like to her?* And Herbert suddenly felt afraid, as he did when he stood by the ocean in San Diego and watched tides come and go, washing away little lives without notice, washing sand castles to grains. And he heard the river racing through the canyon and was reminded of the same thing.

"Come on, Mary Elizabeth. Mom and Dad are waiting for us."

"I'm riding with Chris on the transport."

"You can't do that!"

"Yes, I can. There's ample moon, and the wind's not too harsh. I've never ridden on a transport. I'll be like a dam builder." She flexed both arms.

"Mother won't like it."

"So . . . big deal. Mother doesn't like anything that doesn't fit her picture. She's gonna kill herself and all of us with her notions of perfection."

"She's fighting for our salvation. Come on. Come with us."

"Don't be such a worrier. I'll be fine and won't be much later than you'll be."

"Don't come to me when you're up to your neck in you know what." Herbert fought his frustration as he pushed back through the crowd and the group of admirers surrounding the President. Maybe, if his eyes and Hoover's could meet one more time. . . . He tried to forget his stubborn sister as well as his parents who couldn't stop the urge to go for each other's jugulars. He couldn't arbitrate for any of them right now.

He waited for Hoover to look over and give him some sign of recognition, something like brothers would. Herbert knew what the President must be feeling. How it felt to lose. But Hoover was engaged with the trajectories of pointing fingers showing him this and that, and Herbert Jensen was not noticed.

And then he saw A. P., the aging man with his mass of white hair, someone who never quite seemed tangible to Herbert, even if he had come to dinner and answered a few of his questions. He was a myth Herbert heard about for years, and he'd stepped out of the storybook right into Herbert's living room. He treated Esther as a lady, the family like insiders, and when he sat on the sofa next to his mother as if they really were old friends, he asked her to sing "God Bless America." He'd even gotten sentimental after the song, but A. P. was still a myth to Herbert—a big compared to his little conception of himself and his chances. A. P. was ultra-dignified as he stepped carefully through the construction maze and conversed with other VIPs.

And there the man was, magnified in the artificial light from the electroliers, the Jensens' tether, their terrestrial savior, walking and talking with the President and the Secretary of Interior. He was too involved to notice Herbert trying to lay claim to the inner circle he belonged to, briefly, on the steps of the mess hall.

But, Herbert rationalized, he knew two of these men. Some of the most important in the country and the West. He'd talked with them. Even had one of them in his own home and another of them commenting on his good character. He'd had his share of blessings and shouldn't expect more.

Maybe this was like his one-time encounter with a twelve-point stag near the pines in Ely. He'd been hunting with Jack and his friends. Unable to stand the sight of them skinning the doe they'd shot by accident, he'd gone to sit and think in the thin scattering of snow and the half-light flickering through the junipers. And there it was. The most magnificent animal he'd ever seen. Twelve points on its rack. A gift. The stag watched Herbert, then disappeared into the foliage without a sound, not one twig cracking.

Herbert shivered in the scant snow for four hours in hopes of another glimpse, and as he waited, the stag's glory turned to thin air and uncertainty. Herbert. A doubting Thomas. His necessity to see twice made him doubt what he'd seen, even though he'd never forgotten.

Before he rejoined his parents to tell them about Mary Elizabeth and listen to them lament all the way back to Boulder City, he repeated Hoover's words to establish them firmly in his memory. "Young man. Your kindness is a credit to our nation."

He thanked God for this singular gift. No repeats necessary.

•   •   •   •   •

She stood over her ironing board on New Year's morning, remembering, recasting, reordering the past year in her mind before she made her resolutions for the coming year. Thanks to the Boulder Theater, Esther had made it through 1932. The movie changed four times a week, and since the theater's opening Esther had braved whatever weather and walked three blocks to every new afternoon showing. Sometimes she'd sit by her friend, Conway Mitchell, and they'd both lean back in their chairs and merge with the celluloid images. Maybe Conway was her friend. She wasn't sure.

Their Avenue B home was a vast improvement over cardboard and sheet walls, but when last summer had brought its heat back to southern Nevada, Esther's dream home seemed only a slightly better can in which to seal the Jensens. They had one small electric fan purchased from the Six Companies's store, its cool air coverage a meager four square feet. There was not enough water for a lawn or any peach or apricot blossoms to scent the air outside her window.

All summer, after her early morning ironing, breakfast, the good-byes and the minimal tidying, she fell onto the sofa like a draped sheet. The boiling ocean of air flattened her to the thick cushions. Esther on her side, a fish out of water, one open eye watching for salvation—an ancestor, maybe Uncle Woolley, with an eternal hose full of running water. Only the inviting thought of the dark, cool, Boulder Theater was enough to rouse Esther from her midday naps.

She gave Rebecca three cents to watch Inez (three babysitting jobs plus a one-cent bonus, enough to pay for her ticket to the Saturday morning matinee). Esther left her home embroidering the pillowcases she'd made to sell to laundry customers. But before she closed the front door, Rebecca was already nodding and drifting into the heat's trance.

Even Sunday couldn't compete with the movies during the past six months. The Palm Mortuary where the Mormons met had odors. Even though the mortuary owners bought a pump organ that gave the congregation and Esther a sense of stability, the heat seemed heavier there. Maybe the dead pulled the air closer to wrap themselves in. And when she sat in church, usually without Alf, she couldn't release his absence from her mind. She couldn't turn her heart to Jesus during the sacrament. As hard as she tried to pinch her eyes shut and wait for the smiling Savior holding his arms out to her, she only saw Alf shining his new car, his chamois circling while he angled to see his reflection in the buffed polish. How could he even think of a new car when they barely had enough to clothe and feed everybody, even with Herbert's salary? He seemed to think he could rub the magic lamp of credit and make that green car appear without any effect on anyone. This was January, 1933, when most of the banks across the country were folding up like paper houses. No one was putting on the Ritz, though Alf seemed to think he needed to. Everyone knew who had what and where and when, and there was an unspoken neighborhood ethic on the alphabet streets that no one pretended to have money because no one did.

"My business," he told Esther.

"I can't make those payments," she said. "Six hundred eighty-five dollars would need a gold mine."

"My partner is covering the payments. Don't you worry," he said. "I haven't changed jobs yet. And we've been almost two years in one place. Doesn't that make you happy, Esther?" But she worried anyway. He seemed more of a stranger to Esther than ever, always busy, always talking about his plans that would make them rich, but not really telling her anything. Never home right after work anymore because of those plans, often smelling of some kind of alcohol. She'd always suspected what money would do for him if he had it, and he seemed to be acting out her suspicions lately. When she asked for extras, he said he had nothing more than he was already making at the grocery, but he was certainly acting as if he were personally papered in green treasury bills, especially when he drove around in his new Chevrolet with the running boards, open fenders, and six cylinders.

"It sounds fishy to me," she said often.

"Just a brilliant scheme to provide men with an option to the company store. Myself and Sam Konevic are providing a viable service. Trust me."

So Esther lived for the four afternoons a week she could sit at the picture show in front of the swamp cooler's duct. Then she'd relax, there in the dark cave of the Boulder Theater, images of life on the walls, moving pictures, eyes, smiles, nothing real to deal with except sometimes Conway Mitchell's hand.

"These are nothing more than friendly hands wanting to protect a good friend," he'd say when he enveloped her hand in two of his.

The movies. The cool. The dark. No one to worry about. A way to numb life out so it wouldn't hurt. Forty cents for salvation. Cool. And sometimes Con Mitchell's hand to hold in the dark.

And then, her iron pressing a pleat into a shirt front, she remembered the school committee. She flushed. She'd exerted a tremendous amount of will-power to form that committee after A. P.'s brother's death which suggested the possibility A. P. might follow suit.

Esther did have the idea for the temporary school in the Ranger Station, but she lost her place as chairman after Thelma was so bold. She'd rehearsed her thoughts so many times about the eternal women and children who never seemed an important part of engineering feats. Then she couldn't speak effectively. So vague. So inept. Weak.

All Esther could remember was her futile attempt to speak in front of Mr. Nichols and his magnificent view of the Colorado.

Thelma Parker rescued Esther who failed to speak with certainty. "She's trying to say. . . ." Thelma translated for Esther. Aaron for Moses.

She's trying to say . . . she's trying to say. . . . Maybe I'm invisible, so no one can hear or see me.

Even at the September dedication of the new red-tile-roofed elementary school with its geometric patterns of light and dark brick and the date 1932 set at the top of its east wall, Mr. Nichols introduced Thelma first.

"The backbone of The Mothers for the School Children of Boulder City—Thelma Black," he said. His bow tie bobbed when he swallowed. He asked all three of the committee to stand then, but didn't announce Esther or Dorothy. A. P., who was at the dedication to present a check for $18,800 from Six Companies to pay teachers' salaries, smiled at Esther, but Esther was humiliated. He should have been able to feel pride in her as chairman and organizer, but Thelma had taken it away from her. Rescuer. Bossy. No. Not really. Esther had given it away.

"She's trying to say. . . ." The words stuck in a groove in Esther's head. *Why can't I just say things, not try to say them?*

This was all a blur—Mr. Nichols's tie that spun like a paper pinwheel in her mind, the apologetic stammers Esther made when it was her turn to speak to him about the need for real schools, the bottom-line feeling of being unnecessary because, after all, she was only the wife of the greengrocer who had gotten a job because of a shirt-tail relative who was almost a fabrication in her mind. She shouldn't have tried to speak, she decided. It should be someone legitimate. One of the real people. Why hadn't she sung for Mr. Nichols who seemed so far removed and precise? *Let me sing*, she could have announced. *Then you'll really know what I want to say.* If only she'd been braver. She ground her teeth while she ironed, remembering the committee, her ineptness, even though she'd accomplished her purpose—a temporary— and—since the end of September—a real school.

And Esther had walked every evening after the summer sun gave up for the day. She walked and walked until she hardly knew she was walking any more, like an air current floating over sidewalks. Esther was a common sight walking up and down B, C, D, and F avenues, California, Arizona, Wyoming, New Mexico streets on her broad-heeled black shoes. She never walked on Birch, Ash, or Denver streets where the spacious government houses had been built, every one of them different in some way, individual, gracious, apart. Somehow she didn't belong in that world, but among the rows of boxes built to be bulldozed after the dam was completed. The repeats. The over and over houses like her own. "I'm grateful. I'm grateful," she told herself as she ironed. "I have a home. Children. A husband, sometimes. I have God who loves me. I'm grateful. That's it. Yes!"

Sometimes during her summer walks she saw the hulking shadows sitting on the front steps of their homes, but didn't care to distinguish their faces in the night light or listen to them whispering, "There goes that woman again. Looks like she can't find herself." After sunset, the people were shadows, indistinguishable leaves on trees, opaque cardboard figures of black against shifting configurations of light.

Esther's memories: heat framing a collage of Irene Dunne, Walter Huston, Douglas Fairbanks, Paul Muni, screen faces with soft filters blurring their contours, Ruby Keeler tap dancing, engineers' stern faces, Esther walking and walking. Esther sitting on a folding chair in a row at the Palm Mortuary, chewing sacrament bread and entreating God to hold her hand. Maybe Conway was his messenger. Conway was kind. He understood her need for perfection as a matter of art. But Conway was not her husband, not the one to whom she'd promised her life. The pictures crowded the kitchen while she ironed.

All summer, she'd chosen 4:00 a.m. for her ironing because there were gentle fingers of light crawling through her kitchen window, serenity before the sun blasted out like a bull from its stall at the rodeo. A bull. "Bull" Wilson winking at Mary Elizabeth who was too young to have attention paid her, right in an aisle of the drugstore, right in front of Esther. Chris Johns, the concrete stomper coming by in his car, opening and shutting the door for her daughter, Esther saying "No" to her, Mary Elizabeth throwing a tantrum, screaming "Leave me alone. I know a thing or two." Jack working in an even more dangerous job as a flagman signaling dump trucks as they hauled muck out of the river bottom. Jack waving flags at workhorse trucks with canopies over the drivers' heads to protect them from falling rock. But Jack had no canopy over his head, neither temporally nor spiritually. And Alf disappearing and drinking himself numb. A sea of booze for Alf's boat to sail away.

Now, this first day of January, 1933, Esther also chose 4:00 A.M. to iron because it was the only time no one wanted anything from her. In this quiet, she could enjoy the feeling of something finished. Hung on a hanger. Done. Even though she saw the same articles of clothing week after week, she still loved the look of the blouses, dresses, and work shirts hanging on the rope line across her kitchen. Her reputation for delicately ironed sleeves and collars had grown considerably; the level of dimes, quarters, and nickels grew higher inside her blue teapot, even enough for Christmas. A play tractor for Inez, an angora sweater for Mary Elizabeth, an envelope with college money for Herbert. And always something for the movies.

As she stood ironing, the meetings and the bow ties and the seemingly cool, collected men who lived in brick houses, her tempest of a daughter whose hormones were bigger than her brain, Conway Mitchell's warm hand which reminded her she was no different from Mary Elizabeth who only wanted aliveness after all, flickered in her memory along with flashes of Irene Dunne in *Anne Vickers*, happy to be saved from ambition by love. Whirling. Rows of box houses set in sand like dominoes. A gone-mad ball of sun whitening the entire sky. Rows of Model A's lining the streets. Giant joshuas in front yards of migrating sand that blew away and blew back again in new formations. And the flowing river of workers coming and going on truck transports, plodding down the sand-covered streets in their white shirts, khakis, overalls, and felt halts with sweat stains above the grosgrain ribbon bands. Wooden crosses supporting clotheslines where pillowcases and diapers stiffened into boards. Jack's wedding at the Grace Community Church making Esther cry until she forgot her manners and didn't smile at her new daughter-in-law. The nights waiting supper for Alf, giving up and leaving the plate on the drainboard. Alf driving up one afternoon in a brand new car wearing his new suit and, on the back of his head, a straw bowler she'd never seen before. Esther holding tears back with her fingers and telling him she'd just made the final payment on their absolutely reliable and suitable Model A the day before. Esther borrowing money from her blue teapot for food. Alf telling her she was going insane and he was sick of her jellied backbone that couldn't hold up in any kind of a storm. Esther shouting she was not crazy, only sick for all the things her heart kept asking for. Con Mitchell asking her if she was all right, again and again and even again, sitting by her in the movie theater, holding her hand, and sharing Jujubes. Con Mitchell giving her free admission because she was a loyal customer and saying he was going to have some kind of a talent show in the spring and would she like to sing? And then she tried to swallow the memory of Conway's hand sliding up her thigh, under her dress, his fingers touching her, closer and closer, and Esther wanting the touch of his fingers, but pulling them away, remembering promises, killing her desire in favor of truth she thought she knew. And then seeing Serena Bishop slumping down in the seat of Alf's car when they passed Esther as she walked her ghostly vigil through town. Nights of pacing the streets, up and down, invisible in the night light, a sliver of shadow pacing the town, drifting in and out of night patterns on the sidewalk.

The children swirled into the picture, continual movement at the edges of Esther's iron, their shapes blurring, their words half-heard echoes. Esther, a mannequin ironing blouses, skirts, her children's playclothes, cooking breakfast and dinner each day even when no one felt like eating, drying tears and sweat from children's foreheads and cheeks, mending rips and missing buttons.

Her children had a mother, but only the shell of one. Esther prayed they wouldn't know the difference, prayed she'd be able to hold onto the cord that connected her to them. She felt the cord in her hands every day. Heavy. Thick. Jute. Slipping in her hands, burning the skin. Conway's hand. Esther slipping to hell.

The iron she now held in her hand felt like another burning against her red palms. Always the sensation of burning. Every nerve ending sensitive to the idea of burning, well instructed to fear heat. She breathed deeply, her way of escaping the fire. But maybe she wasn't in the fire. It was winter. The first day of a brand new year. She was home. She was standing at the ironing board, breathing deeply, and remembering who she was and what she had left to do. First step, she had to be prepared mentally when everyone wakened. She'd piece the tatters of herself and her unruly mind together, like scattered scraps from a sewing bag stitched into a quilt. The fire. The white sheets wrapping her like a mummy. Winter-white face, charred body. The memories whirled as she hung the last shirt on the rope line. Finished. Something completed. Done. With the last stroke of the iron, the spinning ball of memories rolled to a corner to rest.

Esther sighed, unplugged the iron, and before she had time to write down her New Year's resolution that she would be calm and satisfied with her lot in life, the phone rang. Her mother, Zina, with news. A. P. had a heart attack during the night. In his basement. In Ogden. He was gone.

• • • • •

The dam site. The river no longer flowed in its course of choice. It had been wrestled into man-made tunnels. Even its bedrock had lost its character and was now a smooth, bland foundation soon to be buried under a mountain of concrete.

"See those crudely painted white dashes on the canyon walls?" Alf held Inez with one arm and pointed for Esther, Mary Elizabeth, and Rebecca's benefit as they stood at the roughhewn Lookout Point, a chain link fence shaped like a batter's cage. "In a few days the dirt fill will reach those marks. They designate the finished contour for the upstream coffer dam that'll keep the river away from the building site. Look at those caterpillars spreading sand and gravel and those jackhammers chopping those grooves to anchor some counterforts."

"This doesn't look like the canyon anymore," Esther said. "It feels wrong."

Cables and footbridges were strung across the canyon. Towers in the shape of pyramids jutted out from high rocks: heavy structural steel enclosed in corrugated sheet iron.

"No wood in those towers," Alf said. "Fire prevention. Those extra steel trestles make it possible for runways to extend out over the edge."

"Those workmen on the trestles look like ants," Mary Elizabeth said, her attention given totally to the indistinguishable men below as if hoping for one to wave in recognition.

"It's not right to do this to the river," Esther said, shaking her head that was covered by a gray cloche to keep the cold wind out of her ears.

"You're just worried about losing A. P.," Alf said. "Look, Esther. Those head towers are seventy-five feet high." Alf accented each number with pride. He could take A. P.'s place for her. Knowledge. Security. She'd been wandering through the few rooms of their house for the past week, unable to remember what motivated her to go in one or out of another. "Tail towers are forty-two. And there's the road where Jack used to drive truck until he got hired on as flagman. See if you can see him down there waving a flag."

"Look at those baskets," Rebecca shouted. "There are men flying in baskets."

"Look more carefully, Rebecca," Alf said. He pointed his finger like it was the sight blade of a rifle on her shoulder. "Those baskets are called skips, and they're hooked to aerial cables that stretch all the way across the canyon. That one right there's Highline number eleven—The Widowmaker. One man rode a load of lumber to his death a few weeks ago. The line broke. And before that there was a hook tender riding an agitator. Same thing."

"Why are you telling her those stories, Alf?" Esther said in that irritated voice Alf heard often these days. "What do you want? Nightmares?"

"Most of the time things are okay, Rebecca," Alf tempered. "See the skip tender standing on that ledge? He'll wave his flag when it's time to slow the skip. Those men in the skips drop seven hundred feet in less than three minutes, where it'd take a man about twenty or thirty minutes to get to the canyon floor if he drove on the highway. See, look! There's the flag waving. He's telling the hoistman to slow the skip."

"Looks like they're riding on sky hooks." Esther said drily, half-present at this family picnic initiated by Alf out of the blue, the wind biting into everyone's warmth and comfort. The picnic lunch Esther prepared would have to be eaten in the car rather than the grassy picnic spot Alf half hoped would appear out of this rocky terrain.

Alf came home early from work the night before. "It's time to do something together," he said to the family. "I realize I've been too wrapped up in my business plans, and want to make amends. Your mother looks a little pale these days. How about taking everybody down to the dam site tomorrow? We'll have a picnic and see how things are coming along on the project."

He'd caught her by surprise. She'd said yes before she remembered to be angry with him over the new car or remembered to be depressed at the prospect of falling into space with no A. P. to catch her. Alf was glad he'd surprised her. He genuinely wanted to do better. She wasn't too good lately, staring into space a lot, not listening to the children, highly irritable when she was distracted from her distraction.

"Those cables carry plate girders, tractors, lots of things besides workmen down into the canyon. They've been there from the very beginning to help men and equipment get down to the shelves where they built the big tunnels. That line's called the Joe McGee. Another deviler. Just last Sunday—"

"Stop telling horror stories," Esther said. "This cliff is frightening enough as it is."

"All right." Alf wanted to please today. "Look across the river, then. See that big hole that looks like a cave?"

"Put me down, Daddy," Inez said, pointing to the diamond shapes pressed into the flesh of her legs.

Alf had unknowingly leaned against the wire fencing that kept tourists and onlookers from falling into the project below. The fencing had bulged out, leaving a gaping hole and space at the tips of Alf's shoes.

"Let me down, Daddy," she screamed. "Big hole."

"Don't be a baby," said Rebecca, who started climbing the fence, wedging her saddle oxfords into the holes between the wire.

"Don't climb up like that," said Esther, snatching Inez from Alf's arms and clutching her extra tightly. "No, honey. That's not a sturdy fence."

Rebecca kept climbing like a monkey. One leg crossing an arm that held onto the fence.

"Alf!" Esther shouted. "Get her down." The chain fence seemed to give with every change in Rebecca's weight, flexing in and out over the edge of the cliff. "Oh, God in Heaven, save that girl!"

"On the wire, on the wire. I am a monkey." Rebecca swang back and forth on the flexible wire. "Can't catch me. Can't catch me. A monkey. A monkey."

Alf grabbed her from behind. "Come on, little monkey. This is a dangerous place."

Her fingers tangled with the wire like frozen claws. Alf pulled from the back while her fingers struggled to maintain their hold. "Stubborn little lady we've got here, Esther. What I'm going to do when she ever lets go is make sure she gets to ride across the canyon on one of those skips. How about that, Rebecca?"

"A monkey, a monkey. Monkeys don't like bas-kets. Monkeys just like tre-e-es."

"Rebecca!" Esther shouted. "Please let go. That wire's not made for hanging. I've got a banana in the picnic basket. A raisin oatmeal cookie too. Come on, baby."

Alf finally jerked her with such force that she lost her grip on the fence.

"I hate you, I hate you," she shouted at her father. "Monkeys hate daddies."

"What are you? Some kind of monster or something?" He cuffed the side of her head.

"Ow-w-w-w," she wailed, running to Esther for protection, holding a fistful of Esther's cloth coat next to the side of her head and pulling on Inez's dangling leg.

"You mustn't say things like that, Rebecca," Esther shouted nervously. "You don't hate your father. He was just trying to get you away from the edge of that canyon wall. That's a long drop. Seven hundred feet."

"Rebecca's a stupid idiot," Mary Elizabeth said. "Everybody in this family is a stupid idiot. Why are we down here looking at cables and skips? This is boring."

"So you could see all the men at the bottom. Ogle their muscles. Their sweat, my sweet one." Esther's sarcasm was more cutting than usual.

"When are you kids going to get a little gratitude?" Alf asked. "When are you going to have a little appreciation for the nice things people try to do for you? The world doesn't exist to serve you, you know."

"All right, everybody!" Esther yelled, a brittle ridge rising in her voice. "We started out on a picnic, and we're going to have that picnic. We're going to be happy today. Right now. Everybody smile. Everybody."

No one smiled.

"Hey, wait a minute," Alf said. "I see somebody I need to talk to." Before he finished the sentence, he was running over toward a small building near the head tower, scrambling over rocks to get a glimpse of the man running the hoist cables. "Dix. Dix Ballard!"

The man turned for a minute, saw who called his name, then turned away, pretending he'd heard and seen nothing. Alf slid over a few loose rocks as he worked his way down to the hoist house.

"Ballard," he yelled. "Where've you been? I haven't seen you for months." Ballard ignored Alfred Jensen.

Alf climbed over jagged rocks, close to the ledge where the head tower was supported by a cable and steel girders, closer to the hoist house.

"Hey you, out of there!" A ranger appeared out of nowhere. "Don't you know you're not allowed past the lookout point?"

"I've got to talk to this man," Alf yelled into the wind. "It's vital."

"Vital, hell. Get your can out of there, mister, or the rangers'll be transporting you to their offices. You might kick some rocks over the edge and kill somebody. What are you, some kind of dimwit?"

"But, Ballard . . . Dix Ballard."

"So, I'll give him a message."

"Tell him . . . tell him." Alf faltered and started back toward the ranger. What kind of a message could he send that would accurately relay his frustration over $50 in cash dropping out of his life when he'd loaned it so many months ago? Fifty dollars was more than a gold mine to Alf. But he knew he could be thrown out of town at Sid Empey's kangaroo court if Empey got a hint of any foul play on his part. But he hadn't done anything wrong, not yet. He'd kept his business on the up and up except for some of the things he dreamed of doing to Dix Ballard if he ever caught up with him.

Alf climbed over the last of the rusted yellow rock poking out of the ground like miniature mountain ranges. "Tell him to be out at the Railroad Pass on Friday night, by invitation of myself and a few friends." He reached out his hand to the ranger.

"What's with you, mister?" The ranger shook his hand. "Hanging out at the Pass? You know it's Prohibition. You from around here?"

"Even the Indians have to get off the reservation from time to time," Alf said calmly, smiling his silvery smile. "The Pass is a friendly place to meet new people."

"Sure," the ranger said. "Stay on the Lookout Point, Mister. You're putting yourself and the men below in high jeopardy."

His family slowly gathered behind the ranger dressed in breeches that hugged his knees, laced leather boots, and a felt hat with a dent in the middle of the crown.

"Sorry, sir," Alf said so Esther could hear him. "Had a friend out there I really wanted to see. I forgot my good sense."

"You sure did," the ranger said.

"My family," Alf gestured to the girls and Esther with Inez on her hip. "Mary Elizabeth, Rebecca, my wife Esther, and baby Inez."

"Nice-looking women to be with someone with absolutely no sense."

"Sorry. I really am." Alf tried to breathe easily, drag big gulps of air into his lungs to calm his jumpy pulse and heart. *Damn,* he swore to himself, *I finally find Dix Ballard. Damn ranger, sticking his officious nose into my business. If something happens to Dix Ballard, it won't be my fault now. Sam tells me I'm a coward not to do something. I was only trying to give him his chance before something happens.*

"Stay on the paths now," the ranger said before he walked back to his car.

"What was that all about?" Esther asked.

195

"Some guy I've been trying to catch up with for a couple of months. That's all."

"What do you need to see him about?"

"Some business deal we had together. Nothing to worry about, Esther. Let's go eat our picnic lunch." Alf lifted Inez out of Esther's arms into his own and kissed her rubbery cheek.

"No," Esther said, "I'm not moving until you tell me what that was about." She looked at him with eyes that mirrored his face and all the things behind it, the thoughts in his interior, the shadows he lived in most of the time.

"The man owes me some money for a favor I did him. That's all. Anything so suspicious about that?"

"No, but you sure seem edgy. What's going on, Alf? Gone more and more, late all the time for dinner, smelling like a keg and preoccupied next to me in the bed. I can hear you thinking at night. Hear the wheels turn in your head, grinding over and over a thing. I don't ever ask you much, but now I want to know."

"I lent him some money." Alf knew it was ridiculous to lie to her, so he didn't try. She always wheedled things out of him anyway like a large mosquito that sucked blood out of a body before it knew it was giving up anything.

"How much?"

"Esther, that's not your business. It's something between me and Ballard."

"How much, Alf? And where did you get money in the first place? You went and got yourself a new car without so much as asking me, when I'd been scrimping and saving your salary and what I can make with ironing and washing to finish the payments for the last one, and here you drive up to the house like some Persian potentate and walk like you were trailed by a cast of thousands. 'Esther,' you said. 'Esther. What do you think of this new car? Lot better than the old one that had to eat dust from Brigham to Nevada. Cars that eat dust die sooner than others.' Oh, Alf, in spite of myself, I thought you were funny, and I laughed even though I was crying inside, 'How in hell's name can we make the payments on a new car now?' "

"Esther." Alf spoke sharply. "This is a picnic today. We brought our family out to have a good time together. I am not allowing you to spoil this day. Do you understand?"

Alf spoke like an animal trainer, knowing Esther couldn't stand to be yelled at, knowing she cowered at the sound of strong language. Alf knew when to pull out his verbal whip and lash at Esther, who seemed more animal than human the way she sensed everything that went on around her.

"You're not going to change the subject, Alf. We've needed to have this out for a long time now." She reached for her baby, but Alf wrapped his arms double around the almost two-year-old girl with curly black hair who started to wriggle and reach for her mother.

"Esther. I planned this day so we could forget history, the past, you know. To help you know that things will be okay, even without A.P. It's a new day. I'm trying to make things better. I came home early last night, I hope you noticed. It seems like I make changes and you never see those. Look. We're together. We have a picnic lunch, so stop making trouble."

"I'm not making trouble. You've been skulking around for the past eight months, half appearing, half disappearing all the time. Neither here nor there. You just come home to sleep and curl into a warm body. You don't care about my feelings building up and building up all the time. You don't care. Your daughter is going wild, a parrot out of the cage, and you don't care. Not about any of us. And I've seen your car parked over on Avenue D time after time."

"Okay," yelled Alf, squeezing Inez until she cried. "Have it your way. Have it out right here at the dam site, right at the edge of a cliff, right in front of God and everybody and your own children, for hell's sake! Don't you have any sense?"

"Look who's talking! You'll have a pregnant daughter or a prostitute and you don't care."

"Mother, I'm not a prostitute," Mary Elizabeth yelled. "You're crazy. You see phantoms every time I move. You're blind!"

"See what I mean. Listen to her. This is what I have to deal with and you're never there to back me up."

Esther started pacing on the slanted gravel path that led down to the chain link fence protecting visitors from the edge. The gravel grated under her shoes. It grated on Alf's nerves: the sound of the loose pebbles sliding against the hard-packed dirt and the fact that Esther wouldn't listen to him. Mary Elizabeth and Rebecca huddled together, pulling and wrapping their gray and blue sweaters tightly around themselves, stretching the wool out of shape as they grouped together to protect each other from the cold wind and the words and the anger flying back and forth. Inez, still in Alf's arms, cried, though her crying seemed more like it belonged to the wind that whipped Esther's hem and Alf's hat brim.

"Give me my baby." Esther charged Alf like a bull.

"You never wanted this baby. You told me yourself." Alf held Inez fiercely while Esther tried to peel his arms away from the child's body.

"You don't care about your children, or me." Esther was screaming. Alf wondered if Dix Ballard was too busy directing the hoist cable or if he was hearing and watching this domestic war. He looked for the ranger's car in the visitors' parking lot, hoping he'd gone on to patrol other areas. Esther was wild, screaming and pulling and kicking him in the shins. Esther was half beautiful like this. Alive, if nothing else. All her absentness and melancholy sitting back in the car and the house. Esther. Queen Esther. Wild woman. Even while he screamed back at her, half of his mind laughed at this passionate scene. Something real. Something screaming in his face instead of passively hovering at the edges.

And suddenly, Alf felt his eyeglass folding into his face, the bridge cutting into his forehead, the temples bowing out from behind his ears.

"Give me the baby, you coward." Esther had turned into a blaze of red, nipping and searing Alf's body with her fists and fingernails. The baby slipped down between them while Alf pushed Esther's palm away from his face, slipped down in the tangle of legs on a bed of loose gravel, and crawled away from the quarrel as fast as she could. Alf grabbed Esther around the middle and squeezed her ribs until she crumpled to the ground. "Get hold of yourself, Esther. Stop. Stop this now." Then he ran after the baby who was crawling toward the chain link fence that bulged out away from the cliff in a singular gaping hole to the bottom where the dam would soon stand against the Colorado.

He grabbed the baby, scraping one of her knees in his haste, and shoved her into Mary Elizabeth's arms. "You girls get in the car. Don't you get out for anything. Do you hear me?"

Tears pooled in Rebecca's eyes. "Mama. Why's Mama on the ground? You hurt Mama."

"She wouldn't stop. I had to stop her. Can you understand that?"

Rebecca ran for the car

Mary Elizabeth stood there in total calm.

"Move, Mary Elizabeth. Now. I told you to get in the car."

"I'll move when you help Mother, not until then."

"You move when I say to move."

"Get my mother."

Alf slapped her. Maybe she looked like Esther just then. Maybe her eyes reminded him of all the accusations he'd seen through the years, or maybe he didn't like her wildness, something he may have given her. He knew where he was going, but she was too young to follow.

His hand stung, the cells and nerve endings on his hand surprised by his action. He could see his finger marks shaped on her cheek, four separate red welts rising under her blue eyes with the heat of white fire in them.

Mary Elizabeth didn't cry. She didn't flinch. She stood like a sandstone monument carved by thousand-year winds while Alf carried his stunned hand upright and walked to the place where Esther slumped on the ground. He bent over the crumpled woman who was holding her ribs with both arms and rocking herself quietly. But when Alf reached out and stroked her arm with a single finger, she turned on him like a wounded animal.

"Get away from me. Don't you dare touch me again." She pulled herself into a crawl and started inching toward the edge of the cliff, away from the chain link fence, over to the side of the cage for tourists and onlookers, over the jutting rocks. "I hate you, Alfred Jensen. I hate you with everything I own, every bit of strength I have. Don't you touch me." Her eyes cut into his like swift swords that would have lanced his pupils had they been steel. "God told me you were no good. God told me. He whispered to me in the night that I should find a new place and a new home with a good man. With a man who loved him and served him."

"You have no idea of my relationship with God." Alf followed her cautiously as she crawled over the chaotic ground.

"You're no good."

"God loves me, Esther. He speaks to me different than he speaks to you. He doesn't talk through you or any other Mormon. Don't tell me about the God who doesn't love me. That kind of god is a stranger to me, and he doesn't exist. No matter what you think you know."

Esther inched closer to the edge, ripping her silk stockings that were already riddled with holes at the tops and the heels. The ground was unpaved here, uncut or marked by human hands, yellow-topped, rusty rocks with serrated teeth. Esther crawled, seemingly oblivious to the jagged points piercing her knees.

"You think you are so blessed by God, Esther. You think you have all the answers about how men are supposed to live. You live in your own little narrow world and expect everyone else to live there too. Well, I've got news for you. I'm not going to be boxed into your world, not now or ever. If you want to live with me, you open up the doors and let some fresh air in, because—listen to me well, my dear Esther—I am a man with places to go and you'd be smart to help me get there. You better stop whining and crying and wishing for the world to match your tiny reality. It's big out there, and I want a woman who'll be big with me. Do you understand? Stop crawling away. Stop running, whining, feeling sorry for yourself. Get up! Now! Stand up and face life!"

Esther had reached the edge, and Alf was right behind her. She looked down into the canyon below, at the tractors, at the ant-men traveling from spot to spot. She looked up at the overhead cables, she looked down again at the footbridges where more ant-men traveled across carrying boxes and bundles and rods and shovels.

"Look what they've done to my beautiful river."

"Esther. I want you to be with me. I really do. I want you to stop being afraid and let the faith you tell me to have work for you. That's why I planned the picnic today. I wanted to make things better for us, for you. I really did! Come on, Esther. Come back away from the edge. We'll talk, I promise."

She sat there, watching, listening, holding her ribs and rocking. "Nothing matters," she said.

"What about those three girls in the car? What about them up there trembling and crying over their mother? They don't understand your pain. They just know whether you're standing up or refusing to move. I think right now the best thing for you is to move."

"My babies," Esther said, the front of her hair blowing in the wind, her cloche crooked on her head. "Blow me away, God, over the edge. I don't want to stay here and take care of Alf and the babies." She held up her arms, waiting for a divine gust of wind. She held them up to the cold winter sun. "Take me. It's my turn."

The wind whistled in Alf's ears as he watched his wife wait. It was time. He knew it now. He'd been suspecting it for a while, even discussed it with Sam and Serena, even Jack and Dr. Spilsbury, but the light seemed clear on the subject today. She was dangerous to herself and to the children. The doctor told him the state mental hospital in Sparks had facilities for nervous disorders. "There are a lot worse cases than Esther there," he said, "but she needs help. People are worried about the way she walks and walks through town, hours at a time, never really talking to anybody, just drifting by like a stray feather, unattached to anything. Her nervous system never recovered from that fire, that's my suspicion."

"So are you going to jump or not?" said Alf, half-hoping in this moment that maybe she'd blow over the edge. A clean, quick end to her troubles. But when the wind stayed gentle, he knew God wasn't going to end things that cleanly, and Alf couldn't stand the thought of his wife flying through the air on her own volition, flying away from him without more thought than that. They'd been through a lot together. It couldn't end like this. She had no wings, and everything would be over too soon if she jumped. Too easy.

He looked down. Esther, still on her hands and knees, was dragging her face against the sawtooth edge of a rock. Blood seeped from her cheek.

"Come on, Esther." Alf bent and held her in his arms. He pulled his handkerchief from his back pocket and flattened it against the wound. "Come on, sweet lady. God knows we've got some repair work to do, but I still love you."

The words surprised Alf because they rang true.

12

She begged until he finally said, "All right, you don't have to go until the talent show is over." When she kissed the brim of his hat six times and thanked him too profusely, he wondered if he had done the right thing. But he wouldn't go back on his word. After all, she could be gone a long time.

The doctor agreed after he'd dropped by the house at Alf's request to size up Esther. "If nothing else, a stay at the hospital will give her rest. Her mind is fractured right now. Splintered. I can get a second signature. Shouldn't be hard. Everybody's seen Esther walking around town the way she does."

"What are we looking at here?" asked Alf.

"What do you mean?"

"I mean, how long? What are her chances?"

"I've seen cases like hers in for six years, but I don't know about getting better. That bad burn doesn't help. She's so sensitive. Every footstep. Every look someone gives her. Her mind is wild trying to figure out the world around her. Most of the time, she just closes the doors. Doesn't look out. Doesn't let anyone in."

"Six years?" Alf asked. "She needs rest, but six years?"

"I hope rest will do it, Alf."

When Alf described the hospital in Sparks to Esther, he said it was her time to be attended by guardian angels. "Everyone will be watching over you, Esther."

At first she'd been hysterical, sobbing in her bedroom and over the evening dishes. "My babies. Who will watch my babies?"

"Jack and Gloria could move in and—"

"Gloria's not raising my babies," she yelled, tightly gripping the handle of the kitchen knife she wiped with a checked towel. "She hates God."

"Calm down! Gloria could cook and keep things straight. Herbert will watch out for the girls. He loves the Church and the babies, Esther. And I'll be here."

"You aren't here now. How will you manage to be here when I'm gone?"

"Mary Elizabeth's old enough to be a mother. Rebecca can fend for herself. The baby . . . we'll find a way. The Relief Society. Sister Parker, especially. You know she loves you."

Esther put the knife in the wooden divider with the other kitchen knives, a collection of knicked silverplate and metal utensils from her mother's kitchen and a few leftovers found in the abandoned drawers of their many rented homes.

"Everything seems so black all the time," she said, "like I'm falling. I grab, but there's nothing to hold onto. Then I'm falling again. It's almost like somebody dug a hole in me once upon a time. But I'm lucky in a way."

"What do you mean, Esther?" Her expression reminded him of a little girl arriving at a birthday party too late for the party favors, and this child in her confused him.

"Nobody can find me when I fall in my own hole, which is nice in a way. But when I can't find myself, it feels too lonely."

Alf avoided the whirlpools in her eyes that might take him down with her. "Do you want me to sing a duet with you at the talent show?" He picked up a broken corner of saltine from the floor.

"Conway knows about the aria I learned from *Carmen*. 'Habanera.' Oooo-ah ah ah-ah," she sang and snapped her fingers like castanets. "He wants me to try it."

Alf hid his smile, not sure if Esther was serious or just crazy. A forty-four-year-old dumpling playing Carmen? An operatic aria for the dam builders? What life should Esther have been born into? What time would have suited this strange being?

"Don't laugh at me. This might be my last time to sing." She whirled and leaned into a slight arabesque in her broad-heeled shoes, looking less round, almost willowy.

At times, thought the surprised Alf, sending her away seemed an absolute necessity, but at times such as this confusing moment, she seemed more like the changing colors of a sunset, a woman shifting through moods, shuffling them like cards. Impermanent. Undefinable. He watched her stand tall, strike a pose in imitation of a haughty Carmen, and switch a copy of *The Relief Society Magazine* back and forth as if it were a filigreed fan. Then, flamenco-style, she stilletoed her heels across the wooden floor and fell beside Alf on the sofa.

"Don Jose," she said, fanning his cheek with the magazine and kissing him passionately on the lips. "It's a waste of time to call love if it suits love to say no. It's a contrary bird. Just as you think you have caught it, it flies away." Esther laughed, stood again to whirl like water in an eddy, and tossed an imaginary flower in Alf's lap. "Aren't you glad Sister Pulsipher taught me a few arias? Frustrated old opera singer hoping her prize student would break out of Brigham City to the Big Times. She shouldn't have taken me to Salt Lake to see two operas. It made me feel bigger than Brigham. Beyond it all. And then I married Alfred Jensen, my Don Jose. He said he could order the world to suit my fancy. I believed every word."

"Sit down." Alf patted the depression in the cushion. "Don't wear yourself out before the show."

She sank into the cushion and nestled into Alf.

"So," he said. "Should we find a way to get you a red dress for your swan song?" He raked her hair gently with his fingers and massaged her scalp. "Red with black lace? A lace mantilla propped high with jeweled combs?"

"Excellent," she said. "And when I'm done with my aria, why don't you come on stage, Don Jose, with your dagger? Everything would be over then. No gasoline wasted on a trip to Sparks. Carmen will lie on the floor to be swept up by the custodians. Then Don Jose can make plans and more plans."

"Esther," Alf pushed her away from his shoulder to a full sitting position. "Stop it! This is real life. Boulder City, Nevada. You're sick. Maybe not for long, but you *are* sick. You need rest."

"Jesus, Savior, pilot me," she sang the old sailors' hymn the Mormons had adopted as one of their own. "Over life's tempestuous sea."

"Esther, Esther, Esther!" He grabbed her face in his hands. "Where are you? What's happening to you?"

"Unknown waves before me roll," she continued. "Hiding rock and treach'rous shoal."

Inez toddled into the room, her curly hair mashed flat on one side from an afternoon nap. "Mama." She ran to Esther's knees and hugged them, touching her cheek lightly to a flower on Esther's skirt.

Esther picked her up and tried to rearrange the unruly curls.

"Mommy, Mommy," Inez sang and twisted her body into Esther's ample chest and soft stomach. She patted one breast with her small fingers. "Let me feel you, Mommy."

"Waif baby." Esther drew a soft circle on the child's cheek with her finger.

"There are plenty of us here," Alf said. "You'll rest easier not having to worry about Inez. Or me, for that matter."

"You think I can sit in a room all by myself and think about nothing all the time? You're dumber than I thought, Alf."

"I think removing a little of the pressure. . . ."

"Shhh," Esther said harshly, putting one finger in the ear closest to Alf and his words. "Don't speak. Let me hold my baby for now."

"But Esther, you know it's right. You agree with me."

"Shhh, I said. Respect my last wishes." She closed her eyes, Alf decided, in imitation of the doomed starlets she'd seen too much at the movies.

"Stop being dramatic, Esther."

"You stop, Alf. Now! 'My light is but a little one,' " she sang to cover the sound of any further words he might have. "My light of faith and prayer. But lo! it glows like God's great sun, for it was lighted there."

Alf mentally counted the days until the talent show. Six. He was a fool to postpone things. He'd have everything ready to drive her up north. He'd pack her things himself. They'd leave exactly at 6:00 A.M. and drive, no stops except for gas, until they reached the doors of the Nevada State Hospital. "Take this stranger," he'd tell them. "A little rest, glue, some rewiring. Fix her, please."

"Shine on, shine on," Esther still sang, "the day is near."

· · · · ·

Esther Carpenter Jensen. Finally on stage at the Boulder City Theater, or at least she would be in a few minutes. Con Mitchell took her hand in his.

"Your hands are cold," he said.

"Cold hands, warm heart." She smiled at this odd friend of hers, one of the few living humans who could read her as she wanted to be read: an artistic woman, essentially a song to be sung rather than an object to be understood or ordered. Conway was her friend. When he sat by her side in the movies, he stroked the paper-thin skin over her knuckles. "Be peaceful," he would say. "I am your friend." He'd be up and down during the movie to check the projectionist booth and the candy counter to make sure there was plenty of freshly popped corn. Sometimes he'd bring a Sugar Daddy to Esther or a striped bag of hot popcorn and tell her he'd be right back. She loved candy that lasted a long time, something she could suck all through the film, something that wouldn't go away too quickly. She thought of the grainy feel of the carmel Sugar Daddy on her tongue and remembered the moments when the white cardboard stick surfaced through the carmel and poked the raw roof of her mouth with disappointment. The end of the movie. The end of the Sugar Daddy. The sun. The heat. Her life.

Con was her friend with the exception of one afternoon during a scene of *Dinner at Eight*. Except for that single occasion, any passion between them found exchange only in the infrequent times they held hands. But maybe the time when his hand crept up the inside of her thigh didn't matter. She'd broken no big promises. And now she was going away. In the morning.

All week long, Mary Elizabeth helped Esther sew the dress. It was red— three tiers of ruffled red cotton and a row of black ricrac at the bottom of each tier. Instead of a black lace mantilla, Esther settled for a yard of red cotton, gathered and fastened to a large comb with thread, and embellished with two streamers of the thin lace floating down over the red fabric. Her fan was small and Japanese and painted with cherry blossoms and branches on black paper. Mary Elizabeth had found it in Woolworth's in Las Vegas during her lunch hour at school. Esther was a Hooverville version of a Spanish gypsy, but a proud one, nonetheless.

Warming up with the do, re, mi, fa, sol, la, ti, do behind the curtains, Esther felt the glow of the red material against her skin, a fire of red that filled her with the wildest possible Carmen anyone had ever seen. Nothing to lose. All of her friends and family knew where she was going in the morning, so she couldn't embarrass them further. And the myriad of dam workers had never seen her face or heard her history. To them she was only Carmen who knew about fire, love, and defiance.

She knew what Carmen was all about even if her portly shape made others doubt she could know. These men poured concrete and dug tunnels and loaded train cars and rode metal baskets across the chasm of the non-Colorado and maybe they were immune to danger because there was so much of it around them all the time. But, they wouldn't be immune to this Carmen. Esther was rich now. She wasn't a blank slate. She had nothing to lose because it was all lost. For the first time, she was rich. She knew about life and could tell of it with her body and her arms and her voice. They would know they were hearing a real Carmen who loved only whom she pleased. Carmen was Carmen in the end, even in a heap on the stage. She was a Capital-C Carmen. Not even Don Jose's dagger could change that.

Alf seemed nervous tonight even though she'd been on her best behavior all week long. "Are you sure you feel like doing this?" he asked her several times. "Do you want me to be backstage?"

"Conway Mitchell will be there," she said calmly. "He's my friend."

All week long she'd sewn and vocalized and practiced in the mirror except when Alf was home. At those times, she cooked and set the table neatly, folding the ironed napkins in a fancy restaurant fold she'd once seen in San Diego when they'd had money for a few minutes. The model mother. The model wife. Alf was also a model husband, home on time, attentive to the children, mild mannered. They almost convinced each other that theirs was a settled, genteel home life, except at night Esther tossed and pulled the covers and tried not to scream and Alf curled into a solitary ball of himself, and they both mentioned how their jaws hurt when they woke in the morning.

"You're on next," Conway whispered to her from where he peeked out to the stage. "You ready? As soon as the juggler finishes with the three chairs, I'll do a very brief introduction, then you get out there in a flash. Okay?"

In a minute she heard him saying, "And here, from Brigham City, Utah, the songbird of the Elberta Theater with her rendition of the "Habanera" from *Carmen*, Esther, the Wandering Gypsy, Jensen!"

The bass of the piano played its Spanish rhythm, setting the stage, the mood. The lights dimmed. "Good heavens, there are people out there," Esther said to herself, putting one leg out from behind the curtain, knowing the other had to follow. She'd seen another Carmen do her stuff, and she hadn't forgotten, but suddenly the same old invisible wall kept her from moving onstage.

"Go on, Esther," Conway whispered, his lips close to her ear.

Esther had told the accompanist to give her plenty of vamp time until she felt ready to launch into the opening line. Suddenly, when she started her slow flamenco with her back arched and her right arm stretched up to its limit, she saw all the heads perched on bodies in the seats of the theater. Thousands of heads, it seemed, a sea of them, and she thought she'd never seen so many heads in her life. Long, large, widow-peaked, eyeglassed, narrow, wide heads bobbing like buoys on the ocean. Her only thin connection to this wide sea was the Spanish rhythm being pumped out by the pianist, measure after measure.

This is like giving birth. It's worse to back away from it. Forward. The only way to go. Push. The first note came out like a baby's head at birth, a sound too wide for the small opening of her mouth. The big sound of the word "love" scared Esther, but despite her trembling, she knew about shows going on. She knew how she'd feel tomorrow if she didn't keep singing. She needed memories to play over in her mind as the car headed north to Sparks.

Good-natured catcalls sifted out of the audience. "What a woman!" "Car-men." "Show your stuff, canary."

Surrounded by the music slipping from her mouth despite her fear that it wouldn't, she found a passageway through the invisible wall, and there was Esther Jensen, Carmen, commanding both herself and her audience to pay attention. This was her moment. "Love is a stubborn and contrary bird that no one can tame." The words ran from her mouth like a ribbon, smooth, flowing, arching over wide intervals, sliding down, chromatic silk. She was in command because it didn't matter what anyone thought anymore or what gossip would go around town about the pudgy older woman who tried to relive her youth and passion like a fool for all to see. She would be gone. Tomorrow. So, tonight.

All she ever felt about love came out with each word and shaped each note, the marginalia of her own story decorating Carmen's song for the dam builders. "Love, love, love, love," each pronouncement a variation of her experience with the word—gratitude, tenderness, spite, begging. Esther dredged the memory of the word love out of herself. The moment of the fire and her blistered skin and her mother's worried eyes checking to see if her little girl Esther was still there. The moment she first saw Alf at the Elberta Theater, both mocking and adoring her. Her childbirthing. Her dead baby twins lying side by side quietly, like dolls on a counter at Woolworth's. She felt Alf making love to her, pumping in and out of her steadily, moaning, hardening, bursting. She remembered twisted gristle coming out of her womb, too soon to love, too soon to be mistaken for a baby with arms and legs. Three times it had pinched out of her. A white, cleanish, twirled-up fist small enough to fit into a cup. And she remembered the electricity when Con Mitchell put his hand on the inside of her leg as Jean Harlow gazed longingly at herself in a gilt-edged mirror in *Dinner at Eight*, his hand inching up under her dress into the sacred territory that was supposed to be protected by her temple garment. The mixed feeling of pleasure and disgust at herself and love.

She was in command, combining her own stories with the one she sang. The storyteller. The minstrel. People sat in a hush at the bareness of the soul before them, reverent, somewhat embarrassed by the raw display of someone else's truth.

She moved when she sang, not so much anything choreographed or especially Spanish, but movement that spoke of her life—hands crossed over her breasts on one measure, her temples pinched tight by the flats of her hands on the next, her hips swaying, feet sliding and stepping.

"If you don't love me, I love you," she sang, knowing the song would be over almost as soon as it had started. One of the finest moments of her life ending, maybe the last time for her to know real aliveness. She didn't know about tomorrow or the day after that, so she leaned into the last appoggiatura as if it was the end of a long day and stayed with the note. The note kept coming out of her, embellished with more of her history so that everyone who heard would know she hadn't come to her present condition like a child on a slide. It had taken time. Her arms spread wider, Esther trying to grab the world or something with them, and then all that was left was the note. All by itself.

The pianist suspended his hands over the keyboard, waiting for the note to end so he could gallop dramatically through the last vivid rhythms to the double bars at the end of the sheet music. Everything was stone still in the audience, everyone waiting for the final resolution of her song. One more note and she would be done with "Habanera," *Carmen*, her debut and finale at the Boulder Theater. And then, instead of the last note, Esther laughed.

She laughed until she bent over holding her ribs with folded arms. She wasn't afraid anymore. Everyone could see her; everyone knew. She laughed and whirled like a top, her arms and mouth wide open, and the three tiers of her dress caught the air like tiny parachutes. The inventive accompanist ran arpeggios up and down the keyboard to make her movement seem planned. At that moment, as she turned and laughed, she knew strength. The power of nothing mattering.

"You did it, sweetheart," Conway said after she walked off the stage carrying herself like an arrogant matador to the sweet music of applause. "You had them in the palm of your hand."

Suddenly, he kissed her square on the mouth. This gesture startled Esther from the cocoon of her triumph. "Conway," she said, "I'm a married woman. The mother of seven children. Don't compromise me."

"Hey," he said, looking at her quizzically, "this is show biz. Don't be so serious."

"Forgive me for holding your hand in the movies," she said with thin lips, "and for letting your hand roam. It was wrong."

"I've got to introduce the next act. Get changed and let me say good-bye. You some stranger now or something?"

Esther walked into the narrow hallway where a sheet was draped on a wire fastened to eye hooks. A temporary dressing room. As she unbuttoned the covered buttons she'd spent hours making, she noticed the wetness under the arms of her new dress: a large circle, a sea of dark red, almost black, down to her waistline. A definite jagged boundary marking an ugly shoreline. Everything that had seemed so right a minute ago seemed so wrong again. Everyone heard her music and shared her soul, but did they have to see how badly she perspired?

Oh Father, she moaned. *Save me. Save me. Where is your promised land? Everything's water and fire. Flooding and burning, dry land that burns, water that never stops. And there's this dam in Black Canyon. Built to trap water that needs to flow. How insane! Look at my new dress. Ruined. Water in this desert. Dry land that burns.*

That night in bed when Esther tried to relive her Carmen performance that everyone said was wonderful and why didn't she try for the big times after she got rested up, she mostly remembered her dress in the dressing room and the unwelcome kiss from Conway Mitchell. A smear of perspiration under her arms, a smear on her lips, Conway thinking she was open to that kind of thing because she held his hand a few times and let his hand wander once or maybe because she was dressed in red. Carmen was, after all, a whore. A fine Mormon lady whose world had twisted into this. By the time she woke in the morning, Esther felt no pride in her performance. It was time for her to be shut away before she disgraced herself further.

13

The cement. One hundred fifty carloads of aggregate and twenty-five carloads of Portland cement were needed on an average day after the pouring commenced. A total of 3,220,000 yards had to be mixed, transported, and poured into a 727-foot-high tapered mass. One step at a time.

The first cement from Lomix was shaped into precautionary three-foot-thick linings in the diversion tunnels. Determined to stay as many steps ahead of the Colorado as possible, the engineers ordered 2,000 tons of steel to bend into semicircular forms that would shape the cement and insure the tunnels' carrying capacity. A smooth-trowel finish on the lining would keep the river from wearing down its surface.

Their first batches were discouraging mixtures of trial and error, the process of hauling and the never-failing heat compacting the cement too soon. Gradually, however, the engineers found a workable mix, and decided it would make more sense to conduct the tests at the pouring site rather than at Lomix.

The cylindrical lining for the tunnel was divided into three parts: invert, side-wall portions, and arch sections. The invert section was the first to be poured into the forms. After rumbling over the cofferdam on a wooden bridge and down a ramp to the tunnel floor, trucks with huge buckets mounted to their flatbeds delivered their loads to a two-legged gantry crane spanning the width of the tunnel like a huge insect. Its transverse bridge was equipped with two hooks for lifting and dumping buckets, as well as with moveable templates for troweling the new surface. The seemingly endless flow of concrete was smoothed and hardened into place. The engineers smiled. "Well done," they said.

For the arch sections, the jumbo carriages that had pushed miners and their drills head-on through a slowly-yielding andesite barrier were converted to drill overhead grout holes. Operation topsy-turvy. New challenges. Wet concrete on the ceiling of the tunnels. In and out, the parade continued— jumbos, miners with drills, stompers, finishers, tuggers, truck drivers, agitators, chutes full of concrete, everyone and everything making preparations for the bridegroom: the water diverted from its own bed into another. A concrete wife. A wide, smooth tunnel. This marriage a serious business.

From the tunnels, the concrete began spreading out on the project— surface for the cofferdam, walls for the spillways, and fill for the deep trench in the middle of the riverbed. Engineers and inspectors measured, gauged, discussed, mixed, and remixed their precious concrete. It spread like chunky fingers of coagulating blood. Hardened arteries. Concrete everywhere, in holes and forms and cracks and tubes.

"Uniformity is essential," the engineers said. "Strict specs for the aggregates, strict ratio of water to cement. Use as little water as possible, almost a no-slump mix. Has to withstand a 2,000-pound test."

At the spillways, two emergency escape routes in Nevada and Arizona in case the soon-to-be reservoir ever reached overflow proportions, the quarter-mile of sloping tunnel needing cement was too steep for regular trucks. First, the engineers tried cable cars on tracks with buckets of cement strapped on, but the jolting cable car ride hardened the concrete in minutes. Not even a jackhammer could make a dent in the hard mass. Next, they tried a hopper and a pipeline, but the heat stopped the cement before it reached the bottom of the pipe. Finally, after a month's lapse, the superintendent opted for highlines. Anything could be transported anywhere by highlines, never mind the crews nicknaming them "Joe McGees" because of their obstinate and unpredictable nature.

One day in the Arizona spillway, nicknamed "Alabama" because so many southerners were on the crew, the carpenters routinely pulled off the shea bolts which held the form in place. The tuggers started to raise the form in preparation for the next pour, due to arrive on a Joe McGee in forty-five minutes. Suddenly, one panel ripped loose, then the rest of the form. Like a sled, it raced down the slope of concrete, four workmen hanging onto coils of cooling pipe. Transforming from Hi-Flyer to barge, the form splashed into the diverted river and into the Glory Hole drop, tossing and falling through the dark tunnel. One man fractured his back, another punctured a lung. Massive bruises. But the tattered crew held on through the roiling waters until a round disc of daylight and volunteer lifeguards greeted them from their boats in the Colorado, ropes in hand. All in a day's work. All in one breath. But they had just begun with concrete. A mere fraction of the three and a quarter million yards, no work on the main structure yet.

On June 6, 1933, the first block of the dam was poured. The Grand Pour, one year ahead of schedule. With the help of Joe McGees, cableway operators, placing crews, concrete stompers, vibrators, finishers, carpenters, signalmen, and inspectors, the concrete oozed into the canyon, rising one giant slab at a time like building blocks set against the river's path.

First, the signalman called for a load of grout from the Lomix plant. The soupy mixture arrived on a Joe McGee and was poured into the form to an inch thickness. Then the crew, using brooms and brushes to work the grout, made a surface which would assure firm contact between the old and the new—no more leakage between horizontal joints which had been a problem plaguing concrete dams in the past. They couldn't take chances with this much water, this much volume, this much pressure. Then another bucket swayed at the bottom of the fall line, a pendulum on a grandfather clock that sometimes bashed into cliff walls, derricks, and unsuspecting workmen.

The thicker mix came in this one. Two at a time, the buckets were mixed and delivered by train on a precarious stretch of downstream track that was balanced on a thin ledge of cliff wall and on long, spidery trestles. Cuts into the walls minimized the overhang of the track, but the trestle carried the bulk of the weight. It stood a hundred feet high in places, a slightly sagging track with creaking trestles under each four-cubic-yard load of cement.

When the railcars reached the track's terminus, workmen placed hooks on each bucket, one at a time, connecting the load to the lower end of a 650-foot fall line. After it lurched across the canyon and stopped swinging, the bucket was lowered to the block where a signalman motioned the placing crew to release its safety latches. To keep out of harm's way, the crew used their long-handled shovels for this task. The signalman then waved a high sign to the cableway operator on the edge of the cliff to dump the load into the 50 x 60, five-foot-deep forms lined with sheet metal. Then puddlers in tall rubber boots, using their shovels for balance, tromped the wet concrete into form edges and keyways interlocking the contraction joints. As they worked, their boots filled with body heat, sweat, and humidity, which, in addition to the setting temperature of the concrete, equalled 160 degrees. The puddlers stopped from time to time to pull off each other's waders and pour them dry.

On rare occasions, forms broke before the block hardened. Puddlers leaped out of the way, some were splashed aside, and a few were buried by the thick lava flow until anxious men in rubber boots rescued them from the gray liquid that was hardening around them. And it kept pouring, twenty-four hours a day. Pouring. The concrete. The wall.

Block upon block, cement poured into the forms, one on top of the next. Several hundred slowly growing columns resembled high-rise buildings with no windows or no space in between. In each of these blocks, various tubes, coils, and paraphernalia were fastened in place: drain tiles, grout pipes, grout stops, cooling pipes, thermometers, strain meters. All to assure proper curing of this cement. Each piece was set in place like a sleeping baby into a cradle—the utmost precision of placement. Each part needed protection from the heavy flow of cement.

Twenty-four hours later, a crew scoured the new green surface with stiff brooms, pneumatic water spray, and compressed air to blast away any scum or uneven particles. The forms were stripped off by tuggers one panel at a time, hoisted by hand winches, and painstakingly reset five feet higher to prepare for the next pour. Then the process began again: placing crews ready at the block, buckets lurching and swaying, inspectors watching every move to safe-guard government specifications, rules, and regulations.

As the columns grew, there was one strange gap at the center of the dam: an eight-foot-wide vertical slot between the crowded towers of the dam's face. It housed pipe coils that connected the cooling and refrigeration plants to the tubing which circulated throughout the concrete blocks. As soon as fifty feet of vertical section cooled to its appropriate temperature with the assistance of this network of pipes, the center slot and the pipes were filled with concrete and grout. But its progress lagged behind the dam wall on either side.

One day, the bolts and braces on a form full of slump gave way, this time to the slot side of the dam. Three pipefitters were matching pipe below, laughing in the shade of the slot, when suddenly ten yards of concrete bathed them and stiffened them and finished them. But it didn't bury them. No one was left to spend eternity entombed in cement. They were dug out with shovels, hands, and regrets.

And the columns grew, block after block, showered with uninterrupted sprays of water for curing. Men with hoses. Sprinkling pipes with 1/8-inch holes. Pumps delivering water twenty-four hours a day. Water to mix concrete. Water to cure concrete, all of which was used to trap water. Water working for and against itself. Concrete. A plug. A dam grew.

• • • • •

Herbert's efforts finally paid off. A better job. He happened to be at the head of the line when a James Thomas stormed in to say he'd had it smelling the burning rubber all the way down the twisting hairpin curves in the canyon. "You come home with shaking knees every night," he said. "You miss a gear and you're in deep you know what. Up to your ears in thin air." He'd had it with the burden of forty trusting men behind him in the A-5 International, even if they were under a canvas cover.

Actually, the employment office didn't assign Herbert to an International or to Big Bertha, the double-decker transport. He was still too lightweight. They promoted somebody else and gave him a Ford truck with an open bed and gates on the sides. Fourteen men lined the flatbed fence, seated themselves on crude wood benches, and clung to gateposts on bad curves. One or two regulars sat on the front seat with Herbert until they scattered to their jobs at Babcock & Wilcox to fabricate penstock header pipe, or to Himix, Lomix, the intake towers, or the jungle of columns at the dam.

During his eight-hour shift, he shuffled materials around the dam site and always waved to his brother Jack when he flagged Herbert forward, hoping the ice would thaw between them soon, the ice created by Jack's departure from the family and its traditions. Miscellaneous tools, sacks of cement for minor patching, missing nuts and bolts. A go-fer job for Herbert. But it was better than busboy, even if he had learned how to make scrambled eggs for 500 men at the mess hall: throw the eggs, shells and all, into the mixer; beat, then strain out the shells. Useful information for somebody else. He was at the dam now.

He liked negotiating his little truck through the Internationals, Morelands, Whites, GMCs, Mack Bulldogs, and hardtails with their solid rubber backs while buckets and lumber and cement traversed high over his head.

One day, while he was waiting for a flag forward from Jack, he heard the loud swishing sound of a loose air hose. Everything stopped abruptly. Herbert looked out of his truck window to see a speck falling through the sky, growing larger. A man falling like a meteor. A shooting star. He fell in a puddle of water next to the rubber-clad toes of three men holding a high-voltage cable

217

up and out of ground water, the lifeline for the electric shovel. He splashed mud on their blue chambray shirts, their overalls, and faces.

"Get those son of a bitchin' trucks moving, Jensen," the foreman on the platform shouted at Jack. "Who in the hell do you think you are, stopping traffic like that?"

"But there's a dead man over there," Jack yelled.

"Get the hell moving, Jensen, or you're fired. That man's not gonna hurt anybody."

Herbert wanted to go to Jack, say something, do anything to redeem his brother, who looked confused. He wanted to go to the dead man too, but then the flag in Jack's hand snapped to move Herbert's truck toward the valve house. There were so many trucks. So much traffic.

Herbert held up his hand as he passed Jack. A silent wave of recognition to his brother who should be home playing his saxophone, not pretending life and death didn't matter because the job must go on. Jack's saxophone. Good memories. Herbert driving away from the scene of the accident. The flag in Jack's hand and the rocks and people falling. Big wheels backing and braking and retreading the dirt while a man whose life was finished was not tended. There should be a moment, a pause, something. This was insanity.

Jack—his only brother. There were twin baby boys born after Rebecca, but they didn't last. Three days old. Herbert missed Jack, who'd been married and buried at the same time it seemed. Jack had gone away with Gloria—gone to places where Herbert couldn't follow. Of course they'd had their brotherly quarrels, their competition, Jack always winning in physical prowess, but Herbert ready with quick fists and a quick temper if Jack needed him. He could be tough when put at a disadvantage, even though he would rather repair than challenge.

But Jack didn't need much defending. Nor did Herbert's sisters, except maybe Inez, who was too little to have a tough skin. Everybody else, though, was thick of necessity, their skins growing a new layer every time they packed their bags and car for a new home, every time they said good-bye and broke ties, fragile wispy ties of affection that seemed to float up in the air and disappear into the irrepressible sky. Onward. Forward. Movement. Never stopping. Never staying. Will-o'-the-wisps never attaching to a place or a thing, always knowing the tearing would happen sooner than later, the ripping, the intrepid *Santa Marias*, *Ninas*, and *Pintas* sailing for new shores, new Americas. Off and away, and yet they'd always been together—the family. Disjointed, but together. Always Alf and Esther and Mary Elizabeth, Jack,

Herbert, Rebecca, and now Inez. Always everybody to count on like the perennial spring green bursting out of brown pods on trees. Always the family until these fragments: Jack and Gloria. Alf and Serena. His mother in a mental hospital, too tightly concocted, strings too tense, high wires stretched inside of her, and Alf, his father, needing something still and peaceful. A reprieve. Herbert forgave his father that need, but the seasons were cyclical. A certain season would come to Alf's life and he'd want the familiar returned, put back in his hand. Alf loved Esther. Herbert watched it many times. And Alf loved him—Herbert, his son who hadn't pleased him the way Jack had.

Jack was looser, not strung so tight. He was an exit sign for Alf, like Serena. Freedom from the intensity of the woman he'd chosen for a wife, from the children who were mixtures and combinations of things he both loved and hated.

Herbert understood Alf, oddly knowing his father was there, loving him from a distance, from a safe place where he couldn't feel the sponginess of a son and a wife who cried too easily and let their hearts show at the tip of their breast pockets.

Closing gaps, wide ones. That's what Herbert prayed for at night. Gaps between brothers, fathers, parents. Gaping holes in his sleep. How to lasso the family and round them up, bring them back together so they could cross over to the celestial kingdom holding hands, adoring each other, lambs and lions together. *Please God.*

And Herbert drove by Jack who was standing in the unprotected open, subject to all manner of falling things, no canopy for his head. He waved his flag precisely and seemed to be growing another layer of skin to cover his fright. Herbert prayed their estrangement would be short-lived, that the brothers would grow into new seasons of respect for each other.

Until then, Herbert would find his way alone. He'd listen, watch, and observe. He'd record things, scratch them onto paper and mold them into something worthwhile. Events would be satisfying that way, because they'd have shape—beginnings, middles, and ends. The ends would be good because they were ends. Nothing happened beyond the last word in the paragraph. Nothing changed the story printed on paper. He'd have the words of the story, the world in those pages, not the world beyond the margins and last paragraph, not the world he'd just watched falling out of the sky into the mud. It was more satisfying on paper: a world with boundaries he could control.

· · · · ·

September 8, 1934

Dear Mother,

You'd be proud of me, Mom. I'm driving the transport truck to the dam now. The road has a 6-1/2% down grade for about two miles and never stops curving. I come home with rubber legs, but I'm proud to be down on the dam instead of hearing about everything secondhand at the mess hall. You should see them pouring that cement. I've never seen anything so big in my life.

Sometimes, I have enough extra to put in my college fund, but my hand seems to find its way into the jar more than it should. As soon as you come home, I'll find a way to school. I promise.

Inie is three now. She's a doll and smart as a whip. She's been going to Dorothy Parker's house during the day while everybody's in school and Dad and I are at work. We are taking good care of the house, keeping it clean for you. Mary Elizabeth doesn't like Gloria. Dad tried to get Jack and Gloria to take over here while he's on the job, but it didn't work too well. She thinks we're a strange bunch, so M. E. told her to take her opinions back to Oklahoma. Jack got kind of mad.

I have a girlfriend now. Edna Pettingill. She's from Willard, Utah. Good Mormon girl. Strong like a farmer's daughter, and she likes me. We'll come up and see you as soon as we get married, which should be soon.

I miss you, beautiful mother. Everyone misses you. Dad's been real busy. He's taken a new job with the business regulations office, trying to move up in the world. He's trying, but it's hard for him. M. E. has a job singing with Jack's band now, though I don't like her out at the Pass. She's only 17. She still goes to church with me. Rebecca too. Sister Parker always sits with us and treats us like we belong. She's a good woman, like you. As soon as I get married, Edna and I are coming for you. You don't belong there.

Your ever loving son,

September 24, 1934

Dear Love Herbert,

Come and get me. I don't belong here with all these crazies. I know I am shaky like a cart with three wheels, maybe. But I know how to stay on the road. I promise I know how. You believe me, don't you, Herbert?

They put me in a tub of cold water under a wet canvas sheet. Towels over my eyes. And they spray me in a shower stall and tell me not to be depressed. At least it's cold, Herbert. You know how much better I like the cold.

I'm glad you found a nice girl. Come and get me, baby. Even up here in Sparks, I can feel the concrete being poured into that dam. I can feel it in my veins. Things are closing in, stopping up my arteries. I don't want to be dammed up anymore. I want my freedom. Please come, Herbert. Kiss Inie for me.

Your mother,

•   •   •   •   •

She finally let him into her bed, finally said she needed a man. Her long legs were warm next to his.

Serena. He'd forget the drive up to Sparks that had been replaying in his mind for months: Esther jabbering like a mynah bird, running off at the mouth, disappearing down a rabbit hole, only the tip of her ears showing from time to time. He hoped she'd found some friends who'd listen to her and take her in like family. Community. She'd always needed community and Alf had robbed her of this, taking her away from friends, pulling her out by the roots every time she'd sink one or two of them down. In the early days, she could usually sing her way into people's lives in a few minutes' time. But her songs were sounding so sad anymore. Damn! Why was he thinking of her now?

She hovered in his mind while this long, willowy woman held him with her legs wrapped around his waist. Pliant rope wrapped his body; another woman surrounded him while he tried to get Esther out of his head. He wanted to savor this beautiful creature, look at the way her dark hair embraced her shoulders, tendrils of it curling around her collarbone, another around her ear. Dark luxurious hair wound its way around his wrist, hair everywhere, sometimes in his mouth, in his face, no breathing without the abundant hair touching something—his chin, his neck. This woman, Serena.

He'd waited. No one who'd watched him go in and out of the front door on Avenue D believed he'd waited, didn't think he had it in him to wait, but he did. He waited until Esther was safe in the hospital, safe in the arms of someone who might know more about her than he did, a new lover. But now, he needed some peace . . . Serena.

He rubbed her belly and thighs and noticed for the first time the feel of her skin. It surprised him because it was leathery. Maybe this was the type of covering that held people together better than the kind Esther had. Her skin was soft, almost like poured cream except for the rough patches that had been in the fire. Cream running all over the place. Nothing binding it. Esther always spilling out for everyone to see, her skin not holding all of her inside as it should.

But Serena's skin felt good next to his and reminded him how he wanted to be. Tougher. Something that wouldn't spill. And maybe now a child would come out of her body to remind everyone how not to weave or miscalculate or doubt.

He touched her nipple again and praised this moment. Serena Bishop, his to hold, to touch, to stroke. Serena at his fingertips. And he kissed her again, her lips not full like Esther's, but well defined. Her firm lips kissed him back with no equivocation. She was his after all those months of him sitting across her kitchen table mesmerized by the subtle throb in her neck. He'd watched her heart beat there, that strong pulse of her aliveness. Serena. His. And he turned further onto his side and stared at the configuration of moles on the side of her cheek, a constellation of dark stars.

He wanted her again and felt his pulse quicken at the thought. He wanted to be swallowed up by her, sucked inside, lost in quicksand. But Serena's insides held him tightly, sucked him in and held him. Not much chance for Alf to rummage around and lose his way. *Serena. Thank you, Serena.*

Serena suddenly laughed. "You know, I thought you were something of a jerk when I met you, even with your handsome face, which by the way is very handsome." She petted both sides of his nose. "I've always thought so."

His wife stopped noticing the fine lines of his face when he couldn't keep a job. "Jerk? Something more eloquent, my dear, please."

"You talk such smooth talk, like you're such a big man."

"You don't think I'm a big man?"

"No, Alf. That's not what I like about you. Surprised?"

He nuzzled into her neck. "Do you like my moustache?" he asked.

"What do I like about you?" She traced straight lines across his forehead to the base of his receding hairline. "I like the way you're cocky. A bullshitter. Yes, that's it. No white knight stuff, even though you pretend to it at times. You're just regular, like me and Sam. Poor Esther. She's trying so hard to be upright and noble she's gone crazy with it."

Alf didn't like hearing Esther's name and didn't want her presence when he was undressed like this. There she was again, looking through him. *You've failed, Alf. I don't know if I can forgive you when you come back, and you know you'll come back. Why did you have to go away in the first place? I don't understand.*

That was the point. She'd never understand how he preferred sitting shoulder to shoulder at a bar with friends who didn't take life so seriously and who weren't obsessed with the hereafter.

"Alf," said Serena, "what are you thinking about? You went away somewhere."

"You don't make an old man feel so good when you say he's nothing fancy." Alf pulled a corner of the crumpled sheet over his nakedness.

"You want to be flattered, or lied to?" Serena sat up, propped her back against the headboard, and lit a cigarette. "I thought you liked honesty, but maybe you need your wheels greased. Do bullshitters need a steady diet of the same to survive?"

"You're tough, Serena." Alf reached for his eyeglasses on the night table and curled the bows around his ears, more comfortable when he could see the sharp outline of everything surrounding him. "Are we lovers or armadilloes in heat?" He leaned on his elbow and stared up at Serena.

She reached for his eyeglasses, put them back on the table, and pulled him down as she slid down. "We're lovers, Alf. You are my lover, and you excite me. And because I don't give out praise very often, you might listen carefully."

Alf turned on his back and closed his eyes when she cupped his penis in both hands as if it were a fragile goblet of water standing alone in acres of sand.

"I like the way you go after what you want, like in Ragtown on that 4th of July. You wanted attention, so you rigged up that phoney speech. Most people pretend they don't care." She bent over him, licked the perspiration from his navel, and circled its perimeter with the tip of her tongue. "And you're decent, Alf, even if you don't appear that way to everybody. You wouldn't dish a man, or a woman for that matter, any dirt. And you stayed faithful to Esther as long as you could. You're decent, Alf."

He rolled back toward her and followed the curve of her arm with his finger, up and down across the skin that was new to him. She was a new kind of woman who had different boundaries where maybe he, Alf, could measure up. Serena.

"I think I love you." He kissed her elbow and tried to shut Esther out of the moving pictures in his head.

"Oh, God," Serena said. "It feels so good to have a man again. So good when you're inside me. Come in me, again. Please, baby."

"God's gift to us peons," Alf said as he kissed her neck, the mole on her left breast, and her long, long torso until it curved into darkness.

• • • • •

Now, sitting day after day in the hospital, instead of staring into interminable space, Esther felt water rising inside—a spring that flowed every time she was reminded of things she loved. She sat on the edge of her bed in her loose gown of coarse cotton. Sometimes she sat on the right side, sometimes on the left, but never anywhere but on her bed. No rocking chair in the sun room, no walks on the ward. She just sat on her bed, looking out the window, reading and rereading the back side of the wrought-iron letters curved in an arch— LATIPSOH LATNEM ETATS ADAVEN—and trying to contain the water that kept leaking from her eyes.

Sometimes, as she tried to ignore the sight of Janice in the bed next to her who behaved like a stone, she felt Alfred driving up out of the water in his new car and new suit. He waved at her as the car wheels floated on the water rising in her. He smiled and said, "It's not as bad as you think, Esther. Enjoy. Be grateful." She grabbed his hand for as long as she could before the water fell out of her eyes, carrying him and his car with it.

And then, there was Baby Inez rising with the water, bobbing up and down and saying words Esther couldn't hear. Herbert, Mary Elizabeth, and Rebecca were laughing at the baby, coaxing her, encouraging her to show off, but Esther couldn't hear them. She could only watch their pantomime.

As the baby splashed the water with her hands, the spray rose in the air until it sheered off its pinnacle and fell on Esther's cheeks where people on the ward thought the water was tears.

"Esther, you don't need to cry so much." Sterile hands held hers, official hands whose bones felt as if they would rather be playing Rook or eating a chicken salad sandwich. All except for Ralph's hands, who not only seemed to like, but needed to hold Esther's. She sensed he needed a mother so much more than his job as an aide, and she squeezed his fingers to reassure him, not so much herself.

"You've got to stop crying," Ralph said. "And you need to eat. You never touch your food."

"I'm not hungry."

"I never saw so many tears," he said. "You'll drown."

Esther, the angles of her body growing sharp, willed herself not to cry. She closed her eyes and buried her face in her pillow, but the water still came in response to the most simple things: the sound of someone singing alone in the middle of the afternoon or the sight of the faithful moon and stars every night, never failing Esther and the women on her ward. These kept the water in motion, a constant high tide.

But when she slept, she could dream, and then she could fly out of the water, even above the water. She could fly from dawn to dusk until the nets of sunset caught masses of salmon-flecked fish. She had a silken body and feathered wings and soared over the streets of Brigham City where she happened to see Alf, the young boy who was brooding about his father who'd left him alone in the world. Alf was talking big, puffing himself up bigger, an expanded chest, a long stride as he walked along Main Street. But Esther didn't need to be bothered with Alf. She could fly over Corinne and back, over the mountains behind the peach orchards in Willard, over the Great Salt Lake. She could fly anywhere she wanted, no limitations, oblivious to weather. Her powerful wings pulled her higher than the seagulls and as far as she could ever wish to go, but she kept remembering the last glimpse of Alf leaning against the window of the Idle Isle Cafe, acting big, so big.

She flew back to Brigham City and lighted gracefully next to Alf. Before he could act any bigger, she wrapped her wings around him to warm him. On Main Street. Young Alf and the angel.

"I grant you three wishes," she told him.

He rested his head against her sleek body. "Esther," he said. "Esther. And Esther."

. . . . .

While Esther dreamed, Alf had nightmares. *Please Serena. Go to Dix. Tell him it wasn't my idea.* Black tunnels. Obfuscated sun piercing the fog. Walls everywhere.

Coward, Serena said through the haze, her eyes cold on his sweating face. *You complain about the money. So, something was done about it, and now you act like a frenzied hen.*

Alf woke in a skim of water, perspiration oozing out of his heels it seemed. The sky outside was still pitch black. He groped in his bed, hoping she would be next to him—long Serena, unaccusing, the woman he knew when he was awake. But then he remembered he was home in his own bed.

Dix Ballard was released from the hospital two months before. Split-T had too much to drink one night and went overboard on his assignment from Sam to remind Ballard of his failings. Word seeped into the community. "Four broken ribs. Ballard's got a broken collarbone. Yeah, at the Pass. A bar fight. He owed Alfred Jensen."

225

Sid Empey questioned him, but Alf could retrace the plot of *The Gay Divorcee* scene for scene and said how well Fred Astaire and Ginger Rogers danced together. Con Mitchell backed his story. Ballard was sticking to his version, though. Telling everybody Jensen was behind the punches and that he had no right being hired on by the city in Business Regulations. "What a joke," he told everybody.

Alf was scared after the Split-T incident. His neighbor knew of an opening in the city offices, and Alf arrived at the right place at the right time. He'd find respect the right way. A white shirt. A tie. No green apron. He was hired because he knew how to type, though Empey warned him he'd better keep his nose clean or he'd be out faster than Haley's Comet.

Almighty hell! Alf turned over to find more darkness in his pillow and now saw Esther under his eyelids, imprinted on his brain. He could feel her melancholy floating over his head, her face magnified on the wall of his mind and never leaving him alone.

"Don't leave me here for long," she had said. Again, he remembered the day he'd said good-bye, the moment before the attendants took her through the heavy doors with caged windows. Her voice was strange to his ears. "Just a little while to rest and sleep until my mind stops hurting, Alf. It spins like a speeding carousel." She coughed, and as he remembered the sound, it was more like a crying sound coughed into her fist. "Everything rushes past my eyes so fast, and my mind can't keep the details." Suddenly, she paused from her whirring speech. "Do you love me?"

She was so pathetic just then, the hospital's freshly laundered pillow-ticking dress shaping her like a stiff tent, canvas slippers gathered around each of her feet.

"That's why I brought you here. Because I care about you. You are sick, my sweet wife."

Remembering her now, her tears seemed bizarre, water puddling until her whole face was covered, everything underwater—her chin, her cheeks, her mouth. "But do you love me, Alf?"

"I've told you a thousand times," he said, wishing she hadn't asked twice. It irritated him. "No matter how many times I say it, you never believe me, so why should I say it again?"

"Because yesterday was yesterday." Her eyes seemed to recede into the water, away from Alf and everything else. Her hands reached out for the attendants on both sides, a little girl walking between two grown-ups who knew the way better than she did. Those were the last words they'd exchanged.

About today. His plans crowded Esther and yesterday to the sidelines. *Remember to tell Herbert I'll be late tonight. Got to get an accounting from Sam. Stupid government's making Six Companies stop issuing scrip! A mandate from the Secretary of the Interior, no thanks to Senator Oddie playing watchdog politician. Why'd they have to do that? My business! I'd like to make it in Business Regulations alone, but it isn't enough for my plans. Maybe some gentle lending behind the scenes? Loans still pay. Maybe we can get a better system worked out. It'll be okay if I just get the right system. No more Ballards!*

"I'll take care of delinquent customers for you," Sam had told him when the scrip finally turned to useless sheets of paper.

"Only if we have an up-and-up loan business," Alf insisted, "or I'm out of the partnership. We'll have contracts, signatures, the whole works. If a man doesn't pay, he just gets more interest added to his principal."

Sam, still impressed with Alf's language that made Sam think there was some essential knowledge he'd missed along the way, promised to keep it straight. He'd try out his new title, Collector, and try to remember the trouble unruly hit men could create in such a small place as Boulder City where Sid Empey kept tabs on every Tom, Dick, and Harry. No more services, he promised Alf, from the likes of the Cooper brothers whose still had been smashed to pieces the weekend after Prohibition was repealed.

They'd thrown a farewell party for five. Serena, Alf, and Verl Cooper sipped gin while Sam and Split-T hurled a sledgehammer at the copper tubes, the boiler, condenser, the wood frame. "Two halves of a chicken," Split-T bragged afterward when Alf asked to hear the history of his nickname. "Perfect halves with two strokes of my wood-handled axe. Like to have barbecued the son of a bitch, but we was in a hurry that night." Alf and Serena were too drunk to be horrified. They laughed and shouted "Split-T, Split-T," the rest of the night and all the way home. The next morning, they asked each other if they'd heard right. After the Cooper brothers packed their money, beds, table and chairs, and drove off in their battered truck, Sam was advised to be more careful in his choice of business associates.

Absolutely up-and-up. But there's no way I can make it without the loan business. Car payment due tomorrow. I can't get ahead on salary.

And Serena. . . . Maybe we can work things out if I can get this Ballard deal straightened out. Yes. Serena who tells me all of a sudden the other day that she'll take Esther's funerals if that's okay with me. Just like that, he snapped his fingers, *she opened her mouth and sang like a bird. Sam said she could sing, but I'd never heard a note.* He snapped a nebulous rhythm in the dark and sat up, looking out the window, seeing nothing, not even his reflection. He got out of bed, went into the kitchen where the yellowed clipping of Bill Watkins's obituary was still tacked to the wall. Pulling aside the curtain Esther'd made out of a fabric with red strawberries falling loosely through space, unattached to any leaves or stems, he saw Esther's blue teapot pushed to a corner behind the oatmeal. The teapot she thought he didn't know about. He could always tell how frightened she was by the level of money inside. Funny what he knew about her that she didn't think he did. He lifted the lid and looked inside. Nothing. Of course. What did he expect? He measured a half-cup of oatmeal and put some water on to boil.

Serena and Alf tried a few duets together after he heard her sing. He hadn't realized how much he missed the music until they harmonized "Heart of My Heart" one night. Serena was good. She had a popular kind of voice, lighter, less trained than Esther's, but he'd recommend her for the funerals Esther couldn't do anymore. People were still knocking on his front door, asking if Esther Jensen was there and could she please sing at a funeral. The death toll on the dam was up to eighty-two now.

He thought of Serena's body and how he liked to slide his hand over the whole length of her. Her Montezuma body. Mysterious. But the children weren't interested in meshing with any substitute woman. They were used to Esther's flabby confidence, her softness, her big pincushion eyes that always looked like they'd been stabbed by a thousand straight pins, wounded by anything with a point to it.

Maybe, when someone waved a magic wand or established a new dispensation of time, maybe then Serena and Alf could create something closer to Alf's vision of things. She had the right kind of hardness, telling him he was a fool when he was a fool, telling him straight when he needed to hear it. She didn't weep about the sadness of the world or let anyone push her aside, not even Alf who never did like it when Esther allowed him to push her around. It was as if his wife expected to be brushed into a dustpan, always waiting to be cancelled, as if she didn't matter somehow. But even mixed in with all the dust and debris, Esther's eyes still shone through. Ancient eyes that knew everything, certainly much more than the rest of her body which seemed to let her down in crises, crumple and fold under her when things got too hard.

Enough of Esther. He mixed his oatmeal into the boiling water, added some salt, and tried to force his mind away from the subject of Dix Ballard who kept pestering Sid Empey to take action against Alf. Dix kept shoving his wrinkled hospital bill under Empey's nose, insensitive to the fact that Alf was working in the municipal offices close to Empey now and that this harassment had to end before Alf's new job did.

"I didn't do anything to Dix Ballard," Alf insisted when Sid Empey questioned him again. "I was at the movies that night, I told you."

"What about the loan you made to Ballard?" Sid asked. That day, he had the look of an owl on a moonless night. His eyebrows poked out like stiff pinfeathers as the little dictator of Boulder City stared at Alf.

"I lent him some money about a year ago which he never returned to me, but I wouldn't harm anybody. I've lost enough in my life. Why should I be a sore loser about something like that?"

"You've got suspicious friends, Mr. Jensen. And, though you've never been caught here on the Reservation, thank your lucky stars, you've been seen drinking out at the Pass. Lucky for you Prohibition's been repealed, but there's still no drinking here in town. I could lean pretty heavily on you if I had the mind to. One slipup and you're not only out of Business Regulations, but out of town. You've got smarts, Jensen. Use them. Understand?"

"I understand, sir. I'm getting my life together. That's why I applied for a job with the city. To bring a little more respect to me and my family."

"How can you even think of playing with fire when you've got those young girls at your house, that's what I don't get." Empey seemed to know everything about everybody.

"We've got things in hand," Alf said, incensed about being pried into by this owl's talons. He wanted to tell Empey he was exceeding the limits of his job as City Manager, but knew it would be foolish.

"Keep it clean," Empey said. "Don't want to see you back here except to report to work."

But Dix Ballard was still taking his case to Empey's secretary, trying to convince her so she could convince Empey to nail Alfred Jensen before he did.

14

Esther's gown was blue and white and the shape of chaos, twisted around her torso more than once. The blue looked old and tired, and it sucked the life from her face as she sat on her bed with her arms folded across her braless chest. Her bed was the third from the end on the ward, and she could see the parking lot where black and green and yellow cars drove in and out of the arched metal gate, a twin to the arched metal headboard on her bed. Both curved like a setting sun.

Alf would be here today. She held his letter in her hand and bent over it one more time:

January 25, 1935

Dear Esther:

I'm coming to see you. It's been a long time since I've looked into your eyes and felt the pain I know you feel. I love you, my dear wife, but I somehow don't think we are good for each other. I'm not the kind of man you need. Maybe you'd get better if I'd change my ways, but I can't. I'm a person too. I just can't believe the same as you.

I need to talk to you about this. I'll arrive on Saturday (my day off). Maybe I can get there by eleven if I drive all night. Everyone sends their love, even me.

Alfred

P.S. Inez is a beauty. I'd bring her if I could, but this is a time for just you and me.

She walked to the window and back to her bed and thought maybe she should wear a pretty dress except she had no pretty dresses anymore. They were all hanging in her closet in Boulder City except for the one she wore when she came here, which was locked away somewhere in a row of metal lockers. The clanking locker door had shut her away from the things of her past like her favorite dress with the white background and lavender flowers and green stems that was folded into a paper sack, waiting for her behind the metal door of locker number 14, until she was well enough to deserve putting it back on.

Alf had liked that dress, too. He said she looked very pretty and fresh like flowers when she wore it. It was a light jersey that never wrinkled, not like the cottons she washed and ironed and wore only a few minutes until wrinkles set into the fabric and reminded her she needed to wash and iron the dress again, sooner than she wanted to, always reminding her that nothing ever stayed done.

Janice, the woman who slept next to Esther, sat on a metal folding chair between their beds. Ever since Esther arrived, Janice had never changed her facial expression. The corners of her mouth sank like rainbow ends into her jowls, and her eyes stared out with a glittering meanness from under untrimmed eyebrows. Sometimes Esther wanted to pet her, to soothe the anger that wouldn't let anyone close, but she faltered when she saw those jaws—set like they were determined to snap. She could calm Janice, she knew. Embrace her like one of her daughters and get her to release those muscles from their bulldog grip of her face. She would, in time. She'd do it as soon as she could lift herself out of whatever it was that was keeping her down, but it felt so heavy. A dense cloak like the heat in Ragtown. A mantle draped and papier-mâchéd over her shoulders. This was not her. This was not Esther.

She rocked on her bed, back and forth, hugged herself with her arms and scratchy wool blanket, and looked around the ward at the other limp gowns, the stiff black hairs growing out of her friend Doris's paper-white cheek. She listened to the sound of shuffling slippers and clinking glasses being carried to the patients on metal trays.

Alf. Her Alf would be coming to see her. Her Alf who made her happy and angry and sad. Her Alf who was like a wheel of color. He dizzied her mind, wanting to get both out of her and into her, and then two lone tears rolled down her face. Her stoic face with two drops running onto her gown where they spattered into dark spots. Water carrying Alf out of her and onto her lap. *Alf, go away from me. Get out of my heart.*

But that was all—those two tears. No more emotion, not even when she saw his car turn under the archway. She read the wrought-iron letters welded to the gate, the back side of which she could read without looking at the sign anymore. She read them through the bars on the window. She read them as she stared at the ceiling and the fan that turned lazily overhead, tired of turning for people who didn't count anymore. Why should the fan have to turn for half-people, non-people who were misshapen, too laden to move or give or return anything to the world?

She showed no feelings when she saw he had a passenger with him who leaned over with a kiss after he parked the car. Esther could see the passenger's grace as she placed her arms on Alf's shoulders and pulled him to her and kissed him like he was going away for a long time, possibly to battle or to war. And Esther recognized the shape of the woman who held her husband. The woman who once gave Esther a bucket for water, and, of course, this made Esther her debtor. Right?

She'd known all along, really. She'd seen the invitation pass between Alf and Serena the first time they'd met. An invitation issued and accepted. Esther wasn't surprised.

And then on a staircase of sunbeams fluttering into the room from the same window, Esther saw her three grandmothers, Grandpa Carpenter's polygamous wives stepping down into the open ward, coming to see her, the sun shining through their transparent bodies.

"Hello, Esther. Do you want a dime for an ice cream cone?"

"But it's not the Fourth of July! What brings you here?"

"We see it's your turn to share now."

"Share what?" Esther asked.

"Your husband." They all giggled, then put their hands over their mouths to shush themselves. The brown liver spots were gone from the backs of their hands. There were no ropy blue veins either.

"You mean Alf?"

"Yes, we do. We had to share Percy." They blushed, and each put one finger to their lips. "But we know a secret. Do you want to hear our secret?"

"If you want to tell me," Esther said, retying the strings that closed her pillow-ticking gown.

"You can't possess anyone." They shook their heads in a mutual no. "Not one whit of them. No man, or woman for that matter, is for possession. They get together to have babies, some pleasure, some companionship, and a bit of security. But not possession."

"You mean, I have no husband?" Esther whispered to them.

"You are a mother of children for the Kingdom of God. Don't be afraid, Esther. God loves you. Nobody else can hurt you because you don't belong to this earth. Don't be shaken by it. Look at us, Esther . . . our arms around each other. We've found peace. Let Alf do what he has to do. It doesn't affect who you are. He can't take anything from you."

The three grandmothers walked slightly off the ground in their gauzy white shoes. The grandmothers with their lily-colored hands caressing Esther's face as she sat on the bed between Janice and Doris, their proud bosoms tucked in veils of white, breasts that had suckled Abraham's seed, the abundant seed spilled into these grandmothers that they might give life, sprout babies, hatch them, birth them. Life. Ongoing like a river, and yet Esther felt a shadow settle over her, like a dam on a river that shaded the grandmothers as they said good-bye and floated up the sun-specked stairs and through the window where Esther could see Alf walking up to the building now. Alone. Straightening his tie. Smoothing his hair with his hands.

And Esther opened her mouth and sang, the first she'd sung in months. It was a thin, wailing note of music that wasn't a song someone had written, and even Janice shifted the corners of her mouth slightly when she turned to stare at Esther.

There were no words to Esther's song. She sounded as if she was crying, and then singing an aria, and then as if she was singing to cover up her ears and eyes with sound. Primitive sound, a high-pitched Gregorian one minute, a shaman's chant the next. A lament, filling the entire ward with surprise, especially the aide who came running to Esther to shake her on the shoulders and tell her to settle down before she disturbed the other patients. Esther put her hands over her ears and squeezed her breasts between her elbows and wailed as if she was inhabited with three centuries of pain.

"Don't do this, Esther." Ralph, the aide, was young with a crowded constellation of pimples on his cheeks. "You're upsetting the others."

"This isn't my home," she sang in the same wailing tone, her words piercingly high as she rocked back and forth in broader arcs, bending clear to her knees and arching her shoulders like wings when she tilted backward.

"Mrs. Jensen. What's happening to you? You're our model patient. We've been thinking you might get better and go home pretty soon. Don't do this, Mrs. Jensen. Please stop."

"It's burning me. I feel my skin going away from me. Help me. I can't stand here and feel my skin become fire and then ash and then nothing. Give me a cool, dark place where there's no fire and where everyone smiles at me and says I am pretty and I can sing to break their hearts and make them feel like they want to live, even with a broken heart. Please find me a place. No more fire."

Ralph sat next to Esther and put both arms around her. He cradled her quietly until her wail stopped as suddenly as it had begun and she crumpled into him, her face in her hands. He reached for her hairbrush and brushed through the matted tangles at the back of her head.

"Esther's very pretty," he soothed her. "She is pretty and everyone loves her."

"Don't lie to me." She spoke into her hands, her words stifled in her palms. "I hate lying."

Another aide dressed in crisp white bent over Esther. "Someone's here to see you, Mrs. Jensen."

"It's been a long time," said Ralph. "Here, sit up. Let me brush the rest of your hair." He gently pulled the brush through the side curls and used his fingers as a comb for her tousled bangs. Opening the drawer to her nightstand, he found a small cosmetic bag with metallic threads and a snap which he opened. He pulled out a worn tube of Miracle Red lipstick and gently dabbed the dark red onto her lips, careful to color her lips just enough, but not so dark as to accentuate the circles under her eyes. Then he found a compact with a flat and frayed powder puff, worn smooth with use, and rubbed it into the thin ring of powder inside.

"Look up," he said, smoothing the powder across her cheeks and nose, rubbing it until there was no line of demarcation, no hint of the artist at work. "There we go, except maybe," he looked inside the cosmetic bag again, "maybe you need a little touch of mascara on your eyelashes. Brighten up those eyes now."

The walk through the ward seemed forever to Esther because she wished her heels backward rather than forward, and the conflict stretched the time it took her to walk past the shadows of selves draped across the iron-frame beds: Alicia with her fifteen dolls lined up on pillow terraces; Margaret with the imaginary flute she played while she dipped her toes onto black tiles, always careful not to touch the white ones; Gabby with her five sweaters, three of them cardigans buttoned haphazardly, one green, one yellow, one beige, all of them with cigarette burns, new buttonholes for Gabby's midmorning buttoning ritual which she always performed with a cigarette in one hand, an ash poised to fall on one of her sweaters and burn another hole.

Alf waiting on the other side of the double door. Alf. Her husband. The father of her children. She straightened herself, pulled in her stomach which had flattened somewhat since she had last seen him. *Alf. I'm ready for Alf.* She nodded her head at Ralph as if to say, "Yes. I can go on my own from here." He must have sensed this shift in her because he gave her back her hand to carry herself.

Ralph, kind Ralph. Nowhere to go. She and the other patients were his kin. Ralph was afraid to go out into the strong light of day with whole people who were too strong, too complete for someone like Ralph.

Her husband wore a new suit. It was almost crisp. He must have hung the jacket while he drove. Put it on for her.

"Hello, Alfred." She put out her hand as if being introduced to him for the first time. Even in her striped institutional gown, she had a presence which seemed to take him by surprise. Had he expected something less sure? she wondered. Something weak, fragile, incompetent? She stood very tall even though she was several inches shorter than he.

He shook her hand in return. "Would you like to sit down?" He pointed to the wooden slat chairs in the visitor's room. "I have a present for you from the girls."

He held out a large box covered with flimsy Christmas wrapping—white candles with yellow flames and red bows on the candleholder. "They wanted you to have something to hold."

Dispassionately, Esther slipped the string off the paper and wound it into a ball, as was her habit. She lifted the paper's edges and it fell to the floor, barely making a sound as it settled near her slip-on paper shoes. The lid lifted off easily, and then there was the tissue paper inside, wrapped around something substantial, and suddenly Esther felt it. A faint something that made her want to tear off the paper as she had years before in her other life. She saw a paw, a cloth paw and then a stubby kind of fur and she knew this bear. Herbert bought it for Inez somewhere in another life and now this bear was here for her.

"I don't need this," she said because she didn't want Alf to know she did. "It's silly for me to have it. Take it back to Inez."

"The girls thought you would like it. It was their idea, not mine."

She turned it over in her hands, the bear she had loved when Herbert brought it home. Her son who was carrying on what Esther knew. Deep in himself, he understood what she and her heart were all about. He was carrying her inside of him. She wouldn't die until he did.

"And I guess I get to hold this bear during the night while you are holding Serena? Don't pretend, Alf. I saw her in the car."

She knew the minute she said it that he never dreamed she would see them, never dreamed she had enough latitude in this place to be close to a window where she could see out into the world and see the stories outside these walls. And yet somehow, he must have wanted her to know. He turned slightly red and then somewhat green and couldn't seem to find any words. She put her hand on his knee.

"It's all right, Alf. I've always known about her. You think I am too caught up in my melancholy to see past my nose?"

Alf put his hand over hers and a timidity glazed his eyes.

"You're wrong about a lot of things, Alf, and most of all you're wrong about me. You don't know who I am. You've been too afraid to find out. So afraid that you don't know there's something out there besides scrambling to the top, something besides having to prove yourself with schemes of money and power. You don't hurt me anymore. You're afraid. Hear me, Alf? Serena is only part of your fear. You can't hurt me with her, Alf."

"Well," Alf said, lifting up his chin and the rest of himself with it. "That's a mouthful from a sick lady."

"I'm no sicker than you, Alf." With her fingernail, Esther dug into an initial carved into the seat of the chair.

"You always were good at making me wrong. Real sharpshooter, Esther." He stood up, his back to Esther, put his hands in his pockets and pulled the fabric until it stretched tight across his buttocks and thighs.

"Nothing to say to me, Alf, after all these years? No regrets? No wish you were heres? But you can't forget me, I know that. We're woven like tight wool. She'll serve you for a time, but she's not the answer."

"It's just been wrong most of the time."

"What's wrong about it, Alf? How are we so different from everybody else?"

"You wanting me to be something I'm not. Me cramping your dreams. We've been in each other's way, Esther. Let's clear the decks."

"Oh, so we'll just sweep all the dirt under the carpet and keep walking on top of it?"

"We've got nothing to clean up anymore."

"You call us nothing?" Esther's hands fluttered to her chest, to the breasts Alf once fondled and the throat he'd kissed.

"No, that's not what I'm saying." The solidity of his back seemed to soften. "Repairs can't help us. Things need to be more clear-cut."

"And how do you propose that?"

Alf cleared his throat and leaned over to brush some dirt from the tip of his shoe. "I thought I knew."

Alf seemed bare to Esther, and she suddenly felt sad for his fear and his ups and downs and all his trying. She wished she could make it right for him. He hadn't wanted all that much, her Alf, the shabby painting of her dream. Something in him stirred her to stand up and find the front of him. "I've always loved you, Alf. Not always well, I know. Go and believe and do what you must, but we're woven. Don't underestimate us."

His eyeglasses hid his eyes from her, and he turned his head when she moved close in to him.

"Look at me, Alfred. Look at me."

He turned his face until she could see his eyebrows, his receding hairline, the mole on his left cheek, but he wouldn't give his eyes to her. Their kiss was brief and to the point. Alf straightened his tie again and held out his hand. A formal departure. Succinct. Clean.

And Esther walked back into the ward. She felt her arms as she walked. She felt her waistline and her wrists and her cheeks and hair. Esther. Here was Esther. She turned in wide, meandering circles as she walked down the aisle. She felt for the pulse in her wrist. A heart was pumping. She remembered that new white and red blood cells were being manufactured. She must be moving inside. She flung her arms wide. "My birthday's coming, everybody. My birthday's coming soon." She was alive. She could dance. She remembered the Lindy. Slow, slow, quick, quick.

"Ralph, do you want to dance?"

Ralph was adjusting a sheet corner on a bed.

"The Lindy," Esther told him. "I learned it in Chicago."

"Oh, so Esther's been to Chicago, has she?"

She stopped. His tone had been solicitous. Then she saw the slight shift in his eyes. She watched his arms raise and motion to someone she couldn't see.

"I'm free now, Ralph. We can dance. You and me." When he ignored her, she waltzed with the teddy bear her daughters had sent. The beautiful brown worn bear with split crystal eyes.

Ralph's face lost every trace of ease. "Esther, what's happening?"

"Don't you want to dance, Ralph? I'll teach you how."

But Ralph didn't like her dancing.

And she looked for the stairs, the swirling sunbeam staircase. It was time to leave. To find a way back to Boulder City and her children. To follow the grandmothers out the window and back into her own life. Esther was a polygamous wife now, just like them. She'd have to recognize Serena and welcome her into the family. She'd have to watch Alf slide his arm around Serena's waist and watch them walk out the door to go to Serena's house until it was Esther's turn again. She'd have to wait while the clock knocked hard against her ears.

But wait a minute. Esther hadn't agreed. The first wife always had a say about other wives. Alf hadn't asked her. He was supposed to ask, not just take liberties, and now there was another woman to deal with, a sharing of her husband, a decree to share everything for the common good of the kingdom, more children, more progeny for God. *But this isn't polygamy, Esther. Polygamy would be easier than this. This is adultery. A broken commandment. This is my other half breaking away, splitting off from me, discarding me, leaving me alone.*

Esther punched the foot of her bed, hit it hard with her fist. Then she punched her pillow and her bear and she flailed her arms and hit her woolen blanket with the flats of her hands, her elbows, her head.

Ralph was prepared. "I'm sorry, Mrs. Jensen. "You'll be back to your normal self in a few days. Guests sometimes do this."

That night as Esther slept in the straitjacket under the crescent head-board and watched mist closing in and then blowing past her face, she saw Janice reach over, quietly so Esther wouldn't hear her, and take the arm of the teddy bear at the foot of Esther's bed. She watched Janice squeeze the bear, wrap her arms around the used fur, embrace it and hold it close and call it Ginko, Sweet Ginko, and she saw the corners of Janice's mouth bend upward for the first time, except she wasn't sure through the sprawl of mist.

15

"*Jesus* loves me, this I know," Rebecca and Inez sang with the other Primary children for the sacrament meeting program. "For the Bible tells me so." Even Inez belonged to the chorus, standing on the front row with the smallest children lifting the hem of her dress up and down to fan herself in the hothouse meeting room. Then she put her arms full circle over her head, round sunshine arms from the "Jesus Wants Me for a Sunbeam" song. Something she'd learned from her mother. A few of the members chuckled out loud.

Sitting between Mary Elizabeth and Edna, Herbert pretended to study the stenciling on the back of the chair in front of him. He masked the pride he felt for his baby sister with a straight face and total concentration on the black stenciled words. *Property of B.C. Ward*, he read over and over. No more *Property of Palm Mortuary*. The ward had their own building and chairs now and were free to breathe clear desert air. No more suspicious smells of catacombs and embalming fluid. Herbert was pleased with his young sisters, his fiancee, himself, and the words: *Property of B.C. Ward*.

The Latter-day Saints were gaining some respect. In the beginning, the riders on his transport teased Herbert about the wives he must have hidden away somewhere, an old saw no non-Mormon could drop even though the Church officially abandoned the policy in 1890. Herbert taught them differently. "Polygamy may be restored in another time and place," he said to their puzzled faces, "but not when the law of the country forbids it." He didn't explain the Mormon beliefs of "another time and place."

For now, polygamy was something mainstream Mormons shunned the way immigrants avoided their native language. Especially Herbert. Embarrassed by the early church practice that caused wrath to be poured on the innocent heads of the Saints, Herbert wanted to be the Boulder City spokesman for Mormons. He wanted to prove their good citizenship and normalcy. Isolation, as they had known in the nineteenth-century days in the Utah Territory, hadn't worked for them here in Nevada. They couldn't, after all, escape the swirls of humanity around them. The old dilemma of keeping to themselves and not coexisting with society was no longer an issue. They were laughing and working side by side, shoveling cement and riding transports with the men who once were labelled outsiders or gentiles, even enemies to the cause of righteousness.

In Boulder City, Herbert gradually developed his own sense of Mormonism in the midst of voices that pulled this way or that, even today as he had listened to Brother Pulsipher. Stake President Pulsipher laid down the law in his sermon: "The church comes first. Before your family and your job. You should be willing to lay down your life for the Restored Gospel of Jesus Christ."

But the week before, Herbert listened to another speaker with slightly different views. Brother Allred, whom Herbert suspected was a Fundamentalist, told the congregation that the Latter-day Saints had sold out to society. He said he exhorted Elohim every night. "Restore the real Gospel—the one Joseph Smith ordained." Polygamy, the United Order, blood atonement, and all, Herbert suspected.

Other lay speakers spoke on other Sundays: "Mormons are a peculiar people, and may they never forget it." "Prepare yourself for eternity. This life is nothing compared to its glory." Promises of realms of glory, kingdoms to rule, seas of posterity. The Restored Gospel of Jesus Christ. "Be in the world but not of the world."

But when Herbert walked out the chapel doors each Sunday into the great sea of sunshine and blue sky, he couldn't refrain from wondering about the humanity swarming around him, rows of them eating in the mess hall, lowering penstock pipe sections over cliffs and into the canyon with moonbeam devices, riding skips on aerial cableways, pouring more and more concrete, finishing the surfaces of the intake towers. The number of dam builders and visitors, engineers, surveyors, carpenters, machinists, *ad infinitum*, made the ranks and claims of Mormonism seem so small.

To reconcile his faith with his doubt, Herbert appointed himself Goodwill Ambassador, a counterpoint to the insularity of some of his fellow Mormons who insisted on separateness. He was a gregarious exemplar, a local liaison, the unofficial Boulder City missionary. He wanted the dam builders to see the gem aspects of Mormonism. Salvation, if they'd only listen. He also suspected they had a few things to teach him, "the sun shining on the just and the unjust alike."

He looked away from the stenciled words now. Inez's clowning and the children's chorus pleased Herbert. And so did the young woman next to him who'd soon be his wife. After their honeymoon at the El Cortez Hotel in Las Vegas for one night, they'd drive to Sparks. He reached into his shirt pocket for the four pieces of letter. Spreading it out on his knee, he read it yet another time.

March 18, 1935

Dear Alfred Jensen:

Since I'm the only doctor at this hospital, as well as the superintendent, I try to release patients when I feel their stay here is not in their best interests. (We have much worse cases and are overcrowded as well.) I don't know as much about mental illness as I'd wish, nobody does, but to the best of my observation, I believe Esther Jensen needs her home more than she needs us. Your wife has been here for eighteen months, and she's wasting away to a pair of eyes that are never dry.

I don't think there is anything wrong with her other than, as one of my aides said, she's dying from a broken heart.

She told me about a dream the other night. "There was a field," she told me. "Sunshine on one side, shadow on the other, a high, huge concrete wall in the middle. Men kept saying it had to be higher, and they poured cement into this wall until it got so high that it blocked all the sunshine out of everywhere. Then, when no one could see sunshine anymore, black clouds got stuck at the top and stayed there forever."

This isn't the place for your wife. She needs to have people she loves around her, and she needs to sing again. She sang when she first came here, sat in one of the rocking chairs and sang for hours, but she won't open her mouth for anything anymore. I'm afraid she's not going to last much longer if she stays here. I'd like you to come and get her.

Yours truly,

When he first found it, the letter was torn through the middle, both ways. Herbert found the pieces when he was emptying the trash in the alley and took them in to the kitchen table to puzzle through the wrinkles. Now, with one hand holding the pieces together, he smiled at the thought of rescuing his mother. He knew her. Knew who she was. He saw the jagged edges of her mind tearing her into pieces, but he knew she wasn't a lunatic. Just too finely tuned for her life. She used to read him stories about King Arthur. She used to gallop her fingers over the tops of his legs—horses off to the rescue. Sometimes, the fingers would gallop over his face, and then she'd kiss him and say he was her special boy, that she could always count on Herbert no matter what. Herbert, the knight on the white horse.

The children were singing the final chorus. "Yes, Jesus loves me. The Bible tells me so," and then, sounding like double-sized elephants on the wooden floor, they pounded off the stage and ran to their seats to beg their parents for pencils and paper to help them make it through the final sermon. Common Sunday bribery.

Rebecca's favorite game was dot-to-dot—a square grid of dots where she and Mary Elizabeth took turns drawing a line at a time from one dot to the next. When one of them closed in a square, they wrote their initials inside. The one with the most initials won.

Herbert felt like a patriarch today, handing out the pencils and paper, telling the girls to be reverent and listen while they drew. The father. The leader. The protection and safety for the Jensens. They gathered around him, petting his knee, leaning a cheek against his arm, asking to sit in his lap. Father hen. And Edna looked at him with eyes mirroring his contentment.

After they listened to one of the brethren give the closing prayer and ask God to protect the workers on the dam from further harm or accident, they walked home in the hot, dry air holding hands, all five of them. Sometimes the younger girls broke out of the chain and ran underneath the frame of clasped hands. Sometimes Inez begged to be carried. Sometimes she twirled, her skirt like an umbrella, in the middle of the fried concrete. They moved through the crisp heat like a company of folk dancers, swinging their arms, oblivious to the overhead sun, disinterested in the sharp tongue of heat that lapped at their arms and legs. They cut across to Coronado Plaza where they serpentined through the oleander bushes, still holding hands and sniffing the heady, almost tropical fragrance. And the heat snapped in the air that surrounded them. Dragonfly wings sawed the air; horseflies brushed past their shoulders.

They all laughed and played Red Rover in the Plaza's spiky grass until they stopped for a minute to watch Serena driving their father's car, waving to them, their father sitting next to her in the front seat. She was a common sight at Alf's side now. She'd helped him drive his car ever since the night he'd come home with a broken arm. "I fell against a stool at the Pass," he told Herbert, but there were too many bruises on his face to blame on a stool.

"Your father and Serena are good friends," Herbert told his sisters after the car turned onto Utah Street. "Dad needs a good friend to help him laugh while Mother is gone."

They agreed. It wasn't good when their father came home drunk or angry. They'd seen his ashen face, accented with a black they didn't understand. They'd seen him lash out at Herbert, telling him he was a Mama's boy with a gelatin spine. They even watched him kick Herbert. Lift the toe of his shoe and kick him hard in the shins. Mary Elizabeth tried to pull her father away from her brother, but his shoe kept striking Herbert's leg like a woodpecker.

"I'm not made of wood," Herbert cried. "That's my leg. Stop it."

"Your mother is a puppet maker," Alf yelled back, "making you into the perfect marionette who perfectly pleases his mother."

"I'm not a puppet. Stop it, Dad." Herbert cried like he was two years old, shameless tears smearing his face.

"How I can have this son? Soft, like Esther. Liquid. Spineless."

"I'm helping you with the children. I'm driving truck now."

"You're cleaning floors on your hands and knees. A woman. Herbert, my son. A woman like Esther."

The final thrust of the shoe broke the skin, and blood darkened the fabric above his folded cuff.

"I have the Gospel," Herbert answered in a shaking voice.

"I have the Gospel," Alf mimicked. "What about you, Herbert? Yourself? Do you have yourself, Herbert, or are you just a package of obedience walking around in skin? Where's your gumption? Kick me back. Show me you have some stuffing in you."

"You have alcohol and the Devil in you."

"Ah now, we hear some talking. Now we see the festering on the insides of the boy."

"You *are* the Devil," Herbert yelled and then slumped into the rocking chair, both hands on his forehead.

"Stopping so soon, Herbie?"

His father looked like a foreigner from hell. His mocking expression hardened into stone while Herbert sat quietly in the chair, all the time rocking and thinking. *The other cheek. You've got one, Herbert. Don't be like him.*

"Say something, Herbert."

He rocked and buried his eyes in the palms of his hands. *I won't say one more word, not if he kicks me again until three weeks from now. I won't answer.* He heard his father's angry breathing.

"Leave him alone, Dad," Mary Elizabeth said quietly. "Just because you're mad, don't take it out on Herbert. He didn't do anything."

"That's the problem," Alf said, turning his head to see his two youngest daughters huddled against the wall. "You're afraid too," he said to them, avoiding his oldest daughter standing in the doorway with her arms folded across her midriff. "Everybody's afraid. I'm sick of it. I'm sick to hell of it."

"You're just as afraid," Mary Elizabeth said as he pushed her aside to pass through the hall doorway. He slammed the door to his room while the girls dampened a washcloth to clean Herbert's shin.

"It really is good he has somebody to help him laugh," Herbert said as they left the Plaza and started back home. "It's better when he's not around too much anyway."

And while they tried to miss all the cracks in the sidewalk on their way home from Sunday School, the dam was filling the canyon, its arteries filling the canyon walls. Columns. Towers. Tentacles. Buckets on cables opening and closing their jaws every hour of that day, dumping more fill, more concrete. Sealing the gap.

While Herbert, Edna, Mary Elizabeth, Rebecca, and Inez held hands and crossed Wyoming Street, someone was troweling cement on the intake towers. Tall turrets behind the dam. Three hundred ninety feet high, reinforced concrete. Soon, they would suck the Colorado River into the underground labyrinth—through their cylindrical gates, through penstocks, drains, pumps, pipes, through wicket gates into turbines, through more pipes and outlets back into the tailrace. The new route for the river—through the labyrinth to rise, fall, whirl, shoot through pipes, tunnels, make a loop out of its course. Water arrested. Sentenced to spin through turbines, one foot of it falling nine feet in one second to make one horsepower or 746 watts of electricity. Water racing through a maze of pipes and tubes until it found its way back to itself—the Colorado.

While Alf and Esther's children decided they should have their mother back home even if they had to set up an around-the-clock schedule to watch and be with her, more conduits at the dam site lengthened. Channels to keep the water from creeping back through rock and bursting through the concrete. Huge, strong, tentacles of penstock pipe to carry the water to the power plant, the generators, the turbines. Steel pipe to carry a river's worth of water in its belly in both high and low water times, season after season, year after year. Steel pipe made by Babcock & Wilcox Company from Barberton, Ohio, esteemed manufacturers of steam boilers and pressure vessels. Steel conduits winding through 14,500 feet of rocky, tunneled canyon walls.

Even as Herbert picked Inez up from a fall and brushed the gravel from her scraped knee, steel pipes were being forged by Babcock & Wilcox, now expatriots of Barberton, Ohio, now pressing pipe in Bechtel, Nevada, one mile from the canyon rim. These same boilermakers waiting for their Olympian trailer to arrive from La Crosse, Wisconsin, designed to transport their 170-ton sections of pipe from Bechtel to the dam.

At that same moment, the Cinderella trailer crossed the Utah-Nevada border, a cumbersome, lumbering, four-wheels-on-a-corner, 37-1/2-feet-long, 22-feet-wide contraption with air-operated brakes and hydraulic steering. Two hundred eleven tons from La Crosse Boiler Company. All sixteen wheels needed continuous rolling action or the drag on the tires could cause a blowout which equaled disaster to the heavy load. Dual axles and a steel pump supplied equalized pressure to a control cylinder nestled between each set of axles. A caterpillar tractor waited to pull the 41-ton trailer plus 170-ton load down the steep canyon road, ready to imprint the paved road with its chain link tracks.

Little men. Big pipes. Big plans. Cableways, networks, pipes, tunnels, labyrinths. Earthworms digging out the earth to turn the river in different directions, hurrying to make the river obey and serve. Serve the little men like Alf, his son Jack, his son Herbert, their wives, their children, the families of those who lost their lives in the path of pouring cement—by asphyxiation in a tunnel, under the wheels of a crane, overcome by impossible heat. The pride of America. A concrete wall filling up a canyon. Brave men rappeling across cliff faces, scraping rocks smooth. Ingenious men devising trailers to carry 170-ton steel pipe, revising jumbo carriages once again, still buzzing into andesite with drills, new places to open. Himix. Lomix. Concrete churning and mixing. Silos to blend cement. Chutes for filling eight-cubic-yard buckets on railroad cars. Agitators. Mixers. Rocks falling through silos, sliding down chutes. Aggregrate dug from quarries, sent on trains to slide through funnels. Earth sliding, moving on train tracks, on truck beds, in chutes, through funnels. Earth falling, sifting, mixing with different equations of itself plus measured amounts of water all to one end: to stop water, divert water, make it subservient to the little men who drove tractors, drafted blueprints, built Fluxo pumps to boost cement along its way to the wall in Black Canyon.

When they opened the door to their empty home on Avenue B, Rebecca put claims on the crispy part of the Sunday pot roast that sizzled in the oven with halved carrots and potatoes.

"If you'll put some Mercurochrome on Inez's knee," Mary Elizabeth told her, "I'll save it for you."

•   •   •   •   •

Alf felt a different sense of himself when he went to work in the municipal offices—a step removed from the average workingman for the first time in his life, a subtle notch of achievement. Cool corridors and white shirts. Less colorful, more guarded language. An illusion of civility, perhaps, but he liked to open the right half of the tall brown doors, swing it open, close it on the sunshine behind him, and walk to his desk. The walls were covered with small glassed documents of one sort or another. Cool. Unemotional. The right setting for Alf who was a torn page like the letter from the State Hospital. Torn into pieces because he didn't know what to do. Hoping for a clean line of demarcation to draw itself across his path, and this job looked as if it might be part of that line. A way to the requisite courage he needed to bring Esther back into his life.

His new position in the Business Regulations department of the municipal offices included a mishmash of odd duties under the title: "Collections and Licenses." The post had been created, Alf decided, to clean up the details Sid Empey didn't care about.

In the beginning, Empey had the sole power of controlling business and residence permits. The government hadn't wanted a boomtown, where any opportunist could drive into Boulder City to hang up a sign or a shingle. Quick fortune and quick exits. A common phenomenon in the West. They'd required formal application for business permits and would have had thirty-one drugstores instead of two, sixteen barbershops and beauty parlors, fourteen restaurants, fourteen filling stations, twelve soft drink shops, plus innumerable others, had they not established strict guidelines. The business field was narrow to begin with because of Six Companies's own department store, mess hall, rec hall, laundry and barbershop. After Sid Empey scrutinized every application with a face that had soured somewhere through his years, picking and combing through every fragment that might be called into question, he tired of that game and found a new one—running a town at his whim. Why, Alf thought, should he bother with the small details, like dog licenses and burning permits?

He joined Sid Empey's fiefdom quite by accident when the job opened like a gaping hole in front of him, the former "Collections and Licenses" man being his neighbor whose mother was dying in Missouri. He never thought he'd want to work under a man as arbitrary as Empey, but he considered this strange windfall a link in his destiny, the one God hinted at on the shores of the Colorado, and submitted to this turn of fate. He'd try to ignore Empey's petty disputes, like the argument with the man who wanted to build a house from native rock. "Absolutely not," Empey told him. "We don't want some hodgepodge town, and you're fired if you go against our aims in this place." Or his quarrel with Robert Hayes over the ranch he'd started south of Boulder City with the help of treated water from the sewage plant to water his oats, chickens, three cows, and one horse. "I hate flies," Empey told him. "Close it up or you're out of here."

"But I've got money in it now," Hayes complained.

"Too bad," Empey said. "Close it down." And Hayes did because there was no court of appeal against Empey, no recourse in a town that was organized by the United States Government.

He'd stay out of trouble with Empey who'd eyed Alf suspiciously during the interview when Alf told him he was pulling his life together, that Empey wouldn't be sorry he hired him. "Not one false step if you want to keep the job!" he'd said to Alf like a father scolding a child. "And stay away from Sam Konevic and the Railroad Pass. Bunch of no-goods out there."

Sid Empey. A meddler. Alf wondered how Empey, who looked like an orphan left by a railroad siding and raised by hungry wolves, could have so much power over others' lives. His face was perfect casting for the stingy landlord Alf had seen in melodramas, and he seemed to have the compulsion to extend that role into his professional life. And why had Alf cast his lot with such a stringent judge? Maybe he needed an arbiter in his life and had unwittingly chosen the harshest he could find.

Respectability temporarily replaced Alf's wild-eyed facts, figures, and hopes. He saw Sam on rare weekends, debated more about the time he spent with Serena, and collected city rent on weekdays—$275 per year for a 40-x-10-foot business lot, or $120 per year for residential ground with a fifty-foot frontage. Something about being employed by the city, by the government, made him feel unburdened of an uneasy guilt, a subdued sense of cheating someone for his own profit. He'd probably picked up this uneasiness from Esther's high-toned moral sense, but still he had his own respect for returns being diffused through an institution; the job seemed cleaner. Alf felt more straightly drawn than he had for some time, though he still couldn't resist Serena or the few opportunities to float a personal loan when someone was down on his luck. After all, he wasn't "Collections and Licenses" forever. The job would probably disintegrate as soon as The Dam was finished, just as the whole town probably would, but he had a good year or two left and figured people weren't drawing sumptuous paychecks anywhere else he'd heard of lately.

The strangely fitting new life changed pace one day. Word flashed through town that Six Companies's records were being seized by the government on authority of a search warrant. Trucks carrying the U.S. Marshal and U.S. Attorney had rolled into town that morning to seize payroll records and deliver them to the courthouse in Las Vegas. A former Six Companies employee, John Wagner, nobody Alf ever heard of, had spilled the beans to the Justice Department and claimed that Six owed $300,000 to the Federal Government in contract penalties—$5 per hour overtime violation. Larry Glavin, chief investigator for Secretary of Interior Ickes, arrived as the trucks departed to investigate Wagner's claims: that Six Companies kept a double set of books, their own and the one they showed to government inspectors. They were in gross violation of the contract which specifically stated that no man should work more than an eight-hour shift each day.

Alf wondered if anybody much would speak up, even though there were plenty of those who'd seen more than eight hours on a workday—both his sons, for instance. There'd been accidents, emergencies, times when a job needed finishing. But it was an unwritten commandment in

Boulder City: Thou shall not blaspheme. Thou shalt reverence Frank 'Hurry Up' Crowe and Six Companies. Besides, Sid Empey might find a way to fire a man for saying too much and paying too little respect to the government and its project. The investigation could have a bad effect. Slow things down. Tie hands. Change the status quo. Forbidden in Boulder City, Nevada, on the Boulder Canyon Project. Not many would say much if pressed because they'd already rationalized that their extra hours were necessary, everything always necessary to this big machine set in motion to stay in motion until its purpose was fulfilled.

"Glavin also wants to check for any irregularities on our business applications," Empey told Alf the next day, one of the few times at work he addressed him directly. "Somebody's been filling his ear about what they consider my arbitrariness, I guess. File them in four categories, Jensen. 'Exclusive' for public utilities, 'Limited' for mercantile, 'Special' for banks, transportation, et cetera, and 'Personal' for doctors and dentists, that kind of thing."

So Alf was given a day's respite from dog licenses and proper receptacles for garbage in the alleys between the avenues, to sort through the hundreds of applications, file them according to Empey's system, and wonder who would come out on top: the Justice Department or the Boulder Canyon Project. Fraud was a heavy accusation. $300,000 worth of it. Six Companies might be greedy in its over-big conglomerate britches, a long distance from the simpler days of those Utah, Idaho, California, and Oregon business firms as entities unto themselves, but Alf would stop short of calling their behavior criminal. After all, he still had some familial pride in the operation, just like everybody else in town. Six Companies couldn't be as negligent as Wagner claimed. Everybody knew that.

When Glavin came to the office to meet with Empey and look at the business applications, he arrived earlier than the solemn Mr. Empey.

"Morning," said Glavin. He held out his hand to Alf.

"Good morning," Alf answered, pushing his latest batch of dog license applications to one side.

"So where's this Mr. Empey I've been hearing so much about?"

"Should be here any minute. He knows he has an appointment with you."

Glavin sat down in the chair next to Alf's desk. "Is he as bad as I've been hearing? I got an earful last night over at the rec hall. Someone said he had his own two-fisted henchmen, namely Buzz Bodell and his ruffians, who pose as rangers and drive him around town to spy into everyone's lives."

"Oh," Alf crossed his legs and swiveled his chair from side to side and began his Empey-in-moderation speech. He didn't know Glavin well enough to say anything else yet. "He makes sure everybody stays within their water allocations, and he keeps close tabs on outsiders, but he has his own sense of fairness. A little Victorian maybe."

"Could he have refused some of these business licenses out of personal vindictiveness?" Glavin lowered his voice. "Or could it be he's a puppet for Six Companies? He's been given an unusual amount of power, you know."

"I don't know about that. He does get on everybody's nerves, even tried to tell me how I was supposed to be running my family life, but as far as being a puppet for Six, I wouldn't go that far. He works for the Bureau, not Six."

"This is hand in glove, man. Don't try to kid me. You know, don't you, he's the only administrator responsible to the Bureau of Reclamation who's an outsider?"

"What do you mean?" Alf straightened his stack of licenses again.

"Every other administrator in this town is a Bureau man, except Empey. I think his son was an executive assistant to Wilbur when he was Secretary over at Interior. Got his own father hired as city manager when he was way too old for the job in the first place and when the job should have gone to a Bureau man. Family influence, pure and simple. The man's in his seventies now and should be retired. He's got to be on somebody's payroll, don't you think?"

"Empey?" Alf laughed out loud. The little dictator hired on by kin? This scenario sounded too familiar, and here was Sid Empey, city manager/dictator who held sway over so many people's lives, his own included. Kin licker. And Empey on somebody's payroll? Keeping the peace with his parsimonious morality when all the time he was on the take? Keeping everybody in line not only for the government but for Six Companies, who was ramrodding its way across the desert and the river and the people who worked the job for them because there was no place else to go? Nice wool over the town's eyes. Nice wool, that is, if it was true.

Alf laughed out loud again. He, Alf, had been called despicable. A schemer. He, a man who'd only wanted to make his way on his own

252

terms. When that failed, as it had lately, he even tried other people's terms. Sid Empey's at the municipal offices, no less. Here was the righteous Empey, maybe deeper into the gears of the machine than Alf ever dreamed of being, and the old codger played his high-handed innocence so well.

"What have you found out about Six Companies's double set of books?" he asked Glavin, feeling cozy with this investigator all of a sudden, cozy with this new insight into Empey, the man who never greeted Alf civilly in the cool corridors of the municipal building, but slipped by instead like a discreet whisper.

"That's for me to know," Glavin said, lighting a cigar and tossing the band on Alf's desk, possibly sensing he'd been too loose with his talk. "But we haven't found what we're looking for, I can say that much. Smart codgers at Six Companies. Got the whole town buffaloed, too. Cat's got the town's tongue."

"Grand schemes everywhere," Alf said, riffling the license applications and suddenly half delirious. He picked them up and spread them like a handful of playing cards. "Me. Six Companies. Sid Empey. Except the difference is in how grand they are! If they're big enough, then everyone kowtows to the schemer like he's king. It's the scale of the thing that makes the difference. The *scale.*" He was burbling, the words tumbling out of his mouth almost incoherently.

Glavin tapped his cigar ash into Alf's empty wastebasket and sat back again to observe.

"That's what I didn't get, Mr. Glavin." Alf was euphoric. A kid at a carnival after he'd knocked over the milk bottles with a baseball. "That's what I haven't understood. Esther's right. I've been shortsighted with my paltry, unimaginative schemes. I didn't think big enough, thinking the problem was fear when really it's scale one needs to consider. A correct perception of scale! Some have big vision. Some don't. Plain and simple."

He put his elbows on his desk, waved Glavin's cigar smoke out of his face, then folded his arms high across his chest and tucked his hands under his armpits. "But . . . the Big Question! THE Big Question. Are you ready?"

Glavin suspended his *Garcia y Vega* natural-leaf cigar near the tip of his ear.

"Who, Mr. Glavin, assigns big or small on the scale? Our fathers who hang themselves? Our mothers who endure? Where's the morality in this, good sir?"

A strong silence followed before Glavin inhaled and blew smoke rings over Alf's desk and noticed Empey's arrival. "I've lost you, my friend," he said quietly, "but not totally. Something's passed here. Let me shake your hand for something I'm not sure deserves congratulations, but nevertheless, my hand."

The two strangers shook hands. Their eyes met briefly, both pairs veined with red irritation from the cigar smoke, both wary of the edge Alf had approached.

"Remember this," Glavin said, standing to greet Sid Empey who was hanging up his coat. "If you want to find fraud, you can. If you decide it's not necessary, then you don't. A word of wisdom from your seasoned investigator who's seen a few games, and not all of them big ones."

"You understand me, then," Alf said, fanning out the pile of license applications like a seashell on his desktop.

"Yes. I think I do."

16

No one noticed when their car rolled into town. They arrived between shift changes and after the usual hours of business and evening pleasure. Edna held Esther with both arms, the farm girl arms that once carried bales of hay and even a sick calf from time to time. She pushed Esther's matted hair back from her eyes. No sheen to it. She blotted the perspiration from Esther's neck and temples.

"We'll nurse her back to health," she said quietly to her new husband. "Lullaby and goodnight, with sweet roses, bedight . . ." Edna sang and then stopped. "What does bedight mean, Herbert?"

"Arrayed. All arrayed in sweet roses."

"Sounds like a funeral to me. Maybe I won't sing that anymore." Edna unbuttoned the top button of her dress, rebuttoned it, shifted her weight under the press of her new mother-in-law's body.

Esther relaxed in the competent arms. "I love my Herbert," she kept saying between lapses into exhausted sleep. "I love Alf too, but I don't need a husband anymore. God is my comforter. Will you tell Alf for me?" she asked.

"Just you be quiet now," Edna said. "Rest your head back." Edna gave a knowing look to Herbert, who seemed to slump slightly into the steering wheel with the prospect of telling his mother about his father and Serena.

The town had changed profoundly in the eighteen months Esther had been away. It even changed in the three days Herbert and Edna were away, grown distant from them because everything was always moving and changing here. Job seekers and train- and truckloads of materials constantly arrived in town, even now in the middle of the night, always a new face for the dam and its city. The Spanish arches built to shade sidewalks in the daytime gaped like hostile black eyes in the dark. The pale and thirsty young trees lining Nevada Highway reflected yellow streetlight, intermittent sprays of leaves blazing like torches in the midst of dark branches, their patterns swirling on the sidewalks and against the car windows.

"Go to Arizona Street, please," Esther whispered. "I don't want to go home just yet."

"You want to see the theater, I'll bet. I've told Edna about it. My mother. Carmen."

"Yes, I was Carmen," she said, sitting up in the middle of the front seat, her hair mussed. "Where's the theater? Is it gone now?"

"We're not there yet, Mother."

"Who will sing at my funeral, Herbert? It'll be one of the few funerals I'll ever attend where I won't be asked to sing."

"We'll all sing," Herbert said. "Me, Edna, the girls. Maybe Jack could play his saxophone and we'll sing 'Dark Town Strutters' Ball.' God'll drive down and pick you up in a taxi. What do you think?"

"Sounds good."

"None of this talk about dying, you two," said Edna. "Your mother's got a lot of life to live. You're going to get better, Sister Jensen."

"You can call her mother, Edna. She'd like that, wouldn't you, Mother?"

Esther didn't answer, drifting into another of her phases. In and out the window.

"It's so soon," Edna said. "No offense, Herbert. When you've had one mother your whole life, and she's been the only one, it seems strange to be calling someone else her name."

"It really doesn't matter," Esther said, her words coming out of her mouth like vapors. "I've seen my Herbert again, met you, Edna. I'll see my girls soon. I'm not sad."

"There's the theater," Edna said.

Esther searched the words on the darkened marquee, *Smilin' Through with Norma Shearer, Leslie Howard, Fredric March*, secretly hoping her name might be there for something wonderful she once did. A bit of Esther in wooden block letters, commemorating her gift to the Boulder City memory. Carmen had sung and danced there on the stage of the Boulder Theater. Carmen in red had outfoxed everyone. They didn't think she could pull it off, but she had. She held them with every seductive subtlety she'd memorized at the movies, every move she'd discovered on her own, even the feeling she had when Con Mitchell touched her thigh during *Dinner at Eight.*

She relished the memory of being alone on a stage and hearing the applause and the cheers, but she knew now it was only a brief thing, unimportant really. A star is bright, then a star fades, but it doesn't matter whether it is bright or faded—it's only on its way to becoming something else. A moment of brightness was a point in a long chain of events, and there was no reason to assign importance to bright or dark, being it was all a continuum. She knew that now. So she kissed her fingers and threw the kiss to the Boulder Theater and the one moment of her life which had seemed so important.

"Mother," said Herbert, "did you know they're dedicating the dam in just a few months? Con Mitchell was asking when you were coming back. He wants you to sing at the dedication of the dam if you're feeling up to it. The national anthem or something like that. He's on the program committee."

"Isn't the President of the United States going to be there, too?" asked Edna.

"My voice went away when I went away. It said good-bye and walked out the double doors."

"But you're home now, Mother. Your voice has come with you."

"What are you two talking about, Herbert?" Edna sat up straighter in the seat and rotated her head to roll out the kinks in her neck.

"Family talk, I guess," said Herbert. "I'd be willing to bet she'll be singing at that dedication. I'd bet on it. Now she's home with us, we'll give her legs to stand on, Edna. Right?"

"Herbert, please," said Esther, "I'm tired. Don't try to put ideas in my head."

The eyes of mother and son met in the dim light of the borrowed car, Alf's not-quite-so-new car lent for the trip. Herbert could never hide from her, nobody could when she looked at them directly. Especially now. The eyes more enormous.

"Just think, Mother. Singing on national radio for a coast-to-coast audience, and Franklin Delano Roosevelt, and Eleanor."

"I said don't put fanciful notions in my head, Herbert. I just want to be in my own bed, not in some scratchy pillow-ticking dress with no tucks or flattering lines."

Herbert laughed at the most unpredictable woman he'd ever known. She elicited unbridled sympathy one minute with eyes looking like two holes being dug through to China, full of all the layers of the earth and the stratas of pressure and molten heat, and then surprised everybody with a good one-liner. "Show business," he said. "Never leaves your system, does it?"

The house was dark, now distinguishable from the row of houses on Avenue B because of the cactus garden Herbert had planted. Nobody wandered into the wrong houses and the wrong beds anymore because people had found ways to make the cottages their own with small picket fences, joshua trees, yucca, painted trim, rock borders. Herbert stopped and turned off the ignition. He'd laid a rock pathway at right angles to the house, a sort of red carpet for his Mother and his new bride.

Herbert, the bridegroom, helped his mother over the old threshold and onto the living room sofa, then returned to the car to carry his new bride over a new threshold. Edna protested. He insisted.

"This is silly," she laughed.

"This is our first home," he said.

A step into this living room was a step onto the floorboards of a cold stage, no audience awake or applauding the players as they switched on the lights. Herbert showed Edna to the bedroom where Alf rarely slept anymore, half-hoping Alf had changed his mind and would be sprawled out on the bed, even if it meant he and Edna would have to use the old surplus cots.

Herbert tucked his mother under a pieced quilt, an assortment of plaids, some of the seams frayed, one that had been with the family in Brigham City, Price, Salt Lake City, Malad, Ely, Ruth, and San Diego. She was so thin now, the only thing still alive seeming to be her eyes. He gently touched her eyelids and closed them. "Sleep, Mother. You're home now."

"Where's Alf?" she asked, her eyes springing open.

"He's on a new shift," Herbert lied.

"I want to see Alf. I have to tell him about God and me."

"Go to sleep now. Tomorrow's a new day. Dream about FDR listening to you sing. 'A nightingale,' he'll say to Eleanor."

• • • • •

Alf lay next to Serena, stroking her, listening to the mechanics of the clock pendulum in her front room, counting the hours and quarter hours before Serena's boarder would come home from his graveyard shift. *Esther will be home by now. I should be there. But she'll suck me back in. I'm pulling myself back together, and I can't be dragged into her undertow. I won't.*

Serena, lying there, asleep, impassive, indifferent. She hadn't disappointed Alf, actually, though she had her own mind, much more of one than

Alf could have imagined in the beginning, fairly well hidden behind the easy smile, but at least she wasn't always floating into backwaters to spin into the vortex of a whirlpool. She hadn't disappointed him, but her tongue was sharp, even like a viper's sometimes when they kissed. He was drawn to the sharpness, the sting. It felt much better than the sentimentality of Esther's lips and mind. Serena wasn't afraid. But her fearlessness was a wall, long and winding, tall, bricked. He'd checked. He'd searched for clefts, erosion, fissures. He couldn't find a gap in the wall.

He'd made a feeble attempt to wedge Serena into his household where she could play house. But as he thought, his children proved reliable in their mother's behalf: Mary Elizabeth throwing her sharp-witted darts at him, smiling at Serena with a much too perfect graciousness; Inez too attached to Mary Elizabeth and Herbert to warm to Serena; Rebecca with her own ideas about eggs, toast, and fruit juice for breakfast when Serena offered to come over and fix it one holiday morning. Serena, after all, was used to black coffee and a leisurely pace. Without words, yet in no uncertain terms, they notified Serena that the Jensen family was complete, no employment wanted, the Jensens fully illustrated. Maybe Esther was missing, but her absence did not erase her place. She could not be replaced, even if she couldn't be found. Nothing narrower, less soft, or less nervous would do.

The baby Serena talked about in Ragtown days didn't come either. As the months went by, Alf heard less and less talk about a baby in her life. He'd been so good at making them before. Maybe if they kept trying. But no sign of babies or domesticity for Serena.

Gradually, it seemed, she laughed louder every time she saw menstrual blood spotted on the sheets. "Maybe I'm saved," she said, "and you too." But she never talked about it except for that, a subject with double edges. Alf sensed she was feeling lucky. Nothing new would replace her. No child would rub her out with its fresh strength. She was impregnable.

Here he was now, Alfred Jensen, his skin touching a sleeping woman—both graceful and desirable—but never fully his if he couldn't find a gap in her wall. The irony of it all, he laughed. A fool like him mesmerized by her lack of fear, but she'd never be fully his if she wasn't afraid of something.

His right arm ached, the one Dix Ballard had twisted back and back until it snapped. He still felt a weakness every time he lifted any kind of weight, the bone never fusing right. To soothe the ache, he placed his hand in the curve above Serena's hip and tried to saddle his mind, tie it to something before it wandered back to the subject of his wife. And there she was, her eyes in full glory. Esther, the pain in his arm, the tightness in his lungs.

He pressed harder against Serena until there was no space between them, but still couldn't find escape into her or sleep. She slept with abandon, her arms wide apart. He began counting. Anything to crowd Esther out. First, he counted carrots on display. Then he counted oranges, balancing them one by one in a growing pyramid. Esther kept interrupting his counting, kept opening the door to his mind and asking for things—a head of lettuce, then a watermelon, then for him to come home. He turned over, told her to go away. After all, he didn't work at the commissary anymore.

He'd given up retailing. The grocery business. The unconscionable smallness of a green apron and stacked oranges, apples, and cantaloupe. After his last night of work, he'd crumpled the green apron into a ball, thrown it at the floor, and dressed for the Pass in the creamy white suit he'd just bought. He was not a sprinkler of vegetables anymore. He worked for the city now. A white shirt. A desk of his own.

Still trying to calm his mind, he counted money—coins, bills. Then pieces of no-good scrip interrupted the steady flow of money into neat piles. Alf turned on his other side and tried remembering faces of customers, new ones, and old ones who still owed him money. But Esther stood in the same line, holding her hand out, asking for a loan. Not for money, but for Alf. "I'm home, Alf. I'm waiting for you."

He tossed again, worried he might waken Serena, half-hoping he would. He needed to hold onto her before he sank back into the swamp. He didn't need to feel responsible anymore. Herbert could give Esther what she needed, which was a caretaker, not a husband. Herbert was like her. Alf didn't need to feel responsible for this woman who'd bailed out on him by jack-knifing into craziness. He'd kept his part of the bargain. She hadn't. Why should he feel responsible? Besides, this new responsibility made Herbert feel important. Alf always wanted him to have a stronger sense of himself, to flash around some importance, some weight. But the boy tried too hard and tripped over his own feet. Not like Jack. Jack was smarter; always had been. Knew how not to try too hard. An art. Herbert would never learn that one. Too much like his mother. Let him have her; they deserved each other.

Customers. Count customers! He'd gotten a reputation for fast, efficient loans, a good one now, and people knew they could depend on him in a pinch. They still asked after his wife, though, and there she was again in line.

You need me, Alf, he heard her whispering. *I bring you respect in this community. Something you've always needed. Boulder City isn't a loose-ends town like Ely, Las Vegas, Ruth. You can't hide here. You're not whole without me. Besides, Sid Empey's watching you.* He grabbed Serena's breast, squeezed it to reassure himself. *Damn it, Esther! Leave me alone!*

And then the sound of water washed over Alf and his counting. He remembered standing by the river, being ordained by God. Called to save himself, and others too. The faces of his children lying on the banks of the river like beached fish, their gills pumping uselessly. Esther. Another wall-eyed fish slumped onto the sofa.

What was he doing? Why was he lying here with a strange woman who wasn't his wife, who was a wall, a blockade like the dam? His hand could feel her strength as she slept. The strength of someone who had nothing to possess, nothing to tie her to the chaos. That's how she did it. That's how she maintained the wall that intrigued Alf and kept drawing him back and back to her. Tied herself to nothing.

Then he knew he couldn't lie next to her for now. Their close skins were sticky, clammy. He peeled himself away. He'd stay calm when he looked at Esther. He could do it now. He'd find a way to make things work, fit all the props in the picture he wanted for himself.

He groped for his shoes in the dark, found his necktie and new white suit. His socks. His suspenders. Boxer shorts. He'd given his bed to Herbert and Edna, so he'd sleep on the floor next to the sofa. He'd be there when she woke up. He'd hold her to him and say he was sorry about . . . about exactly what, he wasn't sure, but he'd say he was sorry things hadn't worked out differently. What more could he say?

•   •   •   •   •

The summer was back, full-bodied, elbowing its way into the house on Avenue B and clinging to Esther with wet threads of hair and strings of perspiration. She lay on the sofa, her nest among pillows and white crumpled sheets, listening to Benny Goodman, Tommy and Jimmy Dorsey on the radio. She told Herbert she didn't want to see anyone for any reason—not her neighbors, not even anyone from the Boulder City Ward who brought tuna fish casseroles and apple pies to their doorstep. Heat was all the company she could handle for the time being.

Alf was in and out of the house, home early some nights and tiptoeing in at three and four on occasion, but always sleeping on the floor next to the sofa when he finally came in. After he made his bed for the night—two blankets folded double beneath him, one sheet on top—he reached through the dark to stroke Esther's hand curling around the piping on the cushion seam. Sometimes he'd know she was awake. They never spoke of things between them anymore, but at night they touched each other's hands like two children who needed to know someone was close by. And in the morning, Alf left again, almost like he disappeared through the walls. Money to lend, interest to earn, and business licenses to regulate before the dam was completed and the whole town dried up and blew away. The end was close; the project was two years ahead of schedule. Six Companies was elated because the U.S. Attorney in Reno had announced there'd be no grand jury on the fraud charges and that formal action was pending. Like all other charges against Six Companies, including Senator Oddie's challenge to the company scrip which took nine months to resolve, these seemed to disappear into the clear Nevada air, subject to eternally pending action. Six had captured America's imagination with its larger-than-life ambition in small-minded, depressed times.

The crews were challenging each other, not with concrete anymore, as the last bucket had been poured on May 29, 1935—the last of 3,240,871 cubic yards of it in the central structure of the dam—but now the race was on to see how quickly the power plant could be built, the turbines put in place, the generators, the accessories. The U-shaped powerhouse, dwarfed by the dam, yet as tall as a nineteen-story building, was being wrapped around the canyon walls, one-quarter mile of steel reinforcements and concrete. Its floor space equalled ten acres, its roof area four city blocks.

But as the power plant grew and Justice Department charges evaporated, another strike threatened the project. Six Companies's wages averaged 71 cents per hour, and the workers wanted the PWA scale at least—a dollar an hour for skilled labor, 75 cents for unskilled. Steelworkers and carpenters had already walked off the job and were trying to convince the electricians, hoisting engineers, machinists, and truck drivers to join them. The truck drivers' union had just voted to remain on the job; Herbert Jensen was one of those voting not to disrupt progress.

As with most desert storms, the fracas between labor and corporate executives intensified into ominous silver-black clouds and erupted like the cosmic anvil, but it would probably end like most desert storms, swallowed in the sand after it ran its headstrong course. Regardless, the water behind the dam that was in place and solid and entrenched started to rise. Lake Mead lapped at old high-water marks, slipping past the chalky bathtub ring left by the Colorado in its worst floods.

At the north end of the basin, fingers of water crawled into the abandoned Mormon settlements of St. Thomas and Callville. They covered the austere adobe houses with chimneys at both ends of each roof, the shelters built by settlers of the Muddy Mission in the 1800s. They floated over Uncle Woolley's almond orchard and other abandoned fields where faithful Mormons had battled alkali, Indians, and scorpions, to grow cotton, wheat, grapes, potatoes, corn, peas, and sugarcane. They covered the wooden floors of the St. Thomas ward house where saints had stomped their feet and clapped their hands to keep time to the one fiddle that played its five-tune repertoire over and over. The Virginia Reel. A quadrille. Two polkas. One waltz.

To the west, the borders of Ragtown and the dismantled remains of the gravel-screening plant were gradually erased by water. At the south end of the basin, at the back of the massive concrete wall, water licked at the base of the four intake towers and at the back of the dam. It was stealthy, slow, steady. Water rising. The project in place despite petty feuds.

One morning before work, Herbert asked Alf to keep Friday night, the last weekend in July, open for a small party. "You could bring her a red rose, Dad," he added. "And she talks about going to Sunday School sometimes. Maybe you. . . ."

They spoke quietly in the kitchen while everyone else slept. Alf fried an egg, easy over.

"I'll see, Herbert, but there's a strike going on, you know that. I'm glad I'm not in the middle of it like last time," he said. "They've got 800 men out as of yesterday."

"I wasn't here for the first one." Herbert buttered his toast. "But the truck drivers voted to hold steady last night. We're too close to being finished."

"I had to rat on some strikers in '31. But I guess I'd do it again if I had to. I'm proud I helped keep things moving even though they used me. No one could've stopped this job before, and no one's stopping it now. The strike's coals to Newcastle at this point. There's never been another project like this in our whole nation. We're making history, Herbert."

"History. Yes. You're right." Herbert pulled a chair up to the kitchen table, a stack of whole wheat toast, and a jar of apricot pineapple jam his grandmother had sent down with a friend passing through to California. "So can you come to the party, Dad? I won't invite too many. It might excite her too much, but just her best friends from the Boulder City Ward and maybe

Thelma Black and Conway Mitchell. Something so she'll know she still counts with us. Can you make it?"

"You don't think I love your mother, do you?" Alf asked.

"I don't know," Herbert said, focusing on the green maze of linoleum on their kitchen floor, swirls of green and white nebulae with black flecks.

"Of course you know what you think. Stand up for yourself, Herbert. What do you think? Do I love her or not?"

"It's none of my business, I guess."

"None of your business!" Alf's whispers imploded. "What do you mean, none of your business when we're talking about your mother?"

"It doesn't seem that you love her, then," he said softly. "If you want to hear what I think."

"It doesn't seem . . . hell, Herbert, say what you think. With conviction. Tell me I'm a jerk. A son of a bitch who hates God and all good things. That's what you think, isn't it?"

"You're my father." Herbert tried to hold his head up, push his chin out, calm the trembling in his voice.

"And what do you think of your father?" Alf pushed his face close into his son's. Herbert could see a string of spittle connecting Alf's lips.

"I think he's lost." Herbert held his breath and waited.

"Do you see me at all, Herbert, or do you only see the man who has disappointed your mother?"

"She only wanted two things. She didn't need a lot, but she wanted you to love the Church and her. That's not too much to ask, is it?"

"Ah ha. Herbert speaks his mind." Alf slipped the egg onto a heavy china plate with a blue border, one of the few remaining plates from the set of dishes he bought for Esther once when he received a bonus at the mines in Ruth. "So, if I let Esther be my guide, even in spiritual matters, then I am a good father. A good man. Right?"

"Each man has to build his own testimony. You could have tried harder." Herbert opened the cupboard to find the sugar.

"What if I have a testimony of something different? What if I believe just as strongly in something else? I'm still wrong, aren't I, because I don't buy your myths?"

"They're not myths, Dad. It's the truth."

"*The truth?*" asked Alf. "That's a lot of truth, I'd say."

Esther appeared at the kitchen door wearing her cotton garments that clung to her back and stomach as if she'd been swimming in them. It was a sacrilege to wear them so brazenly, but the heat had warped Esther's principles.

"Herbert," she said, "it's over. No more talking. It's done."

For once Alf felt unafraid of her eyes. They hardly seemed eyes right then. "Nothing is done, Esther. Everything keeps going, always. It never stops until you do, but even then things keep going, just like the river down there by the dam. Nobody can stop that river. They can change its course, but nobody's stupid enough to think they can stop it. You can't stop things either, even if you die. Something else is always being born."

"I'm not afraid anymore," she said, leaning against the yellow-painted wood table, barely strong enough to stand. "Not of you, not of the cement god with feet of clay blocking my river. So I could die now if I wanted."

"Mother," said Herbert, putting his arm around her shoulders and easing her into a kitchen chair, yellow spindles at her back. "We want you to stay alive. Can't you understand? You make a difference."

"But what about me and what I think?"

"Why be dead?" said Alf. "Just maybe the Lord won't send his angels to carry you to the celestial kingdom where you think you're going. Have you ever thought you just might lie in the ground?"

"It will be cool there," she said. "Dark. No sun."

"But the sun will be shining up above and drying all the leaves and flowers until they crumble and rot. And what if it's boring? What if you don't have anything to do anymore? No kingdoms to populate with good Mormon children. Everybody's notion of eternity is a product of the imagination, the Mormons included. Imagination stops when you do."

"I can't argue." Esther put her head on the straw placemat on the table and closed her eyes. The curls at the back of her neck dripped small jewels of perspiration down her back. "I only know God is my comforter, more than you or any person. God loves me. In the night when I looked up at the ceiling at the hospital and watched spiders walking upside down without falling, I knew then. Something held that spider to the ceiling. Legs attached to God's gravity. I'm no different. You can't hurt me anymore, Alfred."

"Look at me, Esther," Alf said loudly.

She sat motionless, her head still on the table, the woven placemat full of her auburn hair.

"Open your eyes and look at me!" he yelled. "Open those damn eyes of yours. You can't control me with them anymore. All your sadness. All your melancholy. You can't control me and keep me from life anymore."

"Dad," Herbert pulled on his father's belt loops. "She's too fragile."

"Get out of this, Herbert. This is for me and your mother."

"Please stop shouting, Dad. Everyone's asleep. Leave her alone."

"Open those eyes, Esther. Look at me straight on. I'll show you how I can stand up before them now. You can't make me feel like a nothing from the poor Danish immigrants of Brigham City anymore. 'Lost in eleven children. No father. Not enough education.' Your sympathetic words. Your not-so-veiled condescension. Bull shit! You with your little bit of culture and self-righteousness, holding your high-and-mighty self over me."

"You're right, Alf." Her words slipped like insignificance into the kitchen.

"Condescending. That's what you are." He didn't seem to have heard her. "Think you're so damn good."

"Forgive me. I thought I knew how to make everything work." Her hand slipped from the table. It hung at her side and swayed like a wind was playing at its back. She closed her eyes. The lines on her face relaxed. Her jaw too. Her weariness.

"Esther." Alf was on his knees. "Open your eyes. Look at me. I'm not finished talking to you." He grabbed her underarms, lifted her up, "Esther." He shook her like a rag doll. She opened her eyes. Water again.

"She's going to sing at the dedication," Herbert said. "I'll breathe all my breath into her all day every day until it happens."

"It matters that much to you?" Alf asked. "Aren't you weary for her? She's so tired, Herbert. Can't you see that? Stop hanging onto her. Go wet that dishcloth over there on the sink. Let's cool her down."

Herbert returned wringing drops of water from the twisted cloth. "I'm not as green between the ears as you might think. I'm willing to let her go, believe me. But she's always wanted one minute of unadulterated glory. She almost had it at the Boulder Theater, but then she had to go away and people knew it. Everyone in the country will be tuned into their radios to hear the President speak. 'Esther Jensen will now sing 'The Star Spangled Banner,' the announcer will say. You could help her make it. One and a half months. That's all. What do you say?"

"Look at her." She hovered between the fine borderline of wakefulness and sleep.

"But if she knew you wanted it for her, Dad, she'd find the strength."

"Unless she wants it, it's no good. She can't ride my coattails to keep alive."

"She needs you right now."

"I'm not begging her about anything." Alf lifted her hand and rubbed each limp finger. "If she decides for herself, it'll mean more to her. She can stay with us then."

17

September 30, 1935. Franklin and Eleanor Roosevelt, their aides, governors from the six Colorado River Basin states, senators, mayors, Henry J. Kaiser—Chairman of the Board of Six Companies—chief engineers, City Manager Sid Empey, Superintendent Frank Crowe, Bureau of Reclamation heads, Serena Bishop and hopefully Esther Jensen, would soon be together on the platform in the shade of the canopy on the top of the dam. The dedication.

The great dam gleamed in the sun, a bone-white spray of seashell fanning up out of the riverbed. Bold. Monumental. Thick in the canyon—660 feet at the base; 45 feet at the top. Hard next to the rock walls and river bottom. A 727-foot-high barrier set against the river. Beautiful, yet foreign. An alien white monument to science holding back an unreal blue reservoir called Lake Mead where blowing dust, sluggish mud, and a red river had reigned for millions of years, maybe. Who knew for sure what other elements, oceans, or upheavals preceded this giant undertaking, or what might come after?

All these dignitaries, plus thousands of visitors, would witness the dedication of The Dam, though no one was quite sure of its current title—Hoover or Boulder. The official agenda for the dedication seemed confused itself, still referring to the project as Boulder Canyon Project though that particular canyon was miles upstream from Black and soon to be under water.

The people on the dais would clap for the President, the Secretary of Interior, the new commissioner of the Bureau of Reclamation because Elwood Mead had died without a total glimpse of his Bureau's greatest project, for the Six Companies's Executive Committee and their general superintendent,

Frank T. "Hurry Up" Crowe who'd brought the dam in ahead of schedule, and the thousands of men who'd worked twenty-four hours around the clock for five years to accomplish this miracle. No one would mention the cheap labor available because of the Great Depression that made ten and a half million dollars for Six Companies and a $330,000 bonus for Crowe. Those figures might feel uncomfortable to a man who'd drilled or mucked for $4.50 per day and kept hoping, even striking, for more. Nobody mentioned the $100,000 penalty levied against Six Companies for overtime violations or mentioned that Six had billed the U.S. Government $175,000 for extra excavation work. Money, after all, would be secondary today. The dam was a monument to everyone involved, and pride was more popular than complaint on this grand occasion. The Boulder Canyon Project had been a race with time and odds and nature, and these men had won.

"I poured the concrete in the wheel-spoke forms of that intake tower over there." "I helped X-ray the welds on the penstocks." "We did it." "If it wasn't for us. . . ." Most participants in the project were devoted to this mass of concrete and close to violently intolerant of those who carped about unfair labor practices or unequal division of profits in the face of such magnificent accomplishment: a sum greater than its parts.

An appropriate winged statue had been erected for the 110 men and one dog who'd lost their lives during construction—one man for every half-million dollars spent. This, too, would be mentioned, and everyone would clap and swallow the lumps in their throats for those whose memory they cherished. And the dignitaries would bow their heads respectfully when the Secretary of Interior mentioned that four of the original Six Companies's partners had passed away before completion of the project, two of them brothers.

Though neither the Nevada or Arizona wings of the powerhouse at the base of the dam were ready to generate electricity for the Bureau of Power & Light of the City of Los Angeles or the Southern Sierras Power Company, The Dam itself was finished. A marvel. A miracle. Everyone was proud of this child, this project, this time for celebration.

Alf drove the two women and his three girls to the dam early that morning, anticipating the thousands of people crowding the narrow road and space. As he wove through the early crowds and crews of workmen preparing for the dedication, he shook his head, amazed, unable to fathom the fact that his daughters were sitting in the back seat of the car, dressed in straw hats and Sunday best. Mary Elizabeth, Rebecca, Inez. And, miraculously, in the front seat, Esther and Serena sat side by side.

Here I am, driving over the top of a dam that wasn't here a few years ago. The road used to fade out there in the dust. Now it's covered by a blue lake. We're driving across the river like it was never any sort of problem or barrier at all. My wife and Serena sitting together. We're all here. All six of us. Mary Elizabeth so excited for her mother she's forgotten to hate me and Serena for a while. All of a sudden, on the first day of September, Esther pulls herself out of her pool of sweat on the sofa and says she can sing again. "Like a bird," she said.

I'm a lucky man in a strange way. God moves mysteriously.

When Esther had stood up that morning and acted as if she'd only been asleep for a long time, Alf wondered if he dared drive over to the theater and tell Con who'd been waiting for her to come around. Maybe she was responding to the ingrained maxim she'd learned from her mother and the Elberta Theater—the show must go on, once more anyway.

"I can sing," she said quietly, staring through Alf as if he wasn't there. "Serena can sing with me. Like we sang for that boy in the desert."

"I'll be right back," Alf said, then drove down to the theater to find Con Mitchell, still incredulous, glad he hadn't told Esther that Serena's name was already on the program, hoping he'd catch Con in time to make the necessary changes. The doctor said patients like Esther sometimes snapped out of their melancholy for short periods of time and acted as if they'd never been anything but all right.

"They're like those seeds on the desert that don't germinate for sometimes as long as fifty years. Then everything comes together. The conditions are just right—rainfall, temperature, sunshine—and flash, a blossom. Maybe for only a few hours, mind you. . . ."

"Something happened this morning," Alf said before greeting Con with a hello or how are you. He was more breathless than he thought he'd be for a woman who'd worn out his affections. "I know you've been hoping Esther could sing at the dedication. Maybe she can do it now. She's asked for Serena to sing with her just in case."

"The official program's over at the newspaper office," Con said in his announcer's voice that always sounded as if it was introducing the next act, obviously pleased at the news. "Let's run over there. We'll get her name on the program if I have my way."

"But what if she really can't do it?" Alf hesitated. "You know how sick she's been. Maybe this'll only last a few days."

"We'll put her name on there, anyway. Serena can carry it if Esther can't,

271

and Esther sang at enough funerals that she should have her name in print. *Official Singer for The Dam.*"

"A little cavalier?"

"You're afraid for her aren't you, Alf?"

"It was impulsive of me to come."

"What the hell! People don't remember who sings the anthem anyway. Let's put her name on. Nevada still has jurisdiction over a few things around here, right?"

"If you say so, but please," Alf asked as he pushed against the padded theater door and an edge of light cut across the theater's pinwheel carpet, "don't tell Esther we ever put Serena's name in for hers, promise?"

"I won't. Don't worry." Conway inspected a loose chip of paint on the edge of the door. "By the way, did you hear the good news? Dix Ballard moved to Fresno last week. Still sore as a cod about the way Split-T manhandled him. But I convinced him you didn't order the damage."

"Really?" Alf was surprised. He hadn't expected Conway would have thought about him or the Ballard incident after he cleared Alf's name with Sid Empey. "Thanks. I guess I owe you one."

"You've given me one," Conway said, picking up a stray gum wrapper and crumpling it in his fist.

"What do you mean?"

"Esther," he said. "She's been a good friend."

Esther had said the two were friends, but Alf hadn't figured there were two sides in the matter. He thought it was a hello in the lobby kind of friendship. "She's been your friend, too?"

"She's an extraordinary woman, Alf. A little strange maybe, but extraordinary really. Her sensitivity to life." Conway's voice was full of emotion. "Not many could begin to appreciate who she is."

Alf didn't know what to say. No one had congratulated him about Esther in a while. He'd forgotten she was anything besides ill, caught up in endless drama, no intermissions in sight. Now he could sense admiration in Mitchell's analysis of his complex wife, and even affection.

"How do you know so much about Esther?" He'd never considered Esther and another man, but he could see she meant something to Conway. More than a little.

"She likes the movies. What can I say?"

A silence crowded the two men.

"Thanks for everything, Conway," Alf finally said, especially for settling matters with Ballard," and he pushed out into the sunshine wondering at this friendship which seemed much larger than before.

As he negotiated the hairpin curves on the road to the dam, he looked over at her as he would a stranger. She was dressed in white cotton with pastel embroidery on the collar and wore his favorite red lipstick, looking like the Esther he'd always known, but Conway thought she was an extraordinary woman. She sat in the middle of the front seat, Serena by the window.

"Remember, Serena," she said, "when we sang for the boy we found out in the desert, stretched out like a burnt offering?"

Serena fanned herself with her hand, a composite of bronze face and limbs offset by more white cotton, staring out the windshield at something besides the scenery. "Could anybody forget?"

"I'll never forget that day," Esther said, talking to Serena as a best friend on a church picnic outing. She lifted Serena's hand onto her lap and held it in both of hers. "That boy in the desert, stretched out, slowly burning."

Esther played with Serena's fingers. She was like a child, Alf observed, with no memory of any moment before this one.

"Look at that deep gully. Somebody could get hurt." She pointed her finger as if this was a first-time look at a canyon. She laughed when the car hit a dip in the road or a stretch of washboard, like it was a ride at a traveling carnival. "Will the three grandmothers or A. P. be here?"

"They're not here today, Esther," Alf said, a bit uneasy at this new turn of events. She'd seemed normal for the past three weeks, but maybe this heat. . . .

"Who will be here? I'll sing old standbys for the grandmothers. Their favorites. And A. P. loves to hear me sing "God Bless America.""

Alf kept braking on the steep grade, and the smell of burned brakes drifted up from the undercarriage. He worried that it might key something worse in Esther, but so far she wasn't ranting about the cement god with feet of clay. Sometimes during the summer, she'd swiped at her teeth. "Is it gone, Alf? I can still feel it when I put my teeth together."

"What, Esther?"

"The silt. The Colorado in my mouth. It'll drown me, Alf. The dam, too." She babbled through the nights until Alf calmed her. After he slipped through the front door, he lay on the floor in the dark and reached for her delicate fingers. "I'm here now," he said. "You can sleep." He'd had courage in the middle of the night. He was good at touching flesh and could comfort in that way. He stroked her arms, her hands, her breasts.

Serena crossed and uncrossed her legs, pulled her hand back into her own lap, pretending to need it to primp her hair. Esther still responded as a child, awed by the sights, colors, and shapes of rocks.

The President of the United States of America, Alf thought. *Franklin Delano Roosevelt. Little does he know who's singing for him today. Little does he suspect someone might start crying or laughing in the middle of the national anthem. A crazy woman singing "Oh Say Can You See?" I'll write him a letter if anything goes wrong. "Dear Mr. President: I'm sorry about my wife. It's not that she's crazy. Not that. It's just the weight of everything. She wasn't made quite sturdy enough."*

She'll pull through. I've seen her tremble to the point where most people would disintegrate, and still pull through. Singing for Esther is no different from lifting a finger. It's like she's a bird on a telephone wire, just singing because the sun is up. I trust that about Esther.

Or do I?

Serena seemed to be reading Alf's thoughts. He glanced over at her, offset by white, a pair of cotton gloves across her lap, and a white tightness outlining her upper lip. She'd probably heard his doubts. He wondered how she felt about giving up the solo because Esther got up that morning of September first and said she was ready. "Con Mitchell insisted," Alf told Serena that night. "He's always praised the ground Esther walks on. You know that. And he's program chairman." He didn't share his suspicions about Conway and Esther.

Serena uncrossed her legs again and lifted her hair off her neck. The heat intensified as they drove closer to the dam.

"Look at those high cables," Esther said. "Will there be a tightrope walker here today?"

"This is insane, Alf." Serena was sitting with her hands over her face, talking into her rings and fingers. "I'm sitting next to a child, and you want us to go sing on national radio for the President of the United States. I can't believe we're singing together. It's crazy. Really, it's crazy. Alf, why did you get me into this?"

"Serena," Esther said. "Your hands are perspiring. Alf, where's your handkerchief? Let me wipe her hands."

"So why should I stand up there and sing with a woman who's just home from Sparks? We'll make fools of ourselves, Alf. A fool of Nevada, too."

"It doesn't matter," Esther said.

Panic doesn't become you, Serena. The vision Alf had when he first arrived

274

in Ragtown suddenly swelled inside him like the power of the river being dammed behind this structure, rising, growing in volume. *Your trials have not been in vain, Alfred. You are forgiven. Open your arms and receive.*

He watched Serena, squirming for the first time like a butterfly on a corkboard, anticipating the pins being pointed at her wings. Esther placid and trusting, an adult-sized child sitting next to him, smiling into the sun, perspiration spreading across the powder on her cheeks. Surprise at every moment, every new thing, even a license plate from South Carolina.

The girls pointed to a lady with a pink-dyed dog on a leash, the circus of the growing crowd. They craned their heads out of the windows, their mouths open at the height of the canyon wall and aerial cables.

Alfred Jensen, husband of a child or a common sparrow or an overblown woman? Lover of one or two women in the front seat? The shifting perceptions felt like shadows escaping him, disappearing in the dark. And yet the vision still filled his insides: *I am with you.* Serena in profile. More angles to see than he once thought. More that was unable to bend in the wind. *Trust not in the flesh, Alf.* Maybe he'd shaped himself into something beyond either woman, though he wasn't sure if he had a steady fix on who Esther was. So many layers.

Esther groped for his knee and leaned forward to stare up at him with the eyes that had haunted him ever since he first saw her. She was right. He'd been afraid of those eyes, defending himself against them, avoiding the extremities of feeling there. To look into them was usually like watching an invisible point of icicle carve the iris into splinters. But at that moment, he thought he could see a sly smile inside them. A complex piece of music. He felt her gentle touch on the inside of his thigh.

"Alf, it's been a long road. We're almost there aren't we?"

He couldn't speak to her just then, his vision crowded with emotion. "You okay, Serena?" he asked.

"Fine, Alf." She answered as if she were a mechanical doll.

He looked past Esther. Serena's composure was perfect once again except for streaks of perspiration speeding down her neck.

Alf stopped the car to talk with a ranger who pointed him to a special parking lot reserved for senators and mayors and performers. He told everyone to wait in their seats while he opened the doors, *beau geste*, for the ladies. Then he walked through the crowd with both women on his arms, three daughters trailing behind, proud as the President could ever be, and he knew God forgave him his life of doubt, of groveling around at thirty or so different jobs, trying to find a way through the mire to say "I count." In spite of himself, he'd helped Esther hang on. God must have helped, because he hadn't wanted to. He'd wanted her to slip away without anyone noticing, slip out of their mutual lives and take the pain with her. But, against his best judgment, he'd tiptoed across the wooden floor of his front room each night when he could have stayed with Serena.

Was this the prize? Walking with two women on his arms? Walking up to the canopy with fear and strength flanking him? No one the absolute? Esther, frightened, yet walking into the face of power and presidents and concrete and government to sing a song. Serena, frightened, yet wearing the calm exterior that looked like strength.

An usher showed them their places, but they still had hours to wait before the dedication. Alf, manager for the day, poured lukewarm water from their desert bag into the kitchen glasses they'd brought from home. Red and yellow petals were painted on each glass—garden flowers in gentle breezes. "No dehydration today, ladies." As the clock moved closer to dedication time, he unfolded the top of the brown paper sack and passed sandwiches to everyone. They pulled toothpicks out of folded wax paper, ate deviled ham, limp bread and lettuce, and sipped warm creme sodas.

"A toast," Alf said, lifting his bottle high in the air. "To music. To the dam."

The young girls twirled away from their parents to eat their sandwiches, fluttering through the crowds in their Sunday dresses of plaids and checks. When Mary Elizabeth spotted a few friends from Las Vegas High School, she left her half-eaten sandwich on one of the folding chairs. She was keeping the promise she'd made to Herbert to stay away from men today. Everyone had promised not to upset Esther.

Alf protected his white suit with a cloth napkin tucked into his belt. Serena stood to keep from wrinkling even further, bending at the waist to let crumbs and beads of creme soda bypass the skirt of her dress. Before the family picnic was over, Jack arrived with Gloria and Edna who'd become good friends, then disappeared to find the band and play warm-up scales on his saxophone. Herbert was probably caught in the traffic with his loaded transport.

The Jensens. Together. A family event. A baptism. A rite of passage for a concrete adolescent about to enter the serious business of making power and controlling water.

And then the big black car drove through the crowd, the only thing that could pierce the mass of people and noise and cars. The black car with the flag flying from the back end, a flag with red stripes and white stars. Confusion falling out of the doors of the car as they were opened by men in dark, double-breasted suits. Hats for the sun. Eleanor in a white hat with the narrow brim. Franklin with his hair cut high above his ears. Tall, perspiring, waving to everyone. Black tie on white shirt. Franklin's glasses flashing sunlight as he turned from side to side and waved again and again. Eleanor smiling in her white suit. The band playing. Jack playing his saxophone in the middle of the VFW band where Alf couldn't see him as well as he'd like. Alf with Rebecca, Mary Elizabeth, and Inez, seated in the tenth row, waving to the people he knew who stood further in the back of the crowd. Alf important. Waving at Herbert who'd finally found them, at neighbors, at friends from town until people behind him felt impatient with his showboat exuberance but not saying anything because they were feeling their own pride too. Nevada. Important for the first time. Something of value to its country. Dignitaries. The President, even.

"It's time to go up to the podium, Esther."

"What for, Alf?"

"What for? The national anthem, that's what for."

"It's too hot."

Herbert sat down next to Esther in the chair she'd saved for him. "Sorry I'm so late."

"You're here, sweetheart." Esther kissed his hand.

"But Esther," Alf insisted. "I thought this was something you wanted. Your name's in the program and everything."

"No singing right now, Alf. I don't see the grandmothers."

"But, Mother." Herbert joined the protest. "This is what you've wanted your whole lifetime. Right here. Right now. You can do it. I know you can."

"No, Herbert." She stood up abruptly, squeezed past people's knees, and made her way out of the row and to the waist-high wall where she could look over into Lake Mead.

"Isn't this the most amazing thing?" she said to Herbert who'd followed her. "All this blue water. Miles and miles of it. Did you see all that water, Herbert?"

"Please, Mother. You'll regret this."

"No, I won't," she said simply and plainly. "This dam won't last anyway, so why should I sing for it? Thou shalt not worship false idols, don't you remember? Trust not in the arm of flesh. Let's go sit down."

They walked back to the folding chairs sitting on top of thousands of yards of concrete in the middle of the river. Esther sat in the middle, Alf and Herbert on either side, and Serena walked to the platform alone.

The wagon wheel microphone loomed big in front as Serena approached the podium. She stood exactly three feet in front of Eleanor and Franklin and the important people who had drawn blueprints, mapped strategies, superintended crews, and won campaigns.

The Veterans of Foreign Wars band, borrowing a few local boys like Jack to fill in weak sections, began with a roll on the snare drum. The color guard marched from the Nevada side of the dam, and crowds parted for the men in uniform—their garrison caps, their insignia, ribbons, hash marks, high-topped boots shined to reflect the desert sunlight, pure perfection, order, precision. The strips of red and white bending and straightening and blowing and rippling as they passed. Heads up. The flag. Hearts and allegiance. The snare drum rolling and rolling until Alf wondered where the man got such hands to keep a roll going that long. The color guard marching up the aisles of chairs while the crowd and dignitaries rose to their feet, stopping at a platform where a brass stand stood solitary, a repository for the flag. The conductor raising his arms high above his head, waiting for the right moment when his arms would dip and rise again, an upward movement to make music happen.

Alf heard the brass first, almost hearing the air being blown into the trumpet before the sound, waiting to see what would come out when Serena opened her mouth to sing. She looked at the bandleader out of the sides of her eyes, her head bobbing with the upbeat, matching the conductor's gestures and the band's preparation to begin. Her voice lifted with the conductor's arms.

"Oh say can you see."

The words finally came out, the words Alf had played through his mind in the weeks since Esther said she could sing again. "By the dawn's early light." Serena gained strength as she moved into the song, yet lacked an essential something. Esther—short, wan, thin though not slender, depleted fat hanging from her arms—standing next to Alf, her arm in his, listening, mouthing the words. Serena seemed a pastel picture compared to the passionate Esther. He couldn't help himself. He couldn't keep his eyes on anything but Esther. *How could he define her? Like Francis Scott Key writing the national anthem. Like a flag being whipped by the wind. Like a frayed child, but so lost she forgot to be pitiful. She's the inside of the song, the embodiment of the anthem. Alf, you sentimental fool.*

He cried. He stood in front of a folding chair on the top of Boulder or Hoover Dam—it was a dam in Black Canyon was all he knew anymore—and let the tears mix with his perspiration, cousins to all the water behind him and in front of him. Esther had too much life inside of her. Too much for him to handle.

"Oh say does that star-spangled banner yet wave." The drums rolled again, preparing for the climactic event, the word "free." Alf held his breath.

She sang great popular music, Serena did. She knew how to jam the latest love songs with combos in smoky rooms. Esther, on the other hand, was a dramatist. A tragedian. *Esther, Esther.*

"O'er the land of the . . ." Serena was almost there. Next to him, Alf heard a quiet, whispered singing. "O'er the land of the. . . ." She was almost there too, almost to the high point of that song. Alf lifted her hand to his lips and kissed a blue vein.

"Sweet Esther," he said as she sang the word "free" so quietly on the tenth row in front of the President of the United States.

After responding and bowing slightly to the applause, whistles, and cheers, Serena sat on her assigned seat at the back of the stage. Alf looked over at Esther who looked much too used to be sitting in a crowd. The heat again. She fanned herself with the printed program with her name on it, but too slowly to create any movement of air.

Secretary Ickes, master of ceremonies, paid tribute to "The Dam which is hereafter known as Boulder Dam," to Senator Johnson from California, a Republican for Roosevelt, a supporter of the dam. He didn't mention President Coolidge who originally authorized the project; he avoided President Hoover's name too. He introduced the chief engineers, the construction superintendent, the important politicians before the most important one of all. He didn't thank Serena, though. *Too many names to mention,* Alf guessed.

"Ten years ago," FDR read into the spokes of the microphone, "the place where we are gathered was an unpeopled, forbidding desert. In the bottom of a gloomy canyon flowed a turbulent, dangerous river. The site of Boulder City was a cactus-covered waste. The transformation wrought here is a Twentieth Century marvel. . . . Labor makes wealth. The use of materials makes wealth. To employ workers and materials when private employment has failed is to translate into great national possession the energy that otherwise would be wasted. The mighty waters of the Colorado were running unused to the sea. Today we translate them into a great national possession."

Alf heard much of the speech, but he was watching Esther who seemed to be fading in the fluctuating waves of heat. While the President spoke on government credit and industrial expansion, the sun baked the pavement, the canopy, the metal on automobiles. Heat echoed like sound off the black canyon walls. And suddenly, the Esther he'd known didn't seem to be there anymore: she'd evaporated, disappeared into bright sunlight, carried away on the rays of the vision Alf had in the beginning of his southern Nevada days. The sun evaporated this body of water, all the tears, the pools of sorrow, the perspiration. Even though Esther sat there smiling like a wax puppet with a painted face, slowly melting, Alf knew something had happened. He knew she was free. Somehow. He checked to see if Serena had noticed. She was still there, fanning herself, slightly bored, not struggling with anything. And he glanced at Herbert who was so much like his mother, a male reprint of the Carpenters' round, open face where anyone could trample and smash the soft contours with a careless heel, the face which Alf would rather avoid.

"Boulder Dam is an engineering victory of the first order," the President continued. "Another great achievement of American resourcefulness, skill and determination. . . . On behalf of the nation, I say to you, 'Well done.' "

As directed by Secretary Ickes, everyone remained in their assigned places until the Presidential party marched through the crowd to the waiting cars, except for Alf who pressed close behind their wake with Esther draped over his arm. Herbert, who'd found someone to drive his transport back up the canyon, helped situate Esther in the car. Serena said she'd catch a ride back with Jack and Gloria.

"Keep water on her face, Herbert," Alf said. He started for home where he could put Esther in a cool dark room where she'd revive. Autumn was in the air somewhere.

• • • • •

It is cool and dark here though I can see the sunlight as it filters through the silt and green pearl liquid above me. I can relax now. Me. I am water. Every time I hit against a slab of sandstone, it won't hurt me. I'll leap up, spraying into a fan of liquid crystal and fall back into the current where I glide over boulders, abysses, and cliffs. Undifferentiated. Flowing over the rocks. No one can take anything away from me because I'm carried by the flow that's rushing to the Pacific where everything begins again. I'm so cool here.

Esther was vaguely aware of her head in Herbert's lap. "Mama," her son kept saying, cradling her head like it was a baby.

"Cool," Esther mumbled. "It's so cool here. Trust in Jesus."

Drops of water sprinkled from Herbert's fingertips onto his mother's cheeks, running down, curling around her ears.

Sometimes white water. Green. Red sandy water. The particles of silt tumbling towards the sea in this mass of water. I'm cool here. Sun on rocks. Baked rocks. Cool water on all sides. I glide around boulders and rocks, and I'm flowing toward the sea. Spray in the air. Oxygen. The dark crevices under rocks. Cold. Bitter cold out of sunlight. The water. I am water.

"Water," Esther mumbled.

"We're going to be home soon." Herbert rocked his child. "Hang on. There's a free moving picture of the dam construction at the Boulder Theater this afternoon. You love the movies, Mama."

The cars moved like red ants up the canyon road, a string of rosary beads, small prayers to the desert not to burn them, no breeze answering the utterance. A string of beads in a vast land of chaotic rocks and massive fissures and jumbled architecture. Junipers. Creosote. Thousands of years. Birds chirping in trunks of cactus. Lizards blinking on flat rocks, sliding rapidly like drops of ink over the edges of rocks.

"Damn this crowd," said Alf. "Can't get anywhere."

Flashing yellow pierced the insides of her eyes. She focused on the light show, breathing deeply, filling herself with the cutting heat. The light show dazzled on the screen of her eyelids, wheels of interstellar mist, flashing comets, shooting stars. She smiled at Alf's impatience. As if there were anything to be impatient about. She smiled up into the shape of her own face—Herbert carrying her with him. Her son.

Nothing can stop me now. I am water. If they put me in a cup, I'll evaporate. If they hold me in their hands, I'll slip through their fingers. It is cool and dark here with my river. Smooth over flat rocks. Fingers of water splitting into channels, finding new paths. There's always a way through.